THE

TRAVELLING SCHOOLBOYS.

AN INTERESTING STORY.

BEAUTIFULLY ILLUSTRATED.

COMPLETE.

HARKAWAY HOUSE, WEST HARDING STREET, FETTER LANE,
FLEET STREET, LONDON, E.C., AND ALL BOOKSELLERS.

FRANK STAINFORTH

THE TRAVELLING SCHOOLBOYS.

CHAPTER I.

SHOWING HOW THE SCHOOL CAME TO BE ESTABLISHED, TOGETHER WITH TWO OR THREE OTHER PRELIMINARIES WHICH THE READER WILL FIND WORTH HIS WHILE NOT TO SKIP.

IN the year of our Lord 18— an event happened to Dr. Primrose, B.O.D.

He conceived an original idea.

Happily for my readers this wonderful circumstance did not cause him to lose his presence of mind.

He pounced upon it at once, and transferred it to paper.

The doctor was a country clergyman, living in a house—of which we shall know more anon—in the midst of the beautiful scenery of Lake Windermere.

His mania developed itself harmlessly by a profound belief in the angelic disposition of all boys when properly treated; added to this a deep-rooted veneration for his title B.O.D., which had been conferred upon him by a learned society in Glasgow, consequent upon researches after ichtheosauri in his kitchen-garden.

What the mysterious characters B.O.D. might stand for none knew save the initiated.

True, the head-gardener had obtained a fraudulent reputation for sagacity by alleging that the letters stood for "Blessed Old Donkey."

The worthy doctor had been reading a very interesting account of a whipping-match at a public school in the south of England, which would have ended merrily for all parties if the hardened young schoolboy had not taken it into his head to die, and if the afore-mentioned hardened young ruffian's father had not thereupon caused the schoolmaster's imprisonment, on a charge of manslaughter, the law of England being unfortunately too wise to admit that its youths may come to their death by other than natural means.

"And serve him right, too, the scoundrel!" cried Doctor Primrose, perusing the paragraph—which indicated that the playful schoolmaster had been sentenced to imprisonment for life.

Scarcely had he conveyed his new idea to paper, when, viewing it with glowing eye, he exclaimed—

"And why not?"

"Think of me," squeaked a voice, in such lugubrious tones that the doctor pushed his spectacles upon his forehead, and said—

"God bless my soul!"

The tones, so pregnant with ill-omen for the future, came from a large grey-and-pink parrot, which was perched in one corner of the room, and who, being somewhat of a freebooter had been chained by one leg and dignified by the title of "Robin Hood."

"Ah, to be sure, yes, to be sure, Robin; why should I not?" to which Robin responded, in still more dismal tones—

"Oh, think of me!"

Full of his idea, however, the doctor paid no attention to the second appeal.

He rang the bell violently.

It was answered by a stout woman, with red hair and blue eyes, which served the purpose of showing that she was good-humoured and had a terrible temper when aroused.

"I have it!" exclaimed the doctor, excitedly; "Ann O'Dyne, I have it!"

"Have what, doctor dear?"

"Ha," said the doctor, "I perceive that you are in ignorance of that which I have conceived, therefore I will enlighten you, as I want your assistance."

"Doctor, dear," said Ann O'Dyne, when he had unfolded his plan, "don't you have anything to do with thim young imps, and, as for going among them frog-eatin' mounseers, I wouldn't do it for all the gold in the worruld."

"I will show," said the doctor, "that when boys are properly treated they can behave like young gentlemen."

"Don't you do it, doctor, dear!" cried Ann; "sure it's meself that knows the young limbs, and if they don't worry yer into yer grave my name isn't Ann O'Dyne."

"And I will prove," continued Dr. Primrose. "that it is possible for all the nations of the earth to be one vast brotherhood——"

"And make us all eat frogs?" cried Ann.

"The English boy shall get rid of his insular prejudices——"

"And rubbidges!" cried Ann.

"While the foreigner shall learn to thoroughly appreciate our sterling virtues. I will devote myself, and the remainder of my life, to the pioneering of this happy idea. Youth and learning shall walk hand in hand, and we shall no longer have this cry of school terrorism, rising over this unhappy country. I will make my schoolboys happy."

"The heavens be his bed this day, he's gone clean mad!" cried Ann O'Dyne; "to think of giving up his peaceful life here to a parcil of young himps which will worry the life out of him."

"Take me—poor Robin, poor Robin!" cried the parrot, dismally.

The doctor, full of his new idea, turned his house inside out; dormitories were built, a schoolroom was added, the lawn sloping down to the water's edge was turned into a playground. Ann O'Dyne was driven crazy in the purchase of beds, bedding, and a thousand other things necessary for our comfort, which we use every day, and know nothing about.

Then the doctor sent off to the English *Times*, the *New York Herald*, the *Paris Figaro*, and the *Berlin Cross Gazette*, the following advertisement—

" IMPORTANT TO PARENTS AND GUARDIANS.

"A TRAVELLING SCHOOL,"
Conducted by Doctor PRIMROSE, B.O.D.

"A gentleman of high learning and cultivated tastes is about to form an establishment for young gentlemen, which will combine the advantages of travel and education at the same time. As the establishment will necessarily be on a limited scale, each young gentleman should be accompanied by his servant, who will attend to his luggage, clothes, etc., while travelling. Six months of the year will be spent in England, on the shores of Lake Windermere, the remainder will be devoted to travel. For terms, and further particulars, apply to Doctor PRIMROSE, B.O.D.

"Lake Cottage, Windermere."

The doctor found it necessary to add that three months must elapse before he would be in a position to receive his scholars.

Long before that time he had, much to Ann O'Dyne's disgust, completely filled his list, and now our different heroes are hurrying from different countries to their destination.

CHAPTER II.

HOW THEY CAME TOGETHER AND WHO THEY WERE—THE DOCTOR MAKES A SPEECH AND EXPLAINS HIS VIEWS.

SUMMER sunlight streamed upon the purple waters of Lake Windermere and clothed the larch-covered heights of Turner's Fell with golden beams.

This picture of beauty was utterly lost upon mine host of the "Rabbit and Kingfisher" inn on the southern borders of the lake, at whose house was congregated a miscellaneous assortment of boys.

They had begun pouring in the night before from various trains, which, by the way, had rushed off again with a snort and a scream of delight, as though glad to get rid of their troublesome burdens.

Boys were yelling and whooping, waiters were screaming themselves hoarse, mine host of the inn was writhing under the effects of a pea judiciously planted on his nose, when there was a sudden rush to the door by all the assembled youngsters to witness the arrival of a drag.

Among those who strolled quietly up to see what was the matter was a tall, lithe, well-knit, and rather pale young fellow, apparently about fifteen years of age.

"There goes a bully, or my name isn't Frank Stainforth," he said to himself, as he witnessed a sharp cut which the driver of the drag bestowed on one of the mares.

He had no means of pursuing his theory further, for at that moment he received a slap on the back, and a tall youngster, who looked as though he had been thrown together, drawled out through his nose—

"I guess you're one of the pewpils; say, ain't yer?"

Rather annoyed at this unceremonious salute Frank turned to look at his questioner.

His face was brown as a berry, and was set off by a nose turned sharply upwards, as though trying to have a look at the piercing grey eyes which kept it company.

His hair was excessively long and lanky, and his cheeks hollow. Notwithstanding that this gave him a somewhat aged and shrewd appearance, there was a perpetual look of good-humour flitting about his mouth, which won one to him at first sight.

It was this that caused Frank Stainforth to put out his hand, and say, heartily—

"Yes; and I hope we shall be very good friends."

"I hope so, too," responded the new-comer. "My name is Nathaniel Urner; folks call me Nat for short. I come from the States. What's your name, and where do you come from; say."

"My name is Frank Stainforth, and I come from a place about five miles away from here," responded Frank, noticing that his companion had taken a stick from his pocket and was cutting it.

"I always like tew whittle down the talk," said Nat, noticing Frank's glance. "Say, have you got an old man or any sisters?"

"I have one sister and a stepfather," returned Frank, while a shade of sadness passed across his face.

"I am glad tew know that, because I have a sister to home, and I reckon she'll be glad to hear about other feller's sisters. They sent me abroad tew Yewrope so I could get cured of bashfulness. Say, are yew bashful?"

"Not particularly."

"Say, who's that hoosier that's just come up in the waggon?"

"Lord Mouslin De Lain, the Duke of Broadacres' son."

"I swar! what does he do drivin' his own waggon? I thought the bloated aristocrats of Yewrope had plenty of servants?"

"So they have. But that ain't a waggon; it's a drag."

"I don't like him," said the American boy. "Reckon he ain't square."

"What do you mean?"

"Well, he's what we call 'putting on frills' to home. Kinder sneakish, ain't he?"

"I really don't know. You must remember that it is impossible to tell what a fellow will turn out from first sight."

"Wal, look a here. My old man told me if I didn't like a feller at first sight to have nothin' tew do with him, and he's reckoned a smart man down our way."

"Yes."

"Now, I kinder took tew you right off."

"I'm sure I'm flattered."

"Say, sir, yew a pewpil?"

This was uttered as the American boy turned rapidly from our hero to another youth, who was somewhat short in stature, and had one of those jolly, round, good-humoured faces which seems to invite everyone to be as merry as itself.

"Yes," responded the new-comer, "I am fery glad to see you. It sall be fery goot pleasure to me to make friends with you, look you."

"Say," responded the American, with a comical, puzzled look on his face, "what part do you hail from, and whater kinder lingo dew you call that?"

"It was fery good language inteet," responded the youngster, "and my name was Barry Cornwall, at your service, fery much at your service, inteet," continued the young Welshman, bristling up.

"Now, don't you two get quarrelling over your languages," said Frank, hastening to prevent a rupture. "One speaks quite as well as the other. So just shake hands before you have time to lose your tempers."

The American's huge hand was extended and clasped in that of the little Welshman's.

Just then a very thin, slender youth approached Frank.

"Monsieur," he said, "*je suis charmie de vous voir; I do not know de rules of etiquette, but, if you will allow, I sall have much plesair to make your acquaintance. My name was Leon De Gardin. I do not speak the Anglais language very well."

"*Parfaitement bien; et la mien est Frank Stainforth, à votre service!*" cried Frank, brushing up all he knew of French.

Then he introduced the French boy to Nat Urner and Barry Cornwall.

After this the three managed to get along very well, and were evidently much pleased with each other.

"When do we start for the school?" asked Nat, and then, without waiting for any reply, "who's that feller there? He looks like a heron."

This observation was addressed at the expense of a skinny-looking boy, who appeared to be all legs.

"He is a cousin of mine," said Frank.

"I don't like him," cried Nat.

"Nor do I," resumed Frank; "but don't take my not liking him for anything; it is only a fancy, perhaps."

"I wonder where's Deutchy?" cried the volatile American.

"Who is Deutchy?"

"A German that came in the train with me last night. He did nothing but sleep the whole way, except when he woke up to eat some Switzer kase. Ugh! the smell!—then he went off to sleep once more. When we got here he said 'Dinner.' Snakes! you should have seen him hurry down the grub. Then he fell asleep over the table, and they carried him upstairs to bed. That's the last I saw of him. Will you come and have five cents' worth of lemonade? it's a bully drink.—

"A bullion—bully drink—*c'est potage —soup!*" cried Leon.

"No, you duffer, it's lemonade!" cried Nat.

With which observation he led the bewildered Frenchman to the bar.

"M'sieur, m'sieur!" cried a thin, squeaky voice, and the queerest-looking specimen of humanity presented himself.

He was clad in an old fashioned, though perfectly-fitting bob-tail coat of crimson-coloured velvet, on the left breast of which was the cross of the legion of honour; legs, he had scarcely any, and what he had were clothed in knee-breeches and closely-fitting black worsted stockings.

"Jerusalem—what a guy!" exclaimed Nat. "He beats my nigger Squat into fits."

"This is my valet, Pomponet," cried Leon. "He is a good soul, and was once a *brave soldat.*"

"Yes, m'sieur, I have the honour to serve *le grand* Napoleon ven he beat M'Lord Nelson at Trafalgar!" cried Pomponet, proudly, glancing a look of annihilation at the two boys.

Leon explained that Pomponet had once received a sabre-cut in the head, which had had the effect of causing him thenceforth to mix up historical facts in the most marvellous manner.

"Yes, m'sieur," continued Pomponet, "when M'Lord Wellington was at the Nile, *le grand* emperor said to me—'Pomponet, you are one of the old guard, you have the legion of honour,' *Oui, mon général*, I responded. '*Eh Bien*,' he said, 'you must take M'Lord Wellington prisoner.' '*M'foi*,' I replied, 'that is not difficult——'"

At this moment a series of wild yells arose.

They appeared to be a sort of commingling with the war whoop and human shriek.

"*Diable!*" exclaimed Pomponet, and immediately disappeared in an empty flour-barrel.

The three boys rushed out to see what was the matter, and stood there convulsed with laughter.

Nat Urner's nigger, Squat, as he called him, had ventured incautiously near the paddock, where a fine old ram was, in his own opinion, monarch of all he surveyed.

The beast promptly resented the intrusion by rushing upon Squat full tilt, and meeting him in the pit of the stomach; this caused Squat to double up in a trice.

The ram quietly waited until Squat had regained his feet, and then charged him again.

This time Squat, having turned to run, received the charge in an exactly opposite quarter, and gave vent to those dismal yells which had the effect of bringing out the house.

Escape was hopeless, consequently Squat betook himself to a series of manœuvres by which he hoped to free himself of his antagonist.

He dodged and twirled, turned back somersaults, and went through a variety of eccentric performances.

Finding every other method fail, the dwarf resorted to the last weapon in his armoury, and, dropping to his knees, presented his most invulnerable part—his head, to wit—at his antagonist.

This was more than the ram could stand.

His *amour propre* was considerably shaken.

He lowered his head for one grand, final charge, and rushed at Squat.

It is questionable which would have had the best of it.

Both heads were equally well developed in the frontal structure; but at this moment Nat Urner, in some alarm for the safety of his "nigger," rushed in, and, flinging his arms round the neck of the infuriated animal, succeeded in arresting his further progress.

Squat profited by the opportunity thus afforded to make good his retreat, amidst the yells of the spectators, leaving his master in a rather awkward predicament.

If he let go his hold he might expect a charge which would stretch him flat, and, besides causing him no small amount of physical pain, expose him to the laughter which had heretofore been heartily bestowed on the nigger.

If, on the contrary, he held on, he must acknowledge himself vanquished.

At this moment his native wit came to his rescue.

Firmly holding the animal with his left, he extricated his pocket-handkerchief with his other hand, and, by a quick turn, bound the eyes of the irate beast.

Having accomplished this feat, he walked coolly towards the spectators, exclaiming—

"I guess I've about fixed him this bout."

"You Americans always get out with sharpness where bravery will not avail you," said Lord Mouslin de Lain, who had left his dinner to attend the sport, and, by Nat's manœuvre, had been cheated out of some fun.

"Yah!" responded the Dutchman, who stood blinking behind him as though he wished to go to sleep again.

"It was a pity your lordship did not prevent him displaying his wit," said Frank, who was thoroughly disgusted at his remark.

"Perhaps," said Lord Mouslin De Lain, "perhaps I was waiting for you."

"Had I not perceived that his wit was equal to his bravery, your lordship would not have had to wait," replied Frank.

"A fery goot answer," cried Barry Cornwall. "Look you; I could go myself and fight de beast."

"Oh, of course," sneered the young peer; "*post-obit* courage is very delightful."

Nobody paid any attention to this remark, as all were engaged in congratulating Nat Urner; meanwhile a servant was despatched to lead back the ram, which had stood stock-still, to its paddock.

"Squat!" called out the American, "where are you?"

Obedient to this call the nigger presented himself.

He was short, probably not more than four feet high, while his shoulders, rising above his head, so to speak, gave him the appearance of a dwarf.

"Don't call him a nigger, for he ain't!" cried Nat, as this worthy made his appearance. "I'm the only one who can call him a nigger; the fact is he isn't a nigger. He's a South-Sea Islander. My father found him starving on one of the Pacific Islands when he was a boy, and took him aboard the ship; he has followed us about ever since. Come here, Squat."

"Yes, massa; what um want?"

"What do you mean by letting me fight your battles for you?"

"Me like you to fight um battles wid um sheep, massa; do you good."

Then, to the astonishment of everybody, he turned two back somersaults, and finished off by a loud guffaw.

By this time Pomponet appeared, and surveyed the scene with intense disgust.

"I assure you, monsieurs," said he, "if I had known it was but a sheep, *parbleu!* Pomponet would have rescued—"

"Just so!" cried Nat; "we know what you can do. You are good at tall talk, you are."

Further conversation was interrupted by the arrival of the coach.

It was gaily decorated with ribbons, and bore in canvas upon its side—

"Lakeside Academy."

The next few moments were occupied in getting the luggage in and placing the servants to take care of them.

Dr. Primrose had found it necessary to modify his advertisement so that those who came from a distance alone had the option of bringing a servant or not.

Thus it happened that Pomponet, Squat, and a man called Snarly Cool—of whom we shall know more presently—constituted the domestic portion of the young gentlemen's establishment.

"Now then," cried coachee, "we're off!"

"Hold on," returned Nat Urner; "Deutchy has not put in an appearance yet, and Lord What's-his-name is still in the breakfast-room."

"Thank you," responded his lordship, "I'll dwive over in my own dwag."

He was lounging at the window at the time, and, making a movement with his thumb, added—

"That German friend of yours is asleep with his head in a plate; perhaps it would be better if you were to dwag him with you."

Obedient to this advice, Hans Dunderfunk was taken from the table to the coach, where he had not been two minutes before he again fell fast asleep.

"Hurrah!" cried Nat, who was seated on the box with Frank Stainforth, Leon, and Barry Cornwall. "Now we're off, let her rip!"

They had not been journeying for more than three-quarters of an hour ere the rolling of wheels behind warned them that someone was approaching.

"It's Lord Mouslin De Lain!" cried Barry. "He is coming fery fast."

"I swar!" cried Nat Urner. "See here, coachee, don't you let him pass us, and I'll stand a five-dollar bill, a sovereign, I mean."

"I don't want to take noa responsibility," cried the red-faced coachman; "but if so be as Master Stainforth was to take the reins outer moi hands, who, then I ain't to blame."

So saying, he winked mysteriously at Frank.

"All right," responded our hero; "if you say I'm to drive, boys, I don't mind giving his lordship a turn."

"All right, go ahead full speed!" cried Nat. "Hurrah for some fun!"

Frank, accordingly, stepped into the driver's seat as Lord Mouslin De Lain's drag came nearly opposite them.

By a sharp turn of the rein he drove the wheeler across the road, so that if the driver of the drag persisted in his attempt to pass he must have been precipitated into the ditch.

Before he could cross or pass the coach on the other side Frank had lashed his nags to a hard gallop.

It required all his skill in driving to keep the coach from tilting, considering the wonderful pace at which they were going.

The odds for a fair race were by no means equal.

The young peer had four horses and a light drag to carry only two people, while the stage coach was crammed, not only with the boys, but with Pomponet, Cool, Squat, and the luggage.

Frank Stainforth, who saw very well that he would not have a chance should he once allow the peer to pass him, contrived by slurring across the road from time to time to keep his antagonist still in the rear.

This was gall and wormwood to the other.

In vain he tried every feint and dodge.

Frank was too clever for him, and kept him judiciously behind.

"He beant a cochin' on us much, Meister Stainforth!" cried the coachman, as he complacently folded his arms and watched Frank. "I never did think mooch o' they drags, as they calls 'em, not for a country-road."

"How much more of this fun have we got tew do?" asked Nat Urner.

"About twenty yards further," said Frank, "then we turn sharp round the lower bend in the lake, and there we are."

Away they went at redoubled speed. Now they turn the corner.

"'GO AHEAD, FULL SPEED!' CRIED NAT, 'HURRAH FOR SOME FUN!'"

Another spring, and dash, and Frank pulls the chesnuts up directly opposite the door of Lakeside Academy, bringing his nags down to their haunches quivering with excitement, while shouts of triumph go up from the exultant throats of the victors.

About three minutes afterwards Lord Mouslin De Lain drives up.

He had been turned neatly at the last corner, and had, in consequence, been nearly upset in a ditch.

Doctor Primrose was there, with radiant face, all ready to receive his young guests, as he called them.

Immediately behind him was Ann O'Dyne, the matron, while his right and left were flanked respectively by Monsieur Garlic, the French and German tutor, and Mr. Spotworth Grub, who was professor of grammar and *Belles Lettres*, while the butler, Mr. Wedge, was faintly visible in the distance.

This, be it understood, gentle reader, was a finishing school.

The old gentleman shook each new arrival cordially by the hand. He then led the way into the schoolroom, followed by the boys, and, mounting his desk, began his speech of welcome in the following manner—

"We are met together, young gentlemen, under the happiest auspices. We are all desirous of knowledge—'*Scribimus indocti doctique*'—ahem!—Horace. And that knowledge can alone be obtained by travel and by cultivating the friendship and society of those whom the fall of the Tower of Babel condemned to speak a language other than their own."

The doctor paused, and the boys, taking this for the conclusion of his speech, gave forth a wild hurrah.

When silence had, with some difficulty, been restored, the doctor continued—

"Here you will find, while pursuing the studies of the mind, ample recreation for the body. I have been at some pains to find out the best models of sailing and rowing boats, and I think you will not find our navy deficient in that respect."

Another burst of applause greeted the doctor at this point.

"Having spent, I trust, a profitable summer in England, we shall proceed to Paris, and thence through various towns of France and Germany, and——"

At this point a snore interrupted the speech.

It came from Hans, who, having been awakened, and had the speech explained to him, testified his approval by a loud "Yaw," and immediately relapsed into sleep again.

"Tale-bearers and sneaks," continued the doctor, "to use a slangy but very apt phrase, I abhor. Fight, if you must settle your differences in that way, but establish a code of honour amongst yourselves. If anything goes amiss, I shall ask the culprit on his word of honour to plead guilty or not. That will, I trust, prove quite sufficient for the futherance of justice. This is all I have to say at present, young gentlemen," continued the doctor, "except that the remainder of the day will be a holiday. School meets to-morrow at eight A.M."

Ere the doctor's voice had well died away a loud explosion occurred in the hall, which was immediately followed by Ann O'Dyne calling out, in loud tones—

"Murder! murder! Oh, the black imp! Murd-e-er!"

CHAPTER III.

THE FIRST DAY AND THE FIRST NIGHT AT SCHOOL—A DUCKING AND ITS CONSEQUENCES—JOEL SEES A GHOST.

EVERYBODY rushed into the hall in the firm belief that nothing else than murder had been committed.

The cry of murder, coupled with the other exclamation of black imp, etc., made them suspect that Squat had taken a violent fancy for a meal of "short pig" as set forth in the person of Ann O'Dyne.

They were accordingly agreeably disappointed when, on arriving in the hall, they did not see the South-Sea Islander eating up and happy over the murdered body of the matron.

It turned out that Squat, wishing to impress his young master's cleverness upon the matron, had pointed out his gun to her, unconscious of the fact that it was loaded.

Having explained to her the *modus operandi* of sighting a deer, he pulled the trigger, and dropping the gun, or rather being kicked over by it, mingled his cries with those of the terrified domestic.

The situation was fully explained to the doctor, who took occasion to warn the young gentlemen that, in future, fire-arms would be prohibited in the establishment.

"I don't see why I should be prevented from having my gun because that American fellow chose to leave his gun loaded," grumbled Lord Mouslin De Lain.

"I'm right down sorry for it," said Nat Urner.

"What's the use of being sorry for it?" cried his lordship, savagely. "That doesn't mend matters."

"No, I know it doesn't mend matters; but, still, I have done everything in my power to——"

"Of course, of course," said the young peer; "after you have brought all the mischief about it's a very easy thing to say you are sorry."

"I don't see what more I can do."

"Nor I; except try and not be such an ass."

Nat Urner turned red up to his forehead, clenched his fist tightly, and bit his lips in his effort to keep down his temper; then, without making any reply, he turned away from Lord Mouslin, and caught hold of Frank Stainforth's arm.

They were going to have a look at the boats under the direction of Doctor Primrose.

"Say," cried Nat Urner, "I don't exactly know what to do. You know about that gun affair?"

"Yes."

"Well, I apologised, but Lord Mouslin wouldn't take my apology."

"Well?"

"Well, what I want to know is this —ought I to give him a rap on the nose?"

"What for? for not taking your apology? That is too good. No, of course not."

"Well, darn it!" said Nat. "What am I to do? Can't I fight him? Say, you'll be my second, and I'll go back to him and settle the time and place for it."

"I don't think you have sufficient reason for fighting just yet," said Frank.

"Think not?"

"I think," said Leon, who had approached and overheard this part of the conversation, "that it should be an *affaire d'honneur*. I shall have moosh pleasair to be *votre ami.*"

"Nonsense!" cried Frank. "You had much better let the affair drop. If he is such a surly dog as not to accept your apologies I don't see how you can mend matters by fastening a quarrel on him."

By this time they had reached the edge of the lake.

"Gentlemen," said the doctor, mounting on a little knoll, "behold the fleet! I hope it meets with your approbation."

A grand burst of cheering greeted this speech.

Before them, on the purple bosom of the lake, lay boats of every possible build.

"And here," cried the doctor, delighted by the admiration of his young friends, "here is the bathing-house. Remember, I expect every one of my pupils to become expert swimmers—and, indeed, I shall consider myself justified in withholding my consent to boating expeditions until all the parties interested therein shall be able to swim."

Looks of dismay were interchanged among the boys at this speech.

The doctor noticed this and relented a little.

"Of course," said he, "as this is your first day, I will make an exception. You may all try the boats, providing each one contains at least two who can swim."

"Squat can swim like a fish, and so can I," exclaimed Nat, impulsively.

"I can swim, too," Frank said.

"*Et moi aussi,*" exclaimed Leon; "but poor Pomponet is not at home on the water."

"Yes, messieurs," cried Pomponet, "it was the *mal-de-mer* which I suffer from which prevented me from capturing the great English admiral, Nelson, at Brest. The admiral said—'Pomponet, there lies the English fleet. Good! You are a brave man. You must take a boat, go on board the admiral's ship, put a pistol to his head, and say—"Come with me!'" 'There is nothing so easy,' I exclaimed; and I got into the boat."

"Well, what happened then?" asked one of the smaller boys.

"Well, messieurs," cried Pomponet, delighted at having secured an audience, "we went along very well until we were quite close to de Anglaise fleet. Then I was take mit de *mal-de-mer*, and de Anglaise do take me prisonair, because no one can fight mit de *mal-de-mer* in his 'tomach. After that de French admiral he say—'I cannot allow dose *perfide* Albion to make prisonair my brave Pomponet,' so he took them all prisonair."

"How many?"

"Eighty-seven line-of-battle ships, one hundred corvette, four hundred sailors."

"What, all those English taken prisoners at the battle of Brest?"

"*Oui*, messieurs," said Pomponet.

"Why, you old fool, the English won the battle of Brest."

"No, monsieur, your perfidious historians have tell one grand lie; de French have won de great fight."

A shriek of laughter greeted this story, and Pomponet was duly congratulated on his bravery.

By this time the boats were ready.

It was decided that, as there was a delicious breeze blowing, they should go in two of the sail-boats.

Nat Urner, having had great experience in his own country, was given command of one, while Lord Mouslin De Lain obtained command of the boat called the "Partridge."

"Light" was painted in gorgeous colours on the stern of Nat Urner's boat.

Hans was with difficulty persuaded to enter, and then he went sound asleep.

The "Light" proved true to her name. Under Nat Urner's guidance she filled and went off as clean as an arrow.

Not so the other boat, which seemed in difficulties.

But the crew of the "Light," as they sailed away, little guessed what dangers would befal the craft which had been put under the command of the young peer.

The boys of the "Partridge" noticed that Lord Mouslin De Lain allowed the "Light" to get under weigh first, and that he occupied himself in narrowly watching the method by which her young commander got her under way.

At last he gave the order to hoist the lateen-sail.

"Perhaps, if you were to get up the anchor, or let go the buoy-rope——" began Frank.

"I know all about that," said his lordship. "Any fool knows that a boat can't go when she is held by her anchor."

"Then why don't you let her go?"

"I am examining her sailing-points," returned his lordship.

Frank said nothing, although by this time they could hear the other crew jeering at them for not starting.

Snarly Cool sat on the lee-side of the boat, scowling at him from under his shaggy eyebrows.

Barry Cornwall had noticed that on several occasions our hero had evinced an aversion for this man.

They waited for some time, and then Lord Mouslin said—

"Go forward there, some of you, and cut adrift that rope."

"I will go," said Frank.

In a few moments he had cast off the buoy-rope, and the boat, under pressure of a breeze which was every moment increasing, leaped through the water.

Her progress was, however, anything but satisfactory.

She yawed about from side to side, flapped her sails, and trembled all over. Occasionally she would plunge lee-side under.

It became more and more evident every moment that the young peer was absolutely ignorant of her management.

Frank became seriously alarmed about the safety of those on board. Save himself, it was evident that there was no one on the craft who knew how to manage her.

"You seem preoccupied, Stainforth," said the young lord, with a sneer; "rather pale, too. Perhaps the motion of the boat does not agree with you."

"Perfectly," responded Frank.

"You need not be under any alarm," said the young peer, slightly increasing the sneer; "except for the fact of sea-sickness, which I cannot guard against, you are as safe here as on land."

"I may be in error," replied Frank, hotly; "but I suppose I have a right to my own opinion, which is that we are not so very safe."

"Oh, to be sure, but no one else is thereby bound to make themselves uncomfortable."

"Did I say they were?" he asked, fiercely.

"You must excuse Mr. Stainforth, my lord," said Snarly Cool, turning his sleek black eyes upon the peer, and giving him a look which seemed to say, "*I hate him as much as you do.* You must excuse him, sir," he continued, "as he suffers greatly from nervous depression sometimes. It is a family failing."

He gave Frank a glance full of some terrible significance.

The boy paled as he received it, and that same look which was noticeable on his first introduction again came into his face.

They had by this time got out of sight of Lakeside House, and were amongst the numerous group of islands so familiar to the tourists of Windermere.

On the left Nat Urner had brought his boat to the beach of a small well-wooded island, and the whole party had gone ashore.

Lord Mouslin De Lain attempted to follow Nat Urner's example, but the manœuvre was so clumsily executed that she broached-to, and took aboard water by the bucketful; however, no harm was done except to Hans, whom the cold water rudely roused from his slumbers.

Just before supper-time they set sail again, but Frank Stainforth had had time to call Nat Urner aside, and say to him—

"I wish you would keep close to us in your boat; that fool Mouslin will capsize the boat before we get home."

"Do you think so?"

"He knows nothing whatever about managing a boat, and it is getting very squally."

"I would take the tiller away from him."

"I could not do that without an altercation, and perhaps a fight."

"And a fery goot thing too, look you," said Barry; "I am not afraid of him."

"Nor am I," said Frank, quietly; "but it would hardly be the thing to quarrel on the first evening of our arrival."

"True."

"And another thing," said Frank, lowering his voice, and making sure he was out of earshot of anybody, "I see my man Snarly Cool has become very confidential with him. They were talking together just now, and separated in some confusion as I came up."

"Well, what of that?"

"You don't know all," Frank said, in an agitated voice. "If you and I get to be great chums perhaps I may tell you, but at present do what I tell you. You had better take Barry Cornwall in your boat as he cannot swim."

Matters being thus resolved on, they strolled towards the beach.

When the boats had got from under the shadow of the trees they were enabled to perceive that one of those sudden storm-clouds, common enough in the lake districts, was coming upon them.

A dull grey sky had replaced the glorious blue under which they had set sail, and little angry gusts of wind moaned up the lake, and twisted tiny wave-tops into white caps.

The "Light" was the first to get under way, but, instead of squaring away at once for the home run, Nat Urner ran his boat up in the wind, and reefed her down.

"He's afraid of a capful of wind," sneered Lord Mouslin De Lain, as they got under weigh, with better success this time, seeing that their commander had not been slow to profit by experience.

"You will beat him in the race home, at all events, my lord," said Snarly Cool, in a low voice.

"I'll try," responded the peer, as, giving the boat a sheer which nearly capsized her, he ran her before the wind.

"You had better reef down!" called out Nat Urner from the other boat. You'll catch it heavy enough before you get three miles down the lake!"

"Perhaps you had better concentrate your energies on your own boat!" Lord Mouslin De Lain called out, but the words were lost, for they were by this time tearing along at a furious pace.

Presently the light mist and rain hid them from sight of the "Light."

The boat tore through the water, yawing from side to side, owing to bad steering.

Frank was sitting on the starboard, or right-hand side; something seemed to tell him that an accident was about to happen, so he quietly kicked off his boots without being perceived by anyone.

Snarly Cool, who had been watching the progress of events with a gleam of satisfaction in his sinister eyes, said, in an undertone, to the young peer—

"If you were to lean over to the left a little more it would make the boat go along more smoothly."

The young peer, though too high and mighty to take advice openly given, was not above listening to it on the sly; perhaps, too, there was more in the sentence than appeared on the surface, for as Snarly Cool spoke a look of intelligence passed between the two as though they perfectly understood one another upon a certain matter.

In moving his body over Lord Mouslin was so clumsy that, forgetting the importance of the tiller and its action upon the boat, he moved it with him; the result was that the felucca rounded too suddenly.

Her huge after-sail came on board with a crash, and swung over to the lee-side, burying the gunwales under.

A short, sharp cry rose as the sail swept across the place where Frank Stainforth had been sitting, and when it was carried out to leeward he was not to be seen.

Some on board the boat gave one great shout for help, while others simply uttered a cry of horror.

There was but one man who appeared to be perfectly satisfied with the whole proceeding, and that was Snarly Cool.

He could not conceal his look of joy as the boat flew away from the spot where poor Frank Stainforth had disappeared.

The lad's hat floating idly about on the surface of the lake was all that remained visible belonging to him.

The "Partridge" was rolling about from side to side, running off before the wind, while the tutor and Lord Mouslin De Lain, the latter with a face as white as a sheet, were wringing their hands in helpless terror.

But when the boat showed a tendency to run up in the wind, and so come to a standstill, Snarly Cool shifted the rudder by an almost imperceptible movement of his knee, while the smile of Mephistopheles wreathed his fat yellow face.

They were at least one hundred yards away from the spot when Lord Mouslin De Lain suddenly became inspired, and seizing the tiller, he "put it down," to use a nautical term, thus, by a sweep, again bringing the boat up in the wind and half filling her with water.

By this movement the boys, who had been anxiously watching for Frank's reappearance, were again precipitated to the other side, and, in the confusion, Snarly Cool had time to lean over and hiss in Lord Mouslin's ears—

"Fool! if he comes up he will accuse you of having tried to murder him!"

The effect of this speech on the young peer was instantaneous. His face turned livid, and his hands relaxed their grip of the tiller, while his dull eyes seemed to retreat under his overhanging forehead.

"There he is!" shouted one of the boys.

At that instant the "Light" dashed in upon the scene from out of the mist. A pair of small, white hands and a cap were visible, but nothing more was necessary to show Nat Urner what had occurred.

He brought his boat round, right over the spot where Frank had disappeared.

At this moment Snarly Cool, whose eyes were blazing like coals of fire, knocked over Lord Mouslin De Lain.

He fell with him, and, whether by accident or intent, his hand caught the tiller, and pushed it over to starboard.

Under the impulse the boat bounded away from her former course, and crashed into the "Light," making a huge hole in her side, through which the water poured.

"You lubberly, lily-livered brute!" roared the American, "you did that on purpose!"

"You lie!" screamed Snarly Cool, beside himself with rage. "It was you who might have avoided us——"

Before the sentence was finished he had sunk to the bottom of the boat, felled by a blow dealt him by the young American, whose quick blood had caused him to unship the tiller with the speed of lightning and use it as a weapon."

He remembered what Frank had told him. and—well, the blow was given, the insult was avenged for the present, at least. But during this time the others had not been idle.

Before the blow was given there had been a splash in the water, immediately followed by another.

Then two heads came up together, belonging to Leon De Gardin and Barry Cornwall.

The French boy, cool and collected, was preparing to strike out to where Frank had disappeared, when he caught sight of his companion.

His hands alone were above the surface of the water. He was sinking again !

"*Ma foi !*" exclaimed Leon, catching him; "are you not able to swim ? "

"N—n—n—o—ugh ! " panted Barry. "I forgot in the excitement of the moment. Never—ugh—mind. You leaf me—go."

This was the boy who had been counselling prudence !

In the meanwhile a short but most dramatic scene was taking place on board the "Partridge."

After the blow dealt to Snarly Cool, Nat Urner had recovered his *sang-froid* and presence of mind.

"Squat ! Squat ! " he called out.

"Yes, sair," responded that worthy.

"Why don't you go and fish him out ? I guess you're goin' to sleep, ain't yer ? "

"Waitin' for um orders, sar," cried the South Sea Islander, grinning.

"Go ; like greased lightning—skip ! " yelled Nat.

Before the words were well out of his mouth the sleek, oily body of the Kanacka had disappeared beneath the water.

There was a splashing alongside, and Leon appeared, supporting Barry Cornwall.

"I sall do fery well, look you," cried the little Welshman. "Hurry and save him ! "

Once assured that he had firm hold of the boat, Leon turned and swam in the direction where Frank had disappeared.

"Come back ! " called out Nat Urner.

"I guess you're only wasting your time in tryen to foller Squat. He's greased lightnin', he is. You just let him alone, he'll have Frank out."

By this time Barry had clambered on board.

Hans Dunderfunk had embraced Lord Mouslin De Lain, and these two were in turn embraced by Mr. Spotworth Grub and Joel Skimp.

They were clustered together in the stern-sheets white with terror.

"It was all C—C—o—ol's fault," said the young peer. "He t—told m—me to d—do it——"

In short, they were in a deplorable plight. The "Light" was sinking rapidly.

"Stop your bellowing there ! " roared Nat Urner, who was jumping about from one boat to the other with the speed of lightning. "There, Barry, make fast that rope's-end round that cleat; that will do. Now jump on board the 'Partridge,' and make fast a rope I will throw you in the same manner. You lower down those sails, Leon."

He then flung Barry a rope's-end.

This was dexterously caught and fastened.

"Now then, into the 'Partridge,' every mother's son of you, if you want to save your lives ! " cried Nat.

They needed no second invitation.

There was a regular stampede ; in a moment the boat was cleared of them.

Affairs now stood as follows.

The "Light" was full of water, but she was fastened to the "Partridge," so that she could not sink.

The "Partridge" still had her sails up, and was moving slowly through the water.

Leon was about to lower that sail also when there was a cry of—

"There they are—there they are ! "

All eyes were turned in the direction indicated.

At first Squat's sleek, black head and glittering eyes, which glistened like a seal's; then there was a long, pale flash, a gleam of white, and Frank Stainforth's face appeared above the water also.

They made rather slow progress through the water.

The blackman's burden was evidently dead weight.

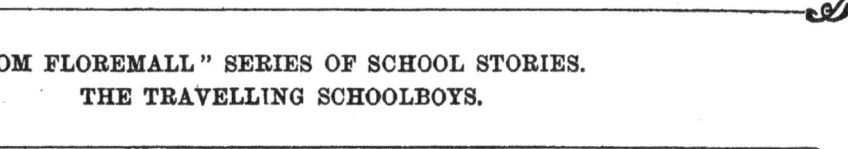

"FRANK TOOK A STEP FORWARD AND INTERPOSED. 'WAIT A MOMENT,' SAID HE."

"I guess I knew Squat would fetch him right out," said Nat. "He's the best diver on this side of the water, he is, for five dollars."

"I entreat your lordship to tell your father that I implored you not to venture," said Mr. Spotworth Grub.

"Let me alone, will you?" retorted the boy, who had now got rid of one fear only to have another, namely—that Frank would say he had intentionally caused him to be knocked overboard.

He was so utterly ignorant of sailing, that he did not know but that his act might not be construed into meaning something of the sort.

Whatever conversation he had had with Snarly Cool, it was enough now to fill him with terror.

Meanwhile, the others were occupied in getting Frank on board.

This was accomplished by hooking a rope to the waistband of his trousers and hoisting him up bodily.

He came up a dead weight.

"I'm afraid he's a gone coon!" cried Nat Urner. "Poor fellow! I've only known him a few hours and I feel as though I had lost a brother."

By this time they had all got round him, and were rubbing away as vigorously as their arms would let them.

Somehow, although they had only known him for a very short time, Frank's charming, quiet, unassuming manners had won them all to him.

Snarly Cool having recovered from the blow Nat gave him, appeared amongst the astonished group.

His face was beaming with smiles.

Nat Urner drew back.

"All right, sir!" cried Cool, with a hearty laugh. "You gave me a round knock; but it served me right, for not knowing my manners to my betters. You see I was anxious on account of my young master."

"You took a curious way of showing it."

"Well, there is no knowing what a man will do when he gets crazy with fright. If anything was to happen to him it would be a sore day for me."

"Umph!" returned Nat. "Supposing, then, that you lend a hand to getting the 'Partridge' emptied of the water that's in her just to show there is no ill-feeling."

"All right, sir; anything to oblige you," he replied, with face brilliant in smiles.

Presently Frank showed some symptoms of returning animation, and a good portion of the water having been baled out of both boats, the boys began to prepare for the remainder of the sail home.

The squall had passed away as suddenly as it had come, leaving behind it a gentle breeze.

They once more put the sail on the "Partridge," towing the disabled "Light," and steered for the academy, where the doctor was awaiting them.

He was in a great state of excitement when he saw the boats come in—one a perfect wreck.

Frank, who had recovered consciousness, was immediately despatched to bed, and a medical man was sent for.

Thither were also sent Barry Cornwall, and Leon De Gardin to keep him company.

The other boys, having changed their clothes, went to inspect the playground, and were subsequently called in to supper.

Lord Mouslin De Lain was strolling in when he met Snarly Cool.

"Your lordship has had a narrow escape," said he, flashing his sinister eyes upon him.

"I don't know what you mean," responded the young peer, haughtily.

"Will you meet me here to-night after supper?"

"For what?"

"I would like to tell you something."

"Very well then, I'll come," he replied, and strolled away.

About ten o'clock the three sleepers were awakened by the other boys coming into their dormitories.

As ill-luck would have it, Joel Skimp's bed was close to Frank Stainforth's.

For nearly an hour the boys kept up a perpetual clatter; and then came silence.

In the midst of this silence there ensued a most dismal croak directly from the head of Joel Skimp's bed.

He woke up and listened.

Gradually his hair stiffened and his face blanched—gradually the lugubrious tones, such as no human tones ever uttered, took shape, and Joel listened, half-frozen with terror, to the words—

"Think of me! "I'll find a way to do him! Think of me!"

Joel shrieked out—

"Oh, Lord! I see a ghost—I hear a ghost!"

But there was another who had just crept stealthily into bed, and the dank sweat of shivering guilt was on his brow as he listened to these—to him—terrible words.

That other was Lord Mouslin De Lain.

CHAPTER IV.

THE CAUSE OF THE UPROAR—THE MYSTERIOUS FOOTMARK—GETTING SHIP-SHAPE.

JUST as everyone had gained the floor with a royal yell, and Joel Skimp was dimly visible on his knees, the moon flung her beams upon the scene.

Presently a golden light vanquished the moonbeams, and Dr. Primrose appeared with a huge red nightcap on his head, and attended by a cohort of sub-tutors.

The doctor held a huge horse-pistol in his hand in such a manner that its discharge would certainly shorten his life.

In his rear came Mr. Spotworth Grub.

"Gentlemen, I must ask you to cease this noise," the doctor began; but ere he finished his sentence there was a rustle of wings and the apparition flew to his shoulder.

Mr. Spotworth Grub shrieked and dropped the candle.

"Gentlemen," cried the doctor, "there is no cause for alarm. The excitement is occasioned by my parrot, Robin Hood, who has by some accident found his way into the dormitory. Will some one oblige me with a light?"

This request was speedily complied with.

When the place was illuminated Mr. Spotworth Grub was found on the floor, while Monsieur Garlic had braced himself against the wall with his legs out at right angles to his body, as a sort of advanced guard which might prevent an enemy from assailing a more vulnerable part.

All the boys were out of bed except Lord Mouslin De Lain.

But here was a singular fact, which, however, escaped general observation. No clothes were on the chair by his bedside, but if one had peeped underneath the blankets which covered the young peer's form it would have been discovered that he had turned in with all his clothes on.

"I wish you fellows wouldn't make such a row," said Lord Mouslin De Lain, with a yawn. "I shan't be able to sleep again all night."

"You must have slept very heavily if you have only just awakened."

"Of course I heard that stupid bird, but I should have thought that some one could have put him out quietly without all this Pandemonium."

"It is my fault," said Doctor Primrose, hastily. "I ought to have seen that Robin Hood was properly secured, but really, in the excitement of the evening, I forgot all about him."

"Not at all, doctor," grumbled Lord Mouslin; "it was not your fault at all. No one can help being a little forgetful at times of other people's comfort. It was that young ass, Skimp, who mistook a bird for a ghost. He must have a very bad conscience, that's all. Good-night."

The doctor, with many apologies for having disturbed them, took his departure.

"What a lark!" cried one.

"Did anybody see Pomponet?" asked Leon.

"Or Snarly Cool?"

"I expect the valiant Pomponet couldn't leave his bed."

"Let's look for him."

"Good!"

Three boys, Frank, Leon, and Nat Urner, immediately got up and hurried on a few clothes.

On the stairway they met the doctor. He was examining something on the carpeting, and wore a puzzled look.

"What is it, doctor?" they asked.

"It is very curious," responded Doctor Primrose. "When I came upstairs to bed the carpeting was perfectly clean now look at it."

He pointed to a broad, muddy foot-mark.

"What do you make of it, gentlemen?"

They could make nothing whatever of it.

Had there been a series of steps, and had these led in any particular direction, they could easily have found out a solution of the mystery by following them up. But here was this solitary imprint of mud as mysterious as even that which puzzled Robinson Crusoe.

After a long consultation, they could not solve the mystery, which they agreed must be left for time to reveal.

"May I ask where you are going, gentlemen!" the doctor inquired.

"If you will go with us we shall be delighted," cried Frank. "The fact is, doctor, Leon thinks that poor Pomponet must be ill, or he would surely have appeared on the scene ere this with his huge sabre."

The doctor agreeing, they searched everywhere for Pomponet but found him not.

At last some peculiar sounds led them to investigate the cellar.

Here they found the hero of Trafalgar sitting on an upturned coal-scuttle.

"What are you doing here?" Leon asked.

"Messieurs," responded the veteran, "I heard a terrible noise and fancied there might be burglars in the house."

"So you ran away to hide yourself?"

"Pardon, messieurs," responded Pomponet, with offended dignity. "I remembered the advice of the great Napoleon. 'Pomponet,' he said to me, at the battle of Austerlitz, 'Pomponet, you have no ammunition, but there are stones. Pelt these perfidious Austrians with them, and they will run.' Messieurs, I did. They ran. Pomponet covered himself with glory. As I said, I remembered this. Who would not profit by experience? I had no ammunition, so I came down here for coals with which to pelt the enemy."

"Come, Pomponet, go to bed, and cover yourself with the bedclothes."

"Messieurs," cried the little man, drawing himself up to his full height, "I am ready to lead you against the enemy!"

Notwithstanding his valour they persuaded him to go to bed, and presently the house was quiet once more.

The following day the boys proceeded to the bathing-house, where those that were not proficient received lessons in swimming.

In this department Squat was invaluable.

When they had bathed, and were strolling by the lake-side, Pomponet came up.

"Ah, monsieur!" he said; "you should employ Pomponet to teach the swim. Lo! it was I who did teach the great Napoleon to swim from St. Helena."

"You must be mad, Pomponet," said the doctor.

"Mad! Perhaps so."

And with a profound bow he departed.

CHAPTER V.

FOUR MONTHS AFTERWARDS—THE FIGHT.

"In fact," said Doctor Primrose, writing to a clerical friend, "despite one or two slight drawbacks I think I can pronounce the school a grand success. I place entire confidence in the boys, although one of them is, to me, a perfect mystery. I should call him the very soul of chivalry and honour, even did I not know that he was the son of my old college friend Arthur Stainforth, who died, you remember in India. Notwithstanding what I have described, a hunted look of fear or guilt steals into his face when it is not animated, a look for which I cannot account; and, on one or two occasions, it has, I might almost say, amounted to absolute terror.

"A man named Cool, whom he has for a servant, has a most extraordinary influence over him. It is very evident to me that the boy does not like him, and yet, when on one occasion his insolence became apparent and I threatened to send him away, young Stainforth entreated me not to do so. What would you advise me to do under the circumstances?"

A matter which had become apparent to the worthy doctor could not but be well known in the school.

It was evident that Snarly Cool had some influence over Frank.

Even Nat Urner, who was his most intimate associate, was no nearer a solution of the mystery than he had been on the first day of his arrival at school.

True, on one occasion Frank had appeared to be on the point of telling him everything, but the young American, notwithstanding his uncouthness, had a keen sense of honour, and perceiving that his companion was labouring under intense excitement, he had begged him to wait until he should be calmed down.

"You might say things now which you would regret by-and-by," said Nat. "And I guess I don't think it would be right for me to listen."

Frank silently pressed his friend's hand and wandered away sadly.

This led to an incident in the playground which more than ever drew the two boys together.

Lord Mouslin, who at the time was being bowled to by little Joel Skimp, noticed how Frank had gone away.

This was too good an occasion to prove his malice to let slip.

"So your friend has given you the cold shoulder, Urner," he said, in those cold, sneering tones of his, which on Nat had the same effect as a red rag shown to a bull.

"I guess you don't know what you are talking about," said Nat, reddening.

"I know perfectly. Who knows but I might go and find him crying and console him?" cried the peer, as a sudden, happy thought occurred to him.

He flung down his bat and strolled towards the spot where Frank had disappeared.

"I reckon you'd better leave him alone," said Nat, resolutely placing himself in the way. "He wants none of your sympathy."

"He might prefer it to that of a cad who is perpetually using slang," returned the great bully.

"Do you mean me?"

"Dear me, you are wonderfully perspicuous this morning."

"Say, do you mean me?"

"If the cap fits you, wear it."

"All right!" cried Nat; "I've put it on. It just suits me exactly."

"I'm glad you think so," sneered the other, as he shouldered Nat out of the way.

He was considerably taller than Nat.

As a result he was utterly surprised when he received a stinging blow under the ear, accompanied by the words—

"If that fits you, you can wear it, too, you lily-livered bully."

Lord Mouslin De Lain with one swift blow felled Nat to the ground, bruised and bleeding.

The blow almost stunned him.

Nothing daunted he rose again, but in a blind sort of way, and had scarcely regained his feet when another sent him to the earth.

Two or three others came running up at this juncture, amongst them Leon and Barry Cornwall.

A little in the rear, Hans Dunderfunk was making his way to the scene of action as fast as his rolling gait would allow him.

"Monsieur," hissed the French boy, boiling with rage, at what he had witnessed, and forgetting his English, "*c'est infamous; vous etes un lache!*"

"*Eh, bien, mon garçon! s'il vous voulez!*" responded the young peer, with a venomous sneer. "*Gardez vous bien!*"

Ere the words had left his mouth his right hand had crushed through the Frenchman's guard, and, landing on his forehead, stretched him beside the American, who was so badly injured as not to be able to rise.

"I thought I should be able to pay that debt off," said his lordship, with a laugh. "There's two of them polished off."

"Dot vas serve dim right!" cried Hans, who had just come up; "py gracious, it was better as goot if you give dem some more."

Barry Cornwall had rushed to assist Leon to his feet.

He turned now, his little Welsh blue eyes flaring with passion, and said—

"It was a cowardly act, neither of them are his match, you sleepy-headed Dutch bully."

"If you calls me by dot name once more I vas lick you wid my belt, dot vas de kind of man I vos."

"Look you, look you," cried little St. David, as they called him; "look you, you are a fery badt bully, as I shall be fery glad to make you eat your words, look you!"

"Give him a thrashing, Hans, he deserves it, and I won't deprive you of the luxury," said Lord Mouslin De Lain; "besides, here is Frenchy, waiting to have another turn."

Leon was sitting on the ground clasping his forehead tightly with both hands.

He had made two or three efforts to get up but without avail.

"Come here and let me lick you," said Hans; " it vas too much droubles to go mit you after, but or you don't koms I was gif you a vorse licking byn-bye, ven I gets you."

"Look you," cried the little Welshman in reply to Hans, "it sall be a fery bad day that you do want to beat me; look you, you shall haf to run a fery little way inteet. Here I am fery near you now," he cried, going up to him.

The German stretched forth his open hand to seize him; but, as he did so, the little Welshman jumped up, giving a sort of bound like a young sprinkbok, and striking out quickly at the same time.

Hans groaned dismally, and put his hand to his nose, from which the blood spurted plentifully.

"Oh, mein nose, mein nose, it was covered mit der blood dat vos run down my face!" howled Hans.

"Look you," screamed Barry, "it sall be that you sall apologise, look you; very humbly, or I sall beat you, look you, very hard inteet!"

"Hurrah for little St. David!" called out a number of boys, while Joel Skimp went to pick up the fallen champion.

"I wish you fellows would hold your row," cried the young peer, glaring at them. "Some of you will get into hot water if you don't."

They had a wholesome fear of him, and this was enough, not only to stop their "row" as he called it, but also to prevent them from giving way to any expression of sympathy towards the vanquished.

"Wait till I gets myself up," cried Hans. "I vos half kill you, you little Welsh tifil."

"I sall be fery gladt to see you do it, look you," cried St. David, who had been "peeling" rapidly.

"But that is irregular," cried one of the boys. "We must have a ring and seconds."

At this moment attention was diverted to Leon, who had, after several ineffectual attempts, regained his feet.

He approached the bully.

"So you want some more, do you, Master Frog? I thought I had effectually cooled your courage."

"Yes," said Leon, "I want some more."

"Come along then, you shall have what you want," cried his lordship, brusquely, putting himself in a posture of defence.

"You are mistaken," cried Leon, calmly.

"Oh! you've had enough?"

"No, monsieur."

His eyes were blazing luridly and his face was deathly pale.

It was evident that he walked with extreme difficulty.

From time to time he pressed his hand to his forehead, as though he would try and collect his thoughts.

"What, then, do you mean? Come, if you want a good thrashing, say so— if you don't, apologise. I have no time to waste over you. There is going to be another fight."

"I hope so," said Leon, slowly.

"Well, come on then. Don't let us have all this fooling. You have surely recovered your wind by this time."

"Yes," cried Leon, panting.

"But, perhaps," sneered his lordship, "it takes Frenchmen longer to come to the scratch."

"Oh, for shame!" cried two or three boys, involuntarily.

"Who spoke?" asked the young bully, looking round, sharply.

"He did, and he, and he," said the young sneak, Joel, pointing out several.

"Perhaps you will be kind enough to favour me with your remarks in person," said his lordship, with his sneering smile.

The boy addressed had, however, no mind to get a licking for nothing, and so he bolted incontinently, and, seeing

Stainforth coming out of the little coppice which skirted the playground, shouted out to him—

"Come here, Stainforth. This row is all on your account!"

"On my account!" cried Frank, in some surprise.

When he was hurrying to the scene Leon had again approached Lord Mouslin De Lain.

"I said this affair was not finished, neither is it," he said. "You have given me a blow, monsieur, and I demand the satisfaction of a gentleman for it."

"And I am perfectly ready to give it to you," said Lord Mouslin, impatiently, putting himself in fighting attitude, ready for the fray.

"I do not fight in your way, monsieur," retorted Leon, bitterly. "I am no match for your English science of fisticuffs, and I do not choose to be butchered——"

"You mean?"

"I mean, monsieur, that there are foils in the gymnasium."

He said this with bitter earnestness.

Lord Mouslin De Lain recoiled.

He turned slightly pale as he said—

"You mistake our English customs, monsieur. I have no mind to be run through the body by a fellow, who wants my life because I have given him a blow."

"True, true! You are wrong, Leon," cried several voices.

"Is this justice?" demanded Leon, with flashing eyes. "Am I to be beaten and insulted by this bully and have no redress? *Sacre!* if this is English honour, the sooner I get back to my own country the better; but I will have my honour satisfied."

"You forget, my friend," observed a perfectly calm voice; "you forget, my friend Leon, it is not your affair of honour, it is mine, and I claim it."

The young Frenchman turned and found Frank Stainforth by his side.

Nat Urner was with him, looking very shaky; he had received some ugly cuts, and was about as badly "punished" as a boy could be.

"Oh! so there is another of them," sneered the bully, looking at the slender, well-knit figure before him with contempt. "We have another would-be champion."

"As a matter of honour, Leon," said Frank, paying no attention to the remark made by Lord Mouslin, "your antagonist, if you wish to fight, having insulted you must abide by the code of honour provided by your country for such occasions. If you insist he must fight you on your terms."

"Oh! you think so?" sneered the bully.

"Stand back. If you touch him before the proper time arrives I'll give you a thrashing, my German bully!" cried Frank, turning suddenly to Hans, who was sneaking towards little St. David.

"Look you, I am not afraid of him!" cried Barry, closing his fists.

"I know you are not," said Frank, "and we will settle that matter at the proper time. At present there must be a truce between you."

"Indeed, we are treated with a lot of fine talk by this melancholy chevalier," said Mouslin. "Pray, who, sir, constituted you an authority on affairs of honour."

"You must remember, however," said Frank, taking no notice of the bully and turning to Leon, "that you and Nat Urner simply took my place; I am the insulted party."

"I got licked bad," said Nat, "and I ain't ashamed to own it. It isn't any disgrace to be licked by a big bully like him, I guess."

"I'll give you another licking, if you don't mind," snarled the young peer.

He didn't at all like the cool, self-possessed manner of Frank.

"Monsieur Urner, if you like, was in your place," said Leon, who had not yet cooled down; "but the other affair is mine."

Frank took a step, half interposing between Leon and the bully, who strode forward savagely to put his threat into execution.

"Wait a moment, if you please," said Frank, quietly. "I am sorry that my friends should have caused this *fracas*——"

"An apology," sneered Lord Mouslin, while the other boys gave Frank a look of contempt, and even Nat Urner and Leon, who believed in him, were disappointed.

"Yes," said Frank, quietly, "an apology due to the others for having been the cause of this *fracas*. I do not think fighting a very gentlemanly or a very brave mode of settling disputes, as I have observed that, except in rare cases, the bully gets the best of it."

"This melancholy chevalier is treating us to a sermon," sneered Lord Mouslin De Lain.

Frank was, however, unmoved by the taunt.

"Yes," he said, "since you call it such. But my sermon is nearly finished. There are occasions in which I consider that no quarrel can be settled without a fight."

"Indeed!" sneered Lord Mouslin.

"This," continued Frank, "where an English boy disgraces his rank and his country, is one of them. Lord Mouslin De Lain, you are a coward and a poltroon!"

Something like a sigh of relief escaped from the young bully's chest as the air rang with hurrahs.

"At last," he said, with grim malice, at the same time moving triumphantly towards Frank, "at last you, too, have let yourself in for a good licking."

"This is not the place to settle it," Frank replied. "We will go to the fighting-ground. Barry Cornwall and Nat Urner are my seconds. Now follow me if you dare."

So saying, he moved away.

"So you are going in for a regular 'mill,' are you?" said Lord Mouslin De Lain, foiled in his intention of striking him at once. "Very well. All I can say is, so much the worse for you, my melancholy-faced game-cock. I would have let you off with a few punches. Now you shall have it hot, I promise you."

Frank made no answer, but continued on his way.

"Here, you two!" said Lord Mouslin, pointing to Hans and Joel Skimp. "You will do as well as any other fellows. It will soon be over."

Again he gave one of his savage grins.

"But who is to be referee?" exclaimed a chorus of voices. "We must have a referee."

Frank turned at this.

"We will have a referee in whose judgment we can rely," he said.

"You had better appoint your French friend, Leon. He knows all about English boxing," sneered the young bully.

"No," replied Frank. "This is an affair which concerns the honour of the whole school. I know of no one so fitted to see that it is vindicated as the principal."

"Doctor Primrose!" they cried, in dismay.

"I'll tell you what it is, Stainforth," said the bully; "you are a sneak."

Frank bit his lip until the blood came.

"You will have an opportunity of making good your words," he said to his antagonist. "Till then it would perhaps be as well if you saved your breath. Has anyone a piece of paper and a pencil?"

One of the boys handed him a note-book.

"I will read you what I have written when it is finished," said Frank, writing rapidly.

There was a moment's embarrassing silence, during which Lord Mouslin De Lain bit his lip and twisted his fingers nervously.

"Look here, Stainforth," he said, "you are forcing me into a false position."

Frank glanced at him quietly as he gave the pencil and note-book back to its owner, and said, with a slight look of contempt on his handsome mouth—

"No, my lord; I am only taking care that all shall know you in your true character. Here is what I have written," he said, as the bully turned red up to his eyes and walked away with, I regret to say, a muttered oath—

"DEAR SIR,—An affair in which the honour of the school is involved is about to take place. Your pupils, knowing the confidence you have placed in them, can give you no better proof of how they reciprocate it than by asking you the following favour:—They wish you to forget for a time the existing relations between you and them, and act for them in a matter which requires the independent judgment of a gentleman. The matter must, of course, be *ex cathedrâ*.

"Signed
"THE PUPILS OF LAKESIDE ACADEMY."

"Bravo!" cried the volatile boys, who now admired Frank as much as they had before despised him.

"Shall I send it ?"

"Yes, yes.   Hurrah!" they cried.

"You will take this, Leon," said Frank.

"You are making grand preparations or your own defeat!" called out Lord Mouslin De Lain.

Frank made no answer.

"I suppose you think I won't lick you as badly when the doctor comes, you little sneak! But you are very much mistaken. I will, if I have to leave here for it."

They walked towards the fighting-ground.

There was a piece of turf smooth as velvet about twenty yards square, which was fringed on each side by tall trees.

These would serve effectually to prevent the sun from entering the combatants' eyes in the event of a conflict, while they, at the same time, acted as a sort of barrier against curiosity.

In short, if the boys had wished to fight without being observed they could have found no better place.

"I reckon you're in for a lickin', Frank," Nat Urner said, as they gained the ground.

"I suppose so," returned Frank.

"You seem to take things mighty coolly.

"What's the use of taking them otherwise?"

"That's so.   Hang it! I wish I could lick that rooster. But he's too almighty big for me, and so there is nothing for it but to put up with what I've got. I tell you what it is," he continued, "I wish you hadn't invited the doctor; it looks bad."

"Yes, it does," said Frank; "but I am sure I have done the right thing under the circumstances. Remember how he has always trusted us, and there is another thing too."

"Go ahead, full speed."

"This fight won't be any child's play. It must come to the doctor's ears, and whatever does happen I want him to see with his own eyes."

"I don't know what you mean," returned Nat; "I only know that the lily-livered brute is a good head and half a shoulder over you, and could give you thirty pounds' weight without minding it."

"Here are your instructions," said Frank.

But as they affect the progress of the story, and show fully Frank's reason for inviting the doctor, I must keep the reader in the dark for a little while longer.

While the two boys were talking the others came up and formed a ring with ropes.

"Won't he get a licking!" cried one. "I'm sorry, for Frank isn't half a bad fellow."

"I'm sorry he asked the doctor," said another. "You see, if he stood a chance of winning I wouldn't mind, but it looks as if he asked the doctor to save himself from getting too bad a licking."

Just then the doctor approached, accompanied by Leon De Gardin.

"Bless my soul, boys! a fight?" he cried.

"And we wish you to be referee."

"But this is most unusual. I—bless my soul!—what am I to do? It is a most unusual—the idea of a principal sanctioning—I—really boys—bless my soul!"

"You are not a principal, doctor," said Frank. "You are simply a gentleman come to see that gentlemen conduct their affairs of honour in a proper manner."

"But this is without precedent."

"So is your school, doctor. You must pay the penalty of having obtained the entire confidence of your pupils."

"I feel immensely flattered; but really the affair is most awkward. What will your parents and guardians think if they know I have sanctioned such a proceeding? Really, my dear boy, I must not allow it. What will they think?"

"They will think exactly as we do, doctor, that strange diseases beget strange remedies. In point of fact, we know nothing of Doctor Primrose,—the gentleman who has honoured us with his society——"

"Very well, then," said the doctor, "I agree. Let me see where I was at. Must you fight? Are you ready?"

Without more ado the boys stripped. The others clustered about the ropes.

Nat Urner went up and whispered to the doctor, who, after divers hems and haws, cleared his throat.

"The conditions are these," he said—"the vanquished one is to apologise to whomsoever his conqueror shall direct him. The conditions are requested by the challenger, and the reason why this is done is because a foreigner, bound by other laws of honour than our own, has agreed to leave his honour in his friend's hands, thus conforming to the laws of the country in which he lives."

Leon looked at Frank, and Frank returned the look with interest.

"Do you not approve, Leon?"

"*Ma foi!*" cried Leon, "you have set yourself a difficult task. I will support you. Yes, my honour is safe with you."

Now indeed the boys gave a loud cheer.

They understood thoroughly what brave and noble Frank had accomplished.

While satisfying the outraged feelings of a foreigner, he had taken the only means by which he could prevent bloodshed.

But they only knew half yet. They were not aware of all the sacrifice Frank was prepared to make.

"We will conduct this most unpleasant affair by the strictest rules, gentlemen," remarked the doctor.

Now the antagonists were stripped to the waists—Apollo and Hercules.

The muscles rolled up on the young peer's broad back as he flung back his arms, and stood out in knots upon his brawny arms.

His face was set in a vindictive grin, which showed his white teeth; he had a handsome, stolid sort of face, of which he was very proud; but its pleasing appearance was marred by the tempest of fierce passions that swept across.

Frank was as straight as an arrow. His face, thoughtful, pale, and handsome, was severely classical, and his figure presented a wonderful contrast to his antagonist. It showed patient endurance and agility.

The other possessed weight and terrible strength.

"Two minutes and a half is the time allowed for recovery," said the doctor. "Poor boy—poor Frank—umph!"

"Remember," whispered Frank, "if I get a knock-down blow you must bring me to in time at all hazards."

"Right."

"No matter what pain you cause me."

"You bet," said Nat; "I know what you mean, and I'll help you as far as I'm able."

The boys advanced amidst dead silence.

"Time," cried one of the boys. "Set-to!"

Frank and the young lord advanced to the centre of the ring.

"Doesn't Frank look well!" cried one. "But I had no idea that Lord Mouslin De Lain was so much bigger than he."

"Poor Frank! he is going at it coolly. Do you know what it is?—I think Frank is going to try and mark him, and then allow himself to be beaten. Look there; by Jove!"

The boys became intensely excited.

To their utter surprise Frank developed powers that astonished them.

The two combatants twisted round one another, their arms shot out like lightning, they dodged, feinted, and gave the soft pat-pat of the gliding guard.

At the end of five minutes both retired to the corners.

This was a revelation to the boys.

It was not fighting hard, it was the science of boxing.

"Well, I never knew that a 'mill' could be such a beautiful thing to look at," cried one of the boys. "Isn't it wonderful?"

"By Jove! did you see the guards?—they were like lightning."

"It's like fencing, only I should say more difficult. Look how Lord Mouslin De Lain seems put out."

Well he might be. He had taken lessons from a great prize-fighter, and yet Frank's superior skill kept him at bay.

"Ah!" cried one of the boys, "now I can understand how terrible must have been those old Grecian boxing-matches where they killed men at a blow."

One observant boy became very much excited.

"Do you observe the angle of their bodies when they hit out?" he said; "they strike with the whole weight of their bodies, not such silly little blows as we do with our arms only, sending in just enough power to raise a lump. If Lord Mouslin De Lain hits Frank a direct blow on the temple he'll kill him."

"Nonsense!"

"I tell you it is so. This is no child's play, and none knows it better than Frank Stainforth."

"Hurrah! hurrah!" suddenly went up from all their throats.

"Oh, Heaven, he is killed!"

CHAPTER VI.

HOW THE FIGHT ENDED.

THAT which had caused the exclamation of astonishment and fear on the part of the assembled spectators was a magnificent throw.

It is a feat in the science of self-defence which even the most expert can rarely accomplish.

To ensure success one must risk everything, and Frank risked his hope on that desperate chance.

As Lord Mouslin De Lain rushed upon him he suddenly dropped, the blow passed over his head, at the same time he caught the young peer by the hips, and, with a slight upward jerk, flung him over his shoulder.

He came down with a crash.

All were astonished at this exhibition of what they supposed to be sheer strength; instead of which it was skill on the part of the bold Frank.

Your books of physics will tell you that a force in motion requires only direction to be self-destructible.

It was this principle which had been applied in this case.

The young peer's rush and weight were well met by Frank.

He fell heavily, and, amidst the plaudits of the spectators, Frank retired to his corner.

The young bully's seconds found him almost unconscious, and it was with extreme difficulty that they got him into his corner, and began sponging him.

Presently he recovered.

"Bravo, Frank!" said Nat; "I didn't think you could do it. He can't punish you very hard after that. By Jove! you even stand a chance of winning."

"You don't know what I have provoked," said Frank; "this will be a fearful round for one or both."

"Ready? time!"

Both boys advanced.

Lord Mouslin gave a cry of rage and forced his blows in right and left.

Frank made no effort just then to return them.

It was all he could do to guard, but, save a few body-blows which were received half spent, he escaped punishment.

Suddenly the young peer presented his face without a guard.

Frank saw what he thought his advantage.

He hit out. •

His blow went true to its mark, but he had much better have let it alone.

It was a decoy.

Receiving the blow with perfect indifference, the young bully countered with his whole weight on Frank's forehead and stretched him senseless.

Poor Frank!

A cry of dismay arose.

Frank went down so much like a log that the spectators feared he was killed outright.

Nat Urner sprang to the assistance of his friend and carried him into his corner.

"Oh, dear, oh, dear! do you throw up the sponge?" asked Doctor Primrose; "do it, for Frank has proved himself both a brave and formidable antagonist."

"No," said Nat, stoutly. "We shall be there, I guess."

"Bless my soul!" cried Doctor Primrose; "you don't mean to say you intend to continue the fight?"

"We are not yet defeated," cried Nat; "we win yet."

All this while he was striving to bring Frank round.

Time was precious; the second-hand of the doctor's watch was travelling round very rapidly.

Leon had his watch in his hand.

"Oh, *mon ami*," said he, "it is all over, I fear. He has only thirty seconds to spare."

"I'll bring him to," returned the American boy, desperately.

"How?"

"He told me not to let him be beaten, and I won't."

"How are you going to prevent it?"

"In this way," whispered Nat.

He produced a pin.

" It is cruel, but it is necessary," he said ; " hold up, Frank."

So speaking, he forced the pin into Frank's arm.

This did not bring him round ; he was therefore obliged to reiterate the operation three or four times.

In consequence of this Frank revived.

" Quick, lad," cried Nat, earnestly, " into the ring ; you have not a moment to spare."

Frank looked round vacantly.

Nat pushed him on his feet.

" Quick—quick ! "

" Where am I—ah—yes—I——"

" Time," cried the boys.

Frank staggered into the ring.

Lord Mouslin made a rush at him, but before his blow reached its destination the young hero, overcome by weakness, dropped to the earth.

Again Nat picked him up.

" That is good," he cried ; " we have gained another two minutes' breathing-time, old boy. Keep on with the drop-game until you get your senses again."

Lord Mouslin was furious that he could not finish his antagonist with a blow.

He himself was beginning to look very groggy.

The fall had done him a deal more harm than was at first apparent.

He began to feel that most treacherous of all symptoms.

He grew ill at his stomach.

During the next five rounds they fought pretty evenly. Frank was on his guard.

But now it was pretty evident that a change was taking place.

As Frank grew better Lord Mouslin De Lain grew worse.

He became decidedly groggy.

Now came gallant Frank's opportunity.

Wily, active, and patient, Frank darted round and round his huge antagonist, seeking for a weak place and yet careful not to expose himself again to one of those treacherous blows which would perhaps have killed him.

Before very long he had closed up his lordship's two eyes, finishing the left with a clean knock-down blow, which lifted the bully off his feet and sent him spinning earthwards.

On the other hand Lord Mouslin De Lain had not been idle.

Frank's cheek was cut across, and the blood streaming from the cut on his forehead so profusely that you would have thought the boys were fighting with knives.

Suddenly Frank threw up his hands, gave a cry, and remained fascinated.

Those who saw him falter cried out that he was beaten ; but Nat, whose eyes were everywhere, at once saw the cause.

Directly behind Lord Mouslin, outside the ring, but looking upon his master with a sinister look on his face, was Snarly Cool.

This was what had caused Frank to hesitate.

Lord Mouslin took advantage of this.

Rushing upon him, he flung him heavily, half twisting him round.

" Take that Snarly away. Order him off the field ! " screamed Nat, as he rushed to pick up his friend.

" Why ? " asked the doctor, shaking with excitement.

" Because he disconcerts my principal," returned Nat ; " I insist upon it."

" Leave the field, sir ! " cried the doctor to Snarly.

" My place is by my master's side," cried Cool.

By this time Nat had got Frank to his feet.

The lad was very pale.

" Are you all right, dear old chap ? " cried Nat ; " a few more rounds will finish him."

" My right arm feels numb," cried Frank, faintly ; " throw some water on my face. Let Snarly Cool remain, but let him keep behind me."

" Right, lad. But let me rub your arm."

He took hold of it.

It lay a dead weight.

Frank uttered a scream of intense anguish.

" You had better stop fighting now," whispered Nat, in a low voice, turning pale himself ; " you cannot fight any more ; give it up."

" No, no."

" You must. Your arm is broken."

" It can't be helped," said Frank. " I won't be beaten while I have life left in me to stand up. I will beat the bully."

The poor old doctor was crying like a child.

"Poor boy!" he cried, wiping away the tears with a huge, red silk handkerchief. "God bless my soul! I'd give a thousand pounds—ay, two thousand pounds, if this had not taken place."

Lord Mouslin De Lain was getting blind.

It became evident that he could no longer see where to plant his blows.

Very often he hit only the air, while Frank, deadly pale, returned the blows with knock-downs.

He fought with only one hand; the other lay useless by his side.

"That's the auctioneer," cried several of the boys, noticing this. "He is keeping that in reserve to finish the fight with."

"I wouldn't like to be in Lord Mouslin's boots when that blow does come," cried another.

Frank heard their remarks and smiled bitterly.

"They little know," he whispered to himself.

Tears of baffled rage and hate burst from the young lord.

In the next round Frank struck his lordship, but the blow was so great that he himself went down.

Nat raised him up.

"You must throw up the sponge," cried Frank, in a voice that was scarcely audible. "I am beaten. I haven't the strength—to stand—on my feet again, and—my arm feels—as if it were—on fire. Oh—I——"

Ere his speech was concluded he fainted dead away.

"Poor fellow, he fought hard for it," said Nat, with the great tears rolling down his face. "To think that that great coward and bully should win, after all. Well, I suppose what must be must be. Here, Leon, hand me that sponge; it goes against the grain, but I must chuck it up."

This was said in a whisper.

The spong was given him.

Hark!

Nat was about to toss it up, when a great cheer made him stop.

To his utter surprise, he saw a sponge in the air in the other corner.

Lord Mouslin De Lain was beaten.

Hans had chucked up the sponge.

At the very last moment Frank Stainforth was acknowledged conqueror.

"Hurrah, hurrah for Frank!" they shouted.

"Hurrah, hurrah!"

In a trice the ropes were flung down.

They crowded about him to offer their congratulations.

Not one went near Lord Mouslin De Lain.

Somebody saw him led away by Hans and Joel.

He was quite blind, and had a head like a vegetable marrow.

Stand back, stand back, all of you, and let him have air!" cried Nat. "Doctor, you must summon medical assistance."

"Bless my soul! nothing serious, I hope," said the doctor, anxiously.

"Oh, dear! oh, dear! He has broken his arm," returned Nat.

"Broken his arm!" echoed the boys.

"Was that why it hung by his side?" asked one.

"Yes, poor fellow," said Nat, who was busy trying to staunch the blood on his face.

"Impossible!"

"It's a fact."

"What a brave fellow!"

"Now we know why he wanted Doctor Primrose."

"He was determined to win."

These and a thousand other disjointed expressions filled the air.

In the meanwhile Doctor Primrose became greatly excited.

"Leon," he said, "run to the house and tell the groom to hasten at once to the village and get a surgeon; lose no time. Nat, take some boys with you, take off the green-house door, and bring it here. Poor boy, poor boy! I am an old fool, and not fit to take charge of boys any more than the man in the moon."

"Ah, doctor," said one of the boys, "you did the right thing after all. If he has gone through so much physical pain willingly to save the honour of the school, what do you think would have been his mental anguish had you forced him into the position of a coward?"

"I declare I don't know what to think, cried the doctor, in great confusion. "You boys are really too wise for your age. When I was a boy we never did these things. God bless my soul! young gentlemen now are as touchy about their honour as if they were grown men. I don't know where this affair will end. I fear it may break up the school."

"TOM FLOREMALL" SERIES OF SCHOOL STORIES.
THE TRAVELLING SCHOOLBOYS.

"BY THE TIME THEY HAD PUT HIM TO BED THE DOCTOR CAME."

"No, doctor," cried one of the boys; "we are all with you in this matter. I believe I speak the sentiment of the whole school."

"Well, well," cried the doctor, "I must think about the consequences some other time. At present this poor boy demands all my care."

Just then assistance approached in the shape of Squat, who was accompanied by Pomponet.

They carried the door between them.

"Messieurs," said Pomponet, "this puts me in mind of the battle of the Nile, where we gave the English such a thrashing."

"Be good enough to hold your tongue, Pomponet."

"But, monsieur, *je vous* assure——"

"Silence!"

Pomponet became dumb.

The door was lifted on the boys' shoulders, and, keeping step in perfect time, so as not to jar the sufferer, they carried him smoothly towards the house.

One of the tutors gave up his room immediately, and thither they took Frank.

By the time they had put him to bed the doctor came and set his arm.

Meanwhile there were hosts of volunteers to sit up with him; but the doctor set his foot down firmly on the point.

"No," he said; "watching sick persons is not the work for boys. You may come in alternately in the day-time, and read to him, after a week or so, but just now he must be left to grown-up men."

Nat went upstairs to see Frank.

"Say, how are you, old chap?" he asked.

"Nat," said Frank, "don't let him come——"

"Whom?"

"Not in the night, for Tom is mad in the night, and I am mad, and we're all merry mad together, except when the hideous phantom comes out of his eyes, and trails itself across us. Ugh! take it away! Not him—don't let him come."

The sufferer's eyes roved vacantly around the room.

"Umph!" cried Nat; "his brain is wandering, but I think I know what he means, all the same."

He found Leon and Barry Cornwall in the playground.

"Look here, you two," he said; "I reckon you know that Frank has a secret?"

"*Oui!*"

"Yes!"

"Well, whatever that secret is, it's got something tew dew with Snarly Cool."

"Yes."

"Whenever that lily-livered skunk is around he makes poor Frank crazy with fear."

"Yes."

"You can bet your boots that now's his chance to work off his hate. Wouldn't it be easy for him some night when we are all asleep to sneak in there and look at Frank, and perhaps drive him into a fever, or twist his wounded arm——"

"Horrible!"

"*Mon Dieu!*"

"I don't care, I believe the skunk would do it. I have a plan."

"What is it?"

"One of us will sit up every night."

"Good——"

"In the passage-way outside, we will thus be able to watch over our champion."

"Yes, *mon ami*," cried Leon, with tears in his eyes. "I love the brave English Frank."

"Since he took care of our honour the least thing we can do for him is to be certain of his safety."

"It sal be a ferry great pleasure, it sal be ferry great inteet," cried little Barry.

"All right, then, old man," said Nat, "we are agreed."

On the other side, Hans, little Joel, and Lord Mouslin, who was very shaky still, were constantly together.

They spent their time in devising a plan for revenge.

"I'll be even with him yet," hissed Lord Mouslin De Lain. "I hate him so, I could kill him."

"It's not such a difficult task just now," said a deep voice.

He turned, guiltily.

Snarly Cool stood before him.

"You're a sweet, revengeful sprig of nobility, you are," he sneered. "Come into the woods, my lord; a word in your ear."

Lord Mouslin changed colour and went with Snarly Cool.

CHAPTER VII.

FRANK SEES A GHOST AND BARRY CORNWALL LAYS IT.

THE affair of watching alternate nights was kept a profound secret by the triumvirate.

The doctor was too much absorbed to notice that they began to look haggard and pale, and that Barry Cornwall had a trick of falling asleep with his head on his desk every third day.

Notwithstanding the doctor's alarm about the affair becoming public property, it was not hushed up.

He wrote to the parents of all the boys, stating the circumstances of the case, which was signed by all the boys in the school.

Strange to say, he had received at the end of a fortnight the unqualified approval of everybody.

Meanwhile, Hans, Joel, and Lord Mouslin had plotted together how they might have their revenge, but as yet the prospects of it seemed very slim indeed.

Whatever Lord Mouslin knew from Snarly Cool he kept to himself.

It was Barry's turn to watch one night.

He was dozing on this particular night, when he woke up with a sort of horror on him.

He was broad awake.

He listened.

Presently he became aware of low moans coming from Frank's room.

This brought Barry to his feet instantly.

He listened.

At first he thought the moans of the boy might be caused by the anguish of the bones knitting.

But it speedily became evident to the young Welshman that Frank was not moaning from pain, he was remonstrating with someone.

That someone was evidently one for whom he had great terror.

It was Squat's turn to keep watch in the sick room.

"Surely," he thought, "if there is anybody in the room Squat would see who it was."

While thus communing with himself he walked softly towards the door, and, pushing it a little wider open, gazed in.

He was for some time completely spellbound by terror, and stood as if frozen.

The thing which had caused Barry's terror was a hideous shroud-shaped figure, which emitted a pale, phosphorescent glow.

A pale yellow, luminous light seemed to come from it, and ascend in ghastly blue wreaths to the ceiling.

Its face was indescribably ghastly, being of a livid pallor, and it held out one hand outstretched, the skinny finger of which pointed towards the terrified sufferer in the bed.

"Beware of me! I come—I come!" it said to Frank, in a most sepulchral voice.

Cold perspiration streamed down the young Welshman's face, but he nerved himself for a desperate effort.

His pent-up feelings could no longer be restrained, and he gave forth a shriek as he rushed at the ghost.

The scream had the effect of rousing Squat, who echoed it with redoubled power.

The ghost turned and fled round the room. Barry sprang after it, and succeeded in catching it by the mantle.

A door opened into the corridor leading to the servants' apartments, and through this went the ghost, dragging the heroic young Welshman after it.

He remembered nothing after that. It seemed to him indeed that he saw the fat, sallow face of Snarly Cool, but, ere he was well conscious of it, he received a blow on the head, which sent him headlong to the floor.

Squat had dashed away down the corridor leading to the dormitory reiterating his cries. Here he was met by a dozen scared boys clad in their nightgowns, and Squat, already frightened out of his senses, and imagining them to be ghosts also, stopped dead short, turned a back summersault, and, uttering a most dismal howl, departed the way whence he had come.

"What is it?" "What's the matter?" came from half a dozen voices.

But Squat paid no heed to them. He rushed madly onwards until he again gained Frank's room, and then, flinging himself under the bed, gave way to his terror in the most heartrending moans.

By this time the doctor had scrambled out of bed and struck a light. He appeared, lightly clad, looking very grotesque in his long red nightcap.

"God bless my soul!" he exclaimed; "what can be the matter?"

"We don't know, sir," cried the trembling boys. "We heard the most appalling screams, and, rushing out, were met full tilt by Squat, who ran away again to poor Frank's room."

"Let us go there at once," cried the doctor. "I fear for poor Frank."

"I am certain I heard Barry Cornwall's voice," said Nat Urner; and, struck with a sudden idea, ran ahead of them all into Frank's room.

He found nothing here to explain matters except Frank moaning.

"Go away; go away! Do not come to me!" he cried.

A dismal groan from beneath the bed caused an investigation, which led to Squat being hauled out by the heels.

When questioned he could not answer. He rolled his eyes, and pointed down the passage leading to the servants' department in evident terror.

When he had regained his voice all he could say for some time was—

"Squat he habber seen de debil! Squat am goin' to die!"

Acting on the hint received from his pointed finger several boys, headed by Leon De Gardin, rushed down the passage, and there found Barry Cornwall lying flat on the ground.

They picked him up, but he sat dazed and trembling for a short period, and in the meanwhile Snarly Cool's door opened, and he appeared, light in hand, with his usual bland smile upon his face.

"May I ask what the meaning of this noise is, young gentlemen?" he said, looking from one to the other.

"Have you seen nothing?" they replied, in a breath.

"What do you mean?" asked Snarly, still blandly.

"Have you seen anyone or the—you know—the Old Gentleman?" asked one boy, casting a look of apprehension over his shoulder.

"Did you hear anything?" queried another.

"I certainly heard a scream," said Cool. "It woke me up, and, when I come to the door, I find one young gentleman upon the floor very nearly dazed, and a lot of others, who look very frightened. But," continued he, "if you ask me to tell you what it all means, I cannot answer you."

"I am fery certain that I did see a fery treadful ghost, look you," said Barry; "and he came from there."

"Where? In the dormitory?"

"In Frank's bedroom."

"You must have been dreaming."

"It sall be a fery badt dream, inteet," said St. David, "look you; it went in there—Cool's room."

Several boys, under the guidance of the bland Snarly Cool, investigated his room, but there was nothing to be found there.

"I think Mr. Cornwall must have been dreaming."

"Perhaps he was walking in his sleep, and saw a ghost," sneered Lord Mouslin, who had just come up.

"He has got his clothes on," said Joel. "What was he doing with his clothes on at this time of night?"

"I tink he knows more about dis ghost den somebody else," said Hans. "I was loose me mine shleep twice by him."

"Gentlemen," said Doctor Primrose, hurriedly, "we must discuss the subject away from here. I beg you will come to my study without further delay."

Accordingly, they adjourned thither. Some dodged into the dormitory as they passed and secured blankets or quilts to enwrap themselves, so that when they assembled they looked like a lot of Indian braves assembled to discuss a war-path.

Barry was incoherent, and vowed he saw a ghost.

Squat was equally certain that he saw the devil.

Both were equally stout in maintaining that they had not slept.

"It is a most deplorable circumstance,"

said the doctor. "If one alone had seen it, I should be inclined to believe that he had been the victim of some psychological phenomenon, but with three witnesses I do not know what to think."

"We don't know that there are three," said Lord Mouslin. "Stainforth was evidently frightened at the noise those two made. Cornwall had a bad dream on the doorstep, and, when he rushed in, he frightened Squat, who no doubt was asleep. Of course, to save himself, he immediately chimed in with what St. David said."

This seemed plausible.

But Barry maintained that he had not been asleep.

"We cannot evidently arrive at the truth of the matter to-night," said the doctor. "Return to your dormitory, young gentlemen, and I will investigate matters in the morning. As the patient appears to be greatly disturbed I will sit up the remainder of the night with him."

Accordingly, they all retired, and discussing the matter, fell asleep.

Nat Urner could not sleep.

He lay tossing about, thinking and thinking what could be the matter.

Presently he heard a soft purr-purr close to his bed.

He looked forth, and his heart beat faster and faster as he saw a large, fierce-looking cat close to his bedside.

It was flashing fire.

He felt a strong inclination to cry out, but he repressed it manfully, and, leaning over the side of his bed, called out softly—

"Puss—puss; poor pussy."

"Mil-row—yow—o-o-w!" said puss, and bounded on the bed.

Nat was startled.

He took a deep breath, and reasoned down his terror.

"The poor thing is full of electricity," he thought. "I have heard that sparks will fly out of a cat's back if she is rubbed the wrong way in the dark."

Thus a little natural knowledge came to his aid.

"Poor pussy," he said, very softly, and rubbed him down the back.

This had the effect of increasing the light, while a strong smell of sulphur revealed to him the whole affair.

"It's Tom," he said, with a sigh of relief, "and somebody has been rubbing her with sulphur for a joke."

He got softly out of bed, and going to Frank's room, found the doctor reading.

"Doctor," he said, "I guess I have found out a solution of this mystery. Come out in the passage."

They went out, and Nat closed the door.

This revealed Mr. Puss in a glow of fire.

"There," said Nat; "somebody has been up to a lark, I guess. The cat must have dashed passed Barry, and woke him up, and Squat, who was scared almost to death."

"Thank you, my boy," the doctor said, quietly; "now go to bed, and say nothing of what you have discovered; I will explain to the others in the morning."

The next morning, after breakfast, in came the doctor to the schoolroom, followed by the head ushers.

Since the school had been formed the boys never recollected having seen him look so grave, or wear such a peculiar expression.

His face was very pale, and this was so unusual a circumstance, with the ruddy-faced, jolly old principal, that they, one and all, felt that something unusual must have taken place.

"Young gentlemen," said the doctor, "I need not remind you of the affair of last night. Before I go any further, I wish to ask you all, on your words of honour, if there is one among you who, prompted by a desire of having 'a lark,' was guilty of covering the cat with a solution of phosphorus?"

No one spoke; the boys looked at one another in silent astonishment.

"I want it distinctly understood," said the doctor, "that I discountenance practical jokes. It is for graver reasons that I ask the culprit to come forward, and I am sure that no fear of the penalty attached to discovery will outweigh the instincts of a gentleman when he becomes aware that his silence may bring suspicion upon the innocent."

Still there came no answer; they remained dumb, and looked from one to the other, as though endeavouring to discover who might be the culprit.

The doctor noted this fact.

"Boys," said he, and his dear, old, kindly voice trembled with emotion—"a most dastardly thing has happened, a thing which I wish it had pleased Providence to spare me the pain of witnessing. A practical joke is at all times to be deplored, but when, either from wanton cruelty or vindictiveness, a person takes advantage of the nervous terror of a boy laid prostrate by an illness brought on by a most chivalrous defence of the public honour, I consider such a fiend in human shape unworthy of the companionship of even the basest of humanity."

This was unusually strong language for the mild-tongued doctor.

"I should consider such a person as beneath the level of common humanity," he continued, "and despite the evidence before me I can hardly believe that anyone in this school could be guilty of such an ingenious scheme for killing a brave but sick boy."

The doctor was so overcome by emotion that he could not proceed.

The boys held their breath in thrilling suspense.

What had been found?

Whom did he suspect?

These questions passed rapidly before their minds while they waited for him to continue.

"I can only add this," continued the doctor; "such a wicked scheme as this comes within the penalty of the law. I leave it to you, boys, to see that this stain which has fallen upon the school be removed. The school is dismissed for the day."

This announcement, which at other times would have been hailed with delight, was now received in gloomy silence.

The boys dispersed to the playground, and gathered in little knots to discuss what the doctor had said.

There were three youths who sneaked out of the schoolroom with white faces, and got laughed at for their pains by a tall man with a smiling yellow face.

Perhaps these three could have told something about the affair.

Their names were Hans Dunderfunk, Joel Skimp, and Lord Mouslin De Lain.

Nat and his two friends were walking together.

"Hang it!" said he suddenly. "What's the use of being gloomy over it—that won't mend matters, say?"

"Look there?" cried St. David, *alias* Cornwall, suddenly! "there is Frank Stainforth. He must have got up out of bed, and yet that is——"

"Impossible!" cried all three together.

They hurried to the spot, but ere they reached the place where they had seen the figure it had disappeared; but, while they were busily employed in discussing the mystery, they caught sight of it again, darting among the trees.

They pursued him; but the figure seemed endowed with incredible swiftness, for they could not catch up with it.

At last it disappeared from view altogether.

Nat flung himself on the ground.

"Look here, old chaps," he said, "I guess I cave in on this thing; I am getting worse into the mystery every day, and don't know my way out of the wilderness; that's what knocks, ain't it?"

"What do you mean?"

"I guess I mean this," said Nat, slowly cutting a stick. "What is the meaning of the mystery which surrounds Frank Stainforth?"

He was answered by silence only.

CHAPTER VIII.

IN WHICH MR. WEEKS THE BUTLER RISES "SOUPERIOR."

THE question which Nat Urner had propounded to his companions constituted what is commonly known as a poser.

The solution to it was found by little St. David.

"It shall be a fery difficult matter inteet to find out, look you." he said; "and I think it is most proper that we do not try to look into affairs and secrets which do not pelong to us."

"That's about the size of it," replied Nat, with a yawn. "Say, this thing is slow; let's go and have a lark."

"What shall we do?"

"Let's go down in the village and have a row with the cads."

"That's all very good for us," responded St. David; "but look you, it shall not be so much fun for Leon, who does not know how to use his fists."

"I'll tell you," said Nat; "we must give him a lesson in boxing. It will never do to let him remain in his present state of ignorance. I can give him a few preliminary lessons, and when Frank gets well he can finish him."

"It will be a finish, *ma foi*," cried Leon, laughing; "supposing he lose his tempaire there will be nothing left of Leon De Gardin."

"I guess we may as well go and have the lessons," said Nat; "since I got so badly used up by Lord Mouslin I feel that to give some feller a black eye would restore me some portion of my lost self-respect."

"That is very grand, *magnifique!*" cried Leon; "to satisfy yourself for being hit by a bully by bullying some-one else."

"I reckon it's human nature, old boy," returned Nat; "so come along to the gymnasium, and look out for a black eye."

Leon received this statement very complacently, and the trio retraced their steps.

After half an hour with the gloves Leon became rather wearied of the *science de fisticuff*, and Nat declaring that he had had sufficient lesson for one day, they adjourned.

"Hickory!" exclaimed Nat, as they passed through one of the corridors waiting for something to turn up. "There goes Weeks with a soup-tureen; I'll bet you he is going to have the soup we left yesterday warmed over."

"*Potage froid*—ugh!" cried Leon.

"It is a duty we owe to suffering humanity to prevent it, look you," cried St. David.

"Right, my little Welshman," returned Nat. "Let's go on the war-path."

Accordingly they crept after the butler, and, going on tiptoe to the pantry, found that Mr. Weeks had deposited the soup-tureen on his right, by the side of which he had placed his hat.

A peculiarity about Mr. Weeks was, that when not in dinner-uniform, he always wore a roundabout coat with enormous side pockets, into which he was accustomed to place such articles as came in his way—a clothes brush out of place, a spoon, a piece of bread— in short, they very much resembled panniers.

Mr. Weeks was stout and florid.

He had a face which resembled parboiled meat, and was the happy possessor of an underdone heart.

No amount of faithlessness on the part of the fair sex could use him up; his heart was full of love.

On the previous evening he had been to a party in the village, and there became enamoured of a maiden fair whose red arms rivalled the colour on her lips, and whose eyes sent lukewarm ecstasy into Mr. Weeks' manly bosom.

"She 'ave give me the 'art ack, that she 'ave," said Weeks. "I must hease my troubled breast by a-writin' on her a line."

He smoothed a sheet of paper, adorned it with a blot which he licked off, smoothed it again, squared his elbows, sighed, planted another dab of ink upon his cheek, stuck his tongue out of his mouth, and wrote—

"DEER, DUCKIE MARI HANN,—My art have been a-bustin' since I sor yer lookin' like the flower of pottery (poetry).

"That's neat," remarked Mr. Weeks, as he went for another penful of ink.

"Not bad," said Nat, *sotto voce*, as he crept closer, and stretched out his hand for the ladle.

Nat had filled the ladle with soup; he quietly transferred the contents to Mr. Weeks' hat.

"And now," exclaimed Mr. Weeks, "to sling in the sentiment."

"Queen ov mi sole, mi 'art is filled with love for thee."

"And my hat with soup," Nat whispered, softly.

Barry and Leon. who were looking on through a crack in the door, stuffed their handkerchiefs into their mouths and began shaking.

"When I think ov mi dooty, yeour himage comes atween me and——"

"The soup," whispered Nat, winking at the boys.

"A WET SPONGE STRUCK THE DOCTOR'S JOLLY ROUND COUNTENANCE."

"When I thinks ov yer lovin' form, a thousand and milyern thorts—burnin' thorts, comes inter mi 'ead."

"And pockets," whispered Nat.

T e butler, deep in the mysteries of composition, did not perceive that Nat had quietly filled both his right and left pocke s with the delectable compound.

"I cannot express mi burnin' thorts in vulgar perose," continued Mr. Weeks, stretching his tongue so far out in his effort of genius, that it almost touched the paper on which he was writing. "Prose is wulgar. Let them as 'as no mind use it, while I mounts mi Pegersis, as they say in books, and sigh to me inharmereter in derlilirous posy."

"Mi deerest, duckie Mari Anner,
I loves you better than——"

"A tanner,' said Nat.

"Enny manner,"

continued Weeks.

"Of men what's false to every vow,
The curs that can't write——"

"Bow, wow, wow!" screamed Nat, and dashed out of the pantry.

Mr. Weeks turned pale, then a flush of anger mounted his poetical brow; he seized his hat to rush after the offenders, and was deluged by a shower of soup.

"Cuss 'em!" cried Mr. Weeks, pitching away his tile and plunging both his hands into his pockets, to be rewarded with more soup up to the wrists.

"Cuss 'em! bust 'em!" moaned Mr. Weeks. "To think as how a poet should come to this."

He stood the very picture of despair, soup dripping from his Apollonian locks —which, by-the-bye, consisted of three straight hairs deftly parted on eithor side—and poetical fingers which had assumed the appearance of mutton driping.

By this time the three conspirators, having secured their retreat, advanced again to parley.

"I'll report you to the doctor for this houtrage," cried Weeks, aware that pursuit was useless.

"I reckon you won't just," returned Nat.

"Oh, woman, woman—lovely tanner,
Don't I wish I had my Mary Anner."

"Ma foi!" cried Leon, "how you like cold soup, barbarian!"

"Look you," said St. David, "it shall be fery wrong of you to steal the heart of a lofely maiden."

"Oh, you naughty, naughty man!" said Nat.

"Oh, you gay deceiver!"

"I were writing the accounts," said Weeks, desperately, wiping his saturated hair with his greasy hands.

"We shall have to tell the doctor, look you; you are a fery dangerous man with the ladies," said Barry.

"I tell you it were the 'counts as I were writin' on," returned Weeks; "and you kaunt make bad out of that, no how."

"Of men that's false to every vow,
And gives us cold soup, bow, wow, wow,"

roared the boys, until Weeks, driven to desperation, chased them down the passage-way, and then departed in search of clean raiment.

CHAPTER IX.

ROBIN HOOD COMES OUT IN A NEW ROLE—MR. GRUB RUBS UP HIS NATURAL

HISTORY, AND DASH TAKES A HAND IN THE PERFORMANCE.

"THERE'S one score settled, I guess," cried Nat. "Any more to pay off?"

They were passing the study at the time.

"Oh, think of me," cried a voice, and, looking in, they behold Robin Hood sissing complacently on his perch, warming himself in the morning sunlight.

"Let's have some fun with him," said Nat. "Pretty Poll!"

"Pretty Robin—Robin Hood!" cried Polly. "Think of me."

"Scratch a pole, Polly," said Nat.

"Oh, mon pauvre joli oiseau," cried Leon, putting out his hand to scratch the bird on the head.

"Sacre-e-e!" he screamed, as Poll nailed him by the forefinger and held on.

Leon jerked him off the perch and swung him round, but Robin Hood held on, fluttering his wings and making the most disagreeable noise.

"*Sacre nom de guerre!* He has bitten off my finger!" cried Leon, when they had finally induced Robin to release his hold.

"We'll serve you out for that, my fine fellow," said Nat.

"That is the second time he has had the bit of us," said St. David. "Look you, what shall we do with him?"

"Give it up."

"We can't hurt him very much, for the doctor is particularly fond of him."

"*Ma foi*—look at my finger!" cried Leon; "I have half a mind to twist his neck."

He made a forward movement towards the bird, who retreated into a corner, and showed fight.

Nat interposed between them.

"No," said he; "I have an idea."

"What is it?"

"We will paint him—make him 'beautiful for ever.'"

"Good."

"The painters have just gone to their dinner, we shall have half an hour undisturbed."

"How can we catch him?"

"You take off your coat, Leon, and cover him with it. I will stand dicky at the door to see that no one comes."

"*Ma foi*," Leon said; "you catch him yourself; I have been bitten enough. Beast! I shall not be able to write to-morrow."

"All right," said Nat; "you go stand dicky."

Despite Robin Hood's cries, the coat was thrown over him, and he was captured.

The three then hurried away with their prize to the green-house, and found no one there.

The floor was covered with pots of all descriptions and colours.

Nat bound a piece of string over Robin Hood's mouth, so that he could not open it.

His legs were next secured, and he lay at their mercy.

"What colour shall we paint him?"

"Red."

"Blue."

"No; black, with gilt wings and tail."

"No, I know; gild his legs and paint his beak alternate stripes of red, blue, and yellow."

Poor Robin Hood, whose plumage was a glossy white, was speedily so changed that his mother would not have known him.

He must have become aware of this fact, for his dejected looks betrayed him to be the most melancholy bird that ever was seen.

His legs and the tip of his beak were beautifully gilt, his body was a coal-black, while his tail showed all the colours of the rainbow.

"What shall we do with him now?"

"Let him wander at his own sweet will and pleasure."

"No; he'd get the paint off."

"Chain him to his perch, and let the doctor see him."

"That would spoil the joke too soon. I have an idea; let's catch a duck and paint him too; couldn't we tie them together, somehow—fasten them together by their legs, and call them the Ornithological Twins?"

"I have a splendid idea."

"What is it?"

"One of you stay here and watch Polly. If the painters come, give them a shilling to keep mum. I'll go and catch a duck. Then we'll dress up Squat as the Baboo Chowdar Ki Kiow, and Pomponet shall be a travelling showman."

"Good. Hurrah! we'll have some fun."

"You will find *un costume de théâtre* in my trunk," said Leon.

"And you will find a duck in the pond. Get that surly old drake that always goes about by himself," cried Nat, to Barry, as he sped away.

In half an hour he had returned with Squat, Pomponet, and the costume, while Barry had tumbled in the duck-pond, and covered himself with mud.

He captured the old drake, though, whose surly temper had vanished beneath the terrible fear that his doom with green-peas had at last come.

The painters put in an appearance at this period of the performance; but Nat "squared" them, as he termed it, by the presentation of a shilling to get beer.

Most of the boys were out on the lake, and those few not nautically inclined were deep in a game of single wicket, so that they were unintruded upon.

The thing which puzzled them most

was how to make the ligature which bound the twins together look natural.

This was a poser.

One of the painters came to their assistance.

"Glue some feathers over the string," he said, and they at once acted upon his advice.

They painted the duck green with yellow spots, and then gilded his beak and legs.

One of the painters put in a few artistic touches, and then spread over them both some sort of composition which had the effect of drying the paint almost instantly.

"Now, old men, it's your turn," said Nat.

Then came the dressing and painting of Pomponet and Squat.

The latter was adorned with goose feathers, painted yellow, blue, and red, which, with daubs across his face, gave him a hideous appearance.

"How are we to get the guys out of here?" said Nat.

"That's the difficulty."

"I tell you what it is, young gentlemen; since you've behaved so liberal, and being how it's a joke, we don't mind lending you our covered cart," said one of the painters.

"And we can get the boat-flags to decorate it with," said Nat, with enthusiasm.

The birds were carefully deposited in the cart, the horses hitched, and away went the madcaps.

Barry Cornwall had contrived to get the flags out of the boat-house without being seen.

"Lor'," said Barry, as they drove off, "who would have thought we could have had all this lark from just going to the library?"

"Such is the power of human intellect, dear boy," cried Nat, loftily.

Away the lads went at a furious pace, until they had got some distance down the road.

Then they stopped and set to work decorating the cart.

They draped it all over with flags and tied ribbons to the horses' manes and tails.

Leon had taken the precaution of securing the house-bell, and Barry bagged a tea-tray, so that they could make noise enough.

Squat was sublimely hideous as the possessor of the bird, and Pomponet entered into the spirit of the affair and rehearsed his part of French show-master to perfection.

It was a long time, however, before he could remember Squat's new cognomen, Baboo Chowdar Ki Kiow.

At last, however, everything was satisfactorily arranged.

"Say, old men, shall we get in with them?" asked Nat.

"No," returned Leon. "It would be bettair not. I sall have de pleasaire to explain to the doctaire that I have found a countryman who is the possessair of the wonderful—— What you call him?"

"The Ornithologica Cassowary Gemini," said Nat, promptly. "Don't you forget it, Pomponet."

"Me know it. The harf-a-holiday ain't the wary oh jemini!" cried Squat, turning a double summer-sault, and shaking his fat sides with laughter.

"No, you ebony-coloured rooster," said Nat. "The Ornithologica Cassowary Gemini."

"Hi, yah! I hab him, Massa Nat," said Squat. "The orti hol jab lass o gowrie oh jemini."

"I say, you fellows in the cart, don't make such an infernal row when you get near the house, or you'll disturb Frank," remarked Nat.

"Blow the music and beat the drum softly," cried Barry.

"All right," said Squat. "Massa best keep his mouf shut, and not give um back talk to Ki Kiow. Ha, ha! omi bah bah."

Before the boys could answer they entered the grounds, and there saw the doctor in company with Mr. Spotworth Grub.

They were acting as umpires to a game of cricket. As the procession came in all the boys came running towards them, shouting at a great rate, and wondering what this might portend.

"What is it, Nat?"

"Hurrah! hurrah! Come along, boys."

"A friend of Leon."

"No; only an acquaintance," said Leon, "He is a good countryman. He wants to see the illustrious Doctor Primrose, to show him the what——"

At this moment Doctor Primrose arrived on the scene.

"Eh? God bless my soul! My dear boys, what have you got there?" he asked.

"The ornithologica Cassowary Gemini," said Nat. "Just come from the Spice Islands, and exhibited before the President of the United States because he couldn't see behind him."

"Ki Kiow ha baboo," cried Squat, suddenly appearing from the cart, and flourishing a war-club made from an overgrown cabbage tied up and richly painted.

"God bless my soul!" cried the doctor; "this is very strange."

Pomponet started off. He had been well drilled, and the lies he told would have made the British tar's hair stand on end.

Despite the fact that he showed an evident tendency to introduce the subject of Trafalgar and Waterloo, he got along very well.

"I will now proceed to show the illustrious doctor, whose fame has travelled all over Europe, and whose new system is an honour to humanity, the great curiosity of the age, which I have obtained permission to exhibit from King ——"

Here Pomponet broke down, but Squat helped him out nobly. Seeing the pause, and imagining that his turn had come, he gave a yell, turned a summersault, flourished his club, and screamed "Hi-hi Poodaw Bamboo!" that being his illustrious title as nearly as he could recollect.

This demonstration having been repressed by a warning glance on the part of Nat, Pomponet continued—

"This great king has consented to exhibit his wonderful curiosity only on condition that he himself is present at every exhibition and shares the profits. The bird is the only living representative of the what——"

"I know the bird," shouted Nat, hastily. "It is called the Ornithologica Cassowary Gemini."

"Exactly," said Leon.

"The harf-a-holiday ain't she a waryun oh jemini!" yelled Squat, with another flourish, thinking his time had again come to say something.

The doctor pricked up his ears, and Mr. Spotworth Grub fancied he detected a well-known strain.

At this the drake began to quake-

-quake, and the macaw, frightened at the tones of its strange companion, made the most appalling noise.

Squat rattled an old chain, and suspicion, if it existed, was quelled.

"The animal, though small, is very fierce," said Leon. "They are obliged to keep him chained."

"Dear me," said the doctor, who was somewhat of a naturalist; "I should like to see him. I don't quite recollect the name, and I fancied I was pretty well read in natural history. But science, dear boys, is only comparative—good gracious!"

The doctor's speech was brought to an abrupt conclusion by the sudden appearance of the twins.

"Stand back, sir, stand back, boys! The bird is dreadfully fierce," said Nat.

The boys scattered to a prudent distance.

It certainly looked a comical object.

The boys had bound the birds so closely together that they resembled one.

Their gaudy plumage and the feathered limb which united them effectually concealed their origin.

"Dear me," said the Doctor, putting on his spectacles; "it certainly is a most extraordinary bird. I do not remember having ever read of it. Umph! the larger of the twain seems to belong to the macaw tribe. Umph! Mr. Grub, do you remember this species?—umph!"

"I think in a book called *Enthologœ Madœ Bibliotheque*, a very rare collection of works in the British Museum, I have come across a description of it," said Mr. Grub, smiling blandly. "Yes; the beak, which has the appearance of being gilt——"

"And the hook-shaped beak of the dexter bird," suggested Nat.

"Exactly," said Mr. Spotworth Grub. "If I am not mistaken, it lives on reptiles."

"You are mistaken, sir," said Leon; "it lives on babies."

"God bless my soul!" exclaimed Doctor Primrose.

"That is to say, the young of any animal," hastily interposed Nat. "My father kept one alive on young rats, though they are fonder of mincemeat made of little niggers."

"You don't say so?"

Just then the parrot, unable to free

himself from his companion, plunged into warfare, and went for the old drake beak and claw.

The drake promptly retorted and the twain kept up a most diabolical concert.

Feathers flew and the glory of paint began to vanish.

Squat kept up the excitement by a *pas seul* and a tendency to scalp Pomponet, who was heard to mutter something about the English and Waterloo.

The boys were almost helpless from excessive laughter.

By this time, too, the doctor was beginning to have a shrewd suspicion that he was being smoked, and several boys had ascertained the nationality of Monsieur Le Directeur by means of several well-delivered peas.

How the affair would have ended we cannot guess, except for the arrival of Dash, the house-dog, who came running up in hot haste, and at once plunged into the affray.

The first act of the unlucky drake was to put his head into the dog's mouth, retiring the next second minus that useful portion of his body.

Happily for Robin Hood, the sacrifice of his twin brother enabled him to gain time to cling tenderly with his beak and claws to Dash's nostrils, and Robin Hood was never known to let go in a hurry, a melancholy fact with which the dog was speedily made acquainted.

In vain he tossed his head in the air and uttered a howl of pain.

Robin Hood rose with the occasion, and, what was worse, when he came down, alighted on the dog's head, from which resting-place it was not in Dash's power to dislodge him.

Dash made a "bee-line" for his kennel, with Robin Hood's two tenacious claws buried in his right ear.

The howls were melody to the boys, who lay on the ground and kicked with delight, keeping up a sort of rippling triplet to Dash's prolonged bow-wo-oh! maintained at the elevation of B flat in the minor key.

A sudden suspicion illumined the mind of Dr. Primrose, and he dashed into his study.

Just then Robin hood dashed in too, and came straight for the doctor through the window.

" Robin Hood ! " cried the doctor.

And the parrot answered—
" Oh ! think of me ! "

" Of course," said the doctor; and soon after he returned to the lawn.

His royal highness Baboo Chowdar Ki Kiow had vanished with the horse and covered cart, carrying with them Monsieur Le Directeur.

In lieu of them Doctor Primrose beheld his pupils rolling over on the ground in convulsions of laughter, while Nat Urner was engaged in the delivery of a story.

" What's become of the—ah, umph !—what's his name ? " asked the doctor.

" He's gone, sir," said Nat.

" Umph ! " said the doctor; " I suppose he's gone to seek redress."

" Yes," cried Nat. " Oh, my ! I shall die with laughter ! He has—g-gone to seek re-dress ! "

" But I don't understand, young gentlemen. It seems to me you are wanting in respect."

" Not for you, doctor; but it was a very good joke indeed."

" Umph," said the doctor; " the black man was——"

" It was Squat, sir."

" And the manager ? "

" Naughty Pomponet."

" And the cart ? " said the doctor.

" It was lent by the painters."

" Umph ! Young gentlemen, I detest practical jokes — umph !—you might have killed Robin Hood. I have seen him, and, dear boys, he don't seem happy."

" We owed him one for the fright he gave us," cried Barry.

" These proceedings," said the doctor, " are very improper, very irregular. Umph ! I pardon you this time, but if it should happen again, I—ah—umph ——"

" It's too good a joke to spoil by repetition, sir," said Nat, with all the cheek in the world.

" I am very angry with you," said the doctor; and stuffing his handkerchief to his face, bolted for the house.

" To see de master rush away puts me in mind of the battle of Waterloo," said Pomponet.

" Where we licked the French badly," said Barry.

" Pardon, messieurs," responded Pomponet; " the French under the great Napoleon swept everything before them."

"You are mistaken, Pomponet," said Leon; "they were not commanded by the great Napoleon."

"By whom, then, monsieur."

"By you, my friend."

"Pardon, monsieur," said Pomponet, laying his hand on his legion of honour, with his beaming smile; "I did not know you were so much acquainted with history."

Pomponet strutted about like a little bantam-cock, to the delight of the boys.

Leon was too high-minded to care a rap how they chaffed Pomponet about the French defeats.

"*Ma foi!*" he said, good humouredly. "Even the bravest cannot always be successful; we have won plenty of victories, but the sea belongs to you barbarians of the ocean. We are satisfied with William the Conqueror, Austerlitz, Fontenoy, Joan of Arc, and lots of others."

But, on the other hand, he was never wearied of telling them tales of French chivalry in the olden times.

"There was no difference between the knights of France and Spain in those days," said Leon. "Sometimes the English knights won. Look at your terrible Black Prince. Ah! *mon Dieu*, he was a warrior. Did I ever tell you about that splendid Breton warrior, Du Guescelin—Bertrand Du Guescelin—and the Black Prince?"

"No; tell us!" cried a number of boys.

"Well, you know, my friends, they were both terrible warriors, and it was never known which was the better man of the two. At the battle of Poictiers, they fought together in single combat for an hour. Du Guescelin had five hundred of his Bretons behind him, and they might have captured the Black Prince; but Du Guescelin was too chivalrous a knight to permit them to do so.

"At last the prince, by a powerful blow from his cartel-axe, brought Du Guescelin to his knees, striking off his helmet; but at the same time he received a blow which sent his axe flying from his hand.

"At this moment the bastard King of Spain rode up, and, seeing the defenceless condition of the brave French knight, aimed a blow at his uncovered head. 'Shame!' cried the gallant Black Prince, opposing his shield to the blow, which was splintered by the shock. 'Yield thee, Du Guescelin, that I may save thee from this assassin.' But, ere the words were uttered, Du Guescelin had sprung to his feet, and pulling the king from his horse, hurled him to the ground, stunned and bleeding, then, turning to the prince, who, not having a sword, was defenceless, he said—

"'I yield me, gallant prince, to the bravest of the brave.'

"The field shook with applause as the prince, returning Du Guescelin's sword, said—

"'Your worth is priceless, brave warrior, therefore I can name no ransom. You are free.'"

"Hurrah!" shouted Barry and the other boys.

"That's a rattling good story. Do you know any more, Leon?"

"Plenty," cried Leon.

"Ah, messieurs," said Pomponet, "chivalry is all very well, but it is nothing to the wonderful wars of the great Napoleon."

"Didn't you capture the Duke of Wellington, Pomponet?" asked Barry innocently.

"*Oui monsieur*," replied Pomponet. "It happened like this. The English army were in full retreat upon Brussels, having been beaten everywhere by the Old Guard. I was slaying thousands when I met *le grand* Napoleon.

"'Pomponet,' he said, 'you are invaluable. I saw that it was you who broke the terrible square.'

"'Ah, *mon empereur*,' I replied, 'you are too good.'

"'Do you see that little cloud of horsemen flying there?' he asked.

"'*Oui, mon empereur*,' I replied.

"'Good,' he said; 'the Iron Duke is there. Capture him and I will give you the *baton* of a field marshal.'

"'*Parbleu!*' I exclaimed, 'it shall be done, and——'"

At this interesting point of the story the dinner-bell rang, and the boys hurried off, leaving Pomponet alone with his glory.

"I guess I'll go and see how Frank is," Nat said, as they went upstairs to wash their hands.

"Good," said Leon.

Nat Urner entered the room softly.

Snarly Cool was in the room with his back half-turned to the door.

Nat started, for he saw him pour a white liquid into Frank's lemonade.

"What does he do that for, I wonder?"

said Nat, as Cool, hearing him, turned with a start.

Then a suspicion leapt into his mind and resolved itself into these words— "Slow Poison!"

CHAPTER X.

THE RESULT OF NAT'S DISCOVERY—SNARLY COOL REMOVES A SUSPICION AND POMPONET MAKES A DISCOVERY WHICH INCREASES IT AGAIN.

As the terrible suspicion leaped into Nat Urner's mind he trembled.

To the brave there is something terribly fearful about the secret assassin.

Nat was brave enough, and yet the sight of this oily villain tampering with his friend's drink, made him stand irresolute and trembling.

This only lasted for a moment, but it was sufficient to give Snarly Cool time to recover himself.

His features resumed their habitual expression, that of a bland smile.

Nat braced himself, set his lips sternly, and walked up to Snarly Cool.

He knew that this serpent-like man bore him no good-will.

They were alone.

It required, therefore, no small amount of cool courage for him to walk up and lay his hand on the tumbler of lemonade into which Snarly Cool had just poured the white liquid, and say—

"Say, what was that you put into the glass?"

He looked him straight in the face, expecting every second that the baffled rogue would fling himself upon him to endeavour to wrest the glass from his clasp.

In this idea he was diappointed.

True, Snarly Cool did not meet his eye, but his features relaxed into a laugh, as he replied—

"I thought you were ill, Mr. Urner, as you entered the room."

"Why?"

"Because you looked as though you had seen a ghost."

"Answer my question."

"Certainly," answered Cool; "it was an opiate. You young gentlemen were making such a noise in the playground that Master Frank could not sleep, so I

was about to give him an opiate, as he looked feverish."

"You are sure?"

"Certain."

"Humph!"

There was a long pause, during which Nat looked steadily at Snarly Cool.

"Well, sir, what did you think it was?"

"Poison," answered Nat, abruptly.

Snarly Cool burst into a loud laugh.

"Well, sir," he said, "what would I want to poison him for? Do you think I have gone suddenly mad?"

Nat was undecided how to act.

He had, he argued to himself, positively no grounds for believing that this man meant mischief except the fact that he both disliked and suspected him; therefore he hesitated.

"I tell you what it is, sir," returned Snarly Cool, presently; "I know you young gentlemen suspect me of being everything that's bad just because Master Frank doesn't happen to like the man whom his father sent to attend on him."

He glanced towards the bed as he spoke, and Nat observed that Frank shuddered.

"He knows best who ought to take care of you, Master Frank, doesn't he?"

"Yes," moaned Frank, feebly.

"And now, sir," said Snarly, "to show you how absurd your suspicious are, I will drink the lemonade, and you can mix him another."

So saying, Snarly Cool raised the glass with a steady hand and drained the contents.

Nat was amazed.

Do what he would he could not drive suspicion of foul play from his mind.

"Very well," he said, drawing a breath of relief; "I believe you now, but I don't believe you always. I come from a land where we read men's faces, and I read something I don't like in yours. Remember you are watched, that's all."

"You have learnt to read faces to very little purpose, sir, if you suspect me," returned Snarly Cool, as he bowed him out of the room.

"I reckon if Frank dies he won't be buried without investigation of the cause; you can bet your bottom dollar on that, Mr. Cool—so good evening to you," replied Nat, as he hurried away to his dinner.

Snarly Cool watched him out of sight.

"Curse you!" he said, turning deadly pale, when Nat had got out of earshot; "I know something that will fix those smart Yankee eyes of yours, that are constantly prying into other people's business, and, by Heaven! I'll fix them before long so that you'll see nothing!"

So saying, he, too, left the room by another door, and Frank was left alone.

After dinner it was customary for the boys to stroll out for half-an-hour for the purpose of digestion.

Nat called Barry and Leon aside for the purpose of telling them what he had seen.

They strolled in the direction of the boat-house.

As they approached their ears caught the sounds of moaning.

"Halloa!" cried Nat; "I reckon there's someone in trouble."

"*Ma foi!*" said Leon, "it sounds very much like Pomponet's voice."

They opened the door, and, after gazing a moment so as to take in the situation, burst into a torrent of laughter.

"Well, I declare," cried Nat, "this beats old Hickory! What's the matter, Pomp?"

The valiant hero of Waterloo, the Nile, and Trafalgar was seated astride an up-turned gig, holding a piece of raw beefsteak to his right optic, and keeping up an incessant shout of *Mon Dieu! pauvres yeux! sacre bleu!* and kindred expressions.

"What's the matter, Pomponet?"

"Monsieur," said the veteran, removing the beefsteak from his eye and revealing the latter all swollen and contused, "you see before you the victim of a grand misfortune."

"What is the matter?"

"Messieurs, my honour have been crush, and my eye have been put out."

"How?"

"I have run against a fist. Oh, *mon Dieu! sacre bleu! mes yeux!*"

"Tell us about it."

"But I vill have my revenge! *S-a-cre nom de noms*, I sall cut him into little bits—*pouf!* I sall not have been *le maitre des d'armes pour rein.*"

"Come, drop all that, and tell who licked you."

"Monsieur, no one licked me, but I haf stop a blow from a fist—a blow, messieurs—wif *mes yeux*"

"Not with both of them," said Barry; "there is only one hurt. Who gave you that black eye? Look you, it is a fery badt black eye inteet."

"Monsieur, it was that *chiffonier*, Monsieur Snarly Cool."

"How?"

"After you have your pudding, messieurs, I leaf de dining-room, and I say to myself—'I vill go down to de boat-house and clean Monsieur Leon's boat.' So I come down. When I get to de boat-house I hear *un grande* noise, and I look in; it was—ugh! oh! ugh! oh, my. Behold, I see Monsieur Cool in the boat. He was leaning over the side and he have *un grand mal-de-mer.*"

"Sick at his stomach, was he?" said Nat.

"*Oui*, monsieur. He was as pale and he—ugh! *mon Dieu!* it was terrible."

"Umph!" said Nat, "this looks strange."

"And then, messieurs," continued Pomponet, "I was glad to think that I haf found a *perfide Anglais* who was sick with de *mal-de-mer*, and I laugh—*mon Dieu!* I laugh until the tears run down from *mes yeux.*"

"And after that?"

"He continued to be sick, messieurs, and I comfort him; I say—'*Bon, mon comorade*, be not *triste*. You are not the first *Anglais* who haf suffered *le mal-de-mer*. I remember your illustrious countryman, Milord Call-in-wood' (Collingwood) 'just before he was taken prisonaire in his vessel, de 'Royal Sovereign' he was dreadful *mal-de-mer aussi*, but I cure him by pat him on de back, and he give me his sword.

"'Pomponet,' he say, 'you have saved my life. I have fought for de honair of my country, but I give de sword to you for having cured me of *mal-de-mer*.'

"Well, messieurs, I said, 'I will do de same for you, *mon ami*,' and I do laugh very mooch—who can help laugh at de *mal-de-mer*? I tump him on de back —I keep on tumping for five minutes, and then he rise to his feet and he say—

"You copper-coloured, garlic-eating, yellow-bellied, monkey-faced son of a swab! There is a thump in return, to teach you how to make fun of a sick Englishman."

"Well, go on," said Nat.

"Well, messieurs, dis was vat he call gratitude. He hit out, and I stops de blow mit my eye, *mon Dieu!* Den de cook she give me beefsteak, and she call me poor leetle French monkey. *Sacre bleu!* he sal fight me wid de sabre!"

"Pomponet," said Leon, quietly, "it serves you right."

"Why?" asked Pomponet.

"Because," returned Leon, "you had no business to insult a sick man."

"But I did not insult him. I did want to do him good."

"You ought to apologise, Pomponet."

"But, messieurs, must I not fight him with the sword?"

"Don't you know that fighting is strictly forbidden since Frank Stainforth broke his arm?"

"*Oui, monsieur;* this is an *affaire d'honeur*."

"Hickory! Jerusalem!" exclaimed Nat. "The honour of a servant! Well, they have some queer notions in Europe."

This was enough for Pomponet. He strolled away disconsolately.

"There, he has found Squat," said Nat, as he watched the two fraternise. "If that nigger doesn't put him up to a bit of revenge on Snarly Cool worth having,

then my name is not Nathaniel Urner, and I don't live in Salem, Massachusetts, when I'm to home. I tell you what it is, lads," he continued, suddenly, after a long pause; "I guess that was poison, atter all."

"How do you know?"

"I'm satisfied," returned the American boy, whittling away viciously at a stick, "that he swallowed the poison to put me off the track, and then took an emetic."

"Impossible!"

"Gospel."

"If he is such a villain he is a very brave one," said Leon.

"Pshaw!" replied Nat, contemptuously. "Any rooster would be brave if he were driven into a corner; and I had him cornered."

"Had we better tell the doctor?"

"No."

"Why?"

"Because it would only distress him?"

"But then consider Frank's life."

"It just amounts to this," said Nat. "That darned skunk ain't going to try his hand at poison again. That little game is played out."

"But he may take some other method."

"True."

"Well, it is a pretty hard line if we can't secure him. He has only got two legs, two hands, and two eyes. We have half a dozen of each, and Squat and Pomponet to spare."

"You forget he has accomplices."

"Who?"

"Lord Mouslin de Lain, the German, and little Joel Skimp."

"Yes, up to a certain point. But they are not the sort of birds to go in for murder. That's ugly work, and, if he wants to do it, he'll have to do it by himself."

CHAPTER XI.

JOEL SKIMP IS SENT ON A MISSION, BECOMES CURIOUS, AND PAYS THE PIPER.

By this time Joel Skimp had become the acknowledged fag and factotum of Lord Mouslin De Lain and Hans Dunderfunk.

There was not the slighest necessity for his being a fag. Fagging was not a part of the school system.

All these pleasantries fell to the lot of Joel Skimp, and for the simple reason that he was a born tody. He gloried in it.

No work was too dirty for him, if by doing it he could retain the favour of his patron. He fagged also for Dutchy. But this was by no means voluntary service.

Hans was a great friend of the young peer, for one thing, and was capable of giving him a good hiding for another, and so Joel fagged and toadied to him also in his spare moments.

As a reward he was admitted into their confidences and plots, and was never wearied in telling his schoolfellows how his friend and chum Lord Mouslin De Lain had asked him to visit his father, the Earl of De Lain's castle, and had promised him that he should go down the Mediterranean with him in his yacht when his lordship began his travels.

There was one especial rule in Lakeside Academy which was strictly enforced. No boy was allowed to drink any sort of stimulant between meals, and liquor of any kind was strictly prohibited being carried into the house.

Hans, who was fond of schnapps, and Lord Mouslin, who was fond of anything he could lay his hand on in the shape of strong drink, found means to evade this rule, and the chosen instrument of their evasion was Joel Skimp.

On this particular night the moon shone brightly and beamed her sweetest smile upon the earth, as though she rather enjoyed these nefarious proceedings.

Joel was lowered from the window, with instructions to procure a supply of liquor. He reached the ground without mishap, peered cautiously round, and, finding no one visible, presently gained the boat-house, and quietly launched the gig.

A few moments more sufficed to send it skimming out on the surface of the lake, and as many more under the shadow of an island, on the northern side of which he speedily disappeared.

He had scarcely disappeared from view of the boat-house ere another form emerged from the schoolroom window, and also betook himself in the direction of the boat-house.

This was Snarly Cool.

He looked somewhat pale under the moonlight ; his habitual smile had vanished from his face, and was replaced by a dark scowl as he pulled steadily on.

He stopped just before he reached the first island, allowed his oars to swing in the rowlocks, and eased his mind by shaking his fist at the only window in Lakeside Academy whence gleamed a light.

There slept in uneasy slumber Frank Stainforth, happily unconscious that his servant was abroad intent on evil.

Fortunately for Joel, this temporary rest on the part of Snarley Cool enabled him to shoot his craft round another island ere his pursuer turned the first one, so that he was not perceived.

The young voyager continued his course for about two miles more, when he pulled to a little wharf, where boats were let on hire.

Joel fastened his boat to the wharf, and taking his basket, ascended to the inn.

The inn was in " full swing," and the bar-parlour resembled cloudland, as Joel Skimp appeared and asked for the landlord.

He speedily appeared ; a fat man with a look of jovial greed in his eye, and the signboard of strong waters upon his nose.

" And," he said, using the conjunction as though it were the connecting link between volumes of thought unspoken and his present address, " what can I do for you this evening, Mr. Skimp ? "

" Skimp, enow ; he do put oi in moind o'a scarecroa, he doa," said a lout, at which there was a guffaw.

" Please don't call me by my name, Mr. Snatchem," said Joel ; " it might get to someone's ears, you know."

" You just put a bridle on your tongue," said the landlord to the lout. " I've seen a many a better'n thou thrown on the road for less."

He scowled fiercely, and the lout's laugh shrivelled and shrank into the veriest whine as he said —

" Eh, it be only a joak, thou knowest well enow."

" Keep your jokes for your own sort, and don't waste 'em on young gents as knows how to pay for what they call for," retorted the landlord.

This bit of satire effectualy cooled the lout's ardour, and turned the laugh against him.

" And what will you have this time, sir ? " said the landlord, turning to Joel again.

"TOM FLOREMALL" SERIES OF SCHOOL STORIES.

THE TRAVELLING SCHOOLBOYS.

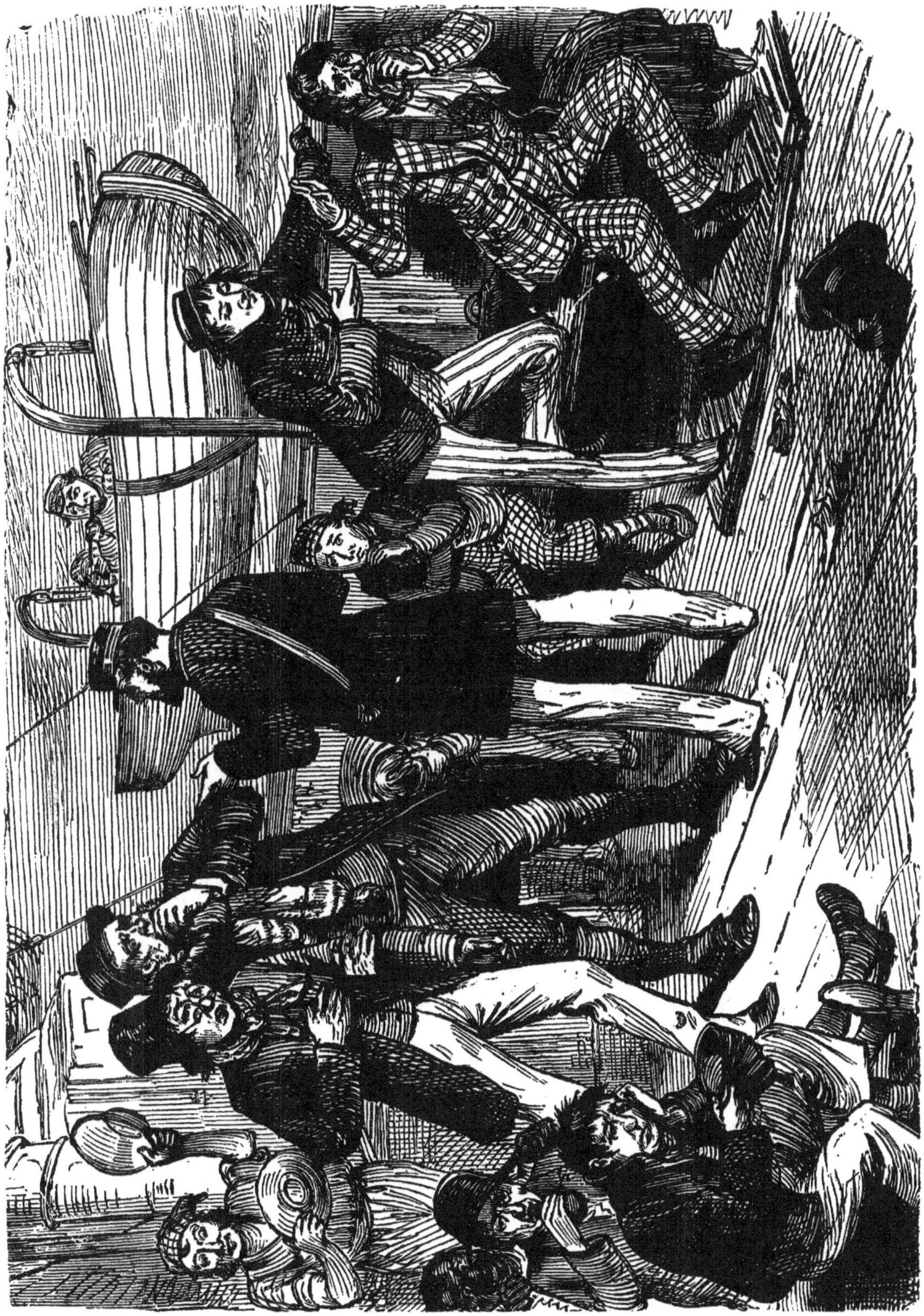

"'I'VE KNOWN SHIPS TO FOUNDER IN LESS WIND THAN THIS.'"

"The same as before, please," returned Joel.

"I have," said the landlord, shutting one eye, and becoming very mysterious, "a bottle of white port wine, the real ding-dong, and no mistake. I wouldn't give it to everyone. What do you say to taking that ?"

"Yes; but be quick, please, for I am in a hurry."

"Very good, sir; in harf a minute," returned mine host, and disappeared.

His half a minute developed into half an hour, the difference between his promise and reality having been taken up in resolving some indifferent Marsala, two or three chalk powders, and some milk, into fine old white port, for which delectable compound Joel was mulcted to the tune of seven-and-sixpence; however, his basket was finally got ready, to his intense relief.

"Perhaps you wouldn't mind taking a drop of something short yourself; it's rather coldish to-night," said the landlord.

Joel said he didn't mind, and he was speedily served with something that brought the water into his eyes.

The landlord saw him to the boat, deposited the basket in the stern-sheets, and, having seen him off, muttered the word—

"Green !"

This referred to Joel, who was soon well on his way homeward.

The "something short" had had the effect of causing him to describe a somewhat zigzag course, so that he skirted an island a little out of the direct route.

Now, had Joel not taken that drop of "something short," his natural prudence would have caused him to hurry homewards; but when he saw a light gleaming through the trees on the island, the "something short" urged him to see what it might be, and he accordingly turned the nose of his boat in that direction.

He reached the beach quietly, and was prudent enough to ground so softly that his boat-keel grazing the pebbles could not have been heard at a distance of five yards.

To his surprise, he found that he had run alongside one of the school-boats.

This more than ever provoked his curiosity; the "something short" had made him bold.

He crept through the bushes towards the light.

Two minutes spent in drawing his short body and long legs through these, served to reveal to him the fact that the light came from a small and evidently unused cottage, for no furniture was visible.

Here were two men standing conversing; they had evidently but just come in, for one of the men—Snarly Cool—was replacing in his pocket a box of matches with which he had just lighted a tallow candle.

The other man was taller than Snarly Cool.

He wore a tightly-fitting black frock-coat, and, what was particularly strange, a red scarf, that gave him the appearance of having received a wound in the breast from which a gush of blood was oozing.

There was something peculiar in this combination of red and black, surmounted, as it was, with a pale face, heavy black moustache, and piercing black eyes that caused Joel Skimp to shudder.

Curiosity, as it often does, unhappily for the victim who falls beneath its influence, overcame Joel's fears and prompted him, like a young snake as he was, to crawl closer and listen.

"And so you have made a mess of the whole business," said the tall stranger, with a slight curl to his black moustache.

"I have done the best I could," returned Cool, with an oath.

"And that was nothing," said the stranger.

"Perhaps you could have done better, since you know so much," cried Snarly Cool; "I tell you they have gotten the idea into their heads that he is persecuted, and they're all down sharp on me."

"Yes; you have managed well," said the other, with another sneering curl of his black moustache, which seemed to curl like a viper over his white teeth.

"What do you send him to that cursed school for, then," returned Cool, "where everything is done on the high falutin' principle, and the boys tell everything that occurs to the schoolmaster ?"

"How could I help it ?" returned the other, savagely. "Didn't I tell you that the guardians suspected something, and insisted on his being sent to school? This school afforded the only chance, since it admitted of young gentlemen" —again came the cruel sneer—"having their servants with them."

"Luck seems to be against us," said Cool.

"We must take care that it turns," returned the other, sternly.

"You won't want that coffin this bout, anyhow," returned Snarly Cool. "I did everything I could, psycho—whatever the deuce its name is—included. I got the boys that hate him to play ghost, and that would have settled him if it hadn't been for a young Welshman who took it into his head to watch outside the door after I had drugged the nigger."

"And the other plan?"

"The other?" echoed Cool, wiping the sweat from his pale brow; "that nearly got me a life imprisonment. They may well call me Cool, for if ever I wanted coolness in my life, it was this afternoon."

"Explain."

"I had got the poison all right. I put some in a young fellow's trunk, named Joel Skimp, whose father is a poor planter in the West Indies, and who, in consequence, couldn't make much of a defence if the thing became traced to him. He had been talking pretty loudly of how he'd fix him if he got the chance, and that was a point against him."

Joel almost shrieked with terror, and shook as if he had a vertigo, when this horrible revelation came upon him.

"To be suspected and hanged for murder! Oh, Heaven! oh, Heaven!" he moaned, mentally; "it is too horrible; I must be dreaming."

"I had fixed all that," continued Snarly Cool, "and the day after the ghost business I chose the time when they were all shouting outside, and I thought I should not be disturbed; the nigger, who is nearly always there, was out of the room for a minute; I knew he had gone to fill his fat stomach; so the coast was clear. I darted to the glass and poured a dose in."

"And———" exclaimed the other, eagerly.

"And," continued Cool, while the dark veins swelled to knots on his forehead, "just then a young American, with an eye like a hawk's and a mind like a steel trap, came into the room and spotted me."

"A pretty bad look-out for you," said the other, coldly.

"I'm a cool hand, I know, and not easily taken aback, but that fetched me."

"So it seems."

"It was fully a minute before I recovered my coolness" continued Snarly, totally unheeding the other's sarcasm, "and, fortunately for me, he was so astonished that he did not cry out."

"Proceed," said the stranger, coldly.

"I believe that boy has nerves of brass; I wouldn't care to come close up to a desperate man in the way he did, and lay my hand on the proof of his guilt within reach of his arm."

"And you did not knock him down, and throw the lemonade out of the window?" almost shouted the other. "Fool! idiot!"

"I did better than that," said Snarly.

"What did you do?"

"I told him it was a sleeping-potion, that they had been making such a noise in the playground as to make him nervous."

"And Frank Stainforth heard you?"

"Yes, and listened, with his eyes rolling round the room, like two full moons, until they seemed to illumine the bed on which he was lying."

"And he did not denounce you?"

"No."

"Then there is something in psychic influence, after all," returned the stranger. "Eh?"

Again he smiled his cruel, snake-like smile.

"I don't know what you call it," replied Cool; "it was good enough to make him hold his jaw. The American boy wouldn't believe me; he told me plump and plain that he believed it was poison, and said something about their being able to read faces in his country, and that mine was a villain's."

"He wasn't far out in his kalk'lation," sneered the other, imitating the American drawl.

"I saw I couldn't make him believe I was innocent."

"Proceed, proceed—the finale; what did you do with it?"

"I drank it!" yelled Snarly Cool, turning livid.

"Then, my friend," said the other, taking out his watch and looking at it coolly, "I am very sorry for you, for in twelve hours from this time you will be a corpse."

"Shall I?" said Snarly, more calmly, wiping the dank sweat from his brow; "I don't think so, for I hurried away and swallowed about half a bar of soap, and the whites of eggs, until I almost turned myself inside out. I was cute enough to go down to the boat-house to do it, too, so that they should not hear me retching."

"In that case," said the stranger, "your admirable coolness has saved your life, and the secret is safe."

"It is," said Snarly Cool, "not so safe as you think."

"How?"

"It's as good as discovered."

"How—quick—speak!"

"A Frenchman, the servant of Leon De Gardin, one of the triumvirate who now constitute themselves the guardian angels of this prince of English boys, as they call him, came down to clean his master's boat."

"Well?"

"Well, he discovered me, and made himself merry with what he called my *mal-de-mer*, until I lost my temper and gave him a thump that will make his jaws ache for a month."

"You should not have lost your temper."

"Lost my temper! I like to hear you say that. Look here, what with braving out a thing, and swallowing poison and emetics until I was as sick as a cat, I'd gone through enough to shake the nerves of any man that was not built of cast iron—and I'm next door to it."

"Yes," sneered the stranger; "brass. After all, it is not of vital importance. The affair must be postponed until he goes to France."

"Postponed! No more poisoning for me; that game is played out. Do you know what that young American said?"

"What?"

"'If Frank Stainforth dies, I'll have his body medically examined.'"

The other turned a shade paler.

"You are right," he said; "the affair must not be thought of until the American is put out of the way."

"And others will rise in his place," said the man, despondently. "It's no use; the boy makes friends wherever he goes. Providence is watching over him."

"Providence? pooh!" exclaimed the other.

A low moan, a half-gurgling sigh fell upon their ears.

Both men started and turned livid.

With one accord they rushed out, to stumble across the body of Joel Skimp.

He had fainted.

"He has heard all," said Cool, with the calmness of a settled purpose.

"What shall we do with him?"

"Put out the light.

It was done.

"He has no business to be out on the lake this time of night," whispered Cool. "He has come for drink. Supposing his boat were to be found drifting bottom up? Supposing he were *found drowned?*"

CHAPTER XII.

WHAT HAPPENED TO JOEL SKIMP.

THE fearful insinuation made by Snarly Cool, relative to the disposal of Joel Skimp, seemed no more to affect the other man than if he had merely asked if he were to put the boy to bed.

"It might do," said the stranger, weighing the chances in his own mind.

"Shall we do it?"

"No; at least, not yet."

"If it is to be done, the sooner the better."

He held the senseless body of the boy over the bank, holding it in such a way that it seemed as if he longed to put his threat into execution.

"In the first place," said the stranger, "gag him. That is necessary under any circumstance."

Snarly Cool laid Joel Skimp down, and proceeded to obey orders.

"Now bring him into the boat, and let us get out on the lake. Who knows? someone else may have been attracted by the light, and may have overheard what we said."

Snarly Cool started.

"It would be just our luck," he said, bitterly.

"That is your opinion only. I think bad luck is frequently the result of bad management," returned the other, taking the oars and propelling both boats out into the open water.

He had previously fastened Joel's boat to the stern of the one they occupied.

"And for that reason," he continued, after a little time, "I think I had better conduct this affair. Remember that my judgment is never at fault."

"As you like," said Snarly, wearily; "I wish I were in my bed. My head is splitting, and I feel all-overish."

"Look at this matter from a common-sense point of view. We think the boy has not been seen, but we are not sure. We cannot be certain."

"True," replied Snarly Cool.

"Someone may have seen him; one never knows about these things; there is always some mischance turning up, to spoil the best-laid plans."

"Yes; you are right; I was foolish to dream of such a thing."

"Take this piece of advice," replied the stranger, while again his snake-like moustache curled and wreathed; "never commit a murder, except as a last resource."

"But about this boy?"

"We must wait until he recovers."

They waited for some fifteen minutes, ere Joel returned to consciousness.

They became aware of this from his low moaning.

"Give him some of that stuff which has got him into this trouble," said the stranger.

"I am afraid, if I remove the gag, he may cry out."

"Let me look at him!" exclaimed the stranger."

He leaned over, and fastened a pair of brilliant snake-like orbs upon the terrified boy. They glittered in the dark like yellow diamonds, and fascinated him.

The stranger continued gazing for perhaps five minutes, at the end of which time he leaned over and whispered in his ear—

"I am going to take the gag from your mouth; if you make the slightest noise, I will kill you! make no mistake about it," he said; "we could have done

so while you were unconscious, but we prefer to save your life, that you may be useful to us. Remove the gag."

Snarly Cool obeyed.

"Drink this," said Cool, handing him a glass of spirits.

"It's not p-p-poison, is it?" asked the boy, with dead white face and chattering teeth.

"Poison, you fool? Do you think we would waste that upon you when we could have killed you comfortably, and dropped your body in the lake ten minutes ago, had we been so disposed? Drink."

This convinced Joel.

He raised the cup to his lips with trembling hands and drained it.

"Now," continued the stranger, while his eyes flashed a deadly fascination, "you have courage to listen to what I have to say?"

Joel nodded his head.

"If we did not kill you just now, it was because we can do it at any time. You are nowhere safe from our power. At any time you may be a corpse, and none will know how you came to your death. Do you comprehend?"

Joel gave him a shivering affirmative.

"Very well then," resumed the stranger; "your life is spared, conditionally on your taking an oath never to reveal what you have seen and heard to-night or shall at any future time become cognisant of. Remember, that if you break it, you will be lost, body and soul. Will you swear?"

"Ye-es," shivered Joel.

"Administer the oath," said the brilliant-eyed stranger to Snarly Cool.

This Snarly did.

It was a horrible one.

"Repeat it after him," said the stranger, and Joel muttered a stammering compliance.

When it was finished, the stranger turned the prow of the boat midst the most profound silence to the other side of the island.

When he reached it Joel saw a small boat, into which the stranger got.

"Farewell," he said; "if you want to communicate with me, use that boy."

He bent his eyes on Joel for the last time, and so doing, rowed slowly away.

"There he goes," said Snarly, propelling the boat in an opposite direction; "if ever the devil could come to earth,

I believe he'd take his shape," he continued, turning to the shivering boy by his side, "and if you don't obey him, you had better have taken service with the devil."

Joel made no reply; the events of the night had proved so horrible that they almost deprived him of the power of motion.

It was well Snarly Cool did not ask him to get into his boat and row, for he could not have accomplished it.

He felt himself weighted and chained for life to a horrible secret, with an unscrupulous, pitiless task-master.

The whole way homeward seemed to him but the consummation of a hideous dream, begun when he had first seen that fatal light.

He scarcely knew how he had parted from Cool at the boat-house, or heard the low growl of Dash ere recognising him.

His two chums were waiting for him.

They had had a long wait, and were prepared to rate him roundly with dark hints of what they would do to him on the morrow; but when they saw his pale face and staring eyes, set as if gazing upon a hideous nightmare, they forgot their wrath in curiosity.

They plied him with questions.

"What has happened?"

"You look as if you had seen a ghost."

He made them no answer, but simply pointing to the basket, staggered to the bed, where he fell a-moaning.

So ended Joel Skimp's journey for "forbidden fruit."

CHAPTER XIII.

PREPARATIONS FOR FRANCE—FRANK'S RECOVERY—LORD MOUSLIN DE LAIN TRIES HIS HAND AT A PRACTICAL JOKE, AND HANS PAYS FOR IT.

You would hardly think that the shadow of crime hung over Doctor Primrose's Travelling Academy for Young Gentlemen a fortnight after the events chronicled in the last chapter had happened.

Frank had recovered sufficiently to be able to walk about with his arm in a sling, and a day had been set apart when they should have a jollification to celebrate his return to health.

Lord Mouslin De Lain felt annoyed at the jollification for the recovery of Frank and, as a result, he pondered how he might pay off a score against them all.

The result was that Joel Skimp was dispatched to the village, whence he returned, bringing with him a small packet, the ultimate fate of which it will be our lot to chronicle.

"Je-rusalem, how time has flown!" cried Nat Urner, as he hopped into bed; "fancy, we have been here over five months."

He tucked himself in snugly.

"And fancy, we shall be in France this day fortnight," remarked Barry, who was already in bed.

"La belle France!" cried Leon, sentimentally; "oh, mon Dieu!"

"What's the matter?"

"Nothing; only I thought there was a pin in the bed. No; it is a what-you-call-him—puce."

"A flea? catch him," cried Nat. "Oh, by Jingo! there is one in mine too."

"Sacre! there are several," cried Leon; "and I am so sleepy."

"Look you, there is a fery great lot in mine, and all big ones!" cried little St. David.

"Oh, Jerusalem! hickory, whiz, slapbang! my bed is all alive! Oh!" cried Nat.

"Oh, mon Dieu, there are millions," said Leon; "c'est bas—I have caught one! Allons, perfide! No; it is gone. Sacre nom de noms, I cannot catch one!"

For some time the boys turned and twisted about, making the night air melancholy with their lamentations.

At last Nat gave a yell and started up in bed.

"I guess I can't stand this; hickory!" he cried, prancing about the room.

"Et moi aussi!" cried Leon, also springing up and dancing round the room.

"Look you—look you, I shall be eaten all up!" cried St. David, joining them in prancing about the room.

"Strike a light, someone," cried Nat.

"Oh, *mon Dieu, ce n'est pas possible*," cried Leon.

"What's the matter?"

"They are all ovair me. I keep scratch—scratch on—*pouf! Sacr--e—e!*"

"I've rubbed off a million, I reckon," said Nat, with a howl and a jump; "and there's more on me. Yeow—yeow! whoop, hickory!"

Then commenced a scene.

The boys pranced up and down, yelling like Comanche Indians.

"I wish you fellows wouldn't make that infernal row," cried a voice. "No fellow can sleep."

"I am fleas all over?" moaned Barry.

"Fleas be jiggered!" roared Nat Urner. "Red hot bloodsuckers, and I haven't caught one yet."

"Oh, Lor'! I'm all on fire," roared Barry.

"You'll have the doctor up presently," cried the same voice. "Can't you kill them and get into bed?"

"I'm on fire," shrieked Leon.

"So am I—red-hot," roared Nat. "Someone go and get a well and put me out."

There was one inhabitant of the dormitory to whom this scene gave great and unmitigated satisfaction.

This was Lord Mouslin De Lain; he shook with laughter.

"If you fellows don't shut up and tumble into bed again I'll call out for the doctor," he said.

"I wish you had 'em all over your carcase," said Nat; "then you wouldn't be in such a hurry to keep silence."

"I'll get out and punch your head."

"For Heaven's sake, strike a light!" cried the victims.

However, a light was not procurable.

"O-hah—ye-ow—hickory! the all-fired things have got on my face!" cried Nat, slapping his cheeks violently.

The row now became awful.

Other boys, unable to sleep, got out and joined in the chorus, throwing pillows at one another, and making short cruises after the water-jug.

Mr. Spotworth Grub appeared at the door, but just then a flying pillow ejected him and put out the candle.

This unusual commotion brought Dr. Primrose.

"Young gentlemen, young gentlemen, this is most unwarrantable——"

A wet sponge struck full upon his jolly round face, and instantly altered it to a countenance of war.

The immediate result of this was to fill the empty beds.

Everybody was asleep when the doctor, holding Mr. Spotworth Grub as a shield, once more entered the room.

Beautiful were the innocent slumbers of the dormitory.

The doctor looked round.

Just then Nat, unable to endure it any longer, gave a yell.

It was piercing, short, and abrupt.

The doctor turned with a startled jump to his bed; but by this time Nat, having relieved his feelings, was apparently sleeping profoundly once more.

While the doctor gazed another yell, with the abruptness of a popgun, awoke the echoes behind him.

This yell came from Barry, and while yet the doctor gazed upon his slumberous countenance, Leon gave vent to his feelings, and caused the worthy principal to jump in that direction; but by this time concealment was no longer possible.

The heat of the bed seemed to reanimate the fleas, who returned to the attack with redoubled vigour, and all the unhappy victims yelled in concert.

Scarcely had the echoes died away when, with one accord, they leaped from their several beds like marbles shot from catapults.

"Gentlemen, this is most extraordinary," said the doctor.

"Fleas?" roared Nat.

"Bugs!" screamed Barry.

"Red-hot!" yelled Nat.

They then, as well as they could, hopping about like kangaroos, informed the doctor that they had been bitten all over.

An examination of their bodies revealed this fact to be true.

Their bodies were literally burning; their bodies being, as Nat had aptly described it—"red-hot!"

"Dear me! God bless my soul! this is very extraordinary," exclaimed the doctor.

"Hi—yow—hoyah!" yelled the boys.

"Mr. Grub," said the doctor, "be good enough to examine the young gentlemen's bedding."

Mr. Spotworth Grub obeyed, and although he found nothing, he speedily felt something, and began rubbing his hands together violently.

"Oh, Lor', oh, dear!" he cried, and the more he rubbed the more painful became the evidence of his suffering, until at last he was obliged to join his cries to those of the boys.

"God bless my soul!" cried the doctor, in amazement; and then, as a sudden light dawned upon him, he said—"Come at once with me, boys; you have been the victims of a most disreputable practical joke."

Away they went, yelling like a troop of wild Indians, to the medicine-chest, where the doctor obtained a quantity of powdered sulphur, and this, having been applied to the surface of the skin, speedily destroyed the small field-insects.

Squat was sent to remove the sheets, and Ann O'Dyne replaced them with clean ones.

All this took time, and it was very far indeed in the wee small hours of the night ere they once more sought repose.

The following morning the victims of the fun met together.

"Now for revenge," said Nat.

"Do you know who put those wretched biting insects in our beds?" asked Leon.

"Of course."

"Who?"

"That thick-headed Dutchman. Do you think I didn't tumble to his pretending to be asleep when we were making that infernal row?"

"He must have had a confederate."

"Who?"

"Joel Skimp."

"No; he would be too much afraid of a hiding, and Lord Mouslin De Lain didn't laugh the whole time, and growled fearfully about having his night's rest broken up. However, they are all in the same boat. Hans must suffer for being in bad company."

"But the revenge?"

"Listen," said Nat.

He then proceeded to unfold his plot, which was carried into effect that evening.

In a retired corner of the playground Hans found the youths round a jar of preserved ginger.

"Isn't this just prime?" cried Nat.

"C'est une bonne bouche grande," echoed Leon.

"It is fery excellent inteet, look you!" said little St. David, making an enormous piece vanish down his throat.

Hans drew near. He was a gourmand, and his eyes watered at the sight of this most delicious compound.

"If I vos to make me frents mit dose poys, perhaps dey vos geef me somedings py dot jar," he said, licking his lips in anticipation. "Donder unt blitzen don't it smell nize!"

"Halloa! Here, Hans, come along."

"Vell, vot you vant mit Hans?" he asked, drawing near with his eyes fastened on the dainty morsels.

"We're going to Germany soon, you know."

"Yah," said Hans, "dat is good."

"Come and tell us something about that half-starved country."

"Dey vonts to make frents mit me," said Hans, mentally. "Perhaps dey geef me some of dose sweet dinks. Vell, vot you vants mit Shermany?" he asked, seating himself by their side.

"Help yourself, Hans. Don't be backward in coming forward. It's good, it is," said Nat, with a patronising air. "We've had our whack; wire in, old man."

Hans jammed his fist into the pot, and hauled out a huge lump, which disappeared, and he went for some more rapidly, as though he were afraid the boys might stop him.

"What's Berlin like? It can't be much, or we should not have so many of the half-starved sausage-eating creatures over here."

"Py gracious, you vos better pelieve it vos better as goot. I be frents mit you, and show you all de places mit me ven ve goes."

Then he said to himself—

"I tells dem all vot I vill do py dem until I haf finish dis pot, den l laugh py dem. Dat was a good choke."

This humourous idea so filled Hans' mind that he laughed till the tears rolled down his face.

"Say, old man," cried Nat, when he had between whiles told them about the glories of "Unter den Linden," and all he would do for them, "say, are you going to collar all that Jamaica ginger?"

"If you vos stingy mit it, it vos better dot you don't give me some at all," said Hans, getting up a show of virtuous indignation.

"Oh, you are like all Germans: you want a lot, so take all you can," said Barry.

"There ain't nothing mean about us," cried Nat. "You can take the pot and swallow it, if you like."

"Yaw," said Hans; "when I finish him, I tells you some stories."

He was as good as his word.

Not only did he eat the ginger, but the liquid also found its way down his capacious throat.

Then he rose solemnly to his feet, and a bland smile of cunning and triumph diffused itself over his fat face.

"I tell you vot," he said; "it vos a goot choke; I humbug you mit myself. I haf eat all dot sweet dings, and ven I gets you by Shermany I gets me all mine frents to lick you. Ha, ha! dat vos a good choke! I haf humbug you to get mit dem sweet dings outside."

"I hope you've had a heap of fun, Dutchy," said Nat. "It's about the healthiest joke you ever had, and I hope, old man, it won't hurt you much."

"Ha, ha, ha!" chuckled Hans; "I go get me some schleep by dot."

"Away, you go, you thickhead; I hope you'll enjoy your sleep. I reckon, old hoss, you won't sleep so easy as you think."

Hans sought a sunny corner, and composed himself for a snooze.

After awhile he began to feel uncomfortable, and thought to work it off by going to play cricket.

In the meanwhile the boys went round and told the story to those on the cricket-field, and, as Hans took the bat, they all shouted—

"Greedy! greedy old thickhead!"

"You bowls me mine ball," said Hans; "it vos a good choke; I did like it."

But just at the ball left the bowler's hand a sudden spasm of pain flitted across the Dutchman's round, greasy face.

He placed his hands on the pit of his stomach, dropped the bat, and doubled up.

The ball was a round-arm shooter, carefully aimed at the middle stump.

This undoubtedly it would have hit, had not Hans, in doubling up, placed his eye in the way, and effectually stopped its further progress.

A scream of pain was heard.

"Oh, murder! mine stomach, mine eye!"

The Dutchman rolled over on the ground, with one hand clasping his eye, while the other embraced the pit of his stomach.

"Oh, mine eye! Oh, mine stomach! I haf a pain mit mine stomach, and mine eye is out!" groaned Hans, as he rolled over and over on the ground.

He had turned a sickly greenish pallor.

"Say, what could you expect, after eating all that Jamaica ginger, old hoss?" said Nat. "Especially," he added, for the edification of those around, "when there were two doses of calomel in it."

This statement produced a shriek of laughter.

Hans turned ghastly, rubbing the affected part and giving forth low moans.

His eye had become so swollen as to be almost closed. But that was evidently nothing to the internal anguish he was suffering.

"Cheer up, old thickhead," said Nat. "Wouldn't you like a little more ginger, say?"

The only reply was a groan.

"Ain't it about time you told us another story of Berlin?" said little St. David. "That was a fery good story inteet."

"Oh, oh! mine stomach!" growled Hans, dolefully.

"I tell you what it is," said Nat, suddenly. "I reckon if he don't get well soon, he'll die. I've heard of those pots having a deal of copper in them."

"That's so," echoed several of the boys, and again Hans gave a most dismal groan.

"Run to the doctor, one of you, and tell him to bring the stomach-pump," cried Nat. "He may be poisoned."

This idea was received with yells of delight.

Away started two of the boys.

They did not go for the doctor, though.

One of them went into the yard and secured the probang, an instrument of farm use, consisting of a flat board with a hole in the centre.

This was used for forcing between the jaws of any cow who might swallow too large a piece of turnip.

The other portion, the ramrod to wit, was then forced down her throat through the little hole in the centre.

Meanwhile another boy had secured a basin of soapsuds from the laundry.

"Drink this right off, Hans, old man," said Nat, handing him a cupful.

The trembling victim complied.

Then they forced open his mouth with the probang, and fastened it behind his ears.

He was too utterly miserable, and in too much pain, to make any resistance.

One of the boys was just preparing to insert the ramrod of the probang by way of tickling him, when the deluge came.

Hans was wretchedly ill, and the probang flew from him.

He continued in that wretched condition for half an hour, during which our three conspirators comforted him by asking him how he liked Jamaica ginger, and wouldn't he tell them some more stories about Berlin.

In this wretched condition he continued until the supper bell rang, and Hans, pale and seedy-looking, was escorted in.

Ill luck pursued him.

Scarcely had he taken his place than his eyes lit on a plate of ginger in front of him.

Squat had helped to lay the table.

Hans, seeing it again, turned pale, left the table, and, as a natural consequence, went supperless and miserable to bed.

Lord Mouslin De Lain marked, but said nothing.

"I suppose it will be my turn next," said he; "but I am not so easily taken in."

Whether he was or not we shall see.

CHAPTER XIV.

FRANK TAKES HIS FIRST WALK, AND THE BOYS HAVE AN ADVENTURE.

A WEEK after that, and while the boys were busily engaged in packing up, the doctor, having to go to town, gave them a holiday.

"What shall we do?"

"I'm sick of fishing."

"So am I."

"Also cricket."

"I'm about tired of that, too. Say, let's go out with Frank, poor old chap; he hasn't stretched his legs for a long while."

"Right you are," said Leon, who had caught up Nat's peculiar phraseology.

This idea was immediately carried out.

They found Frank, and found that he was quite ready to go with them.

He was delighted at the idea of a day's outing in the woods, especially as blackberries were in season.

I am not going to weary my readers with a detailed account of all they did. How Leon, seeking for blackberries, tumbled into a stagnant green ditch; how Barry, going to rescue him, shared the same fate; how they were chased by a farmer; and finally how, almost at dusk, they bethought them of returning home.

"Do you know," said Frank, "we are very near my house?"

"Let's go in," cried Nat, with American brusqueness.

"Not for the world," said Frank, turning a shade pale. "I mean, I should be very glad to see you; but my parents——"

"Look there," said Barry; "there goes Frank's double."

All turned in the direction indicated, and there, sure enough, was Frank Stainforth's second self.

There was no difference between them which could be detected at that distance—hair, eyes, stature, even clothes, were the same.

If one had examined them both closely, he might have become aware that the evanescent haunted look which sometimes crept across our hero's face had, in his double, become a settled one.

"Come on," cried Nat; "let's catch him. See, he beckons us!"

They had for a moment taken their eyes off Frank, and now, as they turned to see if he consented to join them, they found that he had sunk upon the bank, had turned ashy pale, and was trembling like an aspen.

"Why, Frank, old boy, what's the matter?" cried Nat, forgetting the other all in an instant, and laying his hand on his chum's shoulder, while the others crowded round him with looks of concern.

"Don't; please don't," cried Frank, still trembling.

"Don't what, old boy?" asked Nat. "I guess you know very well, old chap, we wouldn't do anything to hurt your feelings."

"Let him go, don't go near him!" said Frank, with his face still covered with his long, pale fingers.

"Right you are, old boy. He may go to Jericho for us, if you like," said Nat.

"Look you," exclaimed Barry, "he has gone, look you, as quickly as he went the other time."

"When—where?" asked Frank, hurriedly.

Barry explained.

"And you did not catch him?" said Frank. "Did not speak a word to him?"

"Not a word," replied Nat. "He ran like a streak of greased lightning."

Frank breathed a sigh of relief.

"It is very unfair, very unmanly of me to give way like this, and excite your curiosity," said he; "but, you know, they say there is a skeleton in every closet. This is mine. Don't ask me to tell you what it is."

"I guess you'd best not say any more about it, old boy," said Nat. "We don't want to know any of your affairs; we are quite satisfied that when the proper time comes, if it is necessary for us to know, you will tell us."

"Yes, yes!" exclaimed Frank, hurriedly.

"*Ma foi!*" said Leon, "let us talk about something else. In another week we shall be in *la belle France*."

"The last time you talked about *la belle France* we hopped out of bed mighty sudden," cried Nat.

And so they changed the subject, and rattled on in light conversation until they got out of the gloomy woods, and Frank became as merry as the rest of them.

Presently they were aroused from their reverie by the sound of voices, and turning the corner of the road sharply, saw a funny old gentleman valiantly engaged in defending himself with an umbrella, which he kept thrusting, now at one, now at the other, at a couple of gipsies, who were evidently bent on plunder.

Just as they came in sight, despite his vigorous defence, he was knocked into a ditch.

They sprang upon him to secure their plunder.

Before they succeeded the four chums gave forth a battle-cry and rushed upon them.

Barry was first in. The valiant little Welshman caught one gipsy by the legs just below the knees, and tripped him up. He then sat on his chest, and despite the man's strenuous efforts to rise, kept his seat.

Leon, who had profited by Nat's preliminary lessons in boxing, dodged a blow which the other aimed at him, and seized him by the neck cloth with a firm grip.

The man endeavoured to shake him off, but, failing in his efforts to do so, dealt him a short blow, which knocked him away half stunned.

Frank had been close behind Leon, and, as he was "floored," the young boxer dealt his antagonist such a blow with his unwounded arm, right under the ear, that he dropped heavily.

By this time the old gentleman had regained his feet, and Barry, despite his efforts, had been unseated, and was rolling in the dust, while his sometime prisoner rose to his feet with a dark scowl, and drew a long clasp-knife from his pocket.

In the gloaming he mistook his antagonists for men.

Strange to say, Nat had remained behind, and had taken no part in the affray.

His reason now became evident; he had a loaded revolver in his hand.

"Say, I guess you'll drop that knife," said he, as the man advanced. "Drop it, or I'll put a bullet through you."

His request was complied with, and the gipsy turned to fly.

"Stay, old hoss, I can hit a wood-pigeon at fifty yards," said Nat, quite coolly, but in a clear, bell-like voice; "so if you try that game you are a dead man."

The gipsy halted, and remained motionless.

"TOM FLOREMALL" SERIES OF SCHOOL STORIES.
THE TRAVELLING SCHOOLBOYS.

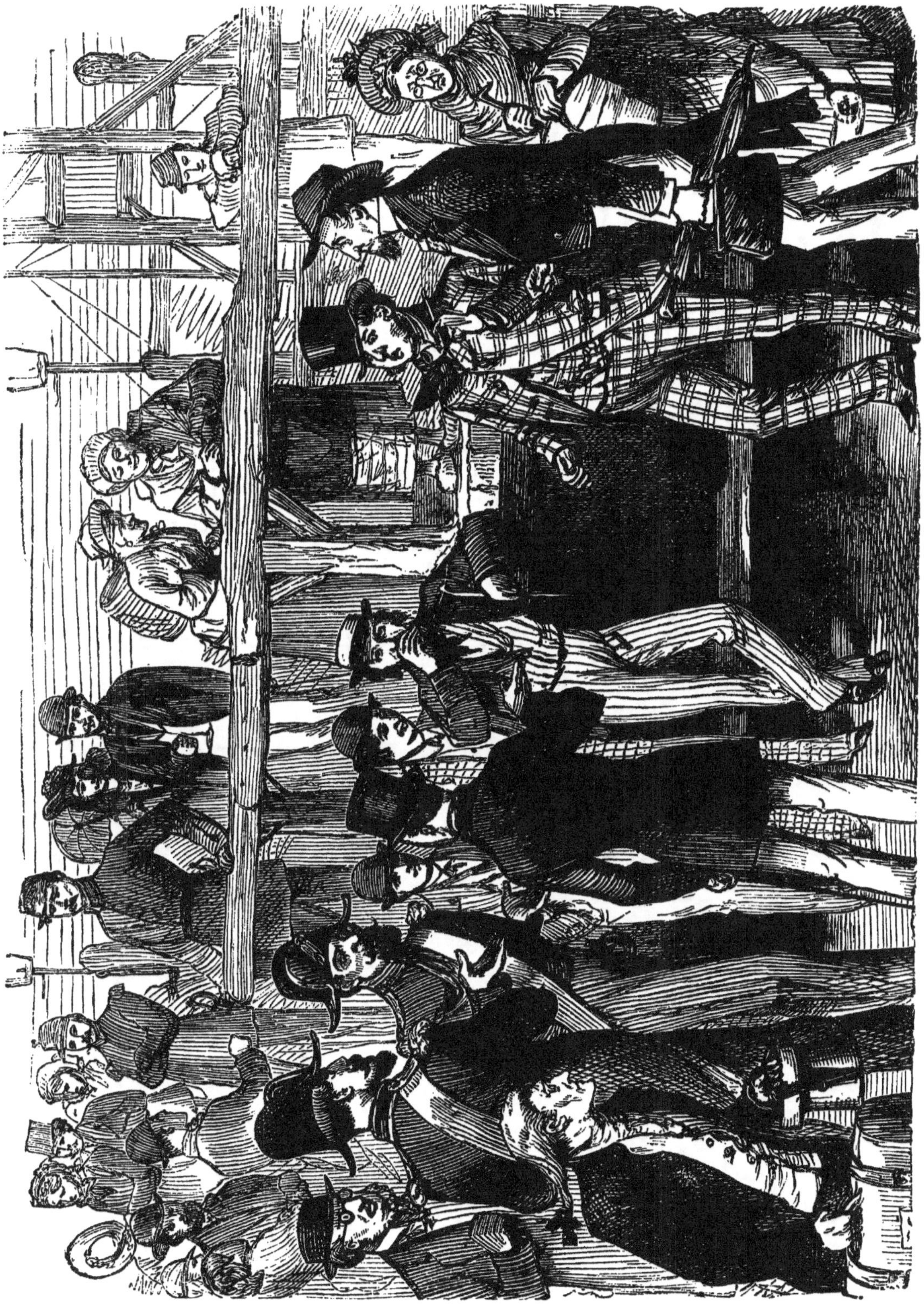

"'OH, LOR'! SOMEBODY TAKE ME HOME,' SAID MR. SWIGGS."

"You too," said Nat, as the other tried to crawl away. "Go alongside of your friend, or you will get the contents of this shooting-iron. Now, Leon, Barry, handcuff them both with you handkerchiefs. Je-ru-salem! I reckon this is better fun than picking blackberries."

"Umph—umph!" cried the funny little old gentlemen, who had a knack of grunting like a pig, speaking with sharp, jerky sentences, which he always preceded with the beforementioned sound. "Umph, umph! obliged to you, boys—umph; they nearly had me—umph! but of course they know what a fool I am—umph!"

"Glad to have been in time, sir," said Frank.

"Umph! of course you are—umph! but how am I to know that?—umph! —what a fool I am!"

A moment was spent in securing the gipsies, who looked remarkably crestfallen.

"Where's that little boy—umph—that caught the ruffian by the legs—umph! Brave boy that, but of course they know that—umph!—as well as I do. What a fool I am!"

"Hope you are not hurt, sir," said Frank.

"Little shaken—umph! Bad thing at my age — umph! Gout—umph! Ruffians get transported—umph! serve them right—umph!"

"If you would like to come to Lakeside House, the doctor, I am sure, will be glad to receive you."

"That's where I was going—umph! Thank you all the same. Doctor Primrose—umph! an old friend, you know—umph! Why should they know what a fool I am?—umph! Do you know a boy there by the name of Barry Cornwall—but of course they do — umph!"

"Yes," said Nat, "a fiery-tempered little brute."

"Why, look you," said Barry, "I know him fery well. He is, look you, a very bad boy."

"Umph! thought so; boys are all scamps, but of course they don't believe me—umph! What a fool I am!"

"Why, look you," said Barry, "if you call us scamps it sall be, look you, that you do impugn our honour, look you, therefore it is that you are no gentlemen, look you."

"Umph! me no gentlemen, you young rascal? umph! but, of course, how do they know I am not a bagman—umph! What a fool I am! Just like me. I warrant that young scamp Barry Cornwall is a disgrace to his relations—umph!"

"Why, look you," said Barry, waxing wrath, "it seems that you take fery great liberties with Parry Cornwall. He has, look you, no relations to pother his head about, except a yellow-faced old uncle in India, who is made of money, and cares nothing about him."

"Who you devil told you that?—umph! but of course, what a fool I am! How is he to know?—umph! Look here, my fine fellow, supposing you were to introduce me to the young scoundrel—umph!"

"Why, look you," said Barry, turning red, "it has gone past a joke. I am Parry Cornwall."

"You? but of course, what a fool I am! Emily's hair and eyes."

The old gentlemen rushed forward, clasped Barry's hand, and shook it heartily.

"Glad to know you, my boy. I'm your uncle. You are a glorious boy—umph! but of course, he knows that—what a fool I am!"

In the sudden demonstration of his joy, the old gentleman seized his umbrella and dealt the captured footpads several blows on the back with it by way of letting off steam.

He then embraced Barry again, by which time the lights of Lakeside Academy were in sight.

CHAPTER XV.

BARRY'S UNCLE MAKES HIMSELF AT HOME—A SUPPER, IN WHICH JOEL SKIMP SHOWS HIMSELF IN A NEW ROLE.

THE introduction of Barry's uncle to Dr. Primrose was characteristic. It is hardly necessary to add that the old gentlemen were delighted with one another.

"As for the boy, Barry—young scamp, umph!—you are making a man of him, doctor—a regular little man. But of course he knows that—umph!"

"Yes," said the doctor; "I am pleased to notice a marked improvement in his classics."

"Classics be hanged, sir!" roared the old East Indian. "He is a little bull-terrier—umph! You should have seen him hold on to the ruffian—umph!—and that other—that pale-faced boy."

"Frank Stainforth?"

"Yes. Umph—splendid boy that. Hit clean from the shoulder, and tumbled the ruffian like a felled ox. Wonderful to see such power in a pale-faced boy like that—umph! What's the matter with his arm?"

"The fact is," said the doctor, turning red, "he had it broken in a fight with a fellow-pupil."

"Umph!—don't you think you're carrying pugilism too far, doctor? By Jove! sir, every one of your scholars are born athletes—umph!"

"I deplore fighting of any description," said the doctor, "as I think it tends to brutalize the mind."

"And yet—broken arm—young boxers umph! Sly old dog—eh?"

He poked the doctor in the ribs, who was dreadfully embarrased. Then came this aside—

"But of course he is. He must be with those young imps. His profession makes him a little deceitful—umph! What a fool I am!"

The four boys smelt the joke, and were bursting with laughter over the absurd idea old Grumpy—for so they had already dubbed Barry's uncle—had conceived concerning Doctor Primrose, namely, that he was a formidable pugilist, who adored fighting, and taught all his boys to be regular hammerers.

It was too late to send the gipsies to the prison that night, so they had to improvise a gaol for them in the out-house, where they were securely bound with ropes, and Pomponet, Squat, and Snarley Cool placed as alternate guards over them.

"I don't like that arrangement," muttered Nat. "Squat is safe, but Pomponet is an ass, and that Cool is a dangerous fellow, quite capable of plotting with the prisoners."

The boys were to have a supper that evening. Old Grumpy had asked them what they would most like, and Nat had retorted—

"A supper."

But he resolved that before going to bed he would see that the prisoners were safe.

"God bless my soul!" cried the doctor, when the supper was mentioned; "don't you get enough to eat, boys?"

"That isn't the point," returned Nat. "We want a regular blow-out, with oyster-patties and roast pheasant and claret-punch—in short, a red-hot supper."

The doctor made a feeble effort to frown this down by saying that "red-hot" suppers were not good for them, but he was overruled by old Grumps.

"Very well, then, young gentlemen," said the doctor; "we will meet for supper"—he laid particular stress upon the word—"at half-past eight. If you would like to invite anyone you'd better say so now."

"It's Barry's feed," said Nat.

"No. On the contrary; it is 'all your feeds,'" said old Grumpy, "if I may use that extraordinary expression you have just made use of."

"Suppose we have Dutchy? It would be good fun to invite him, and then, when he sets his eye on anything, make out that it was prepared for him like the dosed ginger."

"No," said the doctor. "I need hardly point out to you, boys, that the guest should be sacred in the host's eyes. Never play off a trick upon your guest. No matter how you may dislike him, it is your duty to protect him."

"There is nothing like having a small party in perfect harmony with one another," said Frank, by way of cutting short the doctor's sermon. "I vote that just for this evening we don't ask anyone."

"Good."

"Very well, then," said the doctor. "I shall expect you at half-past eight. Till then——"

They did not wait for the conclusion of his sentence, but marched to the schoolroom, where they made the other fellows savage by a glowing description of the feed.

They thought half-past eight would never come, but it did.

What a supper it was! They thought they never could be done eating, and then, when the cloth was cleared away, old Grumpy, rising solemnly, had their glasses filled with a heavenly liquid, which subsequent investigations proved to be egg-hot.

When they were all filled to the brim, Mr. Spotworth Grub proposed the health of "Her Majesty Queen Victoria, God bless her," which was drunk with great gusto, after which old Grumpy solemnly returned thanks to the four boys as follows——

"Young gentlemen — umph! — of course they know they are young gentlemen—it has often been my lot to see danger—umph!—in the jungles—umph! Pig-sticking or potting tigers is constantly throwing one's life on a chance —in fact, I may say—but of course they know all that rubbish. God bless you, boys, and your reverend teacher, who taught you how to use your fists like men—the Church Militant—umph! Nothing like being able to give a good knockdown blow—eh, doctor? Sly dog —but of course they mustn't know that —what a fool I am!"

And all out of breath the old chap sat down, his speech having been received with vociferous cheering.

Then Barry Cornwall proposed the health of Doctor Primrose, who, in response, said he felt it incumbent upon him to remove a certain impression Mr. Cornwall had received relative to the pugilistic tendencies of the school.

He had got no farther when he was interrupted by roars of laughter, through which could be heard the tones of old Grumpy bellowing out—

"Sly dog—umph!—umph!"

So the old doctor could not explain, but, as Frank saw he looked pained, he took an early opportunity of rising to his feet and relating exactly how the school came to have such a reputation for fighting.

He did it so modestly and so well that one would have thought he had got into a very slight scrimmage only, in which chance had given him a broken arm, which served him right. But the others wouldn't accept this version, and Barry Cornwall told the rights of it amidst many remonstrances on the part of Frank, who was overwhelmed with confusion.

Then Mr. Spotworth Grub was asked for a song. He turned red to the roots of his lanky hair, and said he would sing them a trifle of his own composition. and, when silence prevailed, began in a tremulous falsetto—

"My love is in the cold, cold grave
        Beneath the sounding sea,
    I tried her loving life to save——"

"And that's what's the matter with me!" cried Nat, unable to hold in any longer. "Give us something lively."

The others screamed with laughter, while Mr. Spotworth Grub turned purple, despite the doctor's effort to pacify him.

But before he could remonstrate with the boys, old Grump had sprung to his feet, and shouting, "Follow me, boys, in the chorus!" began—

"Oh! in China once, there lived a great man;
    His name was Chi Chow-Ching-a-rang-Tang;
    His legs were long, and his feet were small;
    This festive youth couldn't walk at all."

"Chorus!" bellowed old Grump, and all the boys yelled out—

"Chi, Chow, Chingery, Chang,
    Fiddledee, Toodledum, don't care a hang;
    Chow, Chew, How, How me Fo,
    This Chinaman with the monkey nose,
    This Chinaman with the monkey N-O-S-E!"

The very room rang with the energy of this chorus, and as it died away old Grumps started in with the second verse.

"Oh! Chi Chow Ching-a-rang-Tang fell in love;
    He went to court Miss Dick-a-Dove——"

At this portion of the celestial hero's adventures, the singer stopped suddenly and gazed towards the door, and all the others followed his example, thinking it was part of the song.

But as they turned, the silence became as marked as the former noise and jollity.

A white figure had entered the room, with fixed, staring eyes and noiseless footsteps.

It was Joel Skimp.

His hair was raised as though he were in a state of the most abject terror, while his features worked horribly.

Every now and then he looked over his shoulder and moaned.

"Hush!" said the doctor, in a whisper, "don't wake him. He is a somnambulist. Were he to awake suddenly the consequences might be fatal."

"Pity—mercy!" cried Joel, in agonised tones. "I'll swear—— Away—away! Oh, no, I did not do it; they lie if they said so!"

"What is troubling you?" asked the doctor, in a calm, soothing voice.

The boy turned, still asleep, in the direction of the sound.

"The secret," he whispered, with a look of terror on his face. "The secret! Do you know it? No, you don't. No one knows it but me and him—there he is over there with Frank Stainforth. Frank knows the secret, but he can't tell. Do you know what it is like? It is a nameless horror without any head, a phantom that chills you all day long. There it is by Frank Stainforth. Pity—mercy—mercy!"

And so, moaning and imploring, occasionally working himself up to the most agonised expressions of fear, he slowly walked round the room, and went out again by the door through which he had entered.

They followed him softly, one by one, and watched him up the broad staircase into the dormitory, up which he glided swiftly, like a ghost slipping between rows of beds with rosy faces lying on the white pillows in healthy slumber, unconscious, happily, of the presence of guilt.

He got into bed, and presently his heavy breathing betokened that his troubled spirit was at rest once more.

They returned to the dining-room, where they found Frank pale as death, leaning with his elbows on the table.

He had evidently succeeded in subduing his emotions, for, as they entered, he arose and said, in a voice in which there was scarcely any agitation—

"I wish you good night, doctor. I don't feel very strong, and it is rather late for me."

He smiled faintly, and pointed to his wounded arm.

He had been gone about three minutes, and the other boys were preparing to follow, when Frank's voice was heard echoing through the house—

"Murder! murder!"

Anything like the confusion that ensued can hardly be imagined.

The guests rushed upstairs, pellmell, into Frank's room, and found him trying to staunch the blood which flowed freely from the side of a boy in his bed.

The boy's name was Frank Seymour.

The window was open, and there was a ladder against it, set from the outside.

The room of course speedily filled.

Among the first arrivals was Snarly Cool.

He came in with a look of concern on his face.

"Good Heaven!" cried the doctor, "what can this mean?"

"It means murder, sir," said Frank with the calmness of despair.

CHAPTER XVI.

HOW SNARLY COOL KEPT POMPONET'S WATCH AND HOW ANN O'DYNE'S SCHEME BORE FRUIT.

IF there was one thing in the world which Pomponet hated with his whole soul it was solitude.

He assured the gipsies, when it came to his turn to watch them, that they would be hanged, and finding that this sportive way of beginning a conversation did not draw them out, he recounted all the battles wherein his prowess had been the means of defeating the *perfide*

Anglais; and finding the silence still continue, effervesced and went to sleep, in which condition he was found by Snarly Cool.

"You are a nice soldier; you mount guard well," said Snarly Cool, whereat Pomponet waxed wroth, defied Cool to prove that he had been asleep.

"Look here, Pomponet," said Cool, "I will do you a favour."

"What is that?"

"I see you are tired out. You go and get some supper, my brave Pomponet, have a good sleep, and afterwards awaken at two o'clock and relieve Squat, who will relieve me."

"Good," cried Pomponet, who was delighted at the prospect of getting off for the present.

"But stop!" cried Cool.

"What, monsieur?"

"I have a condition."

"And that is——"

"That you will forgive me that blow I struck you in a moment of passion, and that you will tell me your account of the battle of Waterloo to-morrow."

"Now," said Pomponet.

"Not now," answered Cool, hastily; "to-morrow I promise myself a treat."

"Very good, monsieur," said Pomponet, and leaving Snarly Cool, went in to pay court to Ann O'Dyne.

Ann had no mind for Pomponet's attentions just then.

Her mind was exercised over the fact that a chamber-maid had broken a pane of glass in Frank's bed-room.

At last she hit upon a happy idea, which solved the difficulty.

Young Seymour had the best bed in the dormitory, seeing that it was not exposed to draught either from door or window.

Ann O'Dyne accordingly made a journey upstairs, and bribed Seymour with sundry delicacies in the edible line to change places with Frank for one night, the bargain being sealed with port-wine negus.

She then despatched Pomponet to tell Frank, but Leon's valet found the butler engaged with a bottle of claret, and remained to help him.

Having explained the whereabouts of the relieved guard up to the period of the *dénouement,* it is necessary that we also tell of the doings of the person who relieved him.

Scarcely was Pomponet well out of earshot when Snarly Cool turned to the prisoners.

"Well, men," he said, "you seem to have got into trouble."

They remained silent.

"Keep up your courage; things ain't so bad as they look. Take a nip of spirits."

He handed them a flask of whisky, which the men drank feverishly.

"Tell me how you got captured."

"We was a-walkin' along the road, me and my mate; I just asked an old buffer for a light, when he poked us with his umbreller and commenced for to holler 'Murder!' Afore you could say anything there was a half a dozen young varmints outs on us, and one on 'em, he wer'n't up to my waist hardly, hit me a sledge-hammer whack under the ear that knocked me silly."

"Do you mean to say that two big men like you couldn't have polished off four boys?" asked Snarly, becoming confidential.

The prisoners looked at Cool.

"I'm ashamed of you, mates. It's hardly worth a man's while trying to get yer out of trouble; you'd only get into it, and perhaps split on him."

The two looked at one another in surprise.

Was this a trap?

"I ain't got no cause to love anyone of that lot that got yer into trouble," said Snarly, speaking in a more vulgar way than usual, so as to accomodate himself to their ideas. "If I thought I wasn't going to get into trouble myself perhaps I might have helped you out of yourn."

Again the men looked at one another.

"What do you think of it, Brads?" asked one.

"He's a square bloke," replied his chum. "Look at his eyes when he speaks of the boys."

"You're right, mates," said Snarly; "I hate them. And now, if you could only show me how you could get far enough away by morning to prevent your being scragged again, and chance to blow on me, I wouldn't mind seein' what I could do to let you off."

They pointed out the way to him eagerly.

Up through the lake, and be out of the country before morning.

They knew where there was an encampment of their brothers, and they could lie close there for two or three days.

"Well," said Snarly Cool, "I'll let you go if you'll take this oath to me—that you'll never betray who released you."

They swore it gipsy fashion, crossing their hands and arms over each other's breasts.

"That will do," said Snarly, grimly. "I give you the chance to get away, and if you are caught and break your oath, as to who let you go, you know what to expect."

"You need not have any fear," replied the man named Brads. "We ain't likely to be caught again, now we have the night with us: we wouldn't have been before, if it hadn't been for that young feller with the pistol."

"What fellow?"

He was undoing their bonds as he asked the question.

"A thin, lanky chap, with long hair; he said he'd shoot us if we tried to run, and he were so cool over it that I believe he would."

"You're right, he would," said Snarly. "Curse him, I'll fix him yet."

"Thankee, master," said one of the men, as they stood up unbound. "You've saved us. We won't forget it happen it should come in our way to do you a good turn."

"I'll not forget to ask you if I want your aid," replied Cool. "You wait here a minute till I see is the coast clear."

He went out presently, and returned with the dog.

"You might find him an awkward ustomer, if I didn't introduce him to ou. He don't like prowlers in the night-ime."

One of the men patted Dash on the head, but this did not meet with his approbation apparently, for he growled.

"Best leave him alone," said Cool. "Go down the path yonder; it will lead you straight to the boat-house, where you will find a boat with oars in it; get in, and cast it adrift when you step ashore."

"Good-night, and good luck to you," said the men.

"The same to you," returned Scarly Cool, and looked after them, when their backs were turned, with an evil smile. "No time to be lost," he said, noticing the lights being put out in the dormitories.

While speaking he procured a ladder from the stable, and placed it softly against the window-sill of Frank's room.

Mounting it he peered in, and could just distinguish a figure lying on the bed.

He came down again, and gained the room unobserved, treading stealthily, with cat-like footfalls, until he had gained the window, which he opened softly.

Then he turned, groped his way in the dark to the bedside, and, clenching his teeth, struck one swift, tiger-like blow at the sleeper's heart.

A heavy groan was the response.

He left the knife sticking where he had struck, and, with white face, fled away like a hideous phantom.

Dearly indeed did poor young Seymour pay for his little supper and his port-wine negus; while the assassin gained his room in safety his life-blood dripped slowly down.

Scarcely two minutes had elapsed ere, as already described, Frank appeared on the scene, and alarmed the house.

Medical attendance was instantly summoned, and, in the meanwhile, those about the boy succeeded in arresting the hemorrhage.

"Who could have done this infamous deed?" cried the doctor. "There is the ladder by the open window showing clearly how they came in; it might have, but could—Heaven! it cannot be possible the——"

"Gipsies!" broke in Nat. "Yes, I just thought of that myself, and was going to see how they were getting on, and if secure. Let's go hunt for them."

But their hunt was in vain, although kept up for two or three days.

The prisoners had escaped.

CHAPTER XVII.

OFF AT LAST—GREAT PREPARATIONS, AND A JOLLY FAREWELL—GOOD-BYE, ENGLAND.

AT last the eventful day of departure had arrived. They were going. There could be no mistake about it, as witness the piles of trunks in the hall, the shouting and stamping and running to and fro, the utter suspension of anything like order, the chaos and confusion.

Events had passed rapidly the last two weeks. The attempted assassination of young Seymour—who, by-the-bye, had been sent home the day before departure—had been set down as an effort on the part of the gipsies to revenge themselves upon their captors.

A hundred pounds reward had accordingly been offered for their apprehension, but they remained at large.

Frank, whose arm was strong enough now to be without a sling, Barry, Leon, and Nat Urner occupied one 'bus, which was decorated with the Union Jack, the Stars and Stripes, and the Tricolour.

Lord Mouslin De Lain wished to drive to the station with his four-in-hand, but this the doctor would not allow, as he maintained it made an invidious distinction which he did not wish to see in his school. So the young peer had to swallow his disappointment and mount the 'bus with Joel Skimp, Hans, and Carlos Gomez, a young Spaniard who had come to the school only a few days before.

This 'bus was draped with German and Spanish flags intertwined. Snarly Cool and Mr. Weaks occupied the interior, and made themselves happy with pipes and whisky-and-water.

The doctor, accompanied by Mr. Spotworth Grub and Monsieur Garlic, occupied an open carriage in the rear, from which they could view the proceedings of the "young gentlemen," and see that nothing went wrong. So they bowled along pleasant country roads for hours.

Frank Stainforth's spirit seemed to rise.

Nat Urner remarked upon this.

"Your spirits are rising, I guess. Say, old chap," he said.

"Yes; they are," returned Frank, becoming a little more thoughtful. "I feel as if I were leaving a nightmare behind me."

"I wonder if this double has anything to do with this nightmare that he is leaving behind him; that pale, corpse-like face we saw in the woods," thought Nat, but he said nothing openly.

We will skip over the incidents of the journey.

When they reached London, after travelling at night, all the boys had red eyes and felt particularly seedy.

They all felt wonderfully revived by a breakfast at Morley's Hotel, just by Charing Cross Station, where the old head-waiter could hardly be aroused into animation until Nat hit upon the happy expedient of waking him up with a pea-shooter.

Then came a mad rush to Charing Cross Station, where they found the steam hissing out of the impatient engine, and had just time to take their places when puff—puff—wheugh! they were off and away.

* * * * * *

It was a wild night in the Channel.

The wind is moaning up from the south-west, driving the white spray before it in a chill mist.

The low lights gleam murkily from the town and a chill sweat drips from the glistening masts.

The smoke streams forth in a black, twisting, rolling volume from the black funnel of the Channel steamer, and curls itself away leeward, as though glad to get away from the stormy ocean without.

The vessel rolls at her moorings, and snorts and screams and lashes the water with her great paddles, as though anxious to be off and battle with the tempest.

Men are yelling, women are screaming, children are crying, porters are running against each other, and baggage is being tossed about recklessly.

The boys swarmed aboard and down in the cabin, but, finding it so wretchedly hot, close, and uncomfortable, went on deck again, and watched the process of getting under way.

"Half-turn astern! Cast off that spring! Ease her! Helm a-starboard!"

Swash, swash!

"Steady—port, steady!"

"Steady it is, sir."

Swash, swash! splash! drip, drip!

They are off out through the mouth of the little harbour, past the twinkling lighthouse, into the chop-chop sea.

Onward she goes, her tall, dark hull looming darkly up, with two great eyes —green and red—watching the path across the trackless deep, and one anxious figure on the bridge in ceaseless perambulation to and fro.

The boys soon began to feel the effects of the uneasy motion.

Hans, who had previously done nothing but eat and sleep, was the first to give in.

He turned a beautiful green colour, and sloped for the side of the vessel.

While Barry was making fun of him he suddenly disappeared himself, leaving Leon, who laughed at him to Frank, but departed also, having made, or tried to make, a feeble joke.

Just then Doctor Primrose was supported up the cabin-stairs by Mr. Spotworth Grub, who was looking decidedly weak about the knees.

With much difficulty the doctor was supported to one of the officers of the ship.

During the short conversation he had with him his words were almost inaudible, from the fact that he kept his hand tightly pressed to his mouth.

"Is this what you would call a—a gale?" asked the doctor.

"You might call it a gale," responded the mate.

"God—bless—my soul! but there is no danger, is there?" asked the doctor, pumping up his words and keeping his handkerchief over his mouth.

"I've known ships go down in less wind than this," returned the mate, with a grin, which the doctor, owing to the darkness, did not see.

"How v-ve-ry dreadful!" said the doctor. "The Government should not permit people's lives to be sacrificed by a reckless company in such weather as this for the sake of gain."

"You see, it isn't the shipwreck so much as it is their insides get shaken out of them," said the man, solemnly.

"God bless me! so it is!" cried the doctor. "Mr. Grub, I—God bless me! I feel very ill!"

"So do I," moaned Mr. Grub.

The doctor tried to say something else; but his words were inaudible, and at this moment a sudden lurch sent them both to the lee-side.

Nat was the only one that was not sick on board.

This was due to the fact that he had sailed about a great deal with his father, and so had got his sea-legs on.

Sitting disconsolately on the weather settee he found Lord Mouslin.

The young noble was not "practically ill "—only qualmish.

Nat thought he would complete the task King Neptune had begun.

"How do you think you feel, Mouslin?" he said.

"Go away," growled his lordship.

"I say, you'll be sea-sick if you don't take a remedy."

"What remedy is there?"

"It's a piece of pork," said Nat; "a nice, fat, greasy piece. You swallow the pork and then you are all right."

"Oh, my—oh, my!" groaned Lord Mouslin, hanging pallid over the settee. "You brute — you fiend —you—o-oh, m-y!"

Nat had accomplished the desired result.

Lord Mouslin De Lain was practically ill.

Nat walked away to see what other victim he could light on, when Frank Stainforth passed him.

"I say, Frank," said Nat, "how do you feel?"

Frank made no answer.

"Too ill to speak, old chap? What do you say to a nice piece of fat pork?"

Still he got no answer for his pains.

"I guess it's a shame to torment you," said Nat. "Come down to the bar and have some champagne. It's the only cure to sea-sickness."

Till now the figure had remained motionless, with its back half turned to him, so that Nat was only enabled to see the outlines of the face.

Now it turned full upon him and looked at him.

"Why, what's the matter with you—say?"

It was not that Nat thought his friend sea-sick; but there was a queer expression on his face which he never remembered to have seen there before—a frightened, vavant, awe-stricken look.

"Say," repeated Nat, going forward to place his hand on his shoulder.

But before he could accomplish this the figure gave a laugh—a short, hysterical kind of laugh—and disappeared below.

Nat was about to follow him; but a moment's reflection told him he had better not.

"Perhaps he has got one of his queer fits on him," he said to himself, as he strolled forward. "It's a dirty enough night to give anyone a fit of the blues."

He was speaking his thoughts half aloud, and just then a quivering voice said—

"Is that you, Nat?"

"Yes—who is that?" answered Nat, turning to the settee whence came the sound.

"Frank Stainforth."

"How the deuce did you pass me?"

"What do you mean?"

"Didn't you pass me just now and go into the cabin?"

"No."

"Sure?"

"Certain. I have been sitting here for the last half-hour."

"Then all I've got to say is that I've seen your ghost, old boy, or your double."

"Don't say that—for God's sake don't say that!" moaned Frank.

"It's not a joke, Frank," returned Nat. "As true as I'm standing here, I saw your double."

"Oh, Heaven pity me!" moaned Frank. "I thought I had left the horror behind."

"Rubbish!" said Nat. "I'll go and look for it."

"Stay!" cried Frank, laying his hand on his friend's arm. "Your looking for it would be useless."

He was no longer sea-sick; he was shivering with downright terror.

"Why?" said Nat.

"Because," returned Frank, "because—for God's sake don't betray me—it is a spirit."

"A what?"

"A phantom," moaned Frank, and fell heavily on the settee.

For the first time in his life Nat Urner, looking at this brave young heart by his side, felt the deadly chill of fear creep through his veins.

Calais lights gleamed far off.

The phosphorescent sea moaned about them.

A thousand things awoke to sluggish life in the blackness of the night.

Only two boys remained motionless, listening to the surging of the sea—the pale, ghostly sea.

CHAPTER XVIII.

IN FRANCE—POMPONET AWAKES TO THE SITUATION.

As the boat approached the shore a number of washed-out, seedy-looking people managed to struggle on deck and begin to look after their baggage.

Leon managed to crawl to his feet, assisted by Barry Cornwall, as soon as he heard they were approaching Calais.

"Ah, *mon Dieu!*" cried Leon, with chattering teeth; "I smell *la belle France.*"

"So do I, look you," said St. David, "and it is not a fery nice smell. It smells—pah—like train-oil—ugh!"

"That is nothing, *ma foi*," returned Leon. "Every town must have a smell; it is only the soap-factories, and any smell is better than this wretched sea. I wish someone would give me some eau-de-cologne."

"What light is that, stranger?" asked a tall man with a slouch hat and an unmistakable American accent.

"It is the light from the fort monsieur, to show whether we may come in or not."

"Why in thunder don't they scoop

out the harbour and make it big enough to float a little two-cent concern like this? What air those?"

"Factories for the bobin trade; they are built on the old ramparts."

"What in thunder dew they want ramparts for. I reckon we don't want no ramparts in our United States. No, siree, if we waz to have a muss with Europe we'd send a couple of monitors and blow the hull concern about your ears."

By this time Nat Urner had approached.

"What's that?" he continued, as they got into the inner mole.

"It's the cathedral, monsieur," said Leon, "celebrated for a fine altar-piece by the great painter Vandyck."

"What in thunder dew they want alter-pieces by boss painters for? Reckon we don't hev none of them. Whitewash is good enough for us."

"I guess you'd best give your mouth a rest," said Nat, unable to conceal his disgust. "How high are you? Could you take a tumble?"

The stranger turned in surprise, and, as he stroked his goatee, scowled darkly upon Nat.

"You're a muel, ain't yer?" said Nat, mimicking him; "a boss muel to choaw bullets, heavy on the muscle, all the way from California. How much did you pay for that five-dollar diamond, say?"

"See here, young feller," said the American, looking savagely at Nat; "I guess you don't know who I am?"

"Don't I," cried Nat; "you are one of those beauties that travel all over Europe calling yourself an American citizen, by hickory. That's about how high you are. Do you think I don't know you? You are one of A. T. Stewart's counter-jumpers, you are. How long is it since you got promoted from measurin' dry goods?"

"I guess you don't know who you're talkin' to, young feller," said the man, in a voice that had lost a considerable portion of its swagger. "I am a Missouri man, I am, and I kin chaw up small boys, I ken."

"You can skin alligators and whip snakes, can't yer?" jeered Nat. "Give us a rest, you white-washed fraud, and wash that black dye off your red head. You're a one-horse New-York politician on a European tower."

"You seem to know a good deal about me, young fellow," said the man, making no effort to strike Nat. "Was you ever in the United States?"

"I am an American," retorted Nat, hotly; "and I hate to see my country disgraced by a lot of hoodlums and shoddy aristocrats like you."

"Well, don't give me away," said the man, in considerable confusion; "I reckon there's more beside me that put on the high tone."

"Do you call that high tone?" retorted Nat. "You don't know what high tone is. Take off your false diamonds and your black dye, and behave like a gentleman. Don't go running down every country you come across——"

Nat's speech was here interrupted by the arrival of a third party, who thrust himself into the group without any ceremony, much to Frank Stainforth's annoyance.

"What's the meaning hof of this waiting? You caunt get no satisfaction from them mounsheers."

The new-comer was a contrast to the American; he was oily and short and fat.

He had thin, yellow—or rather, sandy-coloured — whiskers, which were surmounted by a tile stuck jauntily on the side of his head.

While the American rolled a cigar beneath his black moustache the Englishman carried a short pipe between his unwashed teeth, from which no evening breeze could blow away the odours of rank shag.

"Servingt, sir, servingt," he said, elbowing his way in with fussy importance; "caunt you—ha—tell me wot these blooming forineers are going to do with our lugwidge?"

"Reckon they'll examine our plunder at Paris," returned the American.

"Wot a blooming poor-lookin' place it is," said the Englishman, looking round scornfully. "It hain't like London, nor yet Margate. The hair is loaded with 'orrid smells."

"Correct; and I guess you can't get a civil answer from young bloods that think themselves heavy on the high tone."

The boys were very much amused by the duet and rippling over with laughter.

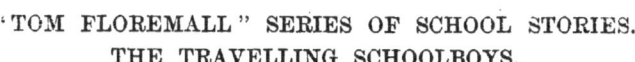

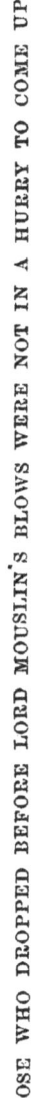

"THOSE WHO DROPPED BEFORE LORD MOUSLIN'S BLOWS WERE NOT IN A HURRY TO COME UP AGAIN."

"You caunt 'elp being mixed hup with a wulgar lot on these boats," said the Englishman, following up the American's glance, and sending one after it in the direction of the boys. "May I hausk your name, sir? There is my keard."

The Englishman produced a huge card, on which was printed—

"CLARENCE HARCOURT SWIGGS."

The American read the name aloud.

"I am pleased to know you, Mr. Swiggs," he said, extending his hand. "My name is Kernal Slapjack. You may have heard of Kernal Slapjack, who led Billy Wilson's Zouaves in the late American unpleasantness. Will you smoke a cigar with me?"

"Sir," said the Englishman, "you do me proud. Will you 'ave a nip of the real thing?"

"I don't mind if I dew. Do you intend to make an extensive tower?" asked the American.

"Hit depends," returned the fat man. "Hif I can endure the worry, hi may stay a week."

"I reckon then, we'd best join company. I ken speak French some."

"There's a sweet specimen of the travelling Englishman for you," said Frank. "No wonder they think us a queer lot on the Continent."

At this moment Pomponet came up to inquire about his master's luggage.

He spoke in French.

Leon winked at Frank, who whispered to Nat Urner, and the three then prepared an excruciating practical joke that should show both Colonel Slapjack and Mr. Swiggs in their true colours.

Frank, when all was arranged, turned to Mr. Swiggs and said—

"I overheard you say just now that you spoke French. Will you help us out of a difficulty? Here is evidently an official of some sort, and I should like you to explain to us what he says."

"Hall right; I don't bear no malice," said Mr. Swiggs, swelling with importance.

Then, strutting up to Pomponet, he bawled—

"*Parlez vous Franky?*"

Pomponet jumped up, startled.

The boys screamed with fun.

"*Oui*, monsieur," said Pomponet, looking confused.

"Ve," repeated Mr. Swiggs, and then considered what he should say next.

Suddenly a happy thought occurred to him.

"*Voulez vous* — that means 'will you,'" he explained to the boys, with a wink; "*voulez vous* tellee me whatee youee wantee, you know, old b—o—y—e?"

Pomponet cocked his head on one side.

He wanted to know whether this man was a lunatic.

"Ze lugwidgee, you knowee, mossoo," cried the fat man, returning to the attack.

"*Monsieur, c'est possible que vous parlez Anglaise, mais je vous assure——*"

Here Pomponet looked perplexed and stopped abruptly.

Mr. Swiggs, thinking he had finished, translated what he had said with a beaming smile.

He said—

"It isn't allowed to talk English when you get ashore. Hurrah for Swiggs!"

At this the boys shouted, and Mr. Swiggs, suspecting that he was being smoked, turned very red in the face.

He mumbled out a lot of French jargon.

Finding that Pomponet was still mystified, he bellowed out—

"I'll not speak your blooming langwidge any more. When I took my ticket they contracted to furnish han interupter."*

"Monsieur," cried Pomponet, in amazement, "I speak English perfectly, but I thought you wanted to speak to me in my own language."

"You misunderstood me," returned Swiggs.

Then turning to the boys, he said—

"He knows well enough what I said, but he pretends not to. The French people like to make us look like fools, they do. It does their heart good, ever since we gave them such a bloomin' lickin' at Waterloo."

Pomponet was up in arms—he looked all fighting.

"Monsieur," he said, "Pomponet will be charitable. He does not think you wish to insult him; he only thinks you are a fool. Behold, monsieur, the Cross

---

* It is to be presumed that he meant interpreter. —ED.

of the Legion of Honour which Pomponet won at the battle of Trafalgar, when
he captured Milord Wellington as he
was hanging over the side suffering from
the *mal-de-mer*. No, monsieur, is only
a fool; he would not like me to run him
through with the small-sword the great
Napoleon gave me. No, monsieur, you
are an Englishman, but we are in
France."

"There," said the fat man, "I knew
them yer boys would get me into trouble.
He's a juke, or one of them swells that
would as soon let daylight hinto a man's
corporosity as look at yer, and my life
not hinsured. Oh, Lor'!"

"Say, old hoss, I'll be your second,"
said the American; "I reckon you can
fix him."

"Perhaps," said Nat, "you'd best take
the insult up; you are pretty good with
the pistol, you know, and you have the
choice of weapons."

"It isn't my funeral to-day," said the
American, hastily. "I don't propose to
get daylight let into me for a man I
only met a second or two ago."

"And yet," said Nat, "not five minutes
ago you expressed yourself ready to tow
France out to sea."

"That was only a joke," said the man,
uneasily. "But this Englishman is the
fellow to fight."

"I hain't got no cause for to fight
him," said the Englishman, hastily. "I
didn't know he was a juke, and, as for
the battle of Trafalgar, he ought to have
been killed there; that's all I can say."

"Monsieur," said Pomponet, calmly,
"I see in your eye you wish to fight me."

"Oh, Lor'! I'll swear I don't!" exclaimed Swiggs.

"Juniper!" said the "kernal."

"I am very sorry for you both," said
Leon, "but you must both fight Pomponet or go to prison."

"Why?"

"It is the law of the land that an
insult must be avenged in blood; therefore, messieurs, your names and addresses
that I may send them to the prefect of
police."

"I won't give mine. I 'ave a wife
and childring at 'ome, in the publican
way, sir," said the Englishman.

"I guess I ain't a-goin' to be shot at.
Not for no one, if I know myself," said
the American.

"Very well then, gentlemen," said
Leon; "I regret to say that it is my
painful duty to place you under arrest."

Two gendarmes, who had just come on
board, and who looked very formidable,
were called up.

"What time does the train start for
Paris?" asked Leon, in French.

"In ten minutes, monsieur."

"And the luggage?"

"Will be examined in Paris, monsieur."

"There, you here," said Leon, turning to the unhappy Mr. Swiggs; "they
say they cannot take your word of
honour, that you must give your Paris
address, and then be escorted there by
them, otherwise——"

"What?"

"Death."

"Oh, Lor'!" groaned the unhappy
Mr. Swiggs, "somebody take me home."

"Be comforted and take courage. It's
only a place like the tower or the dungeons in Lambeth Palace."

"Where I could heat my 'am sand-
witch hevry 'oliday, and wasn't contented
with liberty," cried Mr. Swiggs, as afflict-
ing memories rushed upon him.

"Before you're shot you'll get good
bread and water."

"And this is what they call the plea-
sures of travelling," moaned Mr. Swiggs.

"Never mind," said Nat to the American; "if they kill you, we'll then go
to the American consul, and we'll have
the hull concern towed out to sea."

"What good will that do me? Oh,
Lor'! oh, dear."

"And if they drag you to the guillo-
tine let them beware. Your head may
fall, my brave Swiggs, but we will drench
the streets with gaore!"

"Yes, my braves, we'll have ber-lud,"
cried Barry Cornwall.

"Will they let me write to Hengland,
to my Mary Hann?" asked Swiggs.

"Yes, of course, before they kill you."

"Oh, I wish I stayed at home," cried
poor Swiggs.

"And so do I," said the "kernal."
"This Paris ain't what it was cracked
up to be."

Just then the doctor came up with
Mr. Spotworth Grub, looking decidedly
better; so they hurried on board the
train and were presently being hurried
away to Paris.

In the next compartment they could hear the other two voyagers moaning over the sad fate which had thus untimely come upon them; but the boys, strong in the hope of having some fun out of the incident, kept the knowledge of it to themselves. And now lights— countless flashing lights—glittered beneath the azure firmament.

They were approaching the home of pleasure, the centre of civilisation— Paris!

CHAPTER XIX.

SEEING THE SIGHTS—A FEARFUL ADVENTURE.

PARIS—dear, gay, delightful Paris. Who could live in you and not be happy? Who would see you once yet not leave you with regret?

What a noise and shouting there was! Such a scramble for luggage, such a babel of voices.

"Hotel St. Romain, Rue Dauphin!" said Dr. Primrose, looking round for help.

Our English pilgrims soon found that all French boys were addicted to indulging in a habit—a sort of gesture—which expresses contempt and ridicule in much the same manner as the thumb placed on the nasal organ, as Dr. Ingoldsby has it—

> "The Sacristan, he said no words,
> To indicate a doubt,
> But placed his thumb unto his nose,
> And turned his fingers out.

By the time the boys had got halfway to the hotel—for they walked, having sent their luggage on with Pomponet—they had come to thoroughly understand what the *gamins* meant by this sign.

This so irritated Barry, that he immediately went after one of them and was surrounded by six.

"Let's go and help him, Leon," said Frank, who feared Barry might get injured, and yet did not want to wound the young Frenchman's feelings.

"*A bas la canaille!*" cried Leon, in a loud voice, and with a shrug of the utmost contempt. "They are not worth fighting, they do not know how to do anything but cry and run away. Let him alone, they will be taken by surprise."

He spoke bitterly and slightingly of these street-arabs then, yet afterwards, when the terrible barricades were erected, he thought how vastly he had misjudged their courage.

They clustered around Barry, having enticed him far enough away from his friends, and one tall youth, with red eyes and a ferrety expression of face, poked his finger at our hero.

Upon this Barry knocked him down by a straight blow from the shoulder, a proceeding which elicited from the others cries of surprise and astonishment.

Barry, hearing so much noise, expected nothing less than annihilation, and struck out right and left.

To his own infinite surprise several of the dancing youths went down like grain before the gale, and the rest, to carry out the simile, vanished like chaff.

"Look you," said Barry, as he rejoined his companions, "look you, I shall be fery sorry to fight with them again."

"Why so, St. David?"

"Because, look you, they shall be fery despicable foes, look you, and not worth wasting one's time with."

So they got to the Hotel St. Romain, and were received by Monsieur Le Maître d'Hotel himself.

What a delicious breakfast they had, and how Hans fell asleep in the middle of his breakfast!

Then the doctor gave them a holiday.

He only limited them to take a servant with them.

Leon, Barry, Frank, and Nat sallied off by themselves, telling Pomponet to follow; but as the former knew every inch of Paris by heart, they did not much care whether he came or not.

"What a mean little river it is, after all!" said Frank, looking at the Seine.

"You ought to see the Hudson or the Mississippi," cried Nat, beginning to let off steam. "You could put a dozen Seines or Thames into the Hudson up by Tarrytown, and people would only think it the swash of a river-steamer."

Frank and Leon looked at one another and both began laughing.

Nat reddened a little.

"Well, that was something like bounce," he said; "but you cannot imagine the vast difference between the rivers; we would call both the Thames and the Seine brooks on the other side. What curious little steamboats!"

"About half the size of the Thames boats," said Frank.

"Wouldn't make a deck-house boat for a Mississippi steamer," grumbled Nat.

"There's the Tuileries," said Leon; "there is the very spot. Shall I tell you a story about Napoleon the Great?"

"Yes."

"It was this," said Leon. "Where you see all those beautiful flowers and statuettes, had you lived in Robespierre's time you might have seen on a certain wild, dark night the whole place filled with a mob of flushed, passionate faces, waving their torches, and trampling down these beautiful flowers, listening to the bawling eloquence of fishwives. A poor, pale, beautiful, and good woman sat trembling in one of those windows; her Swiss guard had fled, and, shame to them, the men who had sworn to protect her had left her to the mercy of the rabble. You could just see her pale, careworn face at yonder window, when the glare of the torches lit it up for a moment. This was the mob of 'Liberty, Equality, and Fraternity;' and what do you think they did?"

Leon's frame quivered, his height seemed to increase, and his large grey eyes flashed fire.

"This mob of 'Liberty' stood there insulting one poor woman—one of the hounds hit her! What would you have done had you been there? Would you not have killed the ruffian upon the spot, though you died for it the next moment? Well, a little way apart from the yelling crowd there was a young soldier, a Corsican. He had entered the army as a private, and worked his way up to a colonel's rank. That man did not wish to pull down aristocracy; he had genius and courage to work his way up to it, as you do in your England. He stood watching the crowd, and he muttered between his teeth—'Were I king I would mow them down with grape-shot!'"

"Who was he?" cried the boys.

"Napoleon, when he was simply Colonel Bonaparte, a young Corsican, with an eye like an eagle's, and a temper like polished steel."

"Well, that's a pretty good yarn," said Nat; "but for all that I'm good for taking all the bets I can get upon American liberty."

"Look!" cried Frank, suddenly; "there is a row of some sort going on. Look how the people are all rushing to one spot."

They hurried thither, pierced the crowd, and discovered the cause of all this excitement.

Squat was standing on his head on a pewter pot in the middle of the road, while Pomponet was acting as master of the ceremonies, and taking in sous and centimes by the hatful.

"Beautiful ladies and handsome gentlemen, this wonderful barbarian was purchased by myself from the Emperor of the Cannibal Islands, who was going to have him made into a *ragout à la place Bastile*."

There was a roar of laughter over this.

It was a political hit and told well.

But just then Pomponet experienced another hit.

Barry Cornwall had got his pea-shooter to bear, and St. David was a dead-shot.

"I took him from the English barbarians, who have big toes. *Mon Dieu!* they were the allies of—*Sacre nom de guerre!*"

At the same time Squat received one which brought him to his feet, causing him to make the most frightful grimaces, which the people thought were all part of the performances, and yelled accordingly.

"What a scoundrel that Pomponet is!" said Leon, with a laugh. "He will tell me to-night, upon his word of honour as a veteran who fought under the eye of the great Napoleon, that he hunted for me all over Paris."

"What shall we do now?"

"Shall we go and see the catacombs? Paris is as much a city underground as above ground."

"But there is no fun in going through sewers."

"Yes."

"What fun?"

"Why, these sewers or catacombs are paved with skulls and thigh-bones; it is estimated that over three millions of skulls are buried here."

Nat looked at Frank.

The latter returned his gaze in apparent unconcern.

"*Eh, bien!* come on," said Leon.

"He is not afraid of dead men, whatever he may be of spirits," said Nat to himself, looking at Frank.

A quarter of an hour's rapid walk brought them to the Place de Louis Quatorze, outside the barriers.

Here they found one of the entrances, and, having paid the keeper two francs for the four, they were allowed to descend.

"A guide has just gone," he said; "if the young messieurs hurry up and turn to the right they will catch up with him.

They did as directed.

The place had a very oppressive, earthy smell.

Leon lit a match and showed them that the walls on each side were lined with skulls and bones.

"It's frightfully lonely down here," said Nat.

"And dark, look you," said Barry.

"And the smell is awful."

Another ten minutes passed away.

Then the truth suddenly dawned upon them; they must have taken the wrong turning.

They had lost themselves.

Yet they were not frightened.

"We shall find our way back again presently," said Leon.

"The air is suffocating."

"There is an outlet from here, somewhere."

"What a place to store gunpowder and nitro-glycerine," said Nat. "If those devils of communards had their way——"

"Look! look!" cried Barry, in unfeigned terror.

"What?"

"The double—the double of Frank!"

A thin bluish light smote upon their eyes, a pale phosphorescent glare.

Seated on a throne of ghastly skulls, and laughing wildly, was Frank's "double."

Frank reeled, shrieked, and fell, just as Barry caught sight of Snarly Cool's face, looking pale as death.

Then all was darkness.

Nat drew his revolver and fired.

He could fire no second shot.

The revolver was knocked from his nerveless fingers; they were alone in darkness.

CHAPTER XX.

HOW THEY GOT OUT OF IT—SNARLY COOL PROVES AN ALIBI.

It was not a question of fright but one of absolute terror for our four adventurers.

They were brave enough boys, as they had very well proved themselves to each other; but it is one thing to fight palpable substances and another thing to wage war against the air.

There was something hideously realistic about this pale-faced double of Frank Stainforth.

He had followed them about so unpleasantly that there was no disbelieving him.

"We are going to have some misfortunes, I know we are," said Leon.

Presently Leon heard voices.

They approached nearer and nearer, and Leon could distinguish the clink of sabres and the rattle of rifles.

"Here, here!" he shouted at the top of his voice; "turn to the left, comrades."

In a few moments the boys were surrounded by a detachment of the *garde mobile,* who had come upon them with fixed bayonets.

The young lieutenant picked up the revolver which Nat had let fall.

"This is suspicious," he said.

"I suspect that if you do not get us out of here very quickly we shall all die, *mon lieutenant,*" said Leon, with a shrug.

"But how did you get here?"

"*Ma foi!* on our feet."

"For what purpose came you here armed?"

"If you will restore my young friend

the American to consciousness he will tell why. He is always idiotic enough to carry a revolver. It is a national weakness, *mon ami*, and it has twice been of infinite service to his three friends."

"But why was it fired off?"

"To summon assistance."

"For what?"

"Because we saw a ghost."

"*A bas!* I am not a child."

"It is nevertheless true."

"I must take you before the prefect of the police."

"As you please," answered Leon, carelessly. "We came down; we lost our way; we saw a ghost; we fired a pistol; the ghost and his comrades vanished; you came."

"Oh, so there were other ghosts?"

"*Ma foi!* there were a dozen of them at least, clad in cowls like monks."

"Come, this is too good. You said there was only one. Your ideas are expanding."

By this time they were near the entrance under the Place de la Concorde, up which they ascended.

"Monsieur," said Leon, "a little cold water sprinkled on the face of my friends might save you the trouble of carrying them."

"Good!" said the lieutenant.

Frank shivered as he came to and looked apprehensively over his shoulder.

"Has it gone?" he asked.

"*Oui mon cher*," responded Leon; "it hardly waited for you to faint."

"Don't jest; it's horrible!" said Frank.

By this time Nat Urner had opened his eyes.

The young lieutenant was only waiting for this to march them off, and presently our four sight-seers were in motion, escorted by a file of gendarmes with fixed bayonets.

"If it takes twelve soldiers with fixed bayonets to run in twelve schoolboys who are willing to go, how many would it take to carry a hundred boys who didn't want to go?" said Frank. "There is a sum in proportion for you."

"Perhaps you are not aware that I speak English," said the young lieutenant.

"Thank you very much for not playing the spy," said Frank. "After our affair with the police we hope you will honour us by dining with us."

"If it be proved that you are not *encroyables* I shall be delighted," said the young soldier.

On ascertaining who the boys were, and seeing that their passports were properly made out, the prefect dismissed them at once, apologising for the detention he had occasioned them.

He, however, took down their several statements relative to the figures they had seen flitting about with the ghost, and promised them that the matter should be attended to.

"In France, you know, *petits messieurs*, we do not believe in ghosts."

So they took their leave, and then hurried to the hotel, where they found Snarly Cool, who expressed the utmost astonishment when accused of having been in the sewers.

"What do I want in the sewers of Paris?" he asked; "but perhaps you did see a ghost."

CHAPTER XXI.

THE DOCTOR RECEIVES AN UNEXPECTED TELEGRAM—THE NEW SCHOOL— GOOD-BYE, OLD TIMES.

THE following day they were up at eight o'clock in the morning, and, after prayers and breakfast, ready to go with Doctor Primrose to the new school.

This would not be entirely under his charge, he explained to the boys, but he trusted that everything would go on in a satisfactory manner.

There were about fifty boys at this school, all of them French.

The old doctor did not say that he had been to see the school the day before by himself, and that the inspection thereof had not given him satisfaction.

What the doctor might have said was

prevented from being spoken by the arrival of a telegram.

He read it hurriedly through, and, with much emotion, announced to the boys the death of his old college-friend, whose advice he had so often asked on their behalf.

He had been named executor, and must hasten away at once after introducing them to the new school, leaving them under the care of Mr. Spotworth Grub.

His things were waiting for him in the cab; the minutes were rolling rapidly away, and yet he seemed loth to go.

"Something tells me, dear boys, that I shall not see you on earth again," said the doctor, with tears in his eyes; "and, indeed, I am loth to leave you in this strange land by yourselves. The path of duty does not seem at all clear."

"All right, doctor, we'll take care of ourselves," said Frank, anxious to cheer him up; "don't you worry yourself about us."

"I hope, I hope so, boys."

"You may be sure it."

"Well, well, I must be off. Good-bye, then, boys, for the last time, and God bless you all."

"Good-bye, sir. Three cheers for the doctor, and quick return to him."

"Hurrah, hurrah, hurrah!"

While he got in they clustered round and seemed unwilling to part with him, and cheered his spirits with lusty English cheers.

So he drove off, slowly.

Now he has gone, and they needed all their courage, for they never looked upon his face again.

"Gentlemen," said Mr. Spotworth Grub, "it's time to go to school. Your luggage will be transported thither during the afternoon."

Softly all sallied forth, and, it seemed to them, after an interminable time, they found themselves opposite a sort of prison with a gloomy courtyard shut in from the street by heavily-barred gates.

"This is cheerful," said Frank.

"Looks more like a prison than a school."

"Where is the cricket-green?"

"Look you," said Barry, "there is no archery or rowing, look you."

"There's two stunted trees in the middle of the square, and that's the extent of the vegetation."

"What are those pale-faced boys doing there?" asked Frank, pointing to two boys, who did not even turn round when they made their entrance, but remained steadfastly gazing up the tree.

"They are being punished," said Leon.

"How?"

"They have to watch that tree for four hours, during which time they must not look at anything else."

"And supposing they do?"

"They will get another four."

"And supposing they break that?"

"They will not be allowed to sleep."

"But don't they cane them?"

"No, never."

"Look here," said Nat. "I guess this thing is worse than being caned."

"I tell you what," said Leon, suddenly. "Now I know why Monsieur Le Bon Docteur was so much overcome at leaving us."

"Why?"

"He has been taken in. This is a bad school and he knows it."

"I guess there's enough of us here to make it a good one," said Nat.

"You are mistaken. However, we shall see," answered Leon.

"I know one thing, look you," said Barry. "They shall not make a fool of myself by staring at a tree, look; and it shall be fery queer inteet if I shall lose my sleep, look you."

Thus incipient mutiny had already developed itself before the new-comers had got well within the schoolroom.

Their appearance was greeted by a number of pale-faced students in a variety of manners.

They stuck out their tongues and clapped their left hands to their heads in the most improved French fashion, while the mutterings and peculiar cries, the smell and general nastiness were indescribable.

"Here come the foreigners!" cried one; and then followed a coarse jest about England.

Midst this babel of tongues the head-master, a tall man with a lump of fur on his cheek, struck a gong, and partial silence ensued.

"You foreigners are late for school: our hour is ten o'clock," said the head-master, or Maître d'Ecole; "you look at each other without speaking for a quarter of an hour after twelve-o'clock meal."

This speech seemed to afford great amusement to the French portion of the school.

Mr. Spotworth Grub explained the cause of delay.

"A law once uttered is never altered here," said the *maître*; "it is necessary for discipline."

"But supposing it were made under a mistake?" said Frank.

"You will watch a tree for two hours for presuming to argue with your master," said the *maître*.

Frank felt deeply irritated, but said nothing.

"Because he is a cad, it is no reason why I should prove myself a gentleman," he said to himself.

But Nat Urner viewed things in a different light.

"I'll square old hunk for this, you bet," he said. "He can't come his gun games on us by a darn sight; so we may as well begin as we intend to go on."

"Aren't the English cads getting it heavy; look at their short nails. *A bas! Monsieur Le Poys, vous êtes trop cru —mais je suis Anglais,*" and so on, with a lot of doggerel verses at the expense of Englishmen in general, the points of which will not bear translation.

But this was gall and wormwood to poor Leon.

At last one boy whispered to his neighbour—

"What shall we do with Messieurs L'Internationals after school?" and Leon heard him.

To a Frenchman, the word Internationalist is the worst term you can apply, and there was just sufficient point in the flash of wit to make it particularly maddening to Leon.

"You will see when school is over," he said, in a voice of suppressed passion; "I shall pull all your noses."

"*Vous! vous!*" they cried.

"Leon!" cried Frank, in English.

"What?"

"You will do nothing of the kind."

"But I insist."

"You will offend us all if you do."

"It is this, *mon ami*," said Leon; "even though there was a bully at Lake Windermere I had fair play. Here you are—I will help you; but I assure you this is one of the worst schools in Paris; the good doctor has been taken in."

"I have no doubt of it," said Frank.

The master's chair was erected on a platform; it was a stuffed one with a spring bottom.

By its side was an ivory ball, and line coiled up.

The new-comers wondered what this was for, until they saw the head-master suddenly throw it at a boy who was talking to his neighbour.

So unerring was the head-master's aim from long practice, that he hit the boy exactly on the top of the head.

The boy gave a howl of pain and resumed his studies.

"How brutal!" said Frank.

"If he does that to me I'll crack him up," said Nat.

The principal, to whom, by-the-bye, we may as well give his nickname of Plon-Plon, from a habit he had of suddenly springing a *coup d'état* on the boys, calmly gathered up his string, coiled it round, and waited for another victim.

"Now, you Englis' boys, come here. How aff you learnt? Nodtinks I expect. Tell me no lies, for I assure you it is not possible to deceive me."

"We have not the slightest desire to do so, sir," said Frank.

"You will look at the wall for two hours after supper for ze zecond offence of speak to de mastare without his permission," he said.

"Monsieur," said Leon, speaking rapidly in French, "if you ask me, I think your conduct is infamous. These gentlemen are utter strangers, and you punish them severely for not obeying your laws before they are acquainted with them.

"Silence!" hissed Plon-Plon.

"Monsieur Le de Maître d'Ecole," continued Leon, "I have a very poor opinion of you and your school. I was not treated like this when in England. I had fair play."

"M. Le Vicomte," returned the principal, "I will consider what punishment is adequate to the enormity of your crime; for the present I request silence."

"You've only got yourself in heavy trouble, and done no good," said Nat Urner.

Their conversation was interrupted by the beginning of the lessons.

It speedily became apparent to everyone of the boys that they were better up in every department of school education as taught in *L'Ecole des Jeunes Hommes* than any of the others; they were, in fact, far enough ahead to be put in a class by themselves.

Presently the gong sounded, and Plon-Plon left the room, followed by Mr. Spotworth Grub, Monsieur Garlic, and two other teachers.

Plon-Plon first of all directed the boys how to stand facing one another, to be jeered at during the half hour before dinner by the whole school.

Round they came; they made fun of Hans, who, being a coward, and, besides, somewhat thick-skinned, stood it very well.

They pulled Joel Skimp's hair, and made fun of his long legs.

"Look here," said Lord De Lain. "Leon De Gardin, are these your chivalrous countrymen?"

While he was speaking, a tall, hulking lout of a fellow pulled Lord Mouslin's hair.

His lordship's blue eyes sparkled with anger.

"Hang it—no fellah can suffer that!" he said, and straightway, picking up his huge antagonist as if he had been a bag of straw, he flung him about three yards off, over a desk, and, walking to the little brazier that did duty for the fireplace, stuck his hands in his pockets.

"Bravo!" cried Leon.

"Well done, Mouslin!" cried Frank.

"Bully for you, Rocks," cried Nat. "Hurrah!"

All the quartet forgot their enmity to Lord Mouslin in admiration of his latest effort.

"This thing's a boah," said Lord Mouslin. "What's a fellow to do? Those cads can't fight."

But by this time the other scholars had made up their mind what to do.

They came to the conclusion that it would be well if the Internationalists were taught their place at once.

The first one they pitched upon to sacrifice was Hans, who had gone to a form, and was contemplating going to sleep.

Him they hit under the ear, or rather, one of them did, and he fell under the table yelling.

Then Joel Skimp was caught and tanned, after which they advanced for Barry Cornwall.

Up to this time the quartet had remained quiet, not because they did not care to interfere, but they knew Leon would join them, and they did not want to have him fight against his own country boys if it could be helped; but when Nat Urner's eye was nearly stopped with a paper pellet, and Barry received a cut across the knuckles from a slate, the thing got past a joke.

"Up, boys; let's go for their scalps," shouted Nat.

"I wonder where this row will end?"

"They dare not touch me," said Lord Mouslin.

"Did you ever hear the story of the Quaker?" asked Frank.

"No; what was it?"

"Well——"

Just as he got to this part a ball of soap nearly choked him.

Leon reached out his long arms.

"You have brought it all on yourselves," he said.

"Hurrah! Wire in, boys!" cried Frank.

Then the boys gave a regular English cheer, and charged the crowd that were opposing them.

They charged in form of a wedge, with Frank Stainforth at the head, who bowled over two, right and left auctioneer, by way of opening the ball. Then came Nat Urner on one side, and Leon on the other. Barry Cornwall, being in the rear, stayed behind to get another smack at any adversary who had guarded his first blow, and got knocked down.

In a moment there were half a dozen French boys on top of him, kicking, scratching, snarling, like so many curs.

"Shame!" cried Frank; "let him get up again. Fair play."

"*Mes etoiles!* after we have him down once to let him up and begin all over again; *non, merci.*"

"When I knock you down, I'll let you get up," said Frank, sparring back, just to get weight enough to carry him where St. David was.

"When you do, *ma foi.*"

"There you are, then, old chap," said Frank, rushing forward with a lightning stroke, that sent his antagonist like a pendulum up against another.

Leon scored one, but had to jump back

from a formidable antagonist, whom he found wished to clasp him.

Again the trio were driven back, and again Frank rushed forward like a whirlwind.

"And I guess you'll know a New England trip when you see one again," said Nat, as he sent his antagonist flying, with his head full into the stomach of a friend, who immediately went down.

Lord Mouslin De Lain stood looking at the fight.

"Look here, Stainforth," he said, "you'd better not let that ugly temper of yours get the upper hand or you'll kill someone. I can see you're beginning to hit hard."

"I hate to be mobbed," said Frank, as he backed out of the *melée* of bleeding faces again; "they are like a lot of mosquitos. I've got up to where St. David is twice, and I've been driven back by numbers—sheer dead-weight. They don't know how to do anything but kick and scratch."

"In that case, I don't mind lending you a hand; it amuses one to knock about, so on we go, Frank."

"Hurrah! Shoulder to shoulder," said Frank, "If I can only get St. David in the corner once on his feet you may go and sit down again."

Swish! swish! swish! came the blows from the boys; and soon the brave lads forced themselves through the struggling mass, and, just as they got up to St. David, that youngster managed to gain his feet.

Little St. David had come from a line of warriors.

"Take that, look you!—and that, and that! it shall be ferry good for you, look you!" cried Barry, showering his blows right and left.

"Rush against them; knock them down!" said someone in French. "Those wretched English can only fight while on their legs."

"Go it, lads!" cried Frank; "Mouslin, you'll have to fight now; they are getting savage."

Indeed, some of the boys who had gone off to hammer Hans, the Spaniard, and Joel Skimp, who got very badly hurt, surrounded the trio.

The English boys stood back to back, firm as a rock.

There were certainly fifty boys in that school-room, of these, twenty-five had received some wound in the face or body; and yet Frank Stainforth had not hit out in the manner which had gained for him in England the soubriquet of the sledge-hammer; but he was warming to his work.

Those who received his blows now did not get up in a hurry, and even Lord Mouslin, callous as he was as a rule, became apprehensive.

"Don't lose your temper, Frank," he said, "you might kill one of those curs, and get us all into trouble."

Wouldn't those French boys have liked to have had the English under their feet for five minutes. I promise you they would not have let them get up again in a hurry.

A French boy has no idea of fair play, namely—of giving an opponent a knock-down blow and allowing him to get up again.

Their idea is, once having a foe down to keep him down.

"*Ma foi!*" they would say, "give up our advantage, and begin all over again on the same vantage. That is not war; it is folly."

So the schoolboys would have liked to have had the quartet, or rather it was a quintet now, for Lord Mouslin, seeing the desperate nature of things, had, for for the moment, completely forgotten his feud with the four chums, and only remembered that self-preservation is Nature's first law.

Paul De Cassarand was the name of the boy whom Lord Mouslin had pitched into.

He had recovered himself by this time and was leading the attack with the skill of a general, inciting them to fury by cries of rage, but taking care for his part to keep out of the way of Lord Mouslin's terribly sinewy arms.

At last it became evident that the longer the battle raged the worse off were the French.

They were dropping one by one, and it was noticed now that those who dropped before Lord Mouslin's and Frank's blows were not in a hurry to renew the combat.

Paul De Cassarand saw this.

"*Allons*, comrades!" he said; "these foreigners fight too well with their fists. Let us give them some artillery. Slates, inkbottles——"

"TOM FLOREMALL" SERIES OF SCHOOL STORIES.
THE TRAVELLING SCHOOLBOYS.

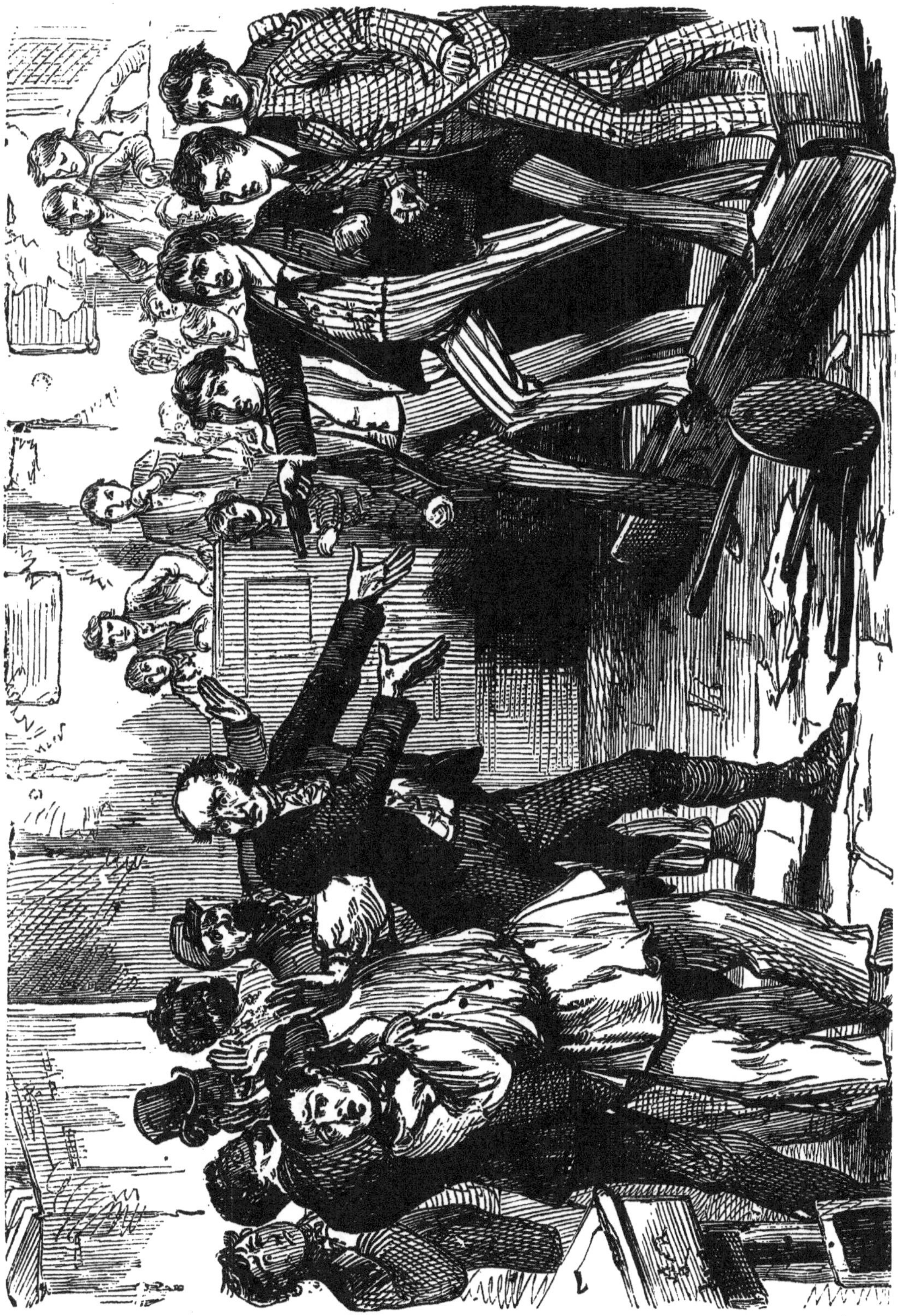

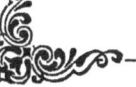

"'SEIZE HIM, COWARDS!' CRIED PLON-PLON, FURIOUSLY."

"Shame, shame!" called out Leon. "Fifty to five, and you must use ink-bottles."

"*Parbleu!*" returned Paul, "we are not more than twenty to five. The rest are *hors de combat;* and it does not seem likely that we can break that beastly square you have formed."

Affairs were getting critical. The French boys' blood was up. They meant mischief.

The English boys were equally determined not to yield, come what may.

It was a wonder the masters did not hear them, for the French boys, with their cries, made enough noise to have awakened the seven sleepers almost.

Before their antagonists got hold of their slates the English boys held a consultation.

What could they do?

There was no means of resisting the shower of missiles that would be poured upon them, and the result of a blow from a slate across the head was not to be desired.

Frank's eye at this crisis happened to fall on a small door, a sort of postern, which led to an alleyway.

It looked very much like flight. But they had no other means of saving themselves for the present.

"Attention, lads!" shouted Frank. "We must make for the door. Keep close together, and make a dash through them!"

As he finished speaking he darted forward. Small need was there for Barry or Nat to use their fists.

He simply cut a straight line through the foe, who fell away on either side.

They gained the doorway almost without opposition, for the foe were too thoroughly demoralised to make the shadow of a stand against them.

They gained the door and slammed it to, 'midst a perfect volley of French exclamations; and not a few slates and inkbottles came rattling against it, showing that their manœuvre had not been executed a moment too soon.

They were now in comparative safety. Through the door they could hear the hum as of bees in a hive.

"We're all right for the present, anyhow," said Barry, "look you, though it is a ferry bad thing that we retreat."

"I'd like to go back and knock spots off them, if I got my head broken," said Nat.

"It is infamous," cried poor Leon, who was weeping with rage. "The curs! the *canaille!* I did not think any of my countrymen could be so base."

"Nonsense!" returned Frank. "You don't suppose we think all French boys are like this? It is not your fault that Dr. Primrose was unfortunate in his selection of a school."

"It's an awful bosh, you know," said Lord Mouslin.

"Still, whatever it is," cried Frank, compressing his thin lips, "we must be their masters."

Just then they heard cries from the other room.

"It is the Spaniard. I reckon they're hammering him," said Nat.

"That decides the matter," said Frank. "I'm sorry we showed the white feather for a moment. Now cautiously, and then a rush. Remember, we must win."

They opened the door, and saw a sight that for a moment caused them to quiver with a sort of sickening sensation.

Young Gomez was standing with his back to the wall preparing for a spring.

He had a cut over his forehead, from which the blood trickled slowly. But that was not what had caused the boys to give forth a shout of dismay.

It was the fact that the French boys had drawn off in fear of the deadly yellow gleam in his eye, which spoke of a settled purpose.

His tawny face was black as midnight. He looked like a panther about to spring upon his prey, and in his hand he held a large hunting-knife.

"Hold!" cried Frank, in a voice of thunder. "Do not move, for Heaven's sake! It is murder!"

He wasted no time in words, for, even as he spoke, he dashed across the space which intervened between him and the crowd, followed by the others.

Another moment sufficed to wrench the knife from the Spaniard's hands and throw it out of the window.

"Hurrah, up and at them!" cried Frank.

Then they went for them. Each boy was desperate.

They meant to win, and they put their souls, as well as their bodies, into it.

In five minutes the conflict was over,

if conflict it could be called, where steady science burst forth, to guide the torrent of passion and sweep everything before it.

Some of the French gained the door and escaped that way, others ran yelling to the windows, flung up the sash, and dropped to the courtyard below, while of the remainder, who were not hurt, some flung themselves upon their knees, and even at full length, upon the floor, grovelling and screaming in downright abject terror.

They had provoked a torrent, and they were terrified because at last it had overwhelmed them.

Four boys were lying on the floor motionless, and it wanted but little prescience to tell whose fearful blows had brought this about.

In every direction boys were moaning, holding their eyes, or striving to staunch the blood which poured from their noses in torrents.

Lord Mouslin, wild with passion, wreaked his vengeance on flying fugitives.

Hans and Joel managed to get up enough energy to go and kick a few prostrate foes who were too frightened to kick back.

Nat Urner and Barry set up shouts of victory.

Leon and Frank bestirred themselves; their natures were too chivalrous to gloat over the defeat of their fallen foe; albeit, the cuts and bruises about everyone showed that the victory had been dearly bought.

They alone went and raised up their fallen enemies, and tried to assist them.

Affairs were in this condition when the principal appeared.

He face was livid with passion as he looked upon the English boys.

"Messieurs," he said, in a thin, tremulous voice, "you come here thinking to subvert the discipline of the school. You shall see that we have a different principle here."

CHAPTER XXII.

FRENCH SCHOOL DISCIPLINE.

THE words of the French principal were dreadfully sinister in their meaning.

Behind him came his assistants, greasy-looking fellows; they were Mr. Spotworth Grub, who looked alarmed, and the ever bland and smiling face of Snarly Cool.

This latter gentleman, to the surprise of not only his master but everbody else, had developed such a marvellous facility for foreign languages that he could now speak French more fluently than his master.

Some even ventured to assert that Snarly, for purposes of his own, had hitherto refrained from displaying his linguistic abilities.

For some moments a deep silence was preserved in the school-room; the whipped French boys slunk back into their places, and the English boys remained standing where they were.

"I make it a rule in this school never to do anything in anger, messieurs," said the directeur; "this day week you will receive the punishment due to your offences."

The boys breathed again.

It couldn't be so very dreadful if he was going to wait a week before inflicting it, and, besides, what had they done?

Soundly whipped a lot of cads who had tried to bully them, and not only whipped them but against most unfair warfare also.

Things passed away quietly enough that day until supper-time.

They wondered at not being let out to play, but supposed that it was part of the punishment allotted to all the school for kicking up a shine.

Precisely as the clock struck six a gong sounded, they were marshalled in military order and marched down a long, stone corridor, to the dining-room.

The building had at one time been an abbey, and, as a result, it was full of gloomy cloisters and corridors.

The candles, burning dimly, reflected weird and grotesque shadows against whitewashed walls, whose plainness somehow sent a chill through one.

The table cloth was dirty, and there were no seats.

Each boy was supposed to take what was set before him, standing.

The fare consisted of some sort of soup —it tasted like dish water—and a small glass of most execrable wine, which tasted very much like vinegar.

All the new-comers made wry faces.

"I say, I guess they scooped out the vinegar-cask to lay in this," said Nat Urner.

"Awful," returned Frank; "won't I have the stomach-ache, that's all?"

"Look at Mouslin!" That spirited scion of the English aristocracy had taken early opportunity of transferring the contents of his glass beneath the table.

Every boy was expected to eat what was set before him, and then turn and walk slowly to another part of the room.

Here, one after the other, they came, stood in a line, at the attention, and waited until the last one had finished. Then, at a given signal, down went their hands to their toes, and back again to the attention.

This manœuvre was repeated four or five times, until the new-comers' backs ached.

All this time not a word was spoken except the principal's commands, delivered in short, sharp, jerky sentences.

Another order, and they marched slowly away, like a funeral procession, to another room, more desolate and gloomy, if possible, than the one wherein they had dined.

This was the study.

Here they remained for two hours, after which, with the same precision which marked their former movements, they were marched to bed.

The boys undressed and popped into bed at the word of command given by one of the tutors.

"Silence is requested!" said the usher, and closed the door.

"I say, Frank," said Nat, "what's your opinion of things?"

"I can hardly say."

"What do you think, Leon?"

"I am going to write to my father to take me away."

"He won't get your letters," said a voice.

"Who spoke?"

"Paul de Cassarand."

"How do you know?"

"Because I have several times tried to get my letters posted, but without success."

"What's their object?"

"To keep matters quiet; for, if it were once known how they treat boys here they would never get any more pupils."

"Oh, I see."

"The school holds the reputation of being one of the best in Paris," continued Paul de Cassarand.

"Well, upon my honour," said Lord Mouslin De Lain, "you fellows deserve it."

"How?"

"Because you're a lot of cads."

"Hold up, Mouslin," said Frank. "Poor devils! I expect the discipline has taken all the manliness out of them."

"You wait until you've been here a month and you'll be just as bad as us," replied Cassarand.

"What, make a row the moment that the old chap's back is turned, and not dare to whisper while he is in sight. You don't know the school or the place we come from."

"I dont; look you, I don't think the punishment is so ferry treadful," said St. David. "It is not so bad as if you got a hiding."

"I guess they don't care about rushing us the same way," said Nat. "That old galoot has found out that we are not the same kind of oyster."

"I don't understand what your friend is saying," cried Paul de Cassarand; "but, from the tone of his voice he appears to be very exultant."

Leon translated what Nat had said.

"Your friend is very much mistaken," returned Paul. "Whenever the punishment is incarceration he allows a week to go by before it begins."

"What do you mean by incarceration?"

"Why, this place is an old abbey, and down beneath there are vaults and strong dungeons, where they chain you and feed you on bread and water."

"What, the scholars?"

"Yes; most of us have been there for a day; they say a week would kill anybody, because their voices give way."

"What has their voice to do with it?"

" Why, look you," said Barry, " if you are there, look you, shouting will do you no good."

" Won't it," returned Paul, " it's the only thing that keeps them away."

" Keeps them away — keeps what away ? "

" Rats ; they come up out of the sewers, and swarm about the cells. They say——"

The boy ceased speaking, and somehow, they knew he was shuddering.

" What do they say ? " asked Leon.

" They say that once a boy was put down there and they forgot him for three days—when they went down, they found his skeleton, only."

" Good Heaven ! "

" They say that's what turned the principal the ghastly, white colour he is."

" Horrible ! " said Frank.

" Yes, it's pretty tough," said Nat, but I guess I don't scare easily."

" If they put me down there I would die of fright," cried Frank.

" Well now, that is curious," said Nat. " Fancy Frank being afraid ; I would back you not to be afraid if you saw a ghost."

" I don't know how it is," returned Frank ; " but somehow—do you believe in warnings ? "

" Well, I don't know ; they had a first-class double-back action ghost to home, when my grandmother passed in her checks, but they discovered afterwards that it was Elder Wilkinson's mule that got loose. Anyhow, she had her warning, and she died the time she said she was going to."

" The whole system of this school is infamous," said Frank ; " what do you say, Leon, to putting our foot down on it and establishing a republic ? "

" *Bravo ! vive la Republique !*" yelled a lot of voices.

" There, you hear, Leon."

" Don't trust them," said the French boy ; " they what you call it, run wiz the hare to-night, to-morrow zey will follow wiz ze hounds ; that English provairb is too true—ah, but you cannot trust them ! "

" I reckon we could knock spots out of them ourselves, with Squat and Pomponet ; and we might get Weeks."

" Weeks and Ann O'Dyne have gone home."

" How do you know ? "

" Pomponet told me ; they were sent home this afternoon ; and probably Squat, Pomponet, and Snarly Cool will be sent away to-morrow, and what about Whilks ? "

" He's gone back."

" Hang it ; you know I can't stand that," said Lord Mouslin. " Hans, did you hear that ? "

" Yaw," snored Hans ; " you lets me get me mine schleep, dots vots I tinks about it."

" I wish the doctor hadn't gone."

" I can foresee a terrible row."

" I tell you," said Nat, " what I can see. I guess they'll find out before they've cut their eye-teeth, that they've tackled the wrong tom-cats."

" Well, we are resolved on one thing —no cellar for either of us."

" You bet ! " returned Nat, with much vehemence.

" Silence ! " cried one of the boys, or rather, whispered one of them. " The directeur is coming upstairs ; he wants to find out who are talking, so as to punish them to-morrow."

" We might as well be hanged for a sheep as a lamb," said Nat, and slipped out of bed.

He crept over to the nearest water-jug, and, seizing it, went out on the passage-way.

It was too dark for him to see anything, except a sort of shadow coming up the stairs.

" I reckon that will cool your ardour," said Nat, to himself, as he emptied the contents of the jug, being rewarded by a shriek, a gurgle, and the fall of some heavy body down the stairs.

Bump—bump—bump ! it went, from one step to another, until the bottom was reached.

Nat, meanwhile, sought the dormitory, replaced the jug and went into bed.

" What have you been doing ? " said Frank.

" I gave him some water to drown his rats," said Nat, in great disgust.

" By Jove ! now we are in for a row," cried Frank.

His predictions were speedily verified The directeur came up, and stole cautiously into the room.

The only difference in his approach was that this time he had a candle with him.

Curiously enough he did not even suspect the French boys. but went straight to that part of the dormitory where the "Travelling Schoolboys" were quartered.

Here some drops of water arrested his attention.

He followed them to the wash-hand stand, by Frank's bed.

Unhappily Frank occupied the side nearest it.

"Monsieur Stainforth," said the directeur, "you will oblige me by opening your eyes."

No answer.

Nat Urner snored hard to prevent his laughter from betraying him.

"Monsieur Stainforth," said the directeur, again, "you will oblige me by opening your eyes, before I bring this cane down upon your ear."

Frank opened his eyes and looked at him.

"You spoke to me?" he said, in a tone of inquiry, which made Nat kick him under the bedclothes, and pretend to have awakened.

"Yes, monsieur," said the directeur, white with passion, but still speaking with the utmost politeness; "I wanted to thank you for that jug-full of water you threw on me. I shall not forget it."

"You are mistaken, M. Le Directeur," said Frank. "I did not throw any water upon you."

"You lie!" returned the master, in a voice quivering with passion.

Frank turned crimson.

"I can only repeat, monsieur," he said, "that I did not throw any water upon you; and now, I must add, that your position gives you no right to insult your pupils."

"Little liar!" cried the man again. "Remember, I never threaten in vain. You will curse the day you allowed yourself the pleasure of throwing water upon your teacher!"

So saying, he withdrew.

"All right." said Nat, in a loud voice; "no one need speak, he is listening outside."

After this piece of information they heard him going down the stairs.

"What a beast he is, look you," cried Barry.

"If he hadn't been the principal he should not have called me a liar twice," said Frank.

"Won't there be a jolly row to-morrow, that's all," Nat returned.

He was mistaken; on the morrow not a word was spoken, nor was the affair alluded to.

This was a mystery to the boys.

CHAPTER XLII.

SAD NEWS—DEFIANCE.

NEARLY a week elapsed after the happening of the above-mentioned incident; a week of the most stupid, dull, heart-sickening routine, and yet nothing was said about the occurrence.

The quartet wished themselves well out of the school; there was nothing to learn, and life was beginning to be simply almost unendurable.

They had to submit to a thousand and one annoyances—in fact, they were in a chronic state of punishment.

The French boys, however, kept perpetually reminding the foreigners that they were in for it.

"Of course, now I know what it is," said Frank, on the fifth morning; "he is expecting Doctor Primrose, and is afraid to do anything that might cause him to take us away. That's the very truth of the matter, you may depend."

He was very much mistaken, however.

After breakfast the directeur called them up before him.

He had a sinister smile on his face which they did not like, something that made them suspect he had news, at once.

"I have the honour to inform you, young foreigners," he said, "that your late preceptor, Doctor Primrose, is dead!"

Had a shell exploded amongst them the boys could not have been more astounded.

Doctor Primrose—dear old Doctor Primrose dead.

"I do not ask you to believe me, gentlemen," said Plon-Plon; "liars seldom believe anyone, as they judge others by themselves. Here is the letter; you will be for the next six months under my absolute charge. I congratulate you."

As he spoke he handed them the letter, in such a manner as if he would say—"take this, your power has vanished from you. Take this piece of politeness from me, and be glad of it, for it is the last you will get."

Frank took the letter, and read of the sudden death of their dear old friend while on his way to join them in Paris, together with his wish that his pet scheme should be so far carried out that they should stay at the French school for six months; for this reason he had appointed Plon-Plon his successor.

"I have advised your parents," said Plon-Plon, "that my coadjutor and myself differed upon one very important point—to wit, the advisability of allowing boys to have men-servants, it leads them into expensive habits—in short, I don't approve of them, and so I have sent them home."

"Sent away Squat?" cried Nat.

"Pomponet!" roared Leon.

"Whilks!" bawled Lord Mouslin.

The only one who did not speak was Frank, but his eyes gleamed brighter.

A load had evidently been taken off his mind by the departure of Snarly Cool.

"Yes," returned Plon-Plon, "I have discharged them all, retaining only the one who, from his intimate knowledge of both French and English, will be the most useful to me."

"Pomponet?" cried Leon.

"Snarly Cool," said Plon-Plon, darting a look at Frank.

"Well," said Nat, "do you know what you have got to do?"

"What?"

"Send for them again right off. I reckon we are the ones who ought to know best what we want, not you. As for your dirty school, I don't care about staying in it now; we don't learn anything——"

"Except to obey, messieurs, and that you shall be taught!" cried Plon-Plon, livid with rage.

His hand was on the ivory ball that lay on his desk; he seized it, and flung it with his full force at Nat Urner's head.

The aim was straight, but it did not catch the American boy unprepared.

He was too good a base-ball player to miss a straight throw, and so, now, as it came full tilt, he caught it on the fly, and returned it.

It was sheer impulse that had caused him to do this; perhaps had he reflected half a moment he would not have done it; at any rate, what was done could not now be undone.

The ball sped true to its mark, and, catching Plon-Plon between the eyes, tumbled him over as if he had been shot.

A cry of horror arose.

"Oh, why did you do that?" cried Frank. "Remember, he was put in authority over us."

"I guess no one was put in authority to bang me over the head with a lump of bone," said Nat, stuffing his hands in his pockets defiantly.

"What are we to do now?"

"I don't know."

"Since you've begun we must back you up," said Frank. "It is very evident that with the death of Doctor Primrose the travelling school has come to an end. What do you say, boys?"

Barry, Leon, and Nat Urner responded in the affirmative.

The others remained silent.

"Solid men to the front," cried Nat, as he saw the directeur rise. "We'll leave!"

The boys moved towards the door.

"Good-bye, Mouslin," said Frank, "I am sorry you won't come with us——"

"A moment," said Plon-Plon, on whose forehead there was an enormous lump. "You cannot leave."

"Cannot leave!"

"No, messieurs, it is necessary that you should be taught discipline, and that is a part of your education that you will find me thoroughly able to inculcate. You, Monsieur Urner, for your little present to me"—he pointed with a ghastly smile to his swollen forehead—"will take a week in the cellars, during which we will find a means of stretching your superfluous muscle."

"The rack!" shouted the boys.

"You, Monsieur Stainforth, will have a week also. Messieurs the Vicomte and

Barry Cornwall, you were pleased to call this school an assemblage of cads, you will be put for two days where you will have an opportunity of displaying your fighting powers."

"Oh, Heaven—the rats!" cried a number of boys in a breath.

The master's quick eye darted round the room; but by this time every head hung down; they were too terrified to dare to meet his eye.

Only the quartet met him undauntedly, giving back his glances boldly.

"After the exhibition of your fighting powers," continued the master, "you will attend on these cads, as you call them, get their meals ready, and help to make their beds in addition to pursuing your studies; we will then see if your marvellous learning will be able to keep ahead of your schoolmates."

"This man is not a schoolmaster," cried Frank, "he is a monster."

"I guess there's only one thing that will prevent us from doing all you say," said Nat.

"And that is, monsieur—I am curious?"

"You can't spell 'able' the right way," shouted Nat. "Come on, lads, let's turn them all out and then make our terms!"

"*Allons, camarades!*" cried Leon. "*Vive la République!*"

Not a voice, or an action answered him from all that cowardly crew; they simply hung their heads.

Plon-Plon marked this, and smiled malignantly—the sinister smile of conscious power.

"They know that I am always prepared for a *coup d'état*. A sudden rising in this school can only have one result—failure."

He rang a bell as he spoke, and the door opened, revealing half a dozen men with masks on their faces standing motionless in the doorway.

"I know one of them," cried Frank Stainforth, impetuously. "Snarly Cool, come away from that crowd!"

Snarly, seeing himself discovered, took off his mask and flung it on the ground.

"To the deuce with such mummery," he said. "I have no reason to conceal my face from him."

"Go upstairs and get my things ready, also pack up the portmanteaus of my three friends. We are resolved not to stay here, since we have heard of the death of Doctor Primrose. You were culpable in not informing me of the death of Doctor Primrose."

Snarly Cool heard, but did not obey.

His smile deepened into a look of bitter hatred, as he looked triumphantly upon Frank and said—

"And I'm not going to do anything of the sort, Master Frank Stainforth; I don't care whether Doctor Primrose is dead or not; you were sent here, and here you've got to stay until the time is up."

"Insolent!"

"It isn't any use for you to come that game now," said Snarly. "We are not in England now, and you haven't that old ass, Doctor Primrose, to run to with your tales about me, so you'd just better keep a civil tongue in your head."

"So you've thrown off the mask at last, have you?" said Frank, in scorn. "Wretch, I know very well that you would not dare be insolent did not another support you in it. Begone, I dismiss you from my service!"

"I'm not in your service," said Snarly, "and so I am at liberty to tell a lot of little secrets if I like, and you give me precious little of your back talk or I will too."

Frank turned pale, but he recovred his firmness almost immediately.

"You may say what you please," he retured; "my friends are not likely to be influenced by your miserable venom."

"You will see your friends fall away from you as if you had the plague," chuckled Snarly, with a low laugh.

Again Frank paled, and this time he felt Leon's hand slipped within his to give him renewed courage.

"Do what you please, you miserable wretch; a poisoner would do anything!"

"Ah!" gasped Snarly, directing a swift look at Joel Skimp, who shivered with terror, and, falling on his knees, cried out—

"I didn't tell, I swear on my soul I did not tell."

"Who said you did. Hold your tongue, idiot!" cried Cool, "or I'll soon find a way to make you."

"Throw down the form in front," said Frank. "They are about to make a rush for us."

His words were speedily verified.

Almost as he spoke half a dozen men, headed by Plon-Plon, made a rush.

At this instant the quartet flung down the form and leaped behind it.

As quickly as they had made the sudden rush so quickly did they stop, for Nat Urner suddenly drew his revolver, and pointed it at the head of one.

"The first that moves a step farther will get a hole drilled through him," said the American boy, coolly. "My father didn't intend me to be eaten by rats when he sent me to school, and I guess he'll back me up. I told you you'd tackle the wrong tom-cats."

For a moment there was a terrible silence.

Then Plon-Plon cried furiously—

"Sieze him, cowards. They are but boys. Are you afraid of a little bravado?"

The men responded by a yell, and rushed forward.

They were restrained by Snarly Cool.

"Don't be fools," he said, "you would simply rush upon your death. I know that young imp, he always means what he says."

"You found out what kind of oyster I was when you put that poison in Frank Stainforth's cup," said Nat.

"It was not poison," said Snarly. "I drank it."

"Yes, and took an emetic immediately afterwards. I hope it agreed with your stomach."

Snarly turned livid.

"That tongue of yours will get you into trouble," he said, huskily.

"Not while I've got an arm and a head to take care of it," returned Nat.

"Put down that pistol and surrender yourself to the properly constituted authorities," said the head master.

"Give us a little rest on that," said Nat. "Properly constituted authorities don't lock boys up in cellars for the rats to eat."

"Unless you give yourself up at once I will call in the gendarmes. We will see if you can shoot them."

"That just suits us to death," said Nat.

"They would have to take us before the justice. So go and get them at once, Monsieur Plon-Plon."

The schoolmaster made no answer.

He dug his long nails into his hands, and compressed his pale brow in deep thought.

What could he do?

In treating the foreigners as he had treated his native scholars he had reckoned without his host.

"Come on," said Nat, "I guess we've had about enough of this thing. Come out!"

As they advanced towards the door one of the men disappeared.

"If you don't get away from that doorway, and let us get into tne street, you can take the consequences," said Nat, extending the revolver. "My fingers are trembling on the trigger, and I'm so nervous that I'm afraid it might go off by accident. Out of that, or I'll drill a hole through one of you!"

There was a precipitate retreat at the conclusion of the speech, not one of that gallant crowd caring about being shot.

Plon-Plon, however, made a hideous face and grinned.

"You are very clever, little messieurs," he said, "but not clever enough for me. The great door is bolted. You are a prisonair."

"The windows," whispered Barry Cornwall, and turning, they ran for one which overlooked the courtyard.

A yell of derision greeted them as they looked out, and saw that Snarly Cool had just locked the great courtyard-gate.

They were trapped.

"Throw down that key or I'll fire," cried Nat to Snarly.

"No, don't," Frank said, earnestly; "you might kill him. Don't let's have murder to account for."

"The dirty skunk!" said Nat.

However, he lowered his pistol.

Snarly, who at first seemed apprehensive, advanced boldly at this, and disappeared in the portico beneath them.

A click caused them to turn round and look in the schoolroom.

They were alone.

Prisoners!

"It is not any use trying to get out this way," said Frank; "even if we stood on each other's backs we could not reach over the wall."

"That's so."

"I am certain of this," said Leon; "after what has passed Plon-Plon would not let us get out of here alive."

"Oh, that is going too far."

"Look you," said Barry Cornwall, "Snarly did not relish what you said about the poison; that exasperated him."

"Hickory," observed Nat, "didn't that fetch him?"

"Did you see his eyes?"

"And little Joel Skimp?"

"Yes; I wonder what he knows about it?"

"Did you notice his terror?"

These and a thousand other queries occupied them for a couple of hours, at the end of which time a bright idea struck Nat.

"We can't get over the walls ourselves," said he, "but we can send intelligence to the effect that we are here."

"Yes, that's a capital idea."

"What shall we say?"

"Here goes," said Frank.

"Good people, four boys are detained prisoners here, and fear that they will be killed. Tell the British ambassador about their condition, or M. Le Comte De Gardin, 18, Rue Rivoli. Signed, Leon De Gardin, Barry Cornwall, Nathaniel Urner, Frank Stainforth."

"Make copies of these, and send them flying," said Frank.

They had no pebbles to attach these missives to, so they used the ink-bottles, tying them by means of the string which was attached to Plon-Plon's ivory ball.

"There is no use in denying it," said Nat; "we are in a bad hole."

"I fear my dream will come true," said Frank, with a sigh.

"What dream was that?" asked Barry.

"You know—about the cellar."

"Well, I reckon we are not there yet," Nat cried, stoutly; "when we do get there it will be time to holler."

"If Pomponet only knew," said Leon.

"If Squat just had about half an idea what was the matter, you'd see him go for Plon-Plon's scalp like a red-skin for a dram of whisky," said Nat.

The time passed away.

Nearly four hours, and it was growing quite dusk.

Still no one came near them.

"I reckon we'll have to camp out here all night," said Nat.

"I am, look you, getting fery hungry," cried little St. David.

"I know what it is," cried Leon; "they want to starve us out."

"Well, I guess they are *euchred* on that little game," said Nat; "we can hold on here for twenty-four hours without any grub, and at the end of that time somebody will have picked up one of those notes."

Thus conversing, the hours slipped away until it grew quite dark.

They had no candle, lamp, or gas; only a faint illumination reflected in the sky from the street-lamps came in through the window to make things dimly visible.

The boys found themselves getting drowsy.

There is nothing makes one so sleepy as having nothing to do.

"It wouldn't do to leave the door as it is," said Frank. "If they won't let us out we must keep them from getting in."

Accordingly they brought up forms and desks and piled them up against the door, so that one could not open it without tumbling the whole lot down.

Nat heard a slight noise outside. He was about to put his eye to the key-hole when Frank pulled him sharply back.

"What did you do that for?" Nat asked.

"Never trust your eye to a key-hole when there is somebody waiting for you on the other side. Look!"

He put a piece of blotting-paper to the key-hole, and a spray immediately came through and wetted it.

"That's Snarly Cool with a squirt," said Nat. "He doesn't get any water in my eye this shot."

"It isn't water," Frank replied. "Feel it, and that will tell you the sort of people we have to deal with."

Nat put his hand on the paper, and presently drew it away with an exclamation of pain.

"What is it?" he asked.

"Oil of vitrol," Frank replied. "I detected it by the smell."

Nat, brave as he was, recoiled in horror.

"Good Heaven!" he said, "that fiend said once he would spoil my sharp eyesight."

"Yes," said Frank. "Had you got that in your eyes once you would **never** have seen again."

Nat Urner gave a wild exclamation of rage and hate. His blood was up.

" I'll pay the skunk back in his own coin," said he.

And, putting the revolver to the door panel, he pulled the trigger.

The door was of stout oak, but the bullet crashed through it.

The report was followed by a scream of agony.

" Good Heaven ! " Frank exclaimed, " You have killed the wretched villain ! "

CHAPTER XXIV.

" NOW FOR MY REVENGE."

FOLLOWING the shriek of agony, in which Frank Stainforth distinctly recognised Snarly Cool's voice, there ensued for a few moment's a terrible silence. Then came the hurrying and shuffling of feet along the passage-way, and a sound as if a heavy body were being dragged along.

" Little rascals," said a shrill voice, following a quarter of an hour's silence, during which they speculated upon what had occurred ; " little rascals, you shall pay dearly for this."

" That's Plon-Plon," said Leon.

" Did I kill that vagabond, Cool ? " said Nat. " I hope I did."

" No, you fiend," returned Plon-Plon, " you did not; but you will be condemned to the galleys for life."

" I'm sorry I didn't kill him," Nat replied. " If you don't get out of that suddenly I'll chance a shot at you, you old kidnapper."

The answer to this was a sudden scampering of feet, as Monsieur Plon-Plon made himself scarce.

The four chums laughed heartily at this fresh exhibition of cowardice on the part of Plon-Plon.

Of course Nat was not in earnest when he said he was sorry he had not killed Snarly Cool.

All four felt as if a load had been taken off their minds when they heard that he was not killed. But they did not want the enemy to think that they were cowed.

Presently they heard footsteps outside again.

" Is that you, Plon-Plon ? " asked Barry. " Look you, you will get shot."

" No, it isn't," answered a voice. " It's I ? "

" Who is ' I ' ? "

" Mouslin De Lain."

" Aren't you ashamed of yourself ? "

" What for ? "

" Well, I thought at one time you were going to turn over a new leaf," said Frank. " Don't you feel like a traitor in going over to the enemy like that ? "

" Look here, you fellows," returned Mouslin De Lain, " it's all humbug for you to talk like that. You've got yourselves into a fearful mess; and I can tell you that Urner stands a good chance of seeing the galleys for life."

" Heavy on the talk," sneered Nat.

" It is a fact," returned Lord Mouslin. " They sent me to you as an ambassador. Plon-Plon will give you one more chance. If you submit, he will not deliver you up to justice."

" That is what we want him to do, look you," replied Barry.

" You just go back and tell Plon-Plon that we don't care worth a cent," said Nat.

" Messages of this sort only show how weak his case really is," added Frank.

" And tell him," said Nat, " that since we are in for the galleys we intend all to go in for the same number of years."

" What do you mean by that," asked Lord Mouslin. " You will go to the galleys. You fired the shot."

" Right you are," said Nat. " Well, you go and tell old Ratskin " (alluding to the blotch on Plon-Plon's face) " that Frank, Leon, and Barry are going to the galleys too, for they intend taking a flying shot, turn and turn about, at Plon-Plon, whenever he shows up this way, or any of his myrmidons."

" I say, Mouslin, what's the matter with Snarly Cool ? " said Frank.

THE TRAVELLING SCHOOLBOYS.

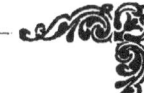

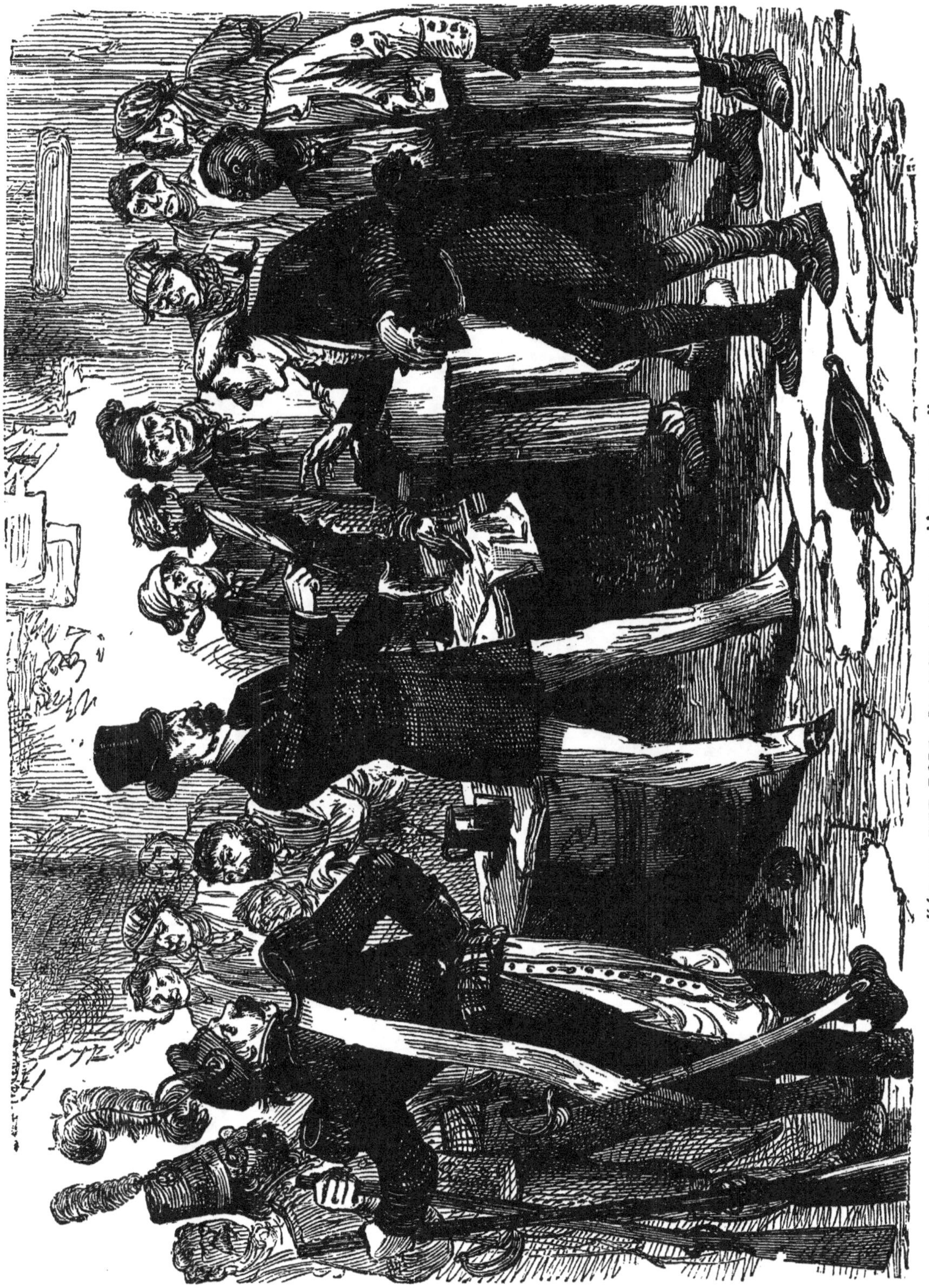

"'SIGN THE ROLL, OR YOU ARE LOST!' SAID HE."

"He's in awful agony. That shot of yours shattered a tin thing he was carrying and spilt the contents—some burning sort of stuff. It spread over his hands and a part of his face. He is in bed now, with cold-water poultices being put on him every three minutes. His cries are appalling. He'll kill you, Nat Urner."

"You give him my compliments," returned Nat, "and tell him I'm just as well able to take care of my life as of my eyes."

"It's all very well for you fellows to brag!" cried Lord Mouslin, using a last argument; "but you cannot hold out."

"Why not?"

"Because there are no means of escape."

"All right; it's good enough to stay here," said Nat.

"Then, in that case, you will be starved out. Plon-Plon says he will wait a week if necessary, but that when his turn does come the longer you hold out the worse you'll get it."

"Who's that prompting you!"

"No one."

"I hear some other voice beside yours. It's Plon-Plon. Stand out of the way; Barry is going to have a shot!"

This ended the interview, for they heard both Lord Mouslin and someone else retreat down the passage-way.

"Well, one thing is certain now," Frank said, presently.

"And that is——"

"That it is war to the knife."

"Yes."

"I wonder what time it is now."

"About eight o'clock. Can you make out the hands of my watch?"

"Here is a match," said Barry. "I have a boxful."

"Good; we shall want them."

They found that it was five minutes to eight.

"Now," said Nat, "here is what we will do. Someone must be on guard all the time to prevent a surprise; so we will divide the night into watches of two hours each. Barry can take the first, Frank the next, Leon the next, and I'll take the morning watch. By that means if there should be anyone on the prowl, we can hear them."

"That's the idea!" Frank replied, "and, although I don't feel sleepy, I'm going to turn in now in order that I may have no inclination to sleep when my watch comes."

"No caulking your watch on deck allowed," said Nat.

In a very few moments, so determined were the boys to obey their self-imposed rule of going to sleep, there was nothing heard save Barry Cornwall's ceaseless tread up and down the room.

The two hours passed.

Barry awoke his successor quietly, and his ceaseless tread went on for two hours more amid profound silence.

He awoke Leon at twelve o'clock, and, having seen that he was thoroughly awake and walking up and down, Frank too went to sleep.

For an hour Leon continued walking up and down.

Once, indeed, he fancied he heard a muffled sound; but, having gone to the door and listened for some time, he heard nothing and accordingly imagined, as he strolled to the window again, that he must have taken the movement of a rat for a human footstep.

Presently an intolerable drowsiness came over him.

He was sitting on a form near the window.

The atmosphere of the room appeared to be getting closer and warmer.

He roused himself and walked up and down; but, despite all his exertions, could not shake off the deadly feeling of lethargy that was creeping over him.

Unconsciously, even while he walked, his thoughts wandered away from him, and he found himself puzzling his brain over matters that were not entirely of the present.

Present and passed seemed linked together in the funniest manner possible.

He knew he was in the schoolroom keeping his turn of watch, and yet he was not there.

His soul seemed lifted out of his body, so to speak, and floating away over the housetops to the sunlit waters of Windermere.

There was Doctor Primrose on the lawn and there the boat-house.

Frank and he were going for a row.

But how could they go for a row if they were prisoners in the school-room?

This was curious.

Presently he was aroused by a noise; some heavy body had fallen down.

He found himself on the ground.

Curious!

How did he get there?

He thought they were on the lake— no, in the schoolroom.

Yes, of course; they were prisoners, and he ought to be walking about.

How hot and smoky the place was!

He was too far gone to see the steady stream of blue smoke that was winding and curling its way into the room through the keyhole.

Suddenly, for a moment, Leon, by some mysterious means, came into possession of his senses.

He staggered to his feet and reeled like a drunken man.

He wanted to go where his comrades were lying to tell them of their danger, but his legs refused to carry him.

He tried to cry out, but his voice died away in a thick, almost inaudible whisper, forming the word—

"Charcoal!"

He reeled again, fell again, and rolled over on his side, desperately clutching the revolver Nat Urner had given him, a victim to Plon-Plon's cunning.

The room was filled with fumes of charcoal; this was what had caused Leon's insensibility.

The other boys lay together on the floor, with their facial muscles contracted, showing that they too felt the effects of the poisonous vapour.

A quarter of an hour passed away, and then there came a crash.

Down came forms, desks, stools, clattering on top of one another.

The door was burst open, and, in the midst of his satellites, stood Plon-Plon.

His ghastly face was wreathed with a satanic smile of triumph.

"Bring them out!" he said, pointing through the smoke; "bring out those little imps who had the audacity to make me hate them! I will show them something that they will never forget!"

Two of the men passed into the room, but retired again, coughing violently, before they could reach where the boys were.

"Bring them out!" cried Plon-Plon, stamping his foot. "Idiots! do you want them to awake before they are secured?"

Again the men dashed in, and this time brought the bodies of the senseless boys in their arms.

In a trice they were securely tied.

"Ah!" said Plon-Plon, with a fiendish smile of triumph; "now for my revenge."

CHAPTER XXV.

HOW POMPONET AND SQUAT TOOK COUNSEL TOGETHER.

THE reader may well suppose that Pomponet and Squat were very much surprised when they received their notice of dismissal, and short notice it was, from their masters.

Both looked very blue over the fact, but from different causes.

Pomponet, being more civilised, readily conceived that perhaps it was true that now they were in France he might not be wanted.

Therefore nothing remained for him to do save a sudden departure to the count's country-house in Normandy.

Previously to arriving at this determination he had called at the count's town-house, in the Rue Rivoli, with his friend Squat.

He found that the family were out of town, consequently he could get neither food, shelter, nor coin.

Accordingly he made his way back to the school, accompanied by Squat, and demanded to see his late master.

This request was refused.

Now Squat's knowledge of French was very limited.

He had, moreover, no very definite idea of employer and employed.

Nat Urner he belonged to; that was a fixed idea in his mind, and, had anybody tried to explain to him in English that he was to go away and not see his master any more he would have stared and wondered what they meant.

As it was, he believed he had done

something to offend Nat who, to punish him, would not see him for two or three days.

So, when Snarly Cool repeated the fact that he was not wanted, he said—

"You tell Massa Nat dat Squat beas sorry for what he do, and nebber do it agen."

He had no very definite idea of what he had done, but he thought it best to apologise on general principles.

The more Snarly cool tried to get the idea into his black head that he wasn't wanted any more, the more Squat requested him to go and tell Massa Nat that he was heap sorry.

At length, tired of talking, Cool shut the door in Squat's face.

Upon this Pomponet turned in a burst of fury to him, and asked him what they should do in their difficulty.

"Squat hungry," replied the obtuse South-sea Islander.

"But we have been dismissed in disgrace. *Parbleu!*" screamed Pomponet, "our honour is insulted."

"Squat heap hungry," responded the South-sea Islander, who had no idea of what honour was. "Massa Nat want Squat to be hungry 'cause him drefful mad wif him."

"You are dismissed. We have our *congé*," cried Pomponet. "What do you intend to do?"

"Go play big Injun. Get money, have heap to eat; come back by-by. Massa Nat not so mad den, I guess."

This seemed a sensible proposition, and Pomponet wondered why he had not thought of it before.

The school was situated not far from the Bois de Boulogne, and thither they went in order to give their entertainment of "Big Indian."

This consisted in Pomponet showing off Squat, who went through a variety of performances, such as standing on his head, bending his back like a hoop, while Pomponet elaborated on the circumstances of his capture in the wilds of the jungle; but all the time they were proceeding thither Pomponet was sorely perplexed what to do.

The Bois de Boulogne was crowded with people, laughing, chatting, and ready to be amused at anything.

In short, they had a splendid chance to make money.

At this moment Pomponet's evil genius came upon him.

His eye fell upon the fat form of the Englishman whom they had met on the Calais steamboat.

In order to understand what follows, it is necessary to know that this unhappy publican had kept to his hotel studiously for a week, being in a cold sweat every time he heard his chamber-door open, for fear that ferocious foreigner might come in and offer him the choice of death by a bullet or small-sword.

This was the first day he had ventured out, having become suspicious that a hoax had been played upon him.

"Messieurs," began Pomponet, in stentorian voice, "look at this barbarian who——"

Here his eye fell upon the fat man, and he immediately stopped his discourse and ran towards him, with a vague idea in his mind of getting him to intercede with Leon for him.

The fat man immediately took to his heels, followed by Pomponet, who called out to him to stop several times, but without success.

Now, as most people are aware, there is this curious fact about a crowd which has nothing particular to do.

If they see one person running, and another trying to catch him, they immediately run too, and everybody who happens to be on the line follows their noble example.

"Stop, Monsieur the Englishman," cried Pomponet.

"Stop!" yelled two or three voices; whereupon a facetious *gamin*, who was passing the fat man, shrieked in his ear—"*A bas l'Anglais!*" and tried to trip him up.

This caused some other sapient individual to call out "Stop thief!" and several gendarmes, hearing this, started in pursuit also.

In a very few moments might have been seen the spectacle of a fat man, with his coat flying open, his hat off, and the perspiration streaming down his face, running for dear life through the park, followed by a mob, which increased every moment in noise and density.

Oh, how he wished that he had never come to Paris as he "stumped it" over the asphalte, making his patent-leathers crack at every stride! and now, to make matters worse, the mounted police, hearing the noise and confusion, galloped up.

The fat man saw them and gave a shriek of fear, thinking his last hour had come.

He turned to the left and darted up a narrow street.

Here he found that his progress was stopped by the fact that a number of police were coming down that way.

The uproar was at its height.

Someone said it was an English lunatic, others that he had just killed a man.

The fat man darted into a shop and through the back-door into an outhouse.

Here he was captured by a detachment of the National Guard, twenty-five strong, who advanced to attack the madman with fixed bayonets.

Pomponet had long since abandoned the pursuit, fearing that, since it caused such an uproar, he might get himself into trouble.

"*Je suis un Anglais!*" bawled the fat man. "*Je claimee* the protection of the English counsel."

"*Quelle horreur!*" cried one of the *sergeants-de-ville*, who had just heard that he had cut a man's throat.

"Kill? Oh, no, mosoo! no, mosoo! I am an Englishman, with a wife and six childring, *et je claimee le protectione* of the British counsel (consul)."

The officers of the law were puzzled.

What had he done?

There were a thousand and one stories told about him, not one of which appeared to have even a germ of truth in them.

He was a foreigner, an Englishman.

They demanded his passport.

He gave them his "Cook's" ticket.

At this moment a gentleman, seeing the confusion, came up.

"I speak English," he said, guessing at the fat man's nationality; "what is the matter with you?"

To him the fat man poured forth a harrowing tale, stating how he remained indoors for a week, and finally how he had been chased by the ruthless ruffian with fell intent and had barely escaped with his life.

"This is some practical joke," said the stranger, who was an Englishman himself; "you have been made the victim of a practical joke."

"Where's my 'at?" exclaimed the fat man, freezing into sudden dignity, now that he knew his life was safe.

Somebody had picked up his hat.

It was handed to him.

"This is a houtrage, sir, for which France shall suffer," said he; "hi'll write to the *Times* about it this very night."

The stranger laughed.

"Poor *Times!*" he said; "what patience the editor must have! But had you not better find out the authors of your fright, and give them into custody?"

"I will," said the fat man, buttoning up his coat and looking fierce.

The Englishman had shown his card to the chief of the police, and it had been quite enough to make him excessively polite.

It was a very plain, simple card, but it proved that the owner of it was one of the countless emissaries that the English *Times* has in every city of Europe, Asia, and America.

Pomponet, being of a volatile disposition, had almost forgotten the incident of his chase.

He was busy exhibiting Squat, when a hand was laid on his shoulder—two gendarmes stood, one on each side of him.

Pomponet was a prisoner.

Gone was his delightful romance of Mumbo-jumbo, which he had just been giving to a highly appreciative audience.

Gone were the joys of accumulating centimes.

If there was one thing more than another of which Pomponet had a horror it was arrest.

They laid their hands on his shoulder, but Pomponet flung open his coat promptly, and showed them the cross of the legion of honour, at which they were obliged to take their hands off again and salute.

The fat man was furious.

Pomponet was puzzled; the stranger was amused.

"The only way of settling it," he said, "is by going before the chief of police."

Thither they went; Pomponet marching proudly, as became a veteran of the old guard, while Squat followed on behind, hardly knowing what to make of it.

One thing was certain; circumstances were very much against his getting anything to eat.

When they arrived at the office the charge was taken.

No amount of explanation would satisfy the fat man, and so poor Pomponet and Squat were sent to durance vile for the night.

It was nearly three o'clock in the afternoon of the next day before they obtained a hearing, and were dismissed with a caution not to do it again, which, seeing they had been doing nothing, exactly suited their case.

"Now that we are branded with dishonour, through that perfidious Englishman, what would you have us do, my friend?" demanded Pomponet.

"Go get suffin to eat," said Squat. "My poor tomach drifful sore—guess Marse Nat get ober his mad fit, when he knows Squat not hab anyting in his 'tomach foh two days."

They went into a cheap eating-shop near the school, and here Squat got rid of his pain, and a bowl of soup, at the same time observing that, as the compound disappeared, so his pain went also.

A man was there, reading his newspaper, and with him Pomponet presently got talking.

From the probable war they drifted into politics, when the stranger, who described himself as a *chiffonier* (ragpicker), grew decidedly "Red Republican," and gave forth doctrines against the aristocracy, which, in Pomponet's frame of mind, were rather soothing.

"Ah, messieurs," he said, finally, "we have destroyed one Bastile, but we have not destroyed enough; there is a Bastile —*sacre bleu!* it is enough to make one's blood run cold to think of the horrors of that old vampire's nest."

He pointed with his finger at the school.

"But you mistake," said Pomponet; "that is a school for young gentlemen."

"*A bas!*" responded the man; "don't I know it, the Bastile! Don't I see their pale faces peering through the gates, sometimes? *Allons!* it is shut now, my friend, because there is some devilry going on in there."

"How do you know—are you sure?" asked Pomponet.

"Sure! *Parbleu!*—do you think I am a man to waste my time on words? Look at that!"

He handed Pomponet a slip of paper, on which was written the appeal which the boys had made to the public.

"It is horrible!" said Pomponet.

"*A bas!* the young aristocrats, it serves them right," said the Red Republican.

"But this is my master's handwriting."

"So much the worse for your master; he is in a bad way, *mon ami*," said the *chiffonier*.

"And it is two days old," cried poor Pomponet.

"Yes; I found it in the sewer, tied round an ink-bottle."

"What shall I do?"

"I'm sure I don't know," replied the *chiffonier*. "Come, it is funny; here is a man who lives in the school Bastile, and does not know what is going on?"

Pomponet explained how he and his friend Squat had been served.

"And you really like this young aristocrat, your master?"

"I love him."

"And the slave, does he love the tyrant?"

"He's not a slave," returned Pomponet. "His life was saved by his young master's father."

"*Allons!*" cried the man; "there seems to be some good in these aristocrats, after all."

"What can I do?" cried Pomponet, with the tears rolling down his cheeks. "Alas! Monsieur De Gardin is not in town, and I don't know where the British Embassy is. I will go to the police."

"It will do you no good to go to either of those places," returned the *chiffonier*.

"Why?"

"Because they will laugh at you both. The police would not make a descent upon such a well-established school except high influence were brought to bear, and, *parbleu!* they would laugh at you if you went to the embassy, and say—'Here comes poor Pomponet, who was turned out of a situation and has gone crazy.'"

"But what are we to do?"

"Trust to me."

"But you have no power?"

"Ha, ha!" laughed the man; "*Le Roi des Chiffoniers* has no power. *Mon Dieu!*"

Again the king of the rag-pickers laughed long and loudly.

"I have power enough to make Paris a boiling hell of blood and fire, my friend, and you will see it some day, with the Cap of Liberty floating in the air above the Column Vendome."

"But about my young master?" cried Pomponet, who cared not one straw about the Phrygian cap so that he came to the rights of things with regard to his master.

"Well," drawled the *chiffonier*, "about your young master?"

"Yes."

"I will save him--if——"

"If—if what?" asked Pomponet.

"If the rats have left him."

"What do you mean?" almost screamed Pomponet.

"I mean, my friend, that the rats are very hungry fellows, especially the grey ones who live in this quarter, for they have not much to live on."

"Well, what has that got to do with it?"

"Simply that they climb up into the dungeons, and, if your friends are confined down there, I would not give you two sous for their lives."

Pomponet turned a deadly colour.

"Oh, for Heaven's sake, monsieur!" he said, "let's hurry. But they dare not—dare not!"

"A chum of mine found the skeletons of two boys there," returned the *chiffonier*, "locked in one another's arms. But perhaps it was not the rats."

"Let us hope so," cried Pomponet, as he staggered out.

"Will you swear not to reveal a secret?" cried the king of the beggars.

"I swear!" cried Pomponet.

"Do you know then that when parents wish to get rid of troublesome children they always send them to the L'Ecole des Jeunes Hommes?"

"Why?"

"Because," returned the man, fixing his cold, grey eyes upon Pomponet, "because so many pupils die there."

CHAPTER XXVI.

A CURIOUS THING HAPPENS IN THE SCHOOLROOM—LORD MOUSLIN IS SURPRISED, AND JOEL SKIMP MAKES A NEW FRIEND.

I BEFORE stated that the school—that is to say, the portion of it not comprised amongst the insubordinates—left the schoolroom in profound silence, obedient to a gesture from Plon-Plon.

A great dread prevailed amongst them and kept them silent, though speculation was rife—the dread of the unknown.

What would be done with the four boys who, for the first time in the history of the school, had dared to oppose—ay, and successfully oppose, too—the terrible puissance of Plon-Plon?

Their imaginations, fed by bygone traditions and weird stories, made them shudder to think what might happen.

They were removed to another portion of the abbey. Books were furnished them, and the school routine went on as usual; but they did not—they could not study; and, when supper-time came, Plon-Plon was found in his place passionless as ever.

Save for the lump placed upon his forehead, and an increased pallor, you could not have known that anything unusual had happened.

Who could guess that beneath that passionless exterior slumbered a volcano ready to break out at any time into a terrible sea of passion?

So passed the time away until bed-time, when Lord Mouslin was called away, and, coming back, informed them of Snarly Cool's mishap and of the fact that the rebels held out as staunchly as ever.

He did not add what they had told him concerning himself; nor did he say that he would, were it not now too late, throw up everything and brave everything in order to throw in his lot with the four brave rebels whose cause seemed now so hopeless.

The night passed away without bringing any noise or confusion.

One boy had, indeed, maintained that he heard the crash of falling desks about two o'clock in the morning; but this was set down to a dream.

Everything was so quiet and regular next morning that they could hardly believe anything had happened.

They were ushered into the school-room.

At the end of the first lesson Plon-Plon ordered them to form circle.

He then addressed them.

"Your companions," he said, "having attempted, without any success, to subvert the discipline of my school, are now undergoing the penalty due to that crime. Resume your studies."

These were the words he spoke, full of terrible significance to those who knew his pitiless soul.

School-life dragged along somewhat monotonously after this for some days.

It was the morning of the third of August when they were told that the first of the exiles would make his appearance.

Who would that one be?

Frank Stainforth was the victim to whom Plon-Plon had alluded. He was led next morning into the school by Snarly Cool, to whom he clung with a terrified air, as though afraid to leave him.

The French boys were thoroughly apathetic.

They had seen this sort of thing before; but Lord Mouslin De Lain was inexpressibly shocked, and a thrill of fear, pity, and horror ran through his selfish soul as he gazed upon the wreck of his former antagonist.

What a change!

What a perfect wreck poor Frank was!

His eyes no longer flashed brightly; his face was a dull, sickly yellow.

That free, firm expression, accompanied by the laughing mouth, had disappeared.

This new arrival was an idiot!

He hung back and hid his face in Snarly Cool's arm, as though ashamed to meet the glare of the inquiring eyes that furtively sought his own from beneath terror-bent lashes, and, catching sight of Joel Skimp, he gave a silly laugh, accompanied by a faint sob, and ran to him.

Joel Skimp and he embraced.

"Dat was very funny," Hans said.

"Well," exclaimed Lord Mouslin, "I should as soon have expected the skies to fall. Oil and water mixing! Certainly the discipline in this school must be terrible."

It seemed as if, in obedience to the wishes of Plon-Plon, Joel Skimp were constituted guardian of Frank.

Discipline had indeed tamed Frank Stainforth.

It had done more. It had made him mad!

What had become of the others?

What had become of that bold American boy, who had not only dared, but had struck and defied that terrible power which sooner or later broke everything that opposed it with the pitiless precision of an automaton?

They had heard about the attempt made to blind him.

God knows what terrible tortures might not be inflicted upon him in those dismal dungeons, which held the shrieks of its victims as closely as their bodies in its granite-bound recesses!

They would have asked Frank, would have questioned him as to what he had gone through, but they were prevented from satisfying their curiosity for two reasons.

The first was, that Plon-Plon had signified that it was his wish no one should speak to him; the second, they could get no coherent answer out of him on any subject.

Of anything that had gone before his mind was a perfect blank.

He had the instinct of a dog, and nothing more.

This was the effect of Plon-Plon's discipline upon one of the quartet who had defied him.

The course of our story will show what he suffered in those terrible dungeons, and how he came in that piteous plight.

CHAPTER XXVII.

THE KING OF THE CHIFFONIERS.

WE return to Pomponet and his new-found friend.

"But, how is it, monsieur," asked Pomponet, "that you who are so well dressed should be King of the Beggars?"

"For this reason," returned the monarch. "They must have someone to look after their affairs for them, seeing that they cannot afford the time themselves; so they give me a salary and I act as their king for them."

"But I thought you were a Red Republican?"

"So I am."

"But Red Republicans do not believe in kings."

"Listen, *mon ami*," replied the king, fixing his steel grey eyes upon Pomponet. "You are a very simple little man indeed; if I get your masters out of this scrape will you do me a favour?"

"Certainly, monsieur — a hundred. What would you?"

"The favour I ask of you is this," said Le Roi. "Never poke that little grey head of yours into other people's affairs, and never meddle with subjects that are too deep for your comprehension."

"*Mais*, monsieur, this is an insult!" he said. "A soldier who has fought with the Grand Empereur——"

"Knows the value of prudence; thereforce, silence!" returned the man, a little fiercely, and Pomponet was awed.

After walking some distance they halted before a rather tumble-downish-looking sort of place in one of the crooked streets for which to this day old Paris is famous.

Pushing aside the light venetian shutters in front of the door the king entered, followed by Pomponet and Squat.

A little bar was just inside, perched upon which was a little cross-legged man, with an enormous nose and yellow teeth, one of which protruded and lapped over his lower lip.

"Good morning, my king," said the little man—at least, in words to that effect, for the salutation, being delivered in *argot*, had a meaning which cannot be translated.

"Good day," responded the king, somewhat ungraciously. "Have you seen Pierre, or London, or the Straits of Dover?"

"They have all been away for the last two days."

"Any news?"

"No, *mon roi*. Everything is quiet, as usual."

"Have you heard again from the *préfect*?"

"Hush," said the man, glancing apprehensively at Pomponet.

"Ah, it is all right, my brave Pipionet," responded the king; it is only a poor devil of a valet who has lost his master, who is locked up in the cellars of *La Bastile des Jeunes Aristocrats*, whom I promised to assist."

"Ah, in that case, all right; only I thought it better to be cautious."

"And a word in your ear," said the king to Pomponet. "If you want to get along amicably down here say nothing about your emperor. We don't like him or anybody belonging to him."

"But, monsieur," said Pomponet, "in that case I should be a traitor."

"Perhaps, then," sneered the king, "you had better liberate your master yourself."

"Monsieur," said Pomponet, in sudden alarm, "do not take offence at every little word I say. If my master were but liberated I care nothing for fifty thousand emperors."

"Very well, then," responded the king; "until we see daylight again, silence, no matter what you hear."

"But where are we going?"

"Into the kingdom of the rag-pickers," said the king.

They passed the bar and went into a little dark room, whence they descended by means of a series of ladders, and Pomponet heard bells tinkling in the distance at every step.

"What are all those bells sounding for?" asked Pomponet.

"To give notice to those below to remove or put up ladders. They are telegraphic bells."

"What a curious idea!" remarked Pomponet. "*Ma foi!* why not leave them all the time and save trouble?"

"That ladder you are on now," said the king, "if it were suddenly removed, would precipitate you fifty feet downwards."

Pomponet screamed and clung to it.

"Have no fear, Pomponet," said his guide. "You are not worth the trouble of putting all our expensive machinery in motion. Here we are at one part of our journey's end."

A glimmering light came through two holes; into these the king thrust his thumbs, and tapped three times with his fingers.

"Who goes there?" cried a voice.

"The king."

"What does he wear?"

"The Phrygian cap."

"What is his colour?"

"Rouge."

"Good," replied a voice, as the door slowly swung back upon a slide, and admitted them to a small, narrow chamber.

It closed again behind them.

Then Pomponet screamed again.

The walls were ascending with fearful rapidity—up, up flew the walls, and Pomponet experienced a sickening sort of qualmish sensation in his stomach, very much resembling the *mal-de-mer.*

Presently a bell rang and the qualmish sensation stopped.

Pomponet opened his eyes.

The door of the little chamber was again opened, and two grotesquely-dressed individuals stood before them armed to the teeth.

They saluted the king as he made his exit through the little chamber, followed by Pomponet and Squat, who was perfectly unconcerned, and simply looked upon their vagaries as one of the multitudinous things white men did which were incomprehensible to the average South-sea Island mind.

The end of this passage brought them to a large, low room, the prevailing feature of which was a dense atmosphere of smoke as thick as a London fog.

Yells of laughter went up, and ghostly forms flitted about from time to time.

At one place a blazing fire was merrily stewing *potage.*

At another men were playing cards or betting furiously.

They all rose, as the new-comers entered, to the cry of—

"*Le Roi Rouge!*"

Then Pomponet discovered for the first time that they were all crippled, patched, or bruised.

The Red King acknowledged the various salutations, and, by a motion of his finger, enjoined silence.

"My children," he said, when this had been procured, "I bring you here two strangers, friends of mine, one a brave soldier who has won the Cross of the Legion on many a stricken field, the other a man and a brother. They will both take the oath of fealty to our brotherhood."

"*Mais, monsieur*——" began Pomponet.

"Silence!" hissed the *chiffonier.* "You must swear or you are lost. Besides, remember your master."

"*Oui,*" sighed poor Pomponet, and, under these circumstances, obeyed.

An intensely ugly-looking customer came up with a Bible, which he caused the valet to kiss.

"Now sign the roll," said he; and Pomponet obeyed.

Poor Pomponet found, to his consternation, that in his zeal to serve Leon he had enrolled himself among the sworn enemies of the empire.

As for Squat, he was prepared to sign his name to anything with charming indifference, or rather to let someone do it for him, for Squat looked upon writing as a sort of fetish which was the exclusive property of the white man.

"Now," said the Red King, "now that we have made a couple of allies, we will go and look for these friends of yours. *Allons,* comrades!"

He seized a torch, and, flinging a bundle of unlit ones to Squat to carry, opened a hanging gateway and let himself into a long sewer, which looked like a street built over.

The place had a close, deadly smell. They could hear the sewage-water trickling past them, and, as they walked, the faint patter as of some thousands of feet, and saw shadows moving away from out of the horizon of light, while dismal, creeping things, begot of the blackness and of the night, slunk away into their filthy recesses.

"*Ma foi!* this is very dismal, *mon ami*," said Pomponet. "Is there any danger of our losing our way?"

"No; no danger of our losing our way," returned the Red King.

"Of what, then, is there danger?" asked Pomponet.

"The danger arises from the fact that one of the water-pipes might burst, in which case——"

"We would be drowned," said Pomponet.

"Exactly."

"*Parbleu!* that is not a very likely contingency, so it does not give me much trouble," said Pomponet, coolly.

"That is not the only danger. Our lights might go out."

"In which case we would have to find our way back in the dark," sighed Pomponet, who was beginning to quake visibly.

"We should never find our way back," answered the king, grimly.

"Why not?"

"Because before our lights had been out ten minutes the rats would not leave a bone of us."

CHAPTER XXVIII.

WHAT BECAME OF THE CHUMS

WHEN the four boys came to their senses they found themselves all lying bound together, completely in the power of Plon-Plon and his assistants.

They returned to their senses almost simultaneously, and looked round in wonder at the change in their fortune.

"How the deuce is this?" asked Nat. "I guess we are about tied, somehow."

Leon was dazed for a moment; and then it all rushed back to him. The dream; the blending of past and present.

"It is my fault," he said. "I fell asleep during my watch."

Plon-Plon watched their dismay, enjoying himself hugely at their discomfiture, and at the punishment in store for them.

"Never mind, Leon. You couldn't help it, old boy," said Frank. "I know by the way my head feels that it was through no fault of yours you fell asleep."

"My head, look you, feels like an empty barn," interpolated Barry.

"I have no doubt you thought yourselves very clever, young gentlemen," said Plon-Plon. "But I told you before I began that I was never beaten in my system of carrying on school discipline. You were rendered insensible by the fumes of charcoal, and now you shall learn what it is to provoke my anger."

"Do your worst," cried Nat Urner. "I defy you!"

"And I will tear every bone out of your body but what I will break that spirit of defiance in you. I have not forgotten that you threw the ball at me, Monsieur L'Americain.

"I'm sorry it wasn't a bullet," cried Nat.

Plon-Plon struck him across the face with a strap he held in his hand, raising a great blue welt and making every muscle quiver with pain.

"You would scarcely be worse off if it had been," he cried, hoarse with passion. "The law is merciful to you young rascals some times; I am not."

"And if you tore us limb from limb you would find every separate member quiver defiance of you," said Barry.

Plon-Plon nodded his head, and some men seized the boys and carried them in through a narrow doorway.

Plon-Plon followed with the light. Along a gloomy passage-way, down stone steps, going round and round in the descent, until the boys' heads turned giddy from the revolution. And then, as the cold, damp air of the dungeons beneath smote upon their faces, they were borne into a square vaulted chamber, which opened into another passage-way, where were a lot of cells buried in profound darkness.

There was a square frame, with a windlass, at one end of this chamber, and the boys seemed to know by instinct what it was, as Plon-Plon pointed towards it with a fiendish smile.

"TOM FLOREMALL" SERIES OF SCHOOL STORIES.
THE TRAVELLING SCHOOLBOYS.

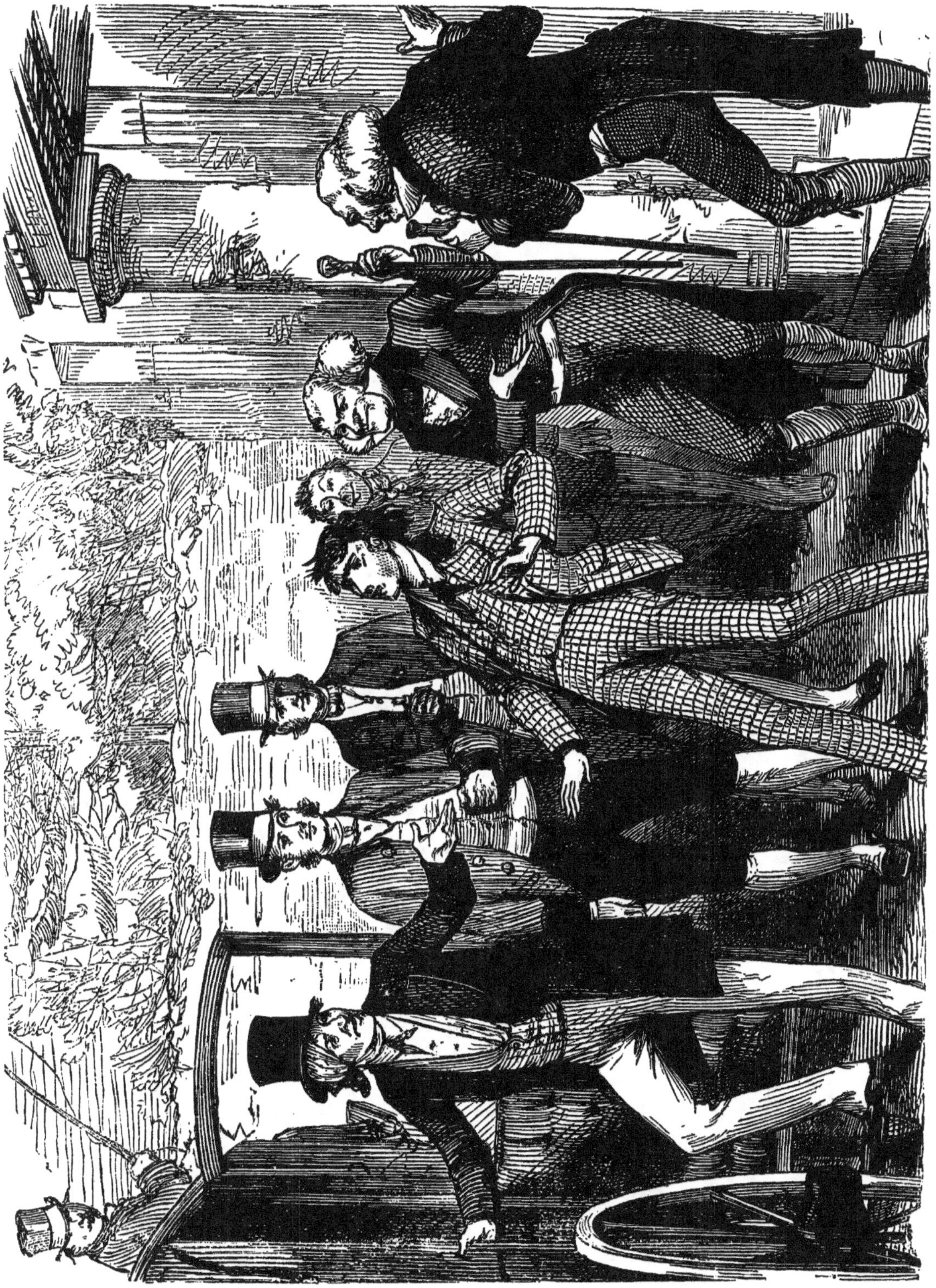

"THE CARRIAGE IS WAITING,' SAID COOL. 'WILL YOU ACCOMPANY ME?'"

"There's what will stretch your limbs, my brave rebels," he said.

And the boys cried together in a breath—

"The rack!"

In another part of the chamber there was a hook and pulley, suspended above the iron staples which went into the floor.

Not far from this stood a charcoal brazier, with a number of iron and copper instruments stuck into it.

Against the wall there was a large, heavily-bound iron chest, but what this was for the boys could not make out.

Stout as were their hearts they could not help shivering with dread as their eyes fell upon these various instruments of torture.

Plon-Plon noticed it with peculiar satisfaction.

"So you begin to appreciate my method," said Plon-Plon, with a sneer

"Do you call this a torture-shop?" cried Nat. "I'd be ashamed to own such a one-horse affair as this. If I went in to torture boys, I'd do it properly."

"You will find it quite effective enough," said Plon-Plon; "and, since you seem to doubt its powers, you shall have first trial."

Resistance was out of the question.

It was no use screaming.

The sufferer's voice could not be heard five yards away.

So poor Nat set his teeth and prepared to bear himself as became a man.

The whole of the time they were putting him on the rack he abused Plon-Plon and made fun of his tortures.

Once one of the tormenters allowed his hand to come near to the boy's mouth, and Nat left a mark on it that the man would remember to his dying-day.

It seemed a foolhardy thing to do, to thus wantonly exasperate his tormentors, knowing that it must recoil on his own head; yet there was much method in Nat Urner's madness.

He hoped that he might drive Plon-Plon into a sudden frenzy of rage, during which, by a blow, he might relieve his victim of all pain by rendering him unconscious.

Once Nat nearly attained his wish.

A bitter taunt had the effect of causing the wretch to spring forward with up-lifted stick, but, seeing the boy expected the blow, he allowed it to fall harmlessly by his side, and gave way to a fiendish laugh, signing to the tormentors to go on.

"No, no," he said; "that was very clever of you, little friend, but Plon-Plon as you call him, prefers to wait for his answer, and insensibility would be too much of a luxury."

It must not be supposed that during all this time that the other three were idle.

Their tongues were the only parts of them left untied, and they used them with unceasing virulence, but all to no purpose.

At last poor Nat's hands and feet were tied and the men gave the rack one turn.

It stretched every muscle in the boy's body and deprived him of the power of speech.

"This is what we call our growing machine," said Plon-Plon. "You will be a couple of inches taller by the time we have done with you," he continued.

"Monster!" exclaimed Frank.

"Wretch!" shrieked the other boys.

Nat Urner could not speak.

His face had turned ashy white.

"Do you like it now?" asked the fiend exultingly.

Nat gave no answer.

"I am accustomed to be answered," said Plon-Plon. "Answer!"

He motioned to the men, who gave the machine another turn, and the others heard a cracking noise as a fearful scream broke from the white lips of the tortured boy.

"Ah!" said Plon-Plon, "I thought my 'one-horse' torture-chamber, as you call it, would prove effective. Are you sorry for what you have done?"

No answer came from the sufferer; his eyes were fixed and staring, a slight, blood-stained, white foam was on his lips.

Plon-Plon nodded his head.

Again the windlass shrieked, and again a piercing, bitter scream awoke the echoes of that dismal cavern.

Plon-Plon's attention was wholly directed towards his victim.

He did not notice the other boys, who were shrieking every epithet at him which hate could inspire, all save one.

That one was Barry Cornwall.

He was lying sideways behind Frank Stainforth, gnawing his bonds like a young rat.

Presently there was a wrench, a snap, a swift untying of feet-bonds.

Plon-Plon happening to turn discovered him as he sprang to his feet.

He gave a cry of alarm.

One of the tormentors gave the door a bang-to and locked it, the others let go their hold of the windlass, and turned with him to capture the boy.

Frank ran to the other end of the vault, the purple veins swelled on his forehead.

There was madness in his eye.

Barry rolled over to where Leon lay, and began gnawing at his bonds with feverish energy.

Oh, if they could only get up in time to help Frank!

What could he do?

Our young hero against four men.

They forgot the terrible prowess born of despair.

Life to him was nothing; vengeance, everything.

With a swift bound Frank was across the vault to where the brazier lay.

He seized it and snatched one of the iron implements from it with his left hand; at the same instant his right caught it up and swung it backwards among his pursuers.

It missed Plon-Plon, but crashed into the face of the man behind him, sending him reeling to earth.

Shifting his weapon—which was a short, heavy poker, such as tinkers use—from his left hand to his right, Frank gave a yell of rage and hate and rushed upon Plon-Plon.

The latter saw him coming, saw the devil that was in his eye, and, coward-like, turned and fled.

Frank, baffled in his first attempt to strike him to the earth, gave another shrill cry of rage, and pursued him.

If Barry could have gnawed Leon free then they had been saved.

"Stop him—stop him!" yelled Plon-Plon, as he ran round the room; but his satellites were too much terrified at that mad boy and his short piece of iron to interpose between him and his prey.

They, however, did one thing which ultimately was effective.

They secured other weapons from among the *débris* of the brazier.

Then they hastened after the fugitives, not daring to intercept, waiting an opportunity of striking from behind.

Frank came within striking-distance of Plon-Plon.

He let out for his head, but the blow fell short and struck him on the shoulder, instead of sending him heavily to the earth.

Frank gave a shriek of delight at this, and, in his madness, thinking of nought else, jumped upon the screaming wretch and hit him on the back of the head.

He was too excited to strike true, so that the weapon merely touched it and descended a second time upon Plon-Plon's shoulder.

It was sufficient to render him senseless instantaneously.

Had it been true to its aim he must have been killed.

Ere Frank's weapon could again be uplifted and again descend it was caught from behind, and he was flung forward, face downwards, upon his victim.

His desperate resistance was ineffectual; a knee pressed heavily between his shoulder-blades, and his hands were forced behind him.

What could he do?

One man sat on his legs.

They bound him securely.

Meanwhile another went over and rolled Barry away from Leon as his task was almost completed.

True, Plon-Plon was incapacitated from carrying out his torture; but the boys were again prisoners.

Frank's desperate efforts had gone for nothing.

"They've got me again, Leon," he said, between his heaving breaths; "but I've paid that devil out for his treatment of Nat Urner."

"*Parbleu!* he is dead!" cried one of the men, turning over the body of Plon-Plon.

His face was a dismal grey pallor, making the mouse on his cheek more hideous by contrast.

From the back of his head a thin, bright crimson stream of blood trickled slowly down.

"If he is, then, it's a bad look out for us, comrades."

"Why so?"

"Why, explaining the manner of his death might be awkward.

"True."

"Release us, and I promise you that you shall have nothing done to you!" cried Leon, quickly. "Nay, more; you shall be richly rewarded."

"Oh, ay; piff-paff! we have heard of that sort of talk before. You don't catch old birds with chaff. We can save ourselves without trusting to anybody."

"How?"

"By simply leaving you here to keep Plon-Plon company."

"But you lose the reward we mean to give you."

"Have you any money?"

"No, but we will write to our parents for some."

"Ah, bah!" said the man. "Do you think that we do not know that your parents sent you to Plon-Plon to be put out of the way?"

All four boys burst out laughing.

"Who told you of that absurd idea?"

"Don't we know that every time a boy dies of 'consumption'—*sacre bleu!*—Plon-Plon gets a lot of money?"

"Horrible!"

"Horrible if you like, but true all the same."

"But don't you know that we are from an English school?"

"And for that reason sent to France to die of consumption. Pay us! If your parents, or those most interested in getting rid of you, knew we had been the means of liberating you, instead of giving us money they would contrive that we should see the inside of the galleys."

Just then a happy thought occurred to Leon.

"If you will go into the country with a note I will give you to my father he will give you money. You can then see whether he loves me or not. What say you?"

"Umph!"

"If you find that he loves me, come back and liberate us; if he doesn't, you have only to let us stay where we are, and you will be the richer by some hundreds of francs.

"*Sacre bleu!* that is not half a bad idea."

"You will go?"

At this moment Plon-Plon groaned.

"He is not dead!" exclaimed one of the men, going over to him. "How stupid we were! It is but a scalp wound the young tiger-cat gave him."

CHAPTER XXIX.

IN THE DUNGEONS—A TREATY OF PEACE.

PLON-PLON'S renewed interest in the affairs of this world was signalised by a groan.

This had the effect of bringing the four bravoes to his side.

Then he tried to sit up, and clapped his hands to his head.

This proceeding was followed by another groan.

"Help me out of this," he said; "I am sick and dizzy; that young whelp has nearly killed me. Never mind, he will wish his right arm had been cut off before he lifted it to strike me."

"What shall we do with them?" asked one of their tormentors, pointing to the group.

"Fling them into the dungeons on the right. Load them with irons, and let them have nothing to eat for a couple of days; by that time they will be fit for the torture I intend to inflict on them."

Another moment and Plon-Plon had reeled away, helped out by his two allies.

The others remained behind to fulfil his orders with regard to the four chums.

"The old one is in a precious state. He'll make it hot for you young members of this school before many hours are over your head," said one of the men, as together they proceeded to undo the fastenings which bound Nat Urner tightly to the rack.

Nat came to his senses as they unfastened him, and expressed at the same time his disgust for things terrestrial by a groan.

This was hailed with satisfaction by

the others, as affording evidence that he had not died under the torture inflicted.

"All right, old chap," said Frank, who, having been raised to his feet, was allowed by his tormentors to approach him; "all right, old fellow, brace up."

"Brace up!" groaned Nat; "I reckon I'll never brace up any more; I'm pulled to pieces."

"Poor old chap!"

Before anything more could be said they were all taken up, and removed one by one to a dungeon on the right.

A filthy, vile place it was.

The only difference between it and the huge cavern they had left was in size.

It was eight feet by fourteen.

Here they chained the boys up, putting a heavy chain round their waists.

They had been ordered to put them in separate dungeons; but this order they disobeyed, and here came out a curious fact.

"If ye'd a showed the white feather we'd have let the rats finish you at once; as it is, if you keep on hollerin', you may last till the old bird comes for you."

"Better let us die at once."

No; they'd be blessed if they'd do that.

A spark of pity had been aroused in their savage breasts by the exhibition of courage, and so, in their own brutal fashion, they showed their appreciation of it.

"Bear this in mind," said the man whose face Frank had smashed with the brazier; "holler together."

Being left to themselves, our four young heroes took counsel together.

"What should they do?"

That was a poser.

Any amount of feeble conversation and various suggestions brought no solution of the absorbing question—"What were they to do?"

"I only want to be free and alone with that skunk just for five minutes," Nat managed to gasp between his spasms of pain, "then I could die happy."

"Ugh!" cried Barry Cornwall suddenly, while Leon gave a shrill scream of horror.

"What is it?"

"Something ran over my face."

"There it is again."

"Rats."

"Remember that cut-throat's instructions, lads," said Frank, steadily. "Don't let's be afraid, but shout together."

This they did, making the cavern ring with the noise of their voices.

"That's better," said Leon, at the conclusion. "I don't feel any rats now, d' you?"

"No; they've gone away."

"For a time."

"Yes."

"Perhaps when they come again they won't be so easily frightened away. They'll get used to it."

"Has anybody got a match?"

"I have some in my pocket," said Barry, "but they are no use."

"Why not?"

"Because I cannot get at them; my hands are chained into this iron bolt."

"Perhaps I can reach your pocket with my mouth," cried Leon.

He tried it, but the attempt was a failure.

His chain allowed him to come within a foot of his friend, but no closer.

They had evidently meant to tantalise them.

"We must only take our chances, look you," said Barry, "and not give up our spirits."

Notwithstanding this attempt to cheer up his companions, the poor little chap was himself overcome with the horror of the situation, and felt that at any moment he could shriek shrill, piercing shrieks of terror.

So the hours dragged wearily along; eternities of pain it seemed to them.

Every now and then the rats would come round them in shoals, but the sound of their voices drove them away again.

At last, despite the terrors of the situation, each one felt an intense desire to go to sleep.

To sleep—horrible thought!

It meant to deliver their bodies up to those horrible things that crawled and glided with lightning rapidity about the inky blackness.

At last they made a bargain.

One was to watch and sing all the time, while the others slept.

When he wished to wake one up he was to rattle his chain and shriek.

"Let me be the one to take the watch," said Leon; "I do not feel the least bit sleepy.

They let him have his own way, and Leon struck up the *Marseillaise*, and somehow, in the excitement of the grand old Republican song he forgot dungeon, rats, and sleep, that most dreaded enemy of all.

So he went on for hours, with clear, fresh, strong voice, that apparently did not know fatigue.

Meanwhile the others slept.

Despite the noise of his singing they slept as soundly as though in bed.

About four hours had elapsed when a light glimmered faintly at the bottom of the circular staircase.

This increased, and presently a torch was thrust into the dungeon, and a portion of Snarly Cool's face became visible.

We say a portion of it, for by far the greater portion of it was concealed by flannels and wrappings of various sorts.

Snarly had not yet recovered from the effects of the oil of vitriol.

It was evident that he knew where the boys were confined, for he came straight to the place, and stood for a moment contemplating them in huge delight.

Leon stopped as he approached.

"So you are trying to keep your courage up ? " sneered Snarly.

"With evident success," retorted Leon, glancing at his companions, whose heavy breathing showed how deep were their slumbers.

"Well, you are plucky ones, you four," said Snarly. "Come, wake up there ! Here's something that will revive you."

He offered Leon a bottle, as the others woke up.

The latter, shrinking back, refused it.

"I do not like your draughts," he said.

Snarly Cool gave a hoarse laugh.

"You needn't be afraid of this one," he said, taking a pull himself ; "I never do anything of that sort, unless there is a necessity for it, and at present you are too safe for me to wish you out of the way."

"Briefly, what is it that you want ? " asked Leon.

He took the bottle and drank some of it, finding it to be sherry wine.

It put new life in him.

Snarly handed it to the others, who, with the exception of Frank Stainforth, followed Leon's example.

"You are afraid," sneered Snarly.

"I am not afraid," returned Frank ;

"if you want to know why I decline to take it, it is because I would not accept a crust of bread at your hands, you scoundrel ! "

Even in the moment of his greatest triumph over his victim Snarly Cool felt abashed, and turned away, cursing himself with the knowledge that, despite circumstances, with the boy he hated lay the true triumph.

"So that is the young cub who shot at me, is it ? " he said, giving Nat Urner's prostrate form a savage kick ; "I promised him that I would spoil his sharp eye-sight for him, and I'll keep my promise ; Plon-Plon has had his amusement, but that is nothing to what mine will be."

"He paid for his fun, and so may you, you lily-livered hound," said Nat ; "I reckon you don't take into your calculation the fact that there is an Almighty looking on at you and your little games."

"Bah ! " returned Snarly Cool. "All you've got to do is to wait here with the rats until I come to do what I promised."

"What's that ? "

"Spoil those sharp eyes of yours with a red-hot poker."

"Why don't you do it now ? "

"Because I've got other business to attend to ; all in good time. You needn't be in a hurry, I won't forget you."

"Bah ! give us a rest ; you are all talk, Snarley Cool."

"What brought me here," continued Snarly, "was this. Plon-Plon has gone to the hospital to have his head patched up ; he wants to see Frank Stainforth about releasing you all on certain conditions, provided Frank Stainforth will pledge his word of honour that he will remain dumb from the time he leaves this dungeon until he returns to it again. Unless he consents to this you shall remain for ever in these dungeons."

"So you believe that there is such a thing as honour," sneered Leon.

"Yes, for such fools as you and Frank Stainforth, said Snarly Cool, with a laugh. "You forge your own chains stronger than we could bind them with your foolish notions of chivalry."

They paid no attention to this remark.

They were in deep consultation as to what they should do.

Was it advisable to let Frank go ?

Was this some new villany, or was Plon-Plon thoroughly sick and frightened at what he had done, and wanted to make the best bargain possible, so as to get out of the mess.

After ten minutes' hasty consultation they came to this last conclusion, and resolved that Frank should go.

"It is also part of the agreement that you will make no effort to escape, or to strike me," said Snarly to Frank.

"Agreed," returned the latter; "and now, be as quick about taking off these irons as you can, for I am impatient to see Plon-Plon."

"Mind, Frank," said Nat Urner, "we don't yield an inch; you remember that, old boy?"

"I'll take good care," returned Frank, as he embraced them all, and turned to depart; "I'll be back like the wind to get you out of suspense; so keep up your spirits till I return. As we are negociating for a peace I suppose you might leave them a torch."

"I have no orders to that effect," returned Snarly, coldly.

Frank said no more, but waving an adieu, ascended the circular staircase.

"Keep up your spirits boys; I'll be back soon," were his last words.

Alas! Back soon!

Did he but know to what he was going, could they but have foreseen the treachery that was to deprive them of their leader, better he had stayed in the dungeon with them though the penalty were fifty times the rack.

CHAPTER XXX.

WHERE FRANK WENT TO AND WHAT HE SAW.

AT the first turning to which they came a sudden suspicion entered Frank's mind, and he had insisted on Snarly Cool leading the way.

"I don't care about being stabbed in the back, Cool," he said, sternly; "and I have no doubt you are as great an adept with the stilletto as with the cup of poison."

"Not a doubt of it," returned Snarly, hoarsely. "*Parbleu!* if it were not for your word of honour I would not trust myself in these gloomy corridors alone with you."

"And you might well be afraid to do so," cried our hero, in a sudden burst of fury. "I swear to Heaven I will make you answer to me for all I have suffered these last five years—yes, and not I only, but others. Oh, I have been a blind fool not to see through all your villany! I see it now."

"We will resume this interesting conversation another time," said Snarly, opening a door which led into a suite of drawing-rooms—from the dungeons to a palace. "Meantime I have to remind you of your promise—that you will open your lips to no one."

"It was given," said Frank, coldly.

Snarly Cool said no more, but, muttering something under his breath, hurried away.

Frank was pacing the room to and fro, impatient at the delay, when another door opened, and two gentlemen entered with gold-headed canes to their noses, who looked about the apartment as though they expected to see a thief lurking under every article of furniture.

Each wore a tightly-fitting blue swallow-tail coat, buttoned in front with brass buttons.

Their shirt-bosoms were gorgeously frilled and puffed out, being surmounted by black-stock ties.

They moved about as though actuated by the same ideas, like twin clog-dancers in a burlesque.

When one turned to the right, the other followed his example, and when he reversed his position the other immediately did the same.

They stalked in, looking right and left, sharply moving in perfect time.

Then, perceiving Frank, they halted abruptly, and each one placed his forefinger to his nose and gave a significant smile.

Frank smiled, too, at which they laughed uproariously, but stopped and looked suddenly round as though to make sure that retreat was secure.

"And how are we to-day?" asked one.

"Yes; how are we to-day?" chimed in the other.

Frank was about to speak, but, remembering his promise, kept silence. He, however, answered them by a smile.

"And how is our cousin, the Emperor of China?" continued the first one, poking at Frank with his stick lightly, as much as to say "Oh, you young dog!"

"Yes, how is our cousin?" echoed the other, poking him in turn.

"And your sister, the Empress of Austria?" continued number one.

"Decidedly, the empress," echoed number two.

Frank hardly knew what to do.

These eccentric old "buffers" were evidently having a joke with him.

"So they have been treating you badly, have they?" asked number one.

Frank now perceived the drift of their conversation.

"Ah," he thought, "these are some government officials, perhaps, who have got an inkling of the story of our cruel treatment here and wish to pump me. This is why Snarly Cool wanted my promise of silence. I am outwitted; but it was given, and I cannot break it. Now I know why Plon-Plon was in such a hurry to come to terms."

He therefore held his tongue.

"Come!" cried one of the visitors, "we know you can speak—we were told you could speak."

"This is a trap," thought Frank, and continued to hold his peace.

"You know," continued the other, "that we have come to release you from the power of the fiend who tyrannises over you. Come, won't you speak?"

"Importune me no further," said Frank. "I have promised that I would not speak until a certain event has happened, and therefore your persistence will avail you nothing, though I thank you extremely for your kindness."

"Ah!" said one of the little men.

"Um!" ejaculated his companion.

"So you won't tell us how the Empress of Austria is, or how your cousin the Emperor of China is? Well, give him our respects when you next write to him, and tell him that you will soon be released from the power of the villains who have you in charge. Never fear; we'll destroy them with your favourite recipe for torpedoes—you know, *coculus indicus*—and blow up every English giant in the world, eh?"

"You are both of you mad," said Frank, to himself.

"Let us feel your pulse," said number one, seizing Frank's right hand.

"Yes, let us feel your pulse," echoed the other, pouncing upon his left wrist.

"You are sure the demon has elevated the temperature?"

"Elevated the temperature!" responded number two.

Each pulled out his watch at exactly the same second with a jerk, looked at them, and replaced them in their fobs with another jerk.

Frank became alarmed, and snatched away his hands from them.

"Hush!" said one soothingly.

"Hush!" echoed his companion.

"Look here," said Frank, "it's my private belief that you are both mad."

Instead of being indignant at this, both the funny-looking little men laughed pleasantly, and bowed themselves out, dodging and turning from right to left in precisely the same manner as they had entered.

Frank was glad to be rid of them.

Snarly Cool soon entered.

"The carriage is waiting for your imperial highness," said Snarly, with a sneer. "Will you condescend to accompany me to it?"

Frank made no answer but followed him.

He noted it as singular that they met no one in the passage; but he put this down as an extra precaution which Snarly Cool had taken.

It was very late in the afternoon—almost evening—he noticed, so that they must have been down in that dismal dungeon for many hours.

The carriage was a covered one, and had a coachman and a footman beside him, in addition to whom there were two others standing behind.

"Plon-Plon lives in state, evidently," said Frank Stainforth to himself. "He couldn't keep all that up on the simple salary of a schoolmaster. After all, it looks as though villany paid very well."

In crossing the Rue Rivoli, a light carriage passed them, the occupants of which shook their hands simultaneously at Frank.

They were the two eccentric old gentlemen who had asked Frank about his cousin the Emperor of China.

"Who are those men?" asked Frank.

"What men?"

"Those men in the carriage who shook their hands at me."

Frank looked keenly at Snarly Cool.

"Oh, it is those lunatics you mean? They are government inspectors, who make it their business to go round examining schools. A precious pair of lunatics they are, too, and a lot of good they do!"

"They have evidently done some good in our case."

"May I ask how?"

"They have forced Plon-Plon to treat with us for our liberation."

"Oh!"

"Is it long since you heard from Windermere, Snarly Cool?"

"You must find that out for yourself."

"I have found out," replied Frank.

"Oh, indeed!"

"Yes; just this moment I saw my father-in-law in the street."

Snarly started.

"He had Joel Skimp and Mad Tom with him."

"You have a wonderful eye," sneered Snarly Cool.

"I have, at least, seen too much for your peace of mind, and my father-in-law's also."

"And your mother's too," said Cool.

Frank trembled a little.

"That used to frighten me," he said; "but your motives are only to earn the money my father-in-law pays you as my keeper, and assassin should occasion serve, you miserable wretch! to put me out of his way, so that he may obtain my property."

"I suppose you have told this to your three chums?"

"I have not. But," continued Frank, "I intend to tell them as soon as I go back."

"Will you tell them, at the same time, that you are mad by birth?" exclaimed Snarly Cool, with sudden, savage energy; "will you tell them that your mother is mad, that your father was driven mad on her account, and that your mad brother Tom was once as bright and clever as you are now until he began raving about base conspiracies to deprive him of his property?"

Frank Stainforth shook like one having the ague.

"Will you tell them that you have had to have a keeper to follow you about under one pretence or the other from the time you were four years old, for fear your madness might come upon you—that madness, the terror of which comes upon you sometimes until I have seen you run and moan and cry at sight of a shadow?"

"Nice thing it will be for them to think," he continued, speaking rapidly, "that your madness may come upon you suddenly in the night-time, and that your best friend may have his throat cut from ear to ear to gratify the devil that has taken possession of you! Don't you think that if they knew your secret they would shrink away from their chivalrous, high-spirited young friend with the bold blue eye and chestnut hair as they would from a leper or some whited sepulchre that is so fair to outward view and so rotten within? You'll tell them, will you? Do! Tell them that when you were a child your mother tried to strangle you in one of her mad fits; tell them how your father looked when he ran a-muck; tell them that that same demon has descended to you, and that you may at any moment kill yourself or your friends; tell them that that dungeon they are so anxious to get out of is the fittest place for such madmen as you, and that, if Snarly Cool had his way, you'd be left there to rot, and not have you go about at liberty, a beautiful Bengal tiger, only waiting an opportunity to gorge yourself with human blood!"

Frank groaned. He seemed to be striving to shut out some horrible sight.

"Incarnate devil!" he said, "have you no pity? Well I know that, though the terror of this haunts me night and day, you are the one who calls it up when it has gone to rest. Yes, I know what you do. You can kill me, for if I say they would kill me, you would reply—'He is mad—mad!' Oh, Heaven! I can see the gibing crowd pointing at me as I sit cowering in my cell hounded to madness——"

Convulsive sobs prevented further speech.

Snarly Cool watched him.

Frank's agony was awful.

A torrent of emotion shook his frame.

"What would your friends, who think you the handsome soul of honour, the handsome prize-fighter, who, though but a boy, can knock a man down at a single blow—what would they think, 1 say, if I were to whisper in their ears that that wonderful strength which they admire so much in so slight a youth, was born of madness? Do you think that young lord Mouslin De Lain would not have shivered with terror if I had whispered into his ear at the beginning of that wonderful battle—'Don't fight with him; you cannot beat a madman. You don't know at what moment the handsome young devil may spring upon you like a tiger-cat and bury those pretty white teeth of his in your throat——'"

"Oh, Heaven! oh, Heaven! Wretch! wretch!" moaned Frank.

They had come out of the town by this time.

Just then a dove, pursued by a hawk, dashed in through the carriage-window with a prolonged coo of terror.

It fluttered into Frank Stainforth's breast, while the hawk, seeing into what sort of company he had got, made off through the opposite window of the carriage.

The dove cooed as it nestled in the breast of its young protector, and the act seemed to change the whole tenour of the boy's thoughts.

The hunted dove whispered—"Hope!"

"Snarly Cool," he said, looking fearlessly at his tormentor, "you may take this as part of my madness, that I look upon this bird as a messenger sent from heaven. Do you know what it says to me? It says—'Hope still; take example from me and hope still. At the last moment God will send deliverance.' If He has seen fit to curse my family with madness, I bow to His will, but I will no longer be the victim of man's cruelty."

"Umph!" thought Snarly Cool, "I have gone too far. Hang that bird!"

The carriage turned in through an enormously high gate, which was immediately shut behind them, and Frank, looking out, discovered that they were in a sort of park, surrounded by high walls.

Scattered here and there, like flocks of sheep, were a number of human beings.

Frank wondered why they wanted such high walls.

The door of the carriage opened, and, behold! the two funny gentlemen who had tried to get Frank to enter into a conversation with them.

As Frank got down the two footmen from behind stood by his side.

A number of the people came up and made the most horrible faces at him.

"Good-bye," said Snarly Cool, jumping into the carriage again; "I hope you will enjoy yourself during your long stay here."

"My stay here?"

"Yes."

"I don't understand."

"Then you very soon shall. I have the honour to inform you that you are in a mad-house!"

CHAPTER XXXI.

SNARLY COOL'S LITTLE SCHEME AND WHAT BECAME OF IT.

IT is not my intention to picture as yet the fearful thoughts which took possession of Frank Stainforth when he found himself in a lunatic asylum.

In an instant he comprehended how he had been trapped; but, leaving the recital of his adventures here for another chapter, we will hasten and rejoin Snarly Cool, who is lolling back in the travelling-carriage by which they had come, smoking a cigar, with a look of content upon his ugly face—and well he might be content.

His scheme had so far been a tissue of triumphs, as will presently be seen.

By the time Snarly Cool had almost finished his cigar, the carriage stopped at the Café Royal.

Snarly Cool looked amidst the sea of animated faces for a long while, but did not see the one he wanted.

At last, in one of the recesses, he found the object of his search discussing a cup of chocolate and reading the *Figaro*.

Snarly sat down quietly beside the

black-moustached stranger, and called a waiter.

"Brandy," he said, briefly.

Snarly waited quiety until he returned; then, in one gulp, the liquor departed.

"Something important has taken place," said the stranger, coolly.

"It has."

"Then he is——"

"In the country."

"Secure?"

"As secure as the nature of the case will admit," responded Snarly Cool, lighting a fresh cigar.

"I saw you in the Rue Rivoli."

"And nearly tossed all the fat in the fire."

"How?"

"Because he saw you."

"Well?"

"Well; in a moment a suspicion of the truth rushed into his head."

"My only wonder is that it did not rush there long ago."

"It's all very well to say that; but I can tell you when he sat bolt upright in the carriage and informed me what our game was, it took my breath away."

"You have regained it," said the other, coolly.

"I have," responded Snarly; "and more than that, I've gained——"

"What?"

"Five thousand pounds."

"Half now and half in a month's time," said the stranger; "I suppose that will do?"

"Yes."

He took out his cheque-book, and, with a hand—a long, white hand, like a lady's—which had not a tremor in it, wrote out a cheque for two thousand five hundred pounds.

It was payable to bearer.

Snarly Cool took it and placed it in his pocket.

"It is well earned," he said.

A silence ensued between them.

"I am curious to know how you secured the boy's incarceration," at last said the stranger.

Snarly Cool gave a detailed account of the affair.

"Splendid boy," mused the other, "splendid boy. It is a strange thing, but I love him; I am proud of him."

"But you love your pocket more," sneered Cool. "The young imp, it is not for want of hate that I did not find a way of killing him."

"Enough," said the other, "you were hired to drive him mad, not to take his life."

Snarly Cool remained silent.

This man was his match.

Cunning as Snarly Cool was, and high as was the opinion he held of his own powers, he knew when to stop.

He therefore broke off abruptly now, and sat moodily staring at the wall in front of him, listening like one in a dream to the ceaseless chatter and busy hum that was going on around him.

"Have you any definite plans for the future?" asked the man with the snaky moustache.

"No."

"What do you mean to do?"

"I mean to turn gentleman, and live on that two thousand five hundred pounds and the rest."

"Even so; say five thousand pounds. It will not last you ten years, and then you will find, when your money is gone, that you have contracted expensive habits without the means of gratifying them. Perhaps"—here he fixed his glittering black eye upon Cool, and read him through and through—"perhaps you think that at the end of ten years you might find a way to bleed me."

"No—no!" stammered Cool.

"I wouldn't advise you to try on that game," said the man; "it might not prove to be a paying one."

"I had no idea of doing such a thing," said Snarly, hurriedly. "What my idea is, is this. Long before my money is spent there will be merry music in Paris. Those that are up will go down, down, down, and those that are down will go up. There will be plenty of spoil, and I don't see why I should not be in at the plunder."

"Have you heard that France is about to declare war against Germany?"

"No."

"Then I tell you now," said the stranger.

"Are you sure of it?"

"Certain. To morrow it will be public property."

"Do you remain in Paris?" ask Snarly.

"Not an hour. The society must have funds; I am going to England to get them. You have the papers with you?"

"Here they are," said Snarly Cool.

He took several papers from his pocket, and handed them to the stranger, who opened them, and read (the document was in French, but we give a translation of it) as follows:—

"KNOW ALL MEN.—Know all men whom these presents may concern, that Frank Stainforth, subject of Her Majesty the Queen of Great Britain and Ireland, having been duly examined, and pronounced of unsound mind by Theodore Duplon and Henri Quatre Bras, physicians to the Hôspital des Fous, Department Seine, at the request of his guardians, has been duly committed to safe keeping until such time as it shall please Divine Providence to restore him to a sound mind.

"(Signed) CONQUELON MONTPEITH,
"Justice et Maire."

The other document was a certificate of the two doctors, stating Frank's insanity.

The symptoms, they said, were silence and a monomania.

He believed that somebody was trying to murder him, and that he was first cousin to the Emperor of China.

A feature of his mania was a disinclination to speak.

"And if he is not mad now they will soon drive him mad," said Snarly Cool, with a grin; "for of all the rows that I ever saw kicked up, he made the worst when he saw how neatly he was trapped."

"Where are you going?" asked the other, as Snarly Cool rose to depart.

"To the school. I want to see Plon-Plon, as I have one or two other scores to settle there before I take my leave."

"Does he know of Frank's removal?"

"Yes."

"You told him."

"I could not do otherwise. Had I not obtained his consent I could not have got him away."

"Very well, then tell him I will call to-morrow and take away Frank Stainforth."

Snarly Cool opened his eyes in surprise, but said nothing.

So they parted.

The plot that was to deprive Frank Stainforth of liberty, reason, and life was completely successful.

He was in a mad-house; his friends in prison.

CHAPTER XXXII.

SNARLY COOL'S REVENGE.

IN the meanwhile how had it fared with the three chums.

Fearful indeed were the hours as they dragged their slow length along.

They had taken watch, turn and turn about, valiantly keeping off the dreadful things that crawled about them; and now the pangs of hunger began to gnaw at their vitals.

The place was intensely cold.

Nat Urner's limbs were fearfully swollen and inflamed.

"Will Frank never come?" they kept crying to themselves, and anon trying to keep up one another's courage by promising each other that he would be there presently.

Still he came not.

They had lost all count of time.

To them it seemed an eternity; each moment was an hour, and they were beginning to abandon hope, supposing that Frank had been decoyed away somewhere else from them, when again they were gladdened by the sight of a light; it was carried, as before, by Snarly Cool.

"Here I am," he said, presently, having watched the emaciated faces before him for fully ten minutes. "I have come to give you my adieus, and to hope that you will enjoy yourselves down here."

"Where is Frank?"

"Upstairs, enjoying himself."

"You lie!"

"Thank you."

"Look you," said little St. David, in a broken, tremulous voice. "If you say Frank is up there enjoying himself, while we are down here, you are a fery great liar inteet."

"Have it so," said Snarly Cool; "it doesn't make much difference either way. I am going to leave this concern, so I may as well tell you to your faces that, until you are thoroughly broken in spirit and constitution, Plon-Plon does not intend to let you out of here. As for your other ringleader there "—he pointed to Nat Urner—"I have come to settle my little private score with him."

"You had better let him alone, you villain; he has been tortured enough," returned Leon.

"That has got nothing to do with me," said Snarly Cool. "I promised him something for his spying about, and I always keep my promises."

"You promised to bring Frank back, and you have not done so."

"No, he promised that," returned Snarly, with a grin.

So saying, he set about lighting a charcoal fire in the brazier.

"What are you doing that for?" asked Leon.

"To keep my promise."

"What promise?"

"Oh, a little warmth won't do you any harm," said Snarly Cool, putting one of the short pokers in the fire. "I am going to try the effect of a hot poker on that boy."

"Fiend! monster! you dare not!" they exclaimed in a breath.

"I dare anything," said Snarly, with a horrible laugh.

"Oh, have some pity!" moaned Leon. "Have we not suffered enough. What have we done to you that you should take delight in making us suffer?"

"You!" cried Snarly; "you have done nothing to me, and it is fortunate for you you have not, or you should taste this iron, too. I don't claim to have much pity in me, but I've got a ruff notion of justice; and, if you'll remember, young sir, you hit me on the head with a piece of wood the first day of our acquaintance; you spoiled all my plans, and you nearly sent me to the penal settlements for twenty years. Come, I think the loss of an eye is a very cheap let-off for that sort of work."

He gave a wild, fiendish laugh as he took the iron out of the fire.

It was red hot.

"After all," he said, coming over to where the three boys were, "there is a great deal in that old Jewish law—'an eye for an eye and a tooth for a tooth.'"

"Not my eyes! for God's sake, not my eyes!" moaned Nat Urner. "Man! fiend! have you no pity in you?"

"Ha, ha!" laughed Snarly Cool; "so I have found a way to make my young bantam shriek with fear at last, have I? He doesn't care for the rack—that won't break his spirit; but he cries in terror at the thought of being prevented from peering into other people's business henceforth——"

"Keep back, keep off, man! Not my eyes! Not my eyes!" moaned Nat, as he came nearer and nearer.

The other boys tore madly at their chains, and he flung all his weight against his in a mad effort to be free.

Alas! it was only the fruitless efforts of despair.

The chains clanked sullenly—that was all!

It seemed as if Snarly Cool wished to prolong the agony of his victim.

"My talk has made this cold," he said, going back to the brazier; "I must get another."

He replaced it by one at a white heat, which lit up his cruel face as though he had been the fiend incarnate.

Nearer and nearer he approached his victim.

Nat felt the burning heat of the instrument, stretched out his iron-loaded wrists, and sank moaning to the floor.

"Help, help! Oh! is there no one to help me?"

Then came a roar, a human roar, far more terrible than that of any wild beast — a human being, an enraged soul!

There was a swift rush of a heavy body through the air.

Snarly Cool turned with the white iron in his hand to meet it.

His arm went up, caught at the wrists by a grip of steel; another grip wound round his throat, and sent the blood flying to his cruel brain.

The torrid blood of the South Sea leaped into boiling passion as Squat bore his master's enemy to the ground.

Seeing him lazing listlessly about the playground, or dodging a blow from his young master, none would suspect the fierce strength which was held in his mis-shapen form; more fierce now when he beheld his master about to be sacrificed by an enemy.

Squat at that dreadful moment had in him the strength of a giant.

Whatever Snarly Cool intended to do to the American boy, the penalty he paid was an awful one indeed.

To Squat, brought up in the wild tents of a half-savage tribe, human life was of very little value.

It was probably to this fact that Snarly Cool owed his life.

The rage of the South-sea Islander would not permit him to kill him.

That was not punishment enough for his fierce soul, now for the first time thoroughly roused since Captain Urner had saved him from his fellow-savages. The would-be burner was a reed in Squat's hands.

He sent him backwards in his fierce grip, while his knee pressed inwards upon his chest, and his arm, the right arm, which held the iron, bent like a child's.

Then a fearful scream of agony rent the dark cavern, and, ere the others could spring forward to his rescue, Snarly Cool had paid the penalty for his cruelty, and the black boy, with lurid eyes, was looking upon his fearful work.

Squat had bent back Snarly Cool's hand until he had caused him to burn out his own eye!

The other would have shared a similar fate had not Nat managed to call out to him to hold; and Pomponet and the King of the Rag-pickers clung to the arm which held that fearful weapon with all the strength of their bodies.

Nat's voice, perhaps, had more effect on this half savage than their united strength.

He broke from them and flung himself down upon his master, sobbing like a child.

He nursed him, and cooed to him, and petted him, and wept over him as a mother does over her lost darling.

Pomponet, that hero of a hundred battles, performed the same action for Leon, who, being more a Frenchman, and more demonstrative than are we—we cold-blooded and phlegmatic Anglo-Saxons—thought it not shame to weep back again and to kiss his old valet with all the fervour of a lover.

Nat Urner managed to articulate words which resolved themselves into this, and which were sweet incense to the ears that heard them—

"Bully for you, old woolly head, I thought you would *euchre* them!"

Having seen things reach their proper climax without a word of explanation, it is but right that we explain how the three rescuers appeared at such an opportune moment.

Briefly then.

After a variety of difficulties Pomponet, Squat, and the Red King of the Rag-pickers had arrived at an iron door which faced the great canal.

The Red King's knowledge of subterranean geography revealed to him the fact that this used to be one of the modes of exit from the abbey in days gone by.

A pick, a jimmy, and the vigorous use of a crowbar, had the effect of rolling back this aged obstacle on its rusty hinges, and they found themselves within the vaults.

Their name was legion.

Vault after vault they searched, but to no purpose, and they were about giving up their search in despair when they heard the boys' cries.

An immediate rush forward answered this.

They arrived on the scene of action just as Snarly Cool had made his second advance on Nat Urner.

With the result the reader is acquainted.

Presently they were seated round the little charcoal stove, the men busily engaged in chafing the boys' limbs, and trying by every means they knew to restore animation to their chill frames.

The King of the Reds produced a bottle of cognac, "a little of which applied internally was," he said, "worth a thousand years of embrocation."

Nat Urner speedily came round.

"Have you got anything to eat?" he asked, in a low tone.

Squat dived in his pocket, and found an onion and a dry crust of bread.

Pomponet took a sausage out of his hat. He had saved it from their breakfast, seeing that he could not eat it all and had paid for it.

These were divided into three equal parts, and immediately disappeared.

"How did you find out where we were?" asked Leon.

Pomponet explained by introducing the three boys, with much *empressement*, to his friend the king.

Leon walked over to him.

"May I shake hands with you ?" he asked.

"*Parbleu !* an aristocrat shake hands with a Red Republican!" said the latter, grimly. "Do you want to lose caste, or do you want me to lose caste ? "

"I do not ask you whether you are an aristocrat or a Red Republican," said Leon. "I only know you are my pre-server. Let me thank you, though I cannot thank you as I know you ought to be thanked."

He kissed the king's hand, and two large tears dropped upon the brown palm.

"*Parbleu !*" exclaimed the king; "then the aristocrats have some feeling, after all."

He was much moved. To conceal his emotion he walked towards the other end of the cave, and tapped the strong box with his stick.

It gave forth a solid sound.

"Halloa !" exclaimed the king, "what have we here ? A treasure-chest, may-be. *Sacre bleu !* we shall see."

He gave it a heavier blow, and this time there was an unmistakable ring about it.

Going to the fire he seized one of the white-hot irons, and, returning, burnt out the lock.

"*Parbleu !*" he exclaimed, "this is better than burning out a poor devil's eyes. But what is this."

They shuddered at this. But what could be done ?

The deed had been committed, and, in point of fact, the man had brought it on himself.

It is certain that if he had not made an offensive demonstration against Nat's eyes he would have kept his own.

They went over to see what the Red King was about.

He had almost completed his task by this time, and presently the lock fell in.

It required nearly all his strength to enable him to lift up the heavy lid; but when it was thrown back what a sight met his gaze !

The box was half filled with gold and silver.

"Ye gods !" cried the Red King,

'what a treasure ! So, then, Plon-Plon is a miser, in addition to his other qualifications."

The others gathered round, expressing their wonderment.

"What a lot of gold ! " cried the boys.

"It is not much when divided amongst us all," said the King of the Chiffoniers.

"But it does not belong to us," cried the boys.

"It is the spoils of war," responded the king.

"Look you," said St. David, "I would not touch a farthing of it."

"Nor would I," "Nor I," from the other two ; "it belongs to Plon-Plon."

"Ah, bah ! These aristocrats have very strict notions about things. How do we know that these coins did not belong to some old abbot who fattened his monks here before Plon-Plon was thought of ? "

"The coins are of recent date. There-fore, the chest must belong to Plon-Plon."

"Even so," said the king, sullenly; "I intend to help myself. *Mon Dieu !* I did not risk my life coming through those terrible sewers for nothing ; so, little messieurs, if you have no objec-tion, I will help myself."

What could they do ?

It was surely wrong to suffer Plon-Plon's gold to be taken, no matter what he had done to them.

"If you take that gold while we are looking on we shall be forced to prevent you," said Leon.

"Well, here is aristocratic gratitude!" said Le Roi Rouge, turning up the whites of his eyes and emptying his pockets back again into the chest; but he com-prehended their meaning for all that, for he said—

"I think, messieurs, you had better go up through that staircase, and pre-tend you escaped without any aid. Here is a pistol in case you have to defend yourselves, but I don't think you will find it necessary. Plon-Plon will be too thoroughly scared at the sight of you."

"Good ! "

"Of course, messieurs, you will see that, under the circumstances, it would be impossible for me to accompany you. But I have a favour to ask you."

"What is it ? "

"That Monsieur the American would

lend me his black servant for a companion. The passage of those sewers by one's self is so very dismal."

"True," said Nat. "Squat, you will go with him—*sabe ?*"

The black nodded his head.

"But, in case of emergency, it is necessary that one should be master. Will you tell him to obey me ?" said the Red King.

"Obey him, Squat."

"Yes, Massa Nat, ebery time."

"Good. Now I will say good-bye, young gentlemen, for the present. Remember, that in the future you have nothing to fear, for the King of the Rag-pickers is your friend."

"Good-bye," they exclaimed, and went upstairs slowly, leading Nat Urner between them.

He was very much exhausted.

Scarcely were they out of sight than the Red King gave a grin and whipped a bag from beneath his coat.

Shoving it into the chest, he raked the gold into it with both hands, and so filling with great speed, until the bag was full and the chest nearly empty.

"Massa Nat him say not touch that yeller stone," said Squat, looking as if he wouldn't mind a free fight.

The king gave him a piece of niggerhead tobacco, and reminded him that his master had expressly told him that he was to obey orders.

The Red King tied the end of the sack securely.

"Lower your back," he said to Squat, and, as that worthy complied, he contrived to shunt about two hundred pounds weight on him.

A white man would have dropped it.

Squat got it on his head and waddled after the king like a duck, staggering along under a weight that would have broken the heart of most men.

"This," said the king, as he marched towards the gate which opened out into the sewers, "is Paris, the centre of civilisation, and it is thus we make use of the barbarian—*Vive la Republique!*"

Presently they were in the sewer, where the Red King securely fastened the gate, for fear Plon-Plon should take it into his head to come and look after his treasure with a file of soldiers at his heels.

There was only one left in that dungeon now, left alone with the rats he was so fond of talking about.

That one was the villain Snarly Cool.

* * * * * *

The boys advanced cautiously.

They were resolved not to be taken by surprise.

Barry Cornwall had the pistol.

"Look you," he said, as he neared a door which promised to give them egress once more into civilisation ; "look you, if a man lays his finger on me I will blow his brains out."

"Let's trail the pantry first," said Nat ; "I'm dying for something to eat."

"Yes ; *mon Dieu !* that will give us more courage to face Plon-Plon," said Leon.

No one was in the pantry, and, by rare good chance, some jellies intended for Plon-Plon's consumption stood on the shelf.

These disappeared like a flash of yellow-light, to be in turn followed by some cold meat, and a couple of pattes each.

Some wine—none of the best either—was discovered in one of the cupboards.

It revived them not a little.

Nat Urner, despite his pale face and swollen limbs, which pained so that he could hardly drag himself along, announced that he was prepared to knock the life out of Plon-Plon.

As a means to that end, and in view of the possible re-appearance of the tormentors, he armed himself with the carving-knife.

"Now," said Barry, "we will go and look for Plon-Plon."

"Where do you think he is."

"In the schoolroom."

"Giving lessons on school discipline to some of those pale-faced roosters," cried Nat, forgetting that his own face bore a close resemblance to a shroud ; "I hope he is, anyhow," he added, "for I want to give him what he deserves before the whole school. I'll bet he never forgets the day he put me on the rack."

They opened the school-room door, and stood before their astonished schoolmates like three ghosts.

Dead silence greeted their entrance.

Two or three ushers were in the schoolroom, but Plon-Plon was not visible.

Nat Urner glanced round the room, and his eye fell on their former companion talking to Joel Skimp, and apparently unheeding their entrance.

"Frank Stainforth," said Nat Urner, " I did not think any punishment could have made you so base. You left us to our fate."

"Frank a coward!" almost moaned Leon, while little St. David, who had held up the whole way, at this sobbed like a child.

The boy thus addressed buried his head on Joel Skimp's arm.

"Joel, dear Joel," he said, "don't let that boy with a knife look at me; he wants to kill me."

Everyone was breathless.

CHAPTER XXXIII.

THE THREE FRIENDS ARE MYSTIFIED—IS THIS FRANK?

To say that Nathaniel Urner was surprised at the reception given him by his sometime chum would be to express but very feebly the state of bewilderment he was in.

He looked at his two companions, and they repaid his stare of wonder with interest.

By this time the buzz of wonderment which greeted their first appearance had swelled to distinct exclamations of surprise and sympathy.

"How did you get out?"

"Did Plon-Plon release you?"

And a thousand and one similar questions.

They paid no attention to them, all their thoughts being confined to the schoolmate who they believed had played traitor.

Nat Urner was the first to put these thoughts into action.

He advanced to Joel Skimp.

Frank was leaning on him, in fact, he seemed clinging to him for protection.

"You may well hide your face," said Nat Urner. "Oh, shame! that you, who set us so many bright and noble examples, should at last fall away."

The figure remained motionless; it was Joel Skimp who trembled.

"We might have believed it from another, Frank, but we did not doubt you for a moment," said Leon. "How could you leave us?"

"Look you," said Barry, "it shall not be that we shall judge him ferry severely, look you; it shall be that he shall explain."

The other turned round, and lifted his lack-lustre eyes to meet his companion's half-sorrowful, half indignant glances.

Even in the midst of their anger they were ready to make excuses for the boy they loved so well.

They recoiled a little as his gaze met theirs.

There was no speculation in his eyes, the dull, glazed blank as it fell upon them too surely told them that they were unrecognised.

"Why, what is this, *mon ami?*" cried Leon, coming forward, and forgetting his anger in an instant. "You surely recognise us—you know us?"

"Oh, Frank, Frank! don't you know us?" burst out Nat Urner, as the dismal truth forced itself upon them that their friend had been driven out of his mind by the cruelty of Plon-Plon.

The others in the schoolroom had gathered round them with open mouths, wondering what might happen next.

"Know you? yes, of course I know you," returned the demented one; "you are the friends of Mad Tom. You tried to kill me once, but I was too quick for you. Ha, ha! Frank Stainforth is not killed so easily, my fine fellows; is he, Joel?"

"No, of course not," answered Joel, hastily; "they may put you down in a dungeon, but they cannot destroy your spirit, can they?"

"I should think not," returned the mad boy.

"Poor old fellow!" cried St. David, with tears in his eyes, "they have driven him mad."

"Don't you know me? speak to me, old chum!" cried Nat, while he laid his hand on the idiot's shoulder.

"Speak to him," cried Nat, in a broken voice to Leon, "perhaps he may recognise you."

"*Mon ami*," cried Leon, using the soft French language, which Frank, for Leon's sake, had learnt to love so well; "*mon ami*, do you not know me whom you left in the dark dungeon. Come, we will leave this schoolroom, where it is close and dark. Come, we will go out into the country, where the sun shines and the birds sing merrily, and the sweet flowers bloom. There, *mon ami*, you will get well again, and not think of the terrors which have driven reason from its throne."

Frank turned to Joel in the most helpless state of idiocy.

"Tell me what he is doing that for, Joel?" he said.

"What?" asked Joel.

"Babble, babble, giggledee gobbledee, habblededee," cried the idiot; "what is he doing that for?"

"He is talking to you in French," responded Joel, turning white. "Ever since he came back," continued Joel, all of a tremble, "he has been unable to speak or understand French."

"I don't believe a word of it," said Leon.

"Nor I," cried St. David.

"What do you think, Nat Urner?"

The American boy had been all this while looking at the idiot with intense earnestness.

"Think," he replied, slowly, as though following up an idea in his own mind; "I think that he is not Frank Stainforth at all."

"You remember that 'double' of Frank whom we saw twice in England?" continued Nat.

"Yes."

"That is he."

"Impossible!"

"Who else can it be?" said Nat Urner. "It isn't Frank, although very like him. Do you remember that little brown mole that Frank had on his forehead just between the eyebrows?"

"Yes, of course."

"Well, this lunatic has not got it. So it is very evident that this cannot be our chum, Frank Stainforth."

"Indeed I assure you he is," exclaimed Joel Skimp.

"You seem very anxious that we should think so," retorted Nat, sharply. "May I ask what interest you can possibly have in the matter?"

"He is my cousin," answered Joel.

"And a pretty cousin you have proved yourself to be," responded Nat Urner. "Look here, you dirty little sneak, if for no other reason than the fact of his having contracted such an extraordinary friendship for you at such short notice, I would not believe it was Frank Stainforth."

Lord Mouslin, appealed to, told them briefly that he had entered the schoolroom on the arm of Snarly Cool, had looked decidedly queer, and, in his opinion, was quite mad.

"I always thought Stainforth had a bee in his bonnet," remarked his lordship. "Snarly Cool told me that his mother and father were both mad."

The three chums looked hard at one another.

What could be the meaning of this terrible mystery?

Oh, if Frank had only given them his confidence!

It was too late now.

"Come on," said Nat Urner. "At least we can do one thing. We can look for Plon-Plon. Boys," he said, "you are a set of dirty cowards, from the biggest to the littlest. You let us get nearly killed without making an effort on our behalf."

"I suppose you mean to include me in the list of cowards?" said Lord Mouslin.

"No, I don't," said Nat, boldly; "but I count you as being far worse. You are a dirty, revengful cur, and I would be sorry if my nigger, Squat, associated with you."

"I'll punch your head," said Lord Mouslin, suddenly coming towards them.

But as he was advancing to put his threat into execution he started back terrified.

For the first time in his life he knew what a spasm of fear was.

He saw by the looks in the eyes of the trio that, baited and badgered as they had been, they would stop at nothing which seemed good in their eyes.

"Anybody could be cheeky if they took to weapons," said Lord Mouslin, as he crept back again. "I didn't think you were such cowards."

"You let us alone. We have nothing to do with you," said Leon De Gardin. "The man with whom we have to settle our account of revenge is Plon-Plon."

As he spoke there was a slight movement at the doorway, and Plon-Plon, the author of all their misery, stood before them.

At sight of him the three boys gave one fierce, terrible yell of rage and hate, and rushed at him.

Sick with terror Plon-Plon fled away.

CHAPTER XXXIV.

WHAT HAPPENED TO FRANK AT THE LUNATIC ASYLUM.

THE moment Frank Stainforth comprehended where he was he ducked his head, and, by so doing, allowed the grasp of the two sham footmen to pass over it.

The next moment found them both sprawling upon their backs.

Then Frank, instead of taking advantage of this opportunity to escape, braced himself against the step railings, and began a lecture to the two doctors.

"You see how easily you may be mistaken," he said; and they listened, to do them justice, smilingly, perfectly conceding everything he said. "You see how easily you might be mistaken. Here that villain Snarly Cool has persuaded you that I am insane, and, I suppose, wanted you to take me into your asylum. Just think for a moment what a dreadful thing it would be if you incarcerated a sane man with a lot of idiots."

The doctors smilingly agreed to this point also, and signalled the two men, who had now been rejoined by two others, to secure the orator.

"The fact is," said one, "we are very sorry, but we cannot let you go to-night."

"Not to-night," chimed in his Echo.

"There are certain little legal formalities necessary."

"But I must go away!" cried Frank; "I insist upon going away, and," he added, as his voice rose, "I insist upon going away at once; beware of attempting to detain me against my will now that you know I am not insane."

"Come," cried a great burly man, who carried a riding-whip in his hand, "come, we have had enough of this backing and filling; it never does no good, sirs," he added, touching his hat to the doctors. "Come, you just might as well know it now as know it gradually, which I calls false pity. You are as mad as a March hare. Your friends sent you here to be cured, if it is possible to cure you, and here you must remain until you are cured. So just take this to heart, and behave yourself; do as you are told, and keep quiet, for, according as you treat others, so you will yourself be treated."

Poor Frank, it was a cruel blow, and for a moment it overcame him.

He, mad!

No, he could not, he would not believe it; come what may, he would not believe it.

Liberty was his birthright; he would have it.

Profiting by his collapse the four men had drawn nearer.

Two of them advanced, and were about to lay their hands upon his shoulders, when he swung round short, dropped one fellow with a blow between the temples, and, leaping over his prostrate body dashed away into the lawn.

When he reached the wall, he found it was so high as to be utterly impracticable.

What should he do?

Should he surrender, and make the best terms he could, or should he have one more trial for freedom?

He resolved upon the latter course.

Turning, he stood at bay for a moment, then he ducked his head, and went for them.

As he came towards them he straightened up, prepared to dodge or hit.

He found hitting from the shoulder the most effectual method of dealing with them, for, bred up in France, they had no idea of the English science of boxing.

Again he left them in the rear; again there was nothing to interpose between him and liberty.

He fancied that that portion of the wall immediately in front of him now was a little lower than the remainder.

He might reach it, he thought.

Redoubling his speed he made a tremendous leap, and just reached the top of it with his fingers.

For a moment he paused, unable to lift himself up—indeed, scarcely able to hold on, so greatly was he weakened by his exertions to be free.

Then began the slow process of lifting himself up.

It was desperate work for an exhausted boy, but he was in a desperate strait.

It is a common saying, that "Fortune favours the brave," and a saying that I have found false quite as often as true.

In this case the fickle jade played Frank a scurvy trick.

Just as he had reached the top and got one leg across, up came the burly man of whom I before made mention, and, snatching at the leg which dangled down, plucked our hero from the wall.

Down to the ground came Frank on his hands and knees.

Before he could recover himself, and make one more effort to escape, they were on the top of him holding him down, and pummelling him to make him keep quiet.

They did not get their victim without a struggle.

Poor Frank was unconsciously doing his utmost to convince them that he was as mad as any March hare.

Several of them bore the marks of his prowess upon their eyes, noses, and mouths, and it was not until he was securely bound that he conceived resistance useless.

"You'll get the straight-jacket for this, my young devil," said one of the men, grimly, holding his nose, which looked as though it had been to the wars.

Frank retained a sullen silence.

"And you may consider yourself lucky if you don't get the shower-bath as well."

"We know several ways of taming the devil in you wild birds," chimed in a third.

During this conversation Frank was being carried to the house again.

They met one of the Esculapian twins in the hallway, and, in response from him, carried poor Frank below.

Here he was thrust into a gloomy room, put into a straight-jacket, an ingenious instrument of torture, which prevented him from doing harm to himself or anybody else, and left to his own reflections.

These were anything but pleasant, and so, in the bitterness of his despair, Frank's fortitude gave way all of a sudden, and he burst into a sudden fit of weeping.

This did him good in one respect.

He sobbed himself to sleep, and slept without sedative for several hours.

His first waking thoughts were that he was still in the dungeon with Nat and Leon, but these were speedily dispelled as he ran over the events which had happened to him within the last forty-eight hours.

Surely he had reached the culmination of his misery now.

Fate could not be more cruel than she had been.

His destiny for life was accomplished.

A lunatic!

The next question was—why he should be treated thus.

He turned it over and over in his mind, but could find no solution of the problem, and again came back to the dreary thought that perhaps he was really mad.

As yet he had no suspicion of the real state of the case, of the fearful deception that had been practised upon them.

So, viewing all things together, he came to the conclusion that, as no hope remained from without, he must do as he had often done before—help himself.

Self-help is next to God's help.

He resolved to be circumspect, and give them no cause to think him dangerous; for, unless that belief was done away with, he saw no possible chance of avoiding the vigilance of his keepers.

A couple of hours after that came the burly man with mocking face and sneering voice, and asked him if the devil was out of him yet?

"Thank you, very much," said Frank; "I feel a good deal better."

"Oh!" replied the burly one, altering his tone, "you are calmer now than yesterday?"

"Yes," responded the young fox, artfully. "I was tired and worn and excited yesterday—I was not myself; and, besides——"

"Besides, you were in a devil of a temper."

"No, not that."

"What, then, is your ' besides ' ?"

"Besides," said Frank, pointing an epigram with upturned eye; "even to the mad liberty is dear."

A Frenchman adores an epigram.

"Come," he said, "this young lunatic is not so bad. *Sacre bleu!* that was a famous *jeu d'esprit. Allons, mon garçon,* although you are mad you are clever."

"Thank you," said Frank; "and you are kindhearted."

"*Parbleu!* I ought to be, little English devil, or I should not have forgiven you for the knocks you gave me yesterday—but how did you find out that?"

Frank, who had made up his mind to escape through the instrumentality of this man, paused a moment to think of an artful reply.

"You see," observed Frank, when he had thought how he could best flatter the man, "you are fat, and you have blue eyes, and no one ever saw a fat man with blue eyes yet who could bear malice for any length of time, and who was not kind-hearted."

"Ha, ha, ha, ha!" laughed the burly one; "what wit, my fine fellow! I will get you to touch up my comedy."

"A comedy—I thought so."

"But why?"

"Because you have a head like Shakespeare—the same resemblance that there is between a barn-door and a walnut cabinet," he added, in English—"they are both made of wood."

"Like Shakespeare," said the man, hastily setting Frank free. "*Parbleu!* if you were not mad on one subject I would adore you. And if you are very good you shall read all my comedies and tragedies."

Frank made a wry face on the quiet, but publicly expressed himself delighted.

The man grew wondrously confidential. He looked around. No one was near them.

"Can you keep a secret?" he asked.

"Yes," replied Frank, promptly.

"Then," he said, "you behold before you William Shakespeare."

"Indeed, I am very glad to know you," said Frank, in English.

The burly person did not evidently understand him. Frank repeated his expression in French, and added—

"I am very glad to have the pleasure of seeing so illustrious a man—I thought I could not be mistaken about that face."

He felt dismally disappointed, almost ready to cry, although he put the best face he could upon the matter.

After all his efforts he had only succeeded in making a friend of a lunatic keeper of lunatics.

However, the lunatic got him his breakfast, and that was some comfort. Frank's spirits began to revive. His friend the burly gaoler was mad on the subject of the drama.

He had been an unsuccessful writer for the stage, and it had driven him mad.

When he was not engaged with his duties his pen would fly along at a furious rate, and he would come into Frank's room with hands, hair, and face covered with ink, to recite a passage from one of his plays for him.

He believed there was a combination of modern authors and critics against him to prevent him getting his plays produced. This furnished Frank with an idea. Supposing he made this maniac keeper of his the means of his own escape!

One evening when he was copying out some of his verses he broached the subject.

"Would you not like to have a theatre of your own to produce your own plays in? you could then beat the cries."

"It would be superb," said the dramatist.

"Just think how this would sound," cried Frank, reading some of the play. "That is really splendid, and if you went away from here," said Frank, "you could defy the critics."

"You would make a splendid villain," said the burly one, all aglow with admiration at Frank's reading of his plays. "If I ever get a theatre and you get better I will have you to play the leading parts."

"Thank you, I am sure," returned Frank, still eager to gain his end. "As for the theatre, don't let that be any impediment; I can find the money to hire one."

"You can?"

"Yes."

"How?"

"I have good friends who will advance the sum to me when they have the proof of your genius before them."

The man seemed overcome with astonishment and delight. Suddenly his countenance fell.

"Your friends wouldn't advance you the money; who would trust a madman with money?"

"But I am not mad," cried Frank, eagerly.

An instant afterwards he saw his mistake, and repented it bitterly.

He should not have said that he was not mad.

"I see," said the dramatist, severely; "it is only one of your dodges to get free—good! you have been making a fool of me; you do not believe that I am Shakespeare."

CHAPTER XXXV.

THE CHUMS GIVE CHASE, AND MEET AN UNEXPECTED ALLY.

PLON-PLON made an effort to disguise his fear. He was about as badly scared as a man could be.

In a second he was travelling down the gloomy corridors with lightning speed, banging the doors after him as he went, in the hope of confusing his pursuers as to his whereabouts.

He had no time to lock the doors behind him or to summon assistance from his four bullies. His enemies hung on too closely in his rear.

"Look you," panted St. David, as they ran along, "I shall job this knife into him behind, look you, if we do catch up with him."

"He is fond of stretching people's legs," said Nat. "He will have to stretch his own pretty lively if he doesn't want a bullet through them."

It needed not all these stimulants to urge Plon-Plon forward in his flight.

He had seen enough of the foreign devils to make him wish that he had never had anything to do with them.

At last, finding the house no longer offered a secure asylum, he dashed out through the cloisters into the street, followed in line by Nat Urner, St. David, Leon, with Pomponet bringing up the rear, armed with a hatchet which he had picked up in the meat-room.

Along they went in full swing up the Boulevard.

Now that they had a clear run before them, and no doors to open, they were gaining fast upon the terrified fugitive, notwithstanding his terrific exertions.

He, for his part, was uttering cries of terror and "Murder!" at the top of his lungs.

Such a sight — namely, three boys armed in that extraordinary fashion and chasing a man—is not a sight seen every day, even in the city of wonders. So they speedily found themselves at the head of a crowd, some of whom cried "Stop them!" and some "Stop him!" others "Stop thief!" and all hugely delighted at the affair.

Long before they had gained the Rue Rivoli the crowd had increased to many hundreds.

They were almost close upon their victim when he rushed into the midst of a squad of gendarmes, who came down the street at the double to see what the row was about.

"Save me, messieurs!" he cried. "There are four devils behind me ready to murder me! Get in front of me, or they will kill me in spite of your protection."

It needed but the pale, terror-stricken looks of Plon-Plon to convince the sergeant that something serious was the matter.

Accordingly, he placed the schoolmaster hastily behind him, and, with three soldiers, formed a bulwark which the boys could not pass.

"Let me get at him!" roared Nat, mad with rage, speaking in English.

"They are English lunatics," cried the master, taking advantage of this opportunity. "I give them in charge! Arrest them! They have made several attempts on my life!"

"Arrest him!" cried Leon, who was the first to come to his senses; "arrest him! We give him in charge! He tried to starve us to death!"

The sergeant was mystified.

"What does all this mean?" he asked.

"They are rebellious scholars. They have turned upon me, and would take my life," sobbed Plon-Plon.

At this the sergeant's duty became clear. It was evidently his duty to uphold law and order.

"Give up your weapons and submit to be put under arrest, young messieurs," he said. "If you have any grievance you can tell it in court, but you cannot take the law in your own hands."

But Leon, like most Frenchmen, was all excitability.

With rapid voice and gesture he was telling the crowd how they had been treated, and imploring them to take his part.

Loud and angry tones, and the glances bestowed upon Plon-Plon, who crouched, shivering, behind the soldiers, told how deeply the crowd sympathised with their wrongs.

"Let us take this tyrant from these toy soldiers, and hang him to the nearest lamp-post."

"Hurrah! Let us do it!" shouted the crowd.

Plon-Plon quaked. Right well he knew he deserved it.

His experience as a Frenchman taught him that the tender mercies of a Paris mob are cruel, and that he might expect little mercy if once they set about carrying their threat into execution.

He was rescued from this fate by the boys themselves.

"We do not want to hurt him," said Nat, in French, giving up his pistol to a policeman as he spoke; "but we insist that he be taken into custody."

At this the crowd began to hurry off in another direction, a report having spread that a shell from the Prussian works near Mont Valerian having entered the city.

It was then that for the first time the boys learnt that Paris was invested.

The war had commenced before they entered Plon-Plon's school, but they had not heard of its rapid progress.

Leon, too, noticed by this time that the guard which had taken them prisoners was not the ordinary police-guard.

It was composed of draughts from the National Guard.

When they got to the prefecture the prefect was too busy dealing out remorseless punishment to supposed Prussian spies to pay any attention.

He first of all blew up Plon-Plon for not being able to keep his scholars quiet, and then the latter told him, all in a tremble, that he was in danger of his life from them, adding—"It's all because I tried to whip and starve the Prussian sentiment out of them."

"Infamous liar! Monsieur, I assure you that until a few moments ago we did not know that Paris was invested," shouted Leon.

"Oh!" exclaimed the prefect; "not know what everyone knows; that convinces me that you are afraid of being taken for knowing too much."

"Monsieur," said Leon, "my father, the Comte De Gardin, will speedily convince you that I am not a spy."

"Are you the son of Count De Gardin, Minister of Public Works?"

"I have the honour."

"Then allow me," said the prefect, taking snuff, "to inform you that you are the son of a scoundrel—as great a scoundrel as ever disgraced France."

"Sir!" exclaimed Leon, pale with rage, "you shall answer to the emperor for this insult!"

"The empire has ceased to exist. Your aristocratic ruffians no longer rule the nation and rise in high places."

"I know what you have done, ruffians that you are!" cried Leon, thoroughly carried away by his feelings; "you have waited until our brave soldiers of the empire were away fighting the enemy, and then you have risen like rats."

"Take them away!" cried the prefect, white with rage. "Shoot them all four by sundown."

"Hold!" said Leon, as the soldiers advanced to take him. "Assassinate me if you will; but these" (pointing to Nat Urner and Barry Cornwall) "are English and American; beware how far you carry your temerity!"

"What!" thundered the prefect; "the republic dare to do anything—take them away!"

"I guess not!" said Nat Urner. "I'm an American citizen, I am, and I call in the protection of the American ambassador."

"Take them away!"

"Look you," said Barry, "I call in the protection of the English ambassador. Look you, it shall be fery bad for you if you do have me shot at. It shall be worse than Waterloo and Trafalgar, look you."

"Furies!" shouted the prefect, "will no one move? Take them away, and do what I command!"

Four soldiers advanced.

Before they had time to do anything, however, two young gentlemen moved quietly up from among the throng of excited spectators.

Each thrust away a soldier, and, ere they could retaliate, each one dived in his pocket, produced a small flag, and laid it over the heads of Nat Urner and Barry Cornwall.

Nat had the Stars and Stripes flag covering him.

Barry was covered by the Union Jack.

The utmost surprise and consternation was visible, as one of the young men, Russel, who was attached to the Washington Legation, began in a low determined voice, which had just the least little nasal twang in it—

"The republic of the United States of America hereby throws her protection over a citizen, named Nat Urner, whose life and liberty she will require at the hands of those who now menace it. Her representative is commanded to protect the life of her endangered citizens, if needs be, with his own."

"Thank you. Halloa! the old chap looks as if he were going to order the guards to fire at us!"

"If he does I'll drill as pretty a hole through him as you ever saw, and chance it. I've got as pretty a looking little Colt's Derringer in my right pant's pocket as you ever saw, and another one in the left. Never have had a chance to use them yet."

"Halloa! there's the Englishman going to speak! Well, I swear he has more cheek than you. Look! there goes an eye-glass up to his right eye. I reckon he isn't much in a row, he looks too ike a woman, with his blonde moustache, woman's hands, pink and white complexion, and lardedawdy air."

"Don't you make any mistake, youngster," said Teddy Russel; that's the Hon. Clarence FitzPaget, one of the greatest devils in Paris. There's nothing he cannot do, and he'll do it as if he were born to do that and nothing else"

The Hon. Clarence FitzPaget had drawn forth a small legal document.

"Victoria, by the grace of God, Queen of Great Britain and Ireland, to all powers and principalities greeting: we have by this act thrown our protection over the body of Barry Cornwall, our liege subject."

"Now shoot him, if you dare!' drawled forth FitzPaget.

"I record your protest. Take them to prison," cried the prefect in a rage.

Handing a Derringer from his left pocket to Nat Urner, Russel levelled the other at the prefect.

"Unless you pledge your word that we are permitted to depart unmolested, I shall be under the necessity of letting a little daylight into you, in the name of the United States," said he.

"By Jove! splendid position," said FitzPaget; "a dramatic situation. If you must fire, hit that wart on the prefect's nose, old fellah. It's a bore."

"Look out for yourself, FitzPaget," said Ted Russel. "A soldier has a 'bead' on your head. If you move you're are a dead man."

"All right. Those fellahs nevah can hit, you know; I shall help myself to his rifle when the fun begins."

There was such an utter and beautiful simplicity about Clarence FitzPaget that, in conjunction with Teddy Russel's levelled pistol, it proved too much for the Frenchman.

He was cowed, and knew not why.

"You can go," snarled the prefect.

"Come on FitzPaget," said Ted Russel. "I expect we'll get a mauling now before we get to the embassy."

"Can't you help poor Leon De Gardin?" asked Nat.

"No; I cannot. You see we can only help citizens, and it looks pretty difficult to help them."

"I know the Count De Gardin very well," said FitzPaget. "He plays a first-rate game of billiards. He had to bolt out of France, you know, when these chaps upset the empire. He's staying with my father at Twickenham. How did you know him?"

"I'm not talking about him. About his son, Leon De Gardin."

"Has he got a son? by Jove!"

"Yes; there he is. What were you doing that you didn't hear him tell the prefect who he was?"

"Fact is didn't heah. Was looking through my betting-book until I heard someone call out for the Queen's protection."

"I don't see what is to be done," said Teddy Russel.

"I know," responded FitzPaget, brightening up. "You give me your Derringers, Russel, and take those two boys out of harm's way. There will be a devil of a row, you know, and you'd best not involve your Government in it, you know."

"Don't be a fool, FitzPaget; you are rushing upon certain death."

"I think the question might be settled in a much easier way," said Nat.

"How?"

"I claim the protection of the Queen of England," said Leon.

"Can't help you officially, old boy; you are not a subject," replied FitzPaget.

Plon-Plon smiled malignantly.

"I think I may claim the protection of England," said Leon, slowly; "I was born in England."

"Then, by Jove! old fellow, you are all right," cried the Hon. Clarence, slapping him on the back. "Monsieur Le Prefect," he said, in the same drawling French that he had used before, "I must also call your attention to the fact that, as this boy also claims to be a British subject" (Leon had not said so; he had, in fact, been born at the French Embassy in London), "I throw the protection of her Majesty upon him also."

But by this time the prefect had recovered his temper and his shrewdness.

"Monsieur," he said, "you know that when a doubt exists, the subject upon whom the doubt exists must be remanded to prison until that doubt be cleared."

"Very well, then," said the Hon. Clarence; "we yield our subject into your hands for safe keeping, and will require you to produce him this day week in this court, with the proofs that he is not an Englishmen. Until such proofs be given I hereby declare him to be a subject of Her Majesty, Queen Victoria, and will hold you and the government of France responsible for his life and property. Before this week

is over, the Prussians will be in Paris," he said, in English. "I fear we could not prove you entitled to the protection of England, old boy, but this delay will do you a lot of good."

"And, in the meanwhile," said Russel. "I call upon you, in the name of the United States of North America, to place under arrest the person of Monsieur Caradoc De Beauvais (Plon-Plon), principal of *L'Ecole des Jeunnes Hommes,* and aid us in prosecuting him for alleged cruelty upon a citizen of that nation."

Plon-Plon turned green.

The prefect bowed, and motioned to two of the National Guard, who stepped forward and placed their hands upon Plon-Plon's shoulders.

"Have you anything more to request?" asked the prefect.

"Nothing, thank you; we are quite satisfied."

"Then you will have the goodness to remove your subjects, and let the work of this court proceed."

"With pleasure," drawled FitzPaget.

"Good-bye, Leon, old chap, for the present," cried Barry Cornwall, as the guard came to take him away. "We will come to see you as often as we can, you know; there is no fear for you."

"All right," said Leon. "Try and find something about Frank Stainforth. I am certain that there is foul play somewhere."

"So am I."

"Try and fathom it."

"You bet."

That was the last the young Frenchman saw of his two friends for some time to come.

"How did you know that I was Nat Urner?" asked Nat of Ted Russel.

"I have been on the look-out for you for some weeks," said Ted.

"Why?"

"Because we got a curious document by the last mail which came from America before communication with the outside world was cut off."

"What was it about?"

"Here it is," said Russel, taking a letter out of his pocket and reading it.

"To the Embassy of the United States, Paris.

"GENTLEMEN,—Be on the look-out for my son, Nat. He may get into trouble in a foreign country, as he is a boy who knows what he is worth. You can tell him by his asking everlasting questions, giving sauce where it isn't wanted, and being knock-kneed.

"Yours truly,

"EPHRAIM WHISTLER URNER."

"There's a letter!" said Ted Russel. "We roared over it."

"I don't see anything funny in it," exclaimed Nat; "it fetched you fellows, and that's what he wrote it for. What more do you want?"

This was a poser.

A deal too much logic for them.

So they went away to their dinner.

Ted Russel was willing to take Nat Urner to live with him if he liked, and advanced to him all the money he wanted on his father's account.

But Nat preferred remaining with his chums, and they accordingly hired apartments near the embassy.

They lived very quietly during those weary weeks, seeking in every way to ferret out the mystery which surrounded Frank.

Time meanwhile passed very drearily for Frank in the lunatic asylum.

He was playing a game of bowls one day when, the bell ringing, he became aware that some other victim was about to be added to the list of the asylum.

Impelled by curiosity, he approached the gate just as it closed upon the Prussian soldiers, who held between them a madman—a blind madman, who was gagged and bound.

Frank started.

The face, notwithstanding its distortion, was strangely familiar to him.

"Snarly Cool! is it possible?"

There was no mistaking his response.

It was the maddened cry of the wolf—a human snarl, anger, hate, revenge in one fierce cry.

The lamp in the room was glaring to its full height, and a thick column of smoke wound its way from it to the ceiling.

He sprang up in bed, and, before the sense of terror left him, caught up a pillow for his defence.

That act saved his life.

A hatchet intended for his skull buried itself harmlessly in the shield, and, as Frank sprang backwards, Snarly Cool repeated his blow.

Frank was now thoroughly conscious of his danger.

Alone with two madmen, and a swarm of them perhaps waiting outside to assist.

He looked towards the door.

It was locked and the key was not in the lock.

With the cunning of madness, Snarly Cool had taken the precaution of preventing the exit of his enemy.

"Madman!" cried Frank, "what would you do?"

"Ha, ha! devil's imp, I have you now!" bellowed the madman, striking at the empty air. "I have you; you cannot escape. We will both die and go to the black pit together."

Frank shouted for help until the echoes rang again, and dodged his enemies round the room.

"Lead me to him," cried Snarly Cool; "lead me to the fiend who has baffled me. Ha, ha! did you think to baffle Snarly Cool because you put out his eyes."

"Devil that you are," exclaimed Frank, "you will upset that lamp amongst those papers, and involve not only us, but the whole asylum in destruction."

The mad, wild, wolfish yell of hate, rage, and fiendish triumph which followed this speech Frank remembered to his dying day. It was awful.

Ere its echoes had died away Snarly Cool seized the lamp and dashed it down into the midst of the papers and MSS.

"Ha, ha!" he said, while his companion uttered a shrill sound. "Ha, ha! we will burn him alive. Ho, ho! he shall roast——"

The two began dancing a wild *pas de deux* in the fierce light of the ascending flames.

Frank's situation was a most desperate one.

He heard all this, and he heard, too, the thunders of the keepers as they rushed in, scattering the frightened horde right and left, and begin pounding on the doors.

"Open, open!" they shouted, battering as they spoke.

"I cannot!" screamed Frank. "The place is on fire, and a madman has the key in his pocket!"

Again the pounding at the door was renewed, but alas! that very solidity which they had given to prevent the insane from molesting their keepers now prevented them from gaining entrance.

Meanwhile Frank had not been idle.

Springing to the window he flung it open.

The room was on the second floor of the building. It was a fearful leap to take, and Frank hesitated.

It seemed almost certain death, yet what was he to do?

A moment more and he would have leaped.

"Hold!" cried a voice on his right.

It was the dramatist.

He had flung open the window of the room next to the one where Frank was, and threw him a rope.

"Is it fast?" asked Frank.

He nodded his head.

Frank let himself down from the window with a jerk, and swung like the pendulum of a clock.

He had scarcely left the window when, in the midst of a sheet of flame, an agonised dead-white face appeared, rolling its sightless eyes and yelling in the last death-grip of agony.

So it remained for a moment, and then it fell backwards into the flames.

This was the last our hero saw of Snarly Cool.

"Hurry!" cried his friend, who had been watching his movements with eager impatience; "hurry, for the love of Heaven! or you will be too late. The wall will fall in and involve me in your ruin!"

He got in, helped by the keeper.

The room was like an oven, and in the next they could hear the fire roaring.

Out in the passage-way the flames had burst, and were curling round the banisters with fiery tongue, and gaining headway despite the buckets of water showered upon the furnace behind.

But at length the place was cleared of its inmates, none of whom perished except those who were the direct cause of the fire.

They were encamped upon the lawn surrounded by furniture of every description, while the flames, now no longer checked, streamed forth from every window in bright lurid glare.

Frank went up to the doctors, who were standing together.

"I am very sorry for you, gentlemen," he said, in his low, mellow voice. "I sincerely trust that the public will furnish you with the means of repairing your loss."

One of the doctors pressed his hand.

"Thank you for your sympathy, little English boy," he said, "but I fear we are ruined. Poor France is too distracted now to give heed to private misfortune. Look there!"

He pointed over to the westward as he spoke.

Shell after shell was flying through the air from Montmartre and Valerian batteries, and along the way to Versailles they could see lines of light flashing, proving that the greatest activity prevailed.

"The Versailles troops are going to attack Paris to-night," said the doctor. "I hope to Heaven they may succeed in saving that unhappy city from the fiends who hold it."

"Good gracious, doctor," cried Frank, "what fiends do you speak of?"

"The Red Republicans who hold the city of Paris—the *communards*."

"Are the Prussians fighting them?" asked Frank.

"No, not the Prussians; the Versailles troops, the army which represents the Republican government."

"Was the emperor killed, sir?" asked Frank.

"Of what importance is it to a mad boy whether he was killed or not?" replied the doctor, testily. "No; he was not. He was captured by the Germans. Ask me no more questions."

"Thank you," replied Frank; "I will not."

He had obtained enough information for his own purpose, and was able to fill up the blanks from his imagination.

"If Paris is going to be captured to-night, I'd better be at the capturing of it," he said to himself. "The front rank of an advancing party is not exactly the sort of place in which they think of looking for me."

However, it was no time to stand still and dream, so he procured a short ladder without being observed, and ascended.

Someone saw him as he got on top of the wall.

They set up a shout and gave chase, but he rushed over, caught up the ladder, and dropped it in the road, following it himself.

He knew that without it they could not scale the wall and would have to go round by the gate.

Once free, with the cool breath of night upon his brow, he fled towards the sullen line of red light, with liberty in his heart and the dawn of hope upon his forehead.

About half a mile from the outer line of fortifications he came across a bivouac of officers.

"What do you want?" they asked him

"First of all some supper," Frank said, "and then to be in your troop as a volunteer when you go against those red devils to-night."

"*Allons, mon garçon.*" cried a big-whiskered colonel; "you shall be the first in if you like."

CHAPTER XXXVI.

THE RED KING PROMISES.

UP till this time the two friends had not been able to penetrate the mystery which surrounded Frank Stainforth.

They sounded Ted Russel to see if he could not assist them, and, under his protection, invaded Plon-Plon's establishment, and inquired for their chum.

They saw him; at least, they saw the same pale-faced boy they had seen on a former occasion.

He was, as usual, with Joel Skimp.

"That's not the boy we want to see," cried Nat Urner.

"You said you wanted to see Frank Stainforth," replied Plon-Plon, with a smile on his face, and an evil triumphant look in his eye.

"I know what I said," replied Nat; "and I don't eat my words. I want to see Frank Stainforth, and I mean to, in spite of your tricks."

"Here he is, and he evidently does not want to see you; I know all your tricks, young gentleman, and I am glad that you have left my school. That poor boy whom you call your friend is, for some reason or other best known to yourselves, terribly afraid of you."

"Well, if you are not a first-class liar, then there are no such things as lies in this world, that's all I have to say on this occasion," answered Nat, in an ebullition of rage, which Ted Russel tried in vain to stop."

"Since you are under official protection I must submit," retorted Plon-Plon, casting an indignant look at Ted Russel; "but I warn you that I shall submit a remonstrance to our government upon allowing a citizen to be bullied by the *attaché* of a foreign embassy upon a trumped up and silly story, fabricated by two lying and spiteful boys."

"Besides," said Plon-Plon, "if there were any other proof required to show you that your story is ridiculous, here is the boy's own cousin, Joel Skimp, who was brought up with him, and who ought to know him a little better than you two, who, by their own showing, have not known him a year."

"Look you," cried Barry Cornwall; "I believe, look you, that Joel Skimp is in the conspiracy against him."

"And if Frank is mad, you have driven him mad."

"Here are two assertions in one breath," retorted Plon-Plon, calmly. "In the first place, this is not your friend, I have spirited him away; in the second place, this is your friend, and I have driven him mad. These charges would be infamous if they were not ridiculous; I await with perfect calmness the close of this miserable war, and the appearance of the boy's father, to whom I have written. Meanwhile, gentlemen, I shall have the honour of escorting you to the door."

"It's about the only act you have ever done in your life that I am thankful to you for, you black-browed rascal," retorted Nat.

"Confound it," he said, as they walked away from the sombre pile of buildings; "that beast of a Frenchman is too smart for me. I thought I was pretty level-headed, and could see as far as most people, but he beats me."

"I am afraid you are under a delusion," said Ted.

"Yes; there's no mistake about that, and an artfully planned one, too," Nat replied, with tears of vexation in his eyes.

"I mean, you must be mistaken with regard to the identity of your friend."

"If you had ever seen Frank Stainforth, you could not be mistaken with regard to his identity," returned Nat.

"I tell you what it is," said Nat Urner, suddenly, after a long silence, "Joel Skimp knows all about it, and if we could only capture him——"

"An event clearly impossible, seeing that he is under the protection of the schoolmaster," replied Ted.

"I don't see it."

"Perhaps not."

"Couldn't we abduct him? Paris is in such a riot now, that they would put down anything of that sort to predatory bonds of communists."

"Um!"

They had got by this time as far as the Place Vendome.

Ted Russel pointed to the huge column.

It lay where it had been pulled down by the mob, all the glories of its battle records levelled with the dust.

"If I only knew where to find the Red King he might help me," said Nat, disconsolately.

"You had better let the communards alone," answered Ted Russel; "they are bound to be beaten in the long run by the Versailles troops, and then God help anybody who has anything to do with them."

"There is the Red King!" cried Nat, interrupting Ted Russel's soliloquy by dashing across the street towards a solitary horseman, who was dressed in a blouse, over which were several military decorations.

Behind him came a small body of desperadoes, evidently his body-guard, who kept yelling and shouting, evidently well pleased with themselves, for they kept shouting, "Long live the citizen king of the Cheffoniers."

Nat Urner ran up to him.

"Why don't you take off your hat to the citizen king?" cried a drunken brute. "*Parbleu*, we will teach you manners."

He made a thrust at Nat with his sword.

The boy parried it coolly with the heavy walking-stick he carried in his hand, and gave the would-be assassin such a whack that he rolled over in the mud.

Another sprang to the assistance of his fellow, but the rest held him back, crying—"*Brava!*"

"I guess I don't take off my hat to anyone unless it's a woman," said Nat, fearlessly.

"Bravo!" cried the crowd; "this is a young democrat. We will make him a lieutenant."

"Don't you know me?" asked Nat, of the Red King, still keeping his eyes fixed on his fallen antagonist, who looked dangerous.

"No, I don't," said the latter, trying to think where he had seen him before.

"Don't you remember?" replied Nat. "In the cellars of that bastile my man Squat did you a good turn."

"His man! He is a young aristocrat—despatch him. He keeps a servant—a slave!" shouted the crowd.

"Silence! and put down your weapons," thundered Le Roi Rouge, for Nat was covered by two or three pistols. "Aristocrat you call him, imbeciles! He is an American citizen, and has done more to help the commune than all of you put together."

"Well, that's a good lie, anyhow," exclaimed Nat, in English; "but it doesn't matter. I thought you couldn't forget me," he added, when the *vivas* had died away. "I did you a service then, I want you to do me one now."

"What is it?" asked the Red King.

Nat told him briefly all that had occurred, and what he wanted done.

He knew Ted Russel would not approve of it; so he resolved to keep it to himself.

"I am too busy to assist you now," said the man.

"Is that all you are worth?" grumbled Nat. "You promised to assist me if ever I should want it; but that's always the way with men when they get up in the world. I don't think much of you, that's a fact."

The Red King looked at him in profound admiration.

"You are a brave boy," he said. "Meet me to-night, then, at half-past eight, near Plon-Plon's school. The watchword is 'Liberty.'"

"Correct," cried Nat, and strolled away, while the Red King continued his parade down the street in a ridiculous assumption of pomp.

"What were you talking to him about?" asked Ted Russel.

"The probable price of horse-flesh," replied Nat; and then seeing that Ted looked sharply at him, said, "Look here, old chap, I'm old enough and ugly enough to take care of myself. If I get into trouble I can get out of it again."

"Like you did before?"

"That couldn't be helped. All I wanted to say is this—I'm going to get at the bottom of this mystery. How I am going to do that is my business, but I am won't have you lugged into it."

"Suit yourself," returned Ted, carelessly; "only remember that if you get a bullet through you or a bayonet in your eye it is your fault, not mine."

By this time they reached the embassy door, and as Ted lived close by they went in to dinner.

CHAPTER XXXVII.

THE ATTACK ON THE SCHOOL—FLIGHT OF PLON-PLON—ON TO THE PRISON—A TERRIBLE NIGHT—WHERE IS LEON?—VIVA LA REPUBLIQUE—AT THE BARRICADES.

THOSE who were in Paris on that bloody night when the Versailles troops stormed it, and fought hand to hand with the fierce ruffians behind their barricades, while grape cannister, and the deadly mitrailleuse filled the gutters with a crimson tide, and the streets with hills of slain, have the picture for ever engraved upon their memories.

It was a wild night—an awful night—when Nat slipped quietly out of his house, accompanied by Barry Cornwall.

Nevertheless, mobs paraded the streets, shouting and yelling, headed by the fierce amazons, the she-devils of Paris, who, even in the very heat of battle, could find time to mutilate their victims.

A woman with her sleeves tucked up to her shoulders, and her hair flying in the night breeze, was rolled past them astride of a mitrailleuse.

"Come, my children," she screamed, "we will taste the blood of those who could not keep out the invader. *Allons!* drink; drink!"

Both boys shuddered.

"She is more like a devil than a woman," said Barry.

Just then her eyes fell upon them.

"What are those two young aristocrats doing?" she exclaimed. "Have we not yet killed all the aristocrats? Kill these two, or the breed will grow again. Kill them, my brave comrades, and we will decorate our brave little mitrailleuse with their heads!"

It was a moment of extreme peril.

Someone in the crazy crowd might have shot the two boys in very wantonness, and who so undertakes to explain to a crowd has a troublesome task.

Nat Urner was equal to the occasion. He drew the cockade, given to him by the Red King, from his pocket, and stuck it in his hat.

This was the work of an instant.

"*Viva la commune!*" he shouted, giving the watchword he had received.

At this a couple of men left the crowd, and, beating the others back with their swords, took the two boys under their protection.

"*Brava les petits communards!*" yelled the drunken women, as they drew her away.

"You had better wear the cockade for the rest of the night," said one of the two silent men. "Have you any news for the king?"

If he had not looked so eagerly at Nat when he said this, the American boy might have replied, unhesitatingly, by telling him whom he was; but something peculiar in the man's manner put Nat on his guard.

"He takes me for someone else," he cried to himself; "I must be careful."

"No," he answered, aloud; "I must see the king myself."

"But you cannot see him to-night. He is at the barrier."

"He is not."

"Where is he?"

"Not fifty yards from where you are standing, and he is looking at you and wondering why it is that you are so anxious to pry into his affairs."

Before the sentence was well finished the two men started and slipped away into the darkness.

Just then they came opposite the school. The street was deserted.

The school, a sombre pile of grey, bearing up against a lurid sky, showed not a solitary light.

Nat give a low whistle.

They waited some time for a reply, and presently it came from under an archway on the right, like a faint echo.

In two minutes a couple of figures approached.

" *What* do you want ? " asked one.

" Liberty," responded Nat.

" Good.   *Whom* do you want ? "

" The Red King."

" You are the little American ? "

" Yes."

" Good."

Again a whistle sounded.

This time there were three distinct calls, and, before, the echoes died away, the street was filled with men.

Nat went up to the door of the school and knocked.

After waiting for some time he knocked again, and this time there was a shuffling of feet and moving of bolts.

Only a small window was opened in the massive oak door, however, and a face peered out.

" What do you want ? "

" Plon-Plon."

" What do you want of him at this time of night ? "

" I want to see him on a message of importance from the government of the commune.   Tell him I come from Henri Rochefort."

" We cannot admit anyone to night— you must come to-morrow."

" But we insist——"

The answer to this was the slamming too of the little window in the face of the questioner.

" Comrades," cried the man in black, turning to his companions, " they refuse to admit the messengers of the king. This is treason to the commune. Come, we will make them obey us."

Ere his speech was finished twenty axes flashed out, showing that the Red King had forewarned his companions as to the sort of reception they were likely to receive ; and now blows fell heavily upon the oaken door, and some were mounted on the shoulders of others, and essayed to enter by the heavily barred windows.

Then lights flashed, and presently the face of Plon-Plon appeared at the window.

" What do you want ? " he asked, and, catching sight of Nat Urner, exclaimed—

" Ah, it is you, is it ? "

" Are you going to let us in ? "

" There is your answer," cried Plon-Plon.

Quick as thought he drew a pistol and fired.

The ball just grazed Nat's temple, and sent him to the ground.

A yell of rage and the report of half a dozen pistols was their answer to this challenge.

They resumed their attacks, but now a murderous fire was opened from inside the prison.

" Down with them! down with them! " cried Nat, who had snatched up an axe from a fallen man, and rained his blows upon the oaken doors.

" *Vive la commune!   Vive les petits communards!* " yelled the crowd, which was increasing every moment. " Down with those who defy the committee."

But it was no easy task.

At last, after a desperate resistance, the stout oaken gate gave way.

The crowd swarmed into the courtway, and Nat and Barry found themselves at its head, steering to the portal which led to the schoolroom.

Again a desperate resistance was offered, and again the attacking party was victorious.

Nat and Barry were in a mad passion ; they scarce knew what they did.

Behind them came a surging crowd of devils, ready for any work.

" To the schoolroom! " yelled Nat, to his chum.

They found the boys all huddled up like sheep.

Nat darted forward.

" Down with the young aristocrats. *Vive les petits communards!* " shrieked the blouses, pressing forward.

" No, no! " screamed Nat, his voice scarcely rising above the cries of terror which the unfortunate pupils raised ; " the tyrant is not here. These are the victims—these are my friends. To the dining-room. He is in the dining-room!"

" *Allons!* to the dining-room! " cried the crowd, melting away.

Once the boys saw them retreating they leaped down and rushed into the crowd of scholars.

"Frank, or whoever he is, is not here," said Barry. "Plon-Plon has taken him with him."

Some boy was hiding his head between two others.

Nat's quick eye observed this.

"There is Joel Skimp—there is the boy we want; come out here."

They seized him.

"Save yourselves, the rest of you, before the mob comes back. Stay, who were those that opposed us ?"

"Reactionists."

"Good! be off with you; we have work to do."

The frightened scholars scuttled away as fast as their legs could carry them.

"Now, you sneak, tell us all about this mystery that you are a party to, or we will call our friends back to tear you limb from limb. Where is Frank Stainforth ?"

"I don't know."

Nat Urner blew his whistle.

"Spare me," cried Joel; "I could not help it; I was forced into the plot under horrible threats."

"Speak quickly!"

"He is in a lunatic asylum on the road to Versailles. Snarly Cool put him there."

"And who is the one that represents him ?"

"He is Frank's brother, Tom—Mad Tom."

"Where is he ?"

"Plon-Plon took him away with him. He knew he had a secret place to retreat to, where the mob could never find him. I would have gone, too, only I lost him in the confusion."

"What was his object in substituting mad Tom for Frank ?"

"He is to get ten thousand pounds from Frank's father-in-law! If they can prove Frank either dead or mad, his mother comes into all the property left him by his father. She was driven crazy by the death of her first husband, Frank's father, who committed suicide. During her insanity mad Tom was born. I don't know how her second husband came to marry her. He has terrible power over her, and does what he likes. That is all I know."

"Good! we will find out more for ourselves. Come with us, and if you leave us at all, remember, you will be killed."

Hither and thither they swarmed over the sombre pile of buildings, looking for Plon-Plon, but they found him not.

Allons, my comrades! we have done famously," said the Red King; "the old tyrant will never put boys to the rack any more."

"In the cellars!" roared Nat, inspired by the idea.

To the cellars they rushed.

The sight of the rack and the instruments of torture crazed them.

"Burn down the place, burn it down!" cried one, and away they rushed upstairs again to put the threat into execution.

Nat was appalled; he did not want to go so far as that; but he found now, when it was too late, that starting a crowd was comparatively easy—checking them almost an impossibility.

He reflected a moment; then a bright idea occurred to him.

"To the prison!" he exclaimed; "to the prison; Let us liberate the prisoners! Vive la liberté!"

"Allons! to the prison! they screamed, and away they rushed to the gaol headed by Nat and Barry, who feared that even in the moment of his liberation Leon De Gardin might say something about the canaille, which would cause them to immolate him upon the altar of their wrath.

Hither and thither rushed Nat and Barry, while Squat brought up the rear, dragging Joel Skimp with them.

At last in one of the cells under the street, they came across an emaciated being; at first he did not recognise them or they him.

It was Leon De Gardin!

In another moment he was in their arms.

"Free, old boy, free!" cried Barry, unlocking his cuffs, "Here, wear this red cockade until we can get a chance to get away from the mob."

"The Versailles troops have just made a grand attack on the walls; they have penetrated to the streets. Paris is running with blood."

"Who are the Versailles troops ?"

They explained.

"I will fight for those who liberated me," said Leon. "Allons! to the barricades!"

Away those three mad boys rushed.

On their way they were joined by a

little man, who seemed all wrinkles and white hair.

It was Pomponet; but they had not time for embracing now, scarcely time for congratulations.

They were dimly aware that they had taken part in the madness, and knew they were behind a barricade; but for whom they were fighting, or what they were fighting for, they knew not till afterwards.

Bayonets were in front of them, making desperate efforts to take their position; and then there came a wild shout from three treble voices as a form mounted the barricades, a slender youth, with dead-white face all aglow.

Frank Stainforth!

He had been at the head of a column of soldiers, which had forced the barricade.

Fortunately for Barry and Nat their hats had fallen off.

Frank pushed them back into a door-way.

"Ah! that is the miscreant who shot my comrade," cried a soldier, making a thrust at Nat Urner.

"You mistake!" cried Frank, turning his weapon; "these are my friends. Am I a Red Republican?"

"No, *parbleu*, that you are not," the soldiers cried, "or we should never have taken this cursed barricade."

He passed on.

"Come with me," cried Frank, hur-riedly; "your side are getting beaten everywhere. We must pass the lines before an indiscriminate massacre takes place. If they begin to inquire you three are doomed."

"What have we done?" asked Nat Urner.

"Done! If it had not been for your desperate valour we should have taken that barricade half an hour ago."

"You were that slender youth who led those desperate charges against us. I could not see your face because that broad hat of yours covered it," cried Nat, in surprise. "Good Heaven, Frank, I fired at you four times."

Frank took off his hat; there were two bullet-holes in it.

"I don't know how I came to miss you," said Frank, with a laugh; "I emptied my revolver with strict impar-tiality at three of you."

Just then Barry Cornwall turned white and fainted away.

"There is one of my bullets," cried Frank. "Poor little St. David! I have shot him in the thigh. We must get out of here—out of France as speedily as possible, if we would save our lives. We are all more or less compromised. Come along to the camp at Versailles."

They hurried along. They had come to their senses by this time, and shud-dered at the wanton slaughter of human life they saw going on.

CHAPTER XXXVIII.

ENGLAND.

IT was with extreme difficulty that the four chums succeeded in making their escape from the blood-deluged city.

"What would you advise us to do, Frank?" asked Barry.

"I know what my advice is," ex-claimed Nat.

"What?"

"Hook it," responded the American.

"Short, sweet, and to the point," said Frank. "I quite agree with you. We have seen enough horrors to last us our lifetime."

"Yes," cried Frank. "It beats alliga-tor-shooting, you bet, but there is only one thing that cramps our movements."

"What's that?"

"No coin," said Nat.

"I haven't a penny," cried Frank. "They took all my money at the lunatic asylum."

"Nor I," said Leon.

"Squat hab plenty ob money," said that worthy, breaking in upon the con-versation.

"Where did you get it?"

"Squat hab plenty ob money, Marse Nat."

"Did you come by it honestly?"

"Squat hab plenty ob money," re-sponded the faithful henchman, without change of countenance.

"He isn't going to let us know where his specie mill is, you bet," cried Nat. "Let's take the coin, and be thankful for what Heaven sends. That's my oyster."

"I expect if Plon——"

His sentence was interrupted by the appearance of a number of soldiers on the scene.

"Ha! here is the little Englishman who led the 14th against the last barricade," cried a fat corporal.

"*Vive le petit Englishman!*" they all cried.

"And for doing you this service you would kill me and my friends!" said Frank, calmly.

"Pardon, monsieur, we did not know you—the little hero who gave the Red Assassins their *coup de grâce!*"

As he spoke they saluted with uncovered heads.

"Good!" said Frank; "I may be mistaken again. I want an escort to Versailles."

"As many soldiers as you like, monsieur," cried a *sous*-lieutenant coming up.

"Thank you; eight will be sufficient," responded Frank.

In another moment they were *en route*.

"By Jove!" said Nat, in English, "that was a narrow escape!"

No further adventures happened until they got to Versailles, where Frank went to see the colonel of the regiment whom he had served under.

From him he easily got passports for his party to Calais, and half an hour afterwards they were whirling away towards the sea.

CHAPTER XXXIX.

THE END.

THEY were in England at last.

On their arrival Barry had telegraphed to his uncle, and that old gentleman had come up grumpy and amiable as usual.

When they had given him a particular account of their adventures, he said—

"But who on earth told you that Doctor Primrose was dead?"

"What!" they all exclaimed.

"Don't you know——;" then aside, "but of course they don't; how should they. What a fool I am."

"Do you mean to say that the dear old doctor is not dead?"

"Not a bit of it."

"You see," said Grumpy, "the death of his friend made him very ill; in fact, sent him to death's door. When he recovered a little he had to be sent to the seaside, and there he has been with me."

"Why did he leave us in that den of iniquity?" asked Frank.

"Den of iniquity do you call it?" bawled the old gentleman. "Why there was not a week passed that we did not hear that you were delighted with the school."

The boys looked at one another.

"Well, well," said Frank; "thank God we are clear of it all at last. And now I will tell you of the mystery which enshrouded my life, and which, until lately, I have not been able to clear away."

"From my cousin, Joel Skimp here, whom I have forgiven, as I find he was frightened into doing a great deal of what he did, I have obtained a clue to all the villany that has been set in motion against me.

"Shortly after I was born my father made the acquaintance of an Italian adventurer, who is now my father-in-law.

"He obtained such an influence over him, that he asked him to his house.

"Sometime after that my father committed suicide; the reason for this sad act I cannot ascertain, but enough for me to know that it drove my dear mother mad shortly after she married my father-in-law.

"In this condition she gave birth to my brother Tom, who was known through the neighbourhood as Mad Tom.

"For years of terror I endured the thought which my father-in-law and his valet Snarly Cool had carefully instilled into me, that I had inherited the seeds of madness, and that at any moment I might break out into raving lunacy.

"It was the shame and horror of this which for years kept my lips sealed, and enabled them to all but accomplish what

I believe is their nefarious purpose—namely, to get the property which is mine on coming of age into their hands.

"By the English law a lunatic becomes dispossessed of his property.

"My poor mother! what his dreadful influence is over her I cannot say——"

Frank broke down, and Barry's uncle burst forth impetuously—

"We are losing time—come!"

"Where?"

"To find a lawyer and a detective first, and then to Windermere."

"Can we go?" asked the three chums.

"Yes, of course, I'll pay for all of you," cried old Grumpy. "Now to unmask the villain!"

Leon had found his father in London, and he readily gave his consent that his son should accompany Frank; they had seen his misery, it was hard if they could not witness his triumph also.

The following day saw them at Windermere.

As they entered the gloomy woods which wrapped the stately pile, Frank felt his bosom thrill with strange emotions; both anger and sorrow struggled for the mastery.

The door was opened by a new man-servant, who showed them into the drawing-room.

"Say some friends from the continent," said old Grumpy. "Umph! what a fool I am! of course, he won't believe that."

But he did believe it, and all unconscious came his fate.

The same calm, pale, venemous face they had seen; the same sinister smile and withering moustache, but more curved lines of care or remorse upon the wrinkled brow than of old, and a few dishonourable white hairs.

"What means this?" he asked, and then turned pale.

"It means," said Frank, sternly, "that your schemes have come to naught."

The bitter smile of hate swept across his face; with a bound he was beside Frank, a pistol in his hand.

"At least, you shall not triumph!" he yelled.

But Nat's keen eye had watched him, and, quick as thought, he tripped his egs from under him. He fell heavily.

When they picked him up he was senseless.

In this condition he was carried to gaol and committed for trial.

In one of the rooms they found a poor crazed woman.

Frank's mother!

Let us draw a veil over the sad meeting.

Suffice it for us to know that years afterwards, when kindness and unremitting care had restored her mind, she found strength to tell of the fatal influence the infamous scoundrel had exercised upon her.

He was a mesmerist, and had subjecte her to his will.

Thinking her faithless to him, her husband had shot himself, and this is what had caused her to lose her reason altogether, until she became a mere tool in the hands of the villain.

* * * * * *

Before the trial came on Doctor Primrose was able to be moved.

He was very weak, but the joy of seeing his dear boys again made his resist the advice of Ann O'Dyne and come on to see them.

"Well, doctor," said Frank, "you will take us to Germany under better auspices I trust?"

"No, no, my dear boys," said he; "I have had enough of the responsibilities of trusting young English lads to unscrupulous foreigners. God bless my soul! When I think of all you boys have gone through it makes me shudder."

The trial of Frank's father-in-law came duly on. He was convicted and sentenced to fifteen years' imprisonment. He cast a look of rage and hate at Frank as the boys cheered this announcement that, despite his courage, Frank was glad to know that he was under lock and key.

What a happy time they had when all this was over! What shooting, and rowing, and fishing at Frank's place!

Then Frank sent over to France to try and find trace of his mad brother, Tom; but they could neither ascertain that nor the fate of Plon-Plon.

And now, leaving our heroes at beautiful Windermere for their much-needed rest, we will say—"Here endeth the first part of "THE TRAVELLING SCHOOLBOYS."

Their further adventures—how fate again went against them—will be narrated at some future date.

FINIS.